FREE FROM THE WORLD

FREE FROM THE WORLD

JOHN JOHNSON

Copyright © 2019 John Johnson

The moral right of the author has been asserted.

Apart from any fair dealing for the purposes of research or private study, or criticism or review, as permitted under the Copyright, Designs and Patents Act 1988, this publication may only be reproduced, stored or transmitted, in any form or by any means, with the prior permission in writing of the publishers, or in the case of reprographic reproduction in accordance with the terms of licences issued by the Copyright Licensing Agency. Enquiries concerning reproduction outside those terms should be sent to the publishers.

This is a work of fiction. Names, characters, businesses, places, events and incidents are either the products of the author's imagination or used in a fictitious manner. Any resemblance to actual persons, living or dead, or actual events is purely coincidental.

Matador
9 Priory Business Park,
Wistow Road, Kibworth Beauchamp,
Leicestershire. LE8 0RX
Tel: 0116 279 2299
Email: books@troubador.co.uk
Web: www.troubador.co.uk/matador
Twitter: @matadorbooks

ISBN 978 1838591 779

British Library Cataloguing in Publication Data.
A catalogue record for this book is available from the British Library.

Printed and bound in Great Britain by 4edge Limited
Typeset in 12pt Adobe Jenson Pro by Troubador Publishing Ltd, Leicester, UK

Matador is an imprint of Troubador Publishing Ltd

For Joanna

I hate the very noise of troublous man
Who did and does me all the harm he can.
Free from the world I would a prisoner be
And my own shadow all my company.

> John Clare, The Northborough Sonnets

INTRA SCRIPTUM

He followed her from the building to the station, crossing the road so that he could watch her from an angle, rather than from behind where one glance back might reveal his pursuit. She was obviously a risk, a risk to his boss and so to him. "Try to stop her taking this further," was the instruction he had been given. "We need to persuade her to stop." And so he followed her, watching and waiting for an opportunity, an easy task because she was not walking quickly but more as if in a dream, lost in the events that had just taken place. He had time to think about the best way to discourage her. There were so many possibilities when someone was so unsuspecting.

She did stop after a while, and entered a café. He waited outside. He could see her writing something down as she sat at a table by the front window. Then she suddenly got up, fumbled in her bag for some coins and left them on the table. She looked more than a little lost, he thought, as she seemed to stand still for a while, as if getting her bearings. She did not seem familiar with this area at all. She did not live or work in the city, after all. He could almost see her reconstructing in her mind the route she had taken earlier, and attempting now to plot it in reverse as she looked first in one direction and then in another. The meeting had obviously flustered her, and she was brushed against by one or two passers-by on the pavement as she paused there. She had an undeveloped beauty, he thought, wearing no make-up and a thick coat pulled around her against the autumn cold. She had not been able to disguise the bruising on her face. He'd have felt sorry for her if it were not for the danger she represented, the danger of discovery and revelation, of the inevitable response of authority to what he and his boss had done. Her eyes were lively as she sought to recall her route. But her demeanour was hunched and she seemed dejected. He was a bastard, his boss, and he knew how he might treat a young and naïve woman when they met.

She came to a decision and set off again, this time crossing the road and turning into the next street. An Underground railway station was at the end of the road, he knew, and she must have come by that means. He held back, turning briefly to look at the entrance to another government building so that she would not see his face and recognise him. He had been there at an earlier meeting, though in the background. She might recognise him, he thought, if he was not careful. But that encounter had been in her place of work, where she felt familiar and confident. She did not look as if she felt that way now. She was quickening her pace as she saw the railway sign further down the street, and he had to swerve to avoid people in his way as he tried to reduce the distance between them. He was much closer to her when she turned into the station, and he almost bumped into her when she stopped to search in her purse for her ticket. Lucky, he thought, that he had a season ticket and could pass the ticket collector without having to queue at the small window. He would probably have lost her if he'd had to wait.

She took the ticket from her purse and passed through the gap in the railings that allowed entrance to the platforms. He smiled in scorn as she handed her ticket over for inspection, surprising the collector who usually just waved people through without looking closely and examining individual tickets. He waved his ticket vaguely at the man and followed her onto the escalator, its wooden steps full of cigarette ends and matches stuck between the planks. She stood in the middle of the step, and another traveller jostled her aside as he wanted to pass her. She was so easy to follow, he thought, that she must have no inkling of his pursuit. Whatever he decided to do, she would not be prepared.

At the end of the escalator she checked the two diagrams listing the stations at which trains would stop. Then she walked onto the platform and stopped immediately. She was near the tunnel entrance and standing near, but not too near, the platform edge. Perhaps this was his chance. Journeys through the city were regularly disrupted by incidents in which passengers fell or jumped onto the rails, either electrocuting themselves in the process or being crushed by the trains which could not stop in time. It was the everyday dread of the drivers, he'd been told, that they would have someone fall or jump in front of their train and have to watch helplessly as they advanced inexorably towards the victim – so easy, then, to make it seem like a suicide. And she was clearly distressed after the meeting, as his boss would be able to confirm if he were ever questioned about her. It seemed best not just to scare her but to ensure that she could not cause them any further problems. Once she was out of the way, that other problem could be sorted out.

He took a position on the platform just a little behind her. The platform was filling up with other passengers, and the next train was clearly delayed. She seemed lost in her own thoughts and was looking down on the rails that were in the long gulley next to the platform. She appeared to see something there that drew all her attention. As the minutes passed and the platform became more and more crowded, he pushed past a couple of passengers so that he was directly behind her. Now he could see that she was watching two mice, two small creatures which managed somehow to survive in the tunnels of the Underground and which were scuttling around the gulley beneath the rails. Absorbed in watching the mice, she had even moved more closely towards the platform edge. And now he could hear the vibrations of the rails, the first warning of the imminent arrival of a train. And then he could feel on his cheek the movement of hot air along the platform, pushed forward by the incoming train. As the rails rattled more loudly, people around them started to pick up cases and bags from the platform and to prepare themselves for the train's arrival. Further up the platform, some edged back a little, knowing the train would still be moving at speed as it passed them before stopping.

He stationed himself directly behind her and turned slightly so that his shoulder was almost in contact with her back. If he kept his hands in his pockets, people could not claim that he had pushed her. It would just be seen as the consequence of an overcrowded platform. In the chaos that would follow her fall, he would just slip away and catch a train on the other platform. The vibration of the rails had now reached its highest pitch, and he knew that the train must be entering the platform at its far end. Now was the time, so he moved one foot forward, and as soon as his shoulder reached her back he pushed forward. She was toppling in an instant. The train was trundling towards the spot where she had been, and a woman screamed further down the platform. He stepped back, reassured that no-one had turned towards him, and moved away immediately All those around were looking in astonishment at the space she had occupied, their last sight of her falling almost headlong before the wheels of the train.

CHAPTER ONE

Richard Simms woke up soaked in sweat. The burned landscape of his dreams still lingered on his eyelids – collapsed buildings, smoke and flames flickering in corners, the sky obscured by dust and ash. Only slowly could he focus on the brown ceiling above him. Only cautiously did he lift his head a little off his pillow. He felt nauseous and thought that he might vomit if he moved at all quickly. He could smell the charred bones and the smouldering flesh of the victims. His head sank back, and he felt tears rolling from the corners of his eyes into the furrows of his nose. He raised a hand to wipe them away and squeezed his eyes to staunch the flow. He opened them again and rolled his head from side to side. Then he sat up, looking around as if he sensed that some danger was nearby. The book he had been reading the previous night was still open on the bedside table. A plastic glass containing water was half-empty. His spectacles were in the brown case, left open for easy access. Nothing had changed. It was just another bad dream, another visitation from the past.

Richard shoved the bedclothes back and swung his legs to the floor. He pushed himself up onto his feet, holding the side of the bed as if he were about to fall. He waited while his head cleared and then leaned forward and pulled the edge of the curtain back from the nearby window. Deep fog outside. The mist of the previous evening had thickened and settled, and it was impossible to see anything except the grey cloud that swirled around the edges of the window. He shivered in his pyjamas and decided it was better to get moving and head off towards the bathroom before he became too cold. He bent down to pull an old pair of grey slippers on, and tugged a woollen dressing gown around himself. He took a pair of trousers from the tallboy near his bed, and his shaving bag. But before he moved, he reminded himself — walk slowly, avoid eye contact, pause before speaking.

It was early and no-one else was yet moving. The bathroom was cold, and Richard could see his own breath in the air. He decided against a bath. It was too cold to wait for the slow trickle of tepid brown water to fill the tub sufficiently. He ran the hot tap in the sink, lathered up his shaving brush and applied a layer of white suds across his chin and cheeks, his upper lip and his throat. He looked at his razor. How long since he'd changed the blade? It was a Monday morning, he knew that, and he changed the blade every third Monday. But was today the third Monday? He couldn't remember at all. There was a great flurry the day he'd last changed the blade. He could remember that. He had gone off to do his daily work, and while he was away Winstanley had had a heart attack on the ward. People shouting and running around, and other doctors arriving at speed, the other inmates had said. But was that two weeks ago or three? The shock of Winstanley's death still seemed so fresh in his mind that Richard decided it must have been only two weeks. And so he shaved without changing the blade. He still marvelled at the notion of a safety razor — the sophisticated engineering of the blades and the clever design of the holder that limited the extent of the blade's exposure — so much better than the old cutthroat his father had given him when he first started shaving. And those two years when he was not allowed a razor, and had to go to the barber for a weekly shave, were now a distant memory. It was good to clear the stubble every day.

The razor scraped the lather and bristles from his neck easily enough, but it grated against the tougher stubble on his chin, as if its edge had been blunted. Perhaps it was three weeks after all. He finished shaving, scraped the toothbrush around the near-empty tin of cleaning powder and brushed his teeth. The paste tasted stale and dry, and he could barely summon enough spittle to wet it. He ran the cold tap and raised some water to his mouth with his hand. He swilled the water around and spat it out, rinsing any dregs down the plughole. He pulled his pyjama bottoms off and put on the dark grey trousers he had brought with him, before putting on the dressing gown again. Along with the thick long johns he was already wearing, he should be warm enough for the day. Before he opened the bathroom door he thought again for a moment – walk slowly, avoid eye contact, pause before speaking.

At his bedside, Richard again opened the thin tallboy that held his clothes and other personal items. He took out a collarless shirt and a thick woollen jumper. He took off his dressing gown and hung it up on a hook on the wall, unbuttoned his pyjama top and folded it up carefully, placing it and the matching trousers on a shelf. He pulled the shirt and jumper on and sat down on the bed to pull on his socks and shoes. Across the ward a male nurse came into view. It was Digby. Richard looked down, concentrating on his laces.

"Morning, Richard. Everything OK this morning?" Digby asked.

Richard waited for a few seconds and then replied without raising his eyes. "Yes, I'm going to breakfast, and then my rounds."

"See you later, then."

Richard stood up. He wasn't proud of his appearance. He couldn't be. But at least he felt clean because he had shaved. And so he left the ward and set off on the long walk to the canteen. The quick way was to leave the building by the back door at the bottom of the stairs and take the path to the back door of the Central Wing, but that meant walking in the cold, damp fog. Better to stay dry, if not exactly warm, inside the building. And so he had to walk the whole length of the West Wing of the building, along the main corridor and back down the Central Wing to the patients' canteen. There were other patients headed in the same direction, and nurses and doctors passing him on their way to the wards. Richard kept his head facing downward, so that he stooped a little, and tried to take note of who was around only by noticing their lower bodies. That way he didn't encounter their eyes. He knew the way just by the marks on the floor and the lower parts of the walls.

As he walked, Richard wondered what would happen now that Winstanley was dead. He thought about this most days as he walked to breakfast. All his interviews and discussions had been with Winstanley in the thirteen years that he had been in Ward 44. Any illness or injury had also been treated by Winstanley. The other doctors knew Richard, of course, but they had never treated him. The nurses helped to look after him, yes, but always in ways that Winstanley had directed. No-one had yet said anything to him about a change, but Richard knew there had to be one. His visits to other wards told him that there were now not enough doctors to run his ward and the others that were grouped together at the far end of the West Wing. Three or four were needed, not the two who remained. But what would the change mean for him?

Richard could smell the mixture of boiled vegetables and disinfectant that always hung in the air before he even reached the patients' canteen and pushed one of the double doors open. He thought that someone could take him anywhere in the world, and blindfold him before returning, and that smell would always betray that he had arrived at the Black Roding canteen. It was not yet busy, but some patients had already collected their breakfast from the serving counter and were seated on the benches that ran alongside the long rows of trestle tables. These were more sociable patients, and they grouped together on the benches. Richard already knew what he would do. He took a tray, put a mug of tea and a metal plate on it, and took some partly burned toast from the metal container on the counter. He scraped some butter from a tub and spooned some jam from a large tin. Then he took his tray to an unoccupied table and sat there. Eating alone, and staying silent, was his chosen way.

Finishing his food quickly, Richard stacked his mug, plate and tray on the piles that stood on a table near the exit. He left the canteen and headed for the hospital shop. He needed to know whether the newspaper delivery had been made. The fog might have delayed it, in which case he could not start his rounds.

The shop was one of several rooms in the Central Wing given over to providing services for patients. It was run by volunteers, the Friends of Black Roding. It sold newspapers and magazines such as *Titbits* and *Woman's Weekly*, chocolate bars made by Cadbury and Fry's, Rich Tea and other biscuits, drinks in bright orange cartons, some apples or pears in the autumn, toiletries such as sachets of shampoo and bars of soap, inexpensive stationery, and any other small items that a short-term admission or a long-term patient might need. The volunteers even assisted the patients in buying clothes and other items through postal delivery, if the patients had sufficient funds. Richard admired the volunteers who turned up regularly to do this work, but he knew the risk that this might lead him into careless conversation, an unguarded moment that might betray him. Walk slowly, avoid eye contact, pause before speaking.

The shutter had been drawn up, and Mrs Jones was just starting the task of taking in the newspapers that had been dropped by the porters outside the shop. She still had her hat and coat on, and the brown woollen garments were restricting her as she attempted to shift the piles of newsprint.

"Ah, Richard," she said, "just in time. I was a bit delayed by the fog this morning, and so was the delivery. Could you just lift these in for me? I'm getting too old to do this easily."

Richard said nothing, but picked up the first pile of papers and carried it into the shop. He placed it on the counter, leaving her to cut the string and unwrap the individual papers. He carried the other three piles in a similar way, clearing part of the counter to help her. Then, again in silence, he left the shop and walked further down the corridor. Beyond the shops and offices there was a series of boxed-in spaces used by the hospital workers for their machinery or stores. The final one was a narrow cupboard beneath a flight of stairs in which Richard stored the trolley that he used to carry the shop's goods to all corners of the hospital. He took the cupboard key from his pocket – he was trusted with that – opened the door and went in, switching on the electric light with an automatic movement of his arm.

The trolley still contained the non-perishable items that Richard sold to patients – bags of sweets and biscuits, containers of drinks, a few toiletries, magazines. But he next needed to load the day's newspapers, and any items that patients had asked for the day before. He pulled the trolley behind him as he edged backwards out of the cupboard, and stopped to re-lock the door. Although the cupboard was now almost empty, he did not want anyone to discover the torch that lay in the far corner of the cupboard, next to a half-doorway that seemed to lead nowhere. Then he turned the trolley towards the shop and pushed it along the corridor.

He hoped that he helped other patients as much as possible, but he avoided giving that impression in every way he could. He knew which doctors read *The Times* and which patients wanted *Woman's Weekly*. He listened carefully and wrote down new orders for particular items, and he even lent small sums of money, without telling the volunteers, to patients who were short of cash. If need be, at the end of the week when the heavy black cash box had to be reckoned up, he would put a few shillings from his own pocket in to balance the accounts. His small pension, and the wages he earned as the trustee for the shop's trolley, meant that he could do this without the volunteers noticing.

In the shop Richard started to load the trolley, mostly with the day's newspapers, but also to replenish the goods sold the previous day. Soaps and sachets of shampoo were running down because they were the most common purchases, and he had to open the shop's own stock cupboard to find some of these. He went over and pushed on the stock cupboard door, making sure that Mrs Jones noticed his action.

"What do you need, Richard?" she asked.

He waited. He looked at the floor for a few seconds. "Soaps," he muttered, not looking up. "Shampoos."

"Here," Mrs Jones gave him the key, "get what you need, put the rest of any box on the shelf and write it in the stock book."

He knew how to do all of this. His trustee status meant that the volunteers felt able to give him these responsibilities. Making him a trustee was one of the few good things that Winstanley had done for him. And he was grateful for the ways in which it allowed him to fill his time. He finished loading the trolley and stood near Mrs Jones, waiting while she served another patient who had come into the shop.

"Are you going off now?" she asked. "I'll be going at twelve thirty, and Mrs Dearing will be here when you come back. I'll see you later in the week."

He was able to leave without saying anything more. When Winstanley had first told him how to converse with others around the hospital, or rather how not to converse, he had hated the rudeness that was necessary – it was not his way. So he learned that sometimes he had to refuse to answer people, looking away or down at his shoes. On other occasions his response would be monosyllabic. But now he was indifferent to any offence that he might cause. He had established his status as a patient, and that was all-important. And with Winstanley dead, it was even more important that he not draw attention to himself by any change in his demeanour or behaviour.

His rounds were lengthy. He toured the wards on the ground floors of both wings during the morning, entering the central areas of each ward and avoiding the dormitory areas. He knew, at least roughly, when ward meetings would be taking place, and avoided those times. In some of the geriatric wards he was allowed, once the nurses had seen him, to wheel the trolley along past the beds, in order to draw the patients' attention to the items it contained. Sometimes the nurses bought items for themselves, sometimes even for patients. Doctors bought the newspapers, especially *The Times* and *The Daily Telegraph*. For the basement wards, which were underneath both wings, Richard had to leave the trolley in another ward and go downstairs to take orders, revisiting the trolley to take down the ordered items. He was grateful that at least he had not been consigned to one of these subterranean horrors. Grim and without natural light, they were particularly depressing in their effects upon the inmates. And the improvements in the general order of the asylum and in the care of patients, which he had observed during his incarceration, seemed to have passed these basement wards by.

It took him until lunchtime to complete the first rounds. He wheeled the trolley back into its cupboard, picked up the money box he used for the sales and gathered together the newspapers which had not been sold. He locked the cupboard and returned the newspapers to the shop. Any unsold by the end of the day would be bundled up and collected the next day as the newspaper delivery was made. Mrs Dearing, who seemed always to smile whatever the weather or the situation, had taken over from Mrs Jones, and she counted the money into the till, left the float in the cash box and rang up the overall sales on the shop till. When he had first been made a trustee, and been given the trolley round, Richard had had to keep a record of all the sales, and the volunteers had checked the sales item by item. He had done it meticulously, so that the figures always balanced. After a while the volunteers had decided that such close monitoring was no longer needed. Richard was grateful for the trust shown in him but never revealed to them that he even understood that he had passed that particular test.

"Which paper would you like, Richard?" Mrs Dearing asked, her smile as broad as ever. It was a small perk that the volunteers allowed him. "There is a copy of *The Daily Telegraph* and a couple of *The Times*. You normally like *The Telegraph*, don't you?"

Richard hesitated. "Yes, but I don't mind which," he muttered, as if to himself.

"Take *The Telegraph*, then, and have a good read when you can."

Richard took the paper, folded it carefully, and as he left the shop he discreetly tucked it partly into his trouser waistband and partly under his jumper. He hoped that it would not be noticed. It was better that he was not seen taking any interest in the world outside the asylum. He would read it later when he got away from everyone else. And so he went off to the canteen, to another solitary meal. But at least he could look forward to reading the newspaper, and to the distraction it provided him.

CHAPTER TWO

Ruth Appleton cursed the fog that smothered the road and the nearby houses in a dirty grey shroud. And she cursed herself for not having planned her journey better. When the train had surfaced from its underground tunnel she had been surprised to see the telltale slow white swirls beyond the platform. It had not been like that when she had set out, nor in Central London, but while the train lurched further into the city's eastern suburbs the fog had deepened, so that as she emerged at the end of the line she could hardly see her way, even though it was almost midday. Twice she had to ask passers-by for directions because the scrap of paper on which she had scribbled some names of roads was incomplete and some road signs were missing. And the case of clothing she had to carry pulled at her shoulder and the handle's coarse leather made her hand sore. She realised too late that she should have arranged for a car or a taxi to pick her up, and not assumed that she would find her own way straightforwardly. "Bloody fool," she said to herself, "as bloody usual!"

It had been a long walk just to get to the gates. Now she was finally standing in front of the asylum, she could still see virtually nothing, yet beyond the locked gates she knew there were buildings and people, in number the size of a large village. The huge gates were shut, and although the iron struts were rusted and brown they were an impenetrable barrier nonetheless. Ruth shivered as the clammy fog seemed to slide down the back of her neck. Beyond the gate there had to be some kind of gatehouse, but she could not see it, which meant that its occupants could not see her.

Ruth put her case on the ground and moved right up to the gates. Gripping a metal stanchion in each hand she tried to push her head through the gap to see what lay beyond. The fog, swirling a little, gave her a momentary glimpse of two houses, one on each side of the road, before concealing them again. Ruth decided there was nothing to do but shout.

"Hey! Hey! Anyone there?" Of course, there was no reply. The futility, the absurdity of her position angered her. "Hey!" she shouted louder, trying – but failing – to shake the giant gates. "Hey, open the gate here! What are you doing, you idiots?"

She suddenly became aware that a vehicle had stopped close behind her. She turned and saw that it was a large delivery van, its lights shining brightly at her, waiting to enter the hospital. Momentarily embarrassed by her outburst, she moved aside. The driver rolled his window down slowly.

"What's up? Is there a problem?"

"I don't know," replied Ruth. "No-one answering my call."

"Day like today," he said, "they don't put anyone standing at the gate. You have to hoot."

Ruth resisted making the obvious response. The driver pushed down on the horn and a loud boom sounded through the murk. From beyond the gates there was a movement. A door opened and shut. Keys jangled. And then a uniformed porter appeared, trudging towards the gates, and he grasped the padlock that held the locking bar in place and opened the lock. With difficulty he drew the locking bar back and then pulled the first reluctant gate back into the fog. Having cleared the roadway on the one side, he repeated the action for the other gate and waved the van along the driveway into the fog. Only then could Ruth accost him.

"Hey," she said, startling him as she moved into his sight. "Hey, how do I get in?"

"Depends who you are and what your business is. It isn't visiting time, and everyone with an exeat has already left for the day. You startled me, hiding in the fog there. What do you want?"

"I'm starting work here today."

"Bad luck for you, then," was his grim reply.

Ruth shuddered slightly. Was it the cold or the bleakness of the welcome that caused that involuntary movement? "As a doctor," Ruth said firmly. The porter's response was instant. His insolent, almost aggressive manner was put aside and a new, respectful approach put on.

"Forgive me, miss, er, Doctor, we often get troublemakers at the gate, and on a day like this it has to be kept locked. Lots of people turn up here asking for work, or food, or even to be admitted. Bloody lunatics! There's as many outside as there are in! Come in to the porters' lodge here," and he pointed to the house on the right of the driveway. Ruth stepped towards the doorway from which the porter must have emerged, while he repeated in reverse the cumbersome task of closing and locking the gates. She waited for him, not wishing to be further challenged by entering the lodge alone. He ushered her in. The hallway of the house served as a reception point, and a window in the wall allowed any visitor to communicate with the duty porter in the first room. Ruth could see a gas fire burning, and a kettle stood on an old gas ring in the corner. There were pigeon holes on one wall, many of them already stuffed with envelopes. Another porter was obviously completing the sorting of the mail, for more envelopes and packages were spread on a table in front of the pigeon holes, and he was picking them up and reading their labels. At the sound of two people entering the hallway he turned and looked through the window, scrutinising Ruth as if startled by her entry.

"What do we have here?" he asked of the other porter, as if Ruth were not there. She bristled.

"Be careful, Mick," his fellow urged, "this is Doctor, er... Doctor... what was the name?"

Mick stiffened at the warning. "Is it Doctor Appleton? We didn't have your first name, and we were expecting a—"

"A man, I suppose," Ruth said wearily.

"Well, yes, I suppose so, but certainly a doctor in a car. All the doctors come here in cars. It's out of the way, you see."

"Yes, I discovered that walking from the station," Ruth said tartly, trying not to let exasperation get the worse of her. "I don't have a car, and I was waiting outside in the fog until that van came up."

"I hope Pete explained that we can't leave the gate unlocked on a day like today. Too much opportunity for… well, you know."

"Yes, I think I do. But you should have been looking out for me."

The porter continued as if he hadn't heard what Ruth had said. "If there was no fog, the gates would be open. Most patients are completely free to come and go as they like." Ruth could sense a note of criticism in the information. "But we have to observe everyone, so as we know if anyone unusual is coming or going. Can't do that in this fog. So the gates have to be locked."

"But you could have a bell, couldn't you?" Ruth knew she shouldn't be challenging them, but the fatuous remarks were irksome. "Never get on the wrong side of the porters," a colleague had once said to her. "You'll need their co-operation some time or another." But Ruth was ignoring the advice.

The two porters looked at her silently. Indeed she felt they were scrutinising her, as if some sign should be evident of how much trouble she was going to cause them. There was a long pause, the seconds seeming to stretch into minutes. Mick looked at his fellow porter, not daring to raise his eyebrows but obviously suspecting her of being troublesome.

"Well, I suppose so, Dr Appleton. Perhaps you'd like to suggest that to the powers that be down in central admin." The other porter could not prevent himself snorting a half-smothered laugh.

Ruth sensed her face flushing with embarrassment. "I'll be sure to mention you as well, if I speak to admin," she said, trying to achieve the right balance of jest and threat in her reply.

Once again there was a pause, and Ruth resisted the urge to fill the silence with any further protestation. Finally, Mick spoke again.

"Well, you'd better be going on down to Reception, down the driveway. They'll be expecting you there."

"How far is it?" asked Ruth.

"About half a mile, I'd say. Third building you come to. On your right."

"What about my case? Must I carry that all the way down?"

Mick turned again to his colleague, this time facing away from Ruth, His head seemed to shake slightly as if in disbelief. The other porter answered her, however, "That's all right, er… Doctor, we'll get that down to Reception later when we bring the mail down, and you can pick it up from there."

Ruth was grateful for the offer. "Thanks for that at least. Is it really as much as half a mile?"

"Yes," he replied, "everyone coming new can't believe how big the place is. It may be more than that."

Ruth left the porters' lodge and started to walk up the driveway. She was indeed surprised by its length, although she had known that the hospital was on the site of an old country house. There was just a tarmac road with grass on either side stretching into the grey mist that still concealed everything beyond ten yards. Since there was no separate path for pedestrians, Ruth walked on the edge of the asphalt, listening carefully for the sound of any approaching vehicle. The fog seemed to have quietened everything. It felt unreal to be walking in this way, unable to see where she was going, or indeed where she had just been, with no building or fellow creature anywhere.

As she walked, Ruth could not help thinking over the events of the past four days. The director at The Victoria Centre in Buckinghamshire had called her in to his office only last Thursday morning, to tell her that her training schedule was to be disrupted; that he had agreed to her transfer to Black Roding as an emergency, and that she was to be a temporary senior house officer there; that Black Roding had a staffing crisis that had worsened following a consultant's death from a heart attack; that it would mean a short-term promotion to acting registrar, and the opportunity to see and to take part in the whole range of psychiatric work that went on at Black Roding. Yes, it would be difficult to adjust to the new setting, and yes, its buildings were notoriously unsuitable for a modern hospital. But it was at the forefront of developments in therapeutic care, and some of its work was gaining a reputation for being at the cutting edge. He would not have agreed to the changes if he did not think that Ruth could meet the challenges. He hoped she was not too upset to hear of the sudden change.

But Ruth *had* objected, vociferously. She had argued that it was unfair to alter her progression through training, and she had no experience of so large a hospital, with its no doubt great variety of psychiatric illnesses; that she was being picked on because she was not married or engaged, and that they would not have transferred her if she were attached to someone, or had a spouse or children at home. But her every argument seemed to be turned on its head by her consultant. She had made excellent progress as a trainee and was an outstanding young medical psychiatrist. She needed exposure to all that the psychiatric services had to deal with, which would not happen if she stayed where she was. Yes, she could challenge it, since it was outside the range of her contract, but in the circumstances he would not advise a challenge. It could cause her to be seen as awkward and unhelpful, a potential troublemaker even, and yes, she had no family or other ties to Buckinghamshire, he knew. And that meant that it was only she who was being disrupted, and not others, as would be the case if he agreed to transfer a married doctor.

That last part was certainly true, Ruth reflected. She had no family connections left. Her father had died in the war when she was five. And surely that had had its impact on her mother, who had never seemed the same to Ruth after the terrible day when that news had arrived. Somehow she seemed to shrink into herself, as if she had seen her life's purpose fail. And when she became fatally ill while Ruth was studying Medicine, the little love she had shown Ruth through her childhood and adolescence had disappeared too, as she became sharp and critical of doctors and hospitals, in almost equal measure to the pride she had shown when Ruth had first left home to go to Cambridge.

With no buildings even yet in sight, Ruth had the opportunity to reflect further on the events that had brought her to psychiatry and to this surreal walk through the chilly fog. She had been training as a doctor and intended to become a general practitioner. But all that had changed with that first death on the ward, when she was on weekend duty. It still haunted her. Even as she recalled it, the two lines of beds seemed to appear on either side of the misty driveway, and she felt that she was once again walking down the aisle between the beds. She could recall the nurse hastily pulling the curtains around the bed, and the mother and daughter of the patient crying out, screaming really, as the man in the bed panted for his last breaths. That feeling of inadequacy had gripped her heart and frozen her then, perhaps for the first time in her life, and it suddenly did so again. She stopped in the middle of the driveway. Should she go on? Shouldn't she just turn around now and escape, as she had wished to then? A light appeared in the fog ahead of her, and then another. Ruth could hear the engine of the delivery van, returning now to the front gate. But she didn't move until the driver again leant on his horn, the noise startling her into evasive action.

"Silly cow! Get out of the way!" the driver shouted at her as he passed. "What are you trying to do?"

Ruth stood still on the grass at the verge of the driveway, her shoulders drooped in shock. What, indeed, was she trying to do? To make people well? She didn't seem to have done that for some time. To help people cope? Yes, she'd done some of that, both by prescribing drugs and treatments and by talking to them about their problems. But not everyone had coped, and she had had to prescribe deeper treatments – stronger drugs, electroconvulsive shock therapy. She accepted the necessity of these but wondered if this was how she should spend the rest of her working life. Well, she confirmed to herself again, she'd realised that this emergency placement was at least a way of working out her answer to that question. Six months, long enough to decide if this really was her vocation. If it wasn't, then she would indeed turn around and walk away.

Finally a building appeared on Ruth's right. It seemed to be a three-storey grey brick building, and a path led from the driveway down the side of the building, but still disappeared into the fog that seemed if anything to be even thicker on that side. Looking up, Ruth could make out a sign – 'Nurses' Accommodation (Male)' it said. A row of windows on each floor of the building seemed to denote the bedrooms beyond. Ruth shivered a little. Her own accommodation had not been made known to her yet and already she had misgivings. A single female doctor would not be high up the hospital's accommodation list, she knew. She walked on and came to a similar building but taller. She could not see the roof but could count four storeys of windows that looked out onto the driveway. Again a path led off to the right and along the side of the building. And again there was a sign – 'Nurses' Accommodation (Female)' – that made Ruth wonder what it was going to be like to work and live in so big and isolated an institution as this, a question she had hardly had time to ask herself in the past few days. Only in the biggest of teaching hospitals had she seen nurses' accommodation as large as this, but they were usually in city centres, not stuck out here. Most nurses would not have cars, so what was their life like? And she herself did not drive. What would her life be like for the next few months? A bloody pain, she suspected.

CHAPTER THREE

Richard finished reading the newspaper and stood up. It usually took him half an hour to read all the articles that interested him, so he reckoned that gave him five more minutes before he went back to complete the trolley rounds on the upper floors of the hospital. He walked across to the half-door in the side of the room and looked out. Still all he could see, even from the high vantage point of this room, was the fog. It was not going to clear at all, and so the distant view of London, which he loved so much, was not going to be visible. He put the newspaper down on the pile in the corner where he kept old copies. He looked at the date of the bottom-most *Times* – 8th September 1965 – not quite the four weeks old point at which he usually cleared them out, so no need to do anything about the old copies yet. Winstanley had died on the 13th, he seemed to remember, and that corresponded with today's date being just three weeks later, which he had noted on the front page of the newspaper. Three weeks – they must do something about replacing him soon.

He glanced around the room. The wooden boards that constituted the walls were rough and full of splinters. He avoided touching them if possible. An old noticeboard contained the yellowing clippings he had kept from newspapers long since discarded, which he had pinned to the board. The floor planks were worn smooth, especially near the open space above the half-door that constituted the room's only window. Above this, and attached to the ceiling by a long metal bar, was the old pulley mechanism by which the servants had hoisted up the tools, paints and chemicals with which the water system had been made clean and safe. His seat, positioned to catch the light that came in through this space, was an old wooden dining-room chair that someone had brought up to the room many years before he had started to use it. Against a wall he had placed six wooden beer crates, with two planks straddling the crates, that served him as a desk, and on the top were his exercise books, pen and pencil, and the books he did not want anyone else to see him reading. A metal staircase, turning brown with rust and threaded through by spiders' webs, started in one corner of the room and led up to the space above, in which the vast water tank was housed that had once fed the water system of the country house and later the asylum. The tank had not been used for over fifty years, and all the lower pipework had been removed, but the water tower had never been demolished. Richard was grateful for this, as he was grateful to the retiring porter who had told him confidentially, six years ago, that the cupboard in which he kept his trolley also contained the old doorway into the basement passage that led into the water tower itself. The tower was shut and securely locked up, as far as the asylum authorities were concerned, its doorway into the grounds of the asylum fenced off to prevent any access. And so he had been able to make his way carefully through the basement passage each day, and climb the stone staircase that led to this room, six storeys high in the tower, unknown to any other member of the hospital community. Here was the place where he could read in a period of peace, without feeling the constant need to disguise his true self, to dissemble and imitate the insane, the necessary actions that troubled him incessantly.

Richard pulled the chair over to the desk of crates and sat down. He opened the topmost exercise book and a pencil, thought briefly, and then wrote:

Monday 4th October 1965.

No news yet of a replacement for Winstanley. As the days pass without any change, or any visitor, I realise how much I have been made dependent on one man, a doctor, who showed little thought for me. I regret his death, not as I have mourned other deaths. I never felt any sympathy with or from him, unlike many others. But his absence makes me more anxious than I can recall my father's did, after his death, or even that of my mother, whom I had not seen for many years. How strange it is to have become so connected to a man whose company I would never have sought, and whose ambitions and desires I could not share. And to be left so adrift by his death that I can barely think of anything else. And the absence of any response by the superintendent to his death makes me as bewildered as I am anxious. Surely a replacement will be made soon?

Richard read over the words, decided they were sufficient and closed the book. He stood up, looked briefly at the fog again, as if hoping it might have lifted, but seeing no change he headed for the door and the staircase down. As he went through the door he reached into his pocket for the torch that would be needed lower down. If he left the door open there would be enough light for him to walk down four of the twelve flights of steps. But beyond that he would be in darkness. He turned the torch on, shut the door and started his descent, shining the torch downwards so the light always spilled onto the two steps ahead of him. He held the banister rail in one hand and took the steps slowly. Once before he had slipped on a step, fallen and bruised himself badly. Fortunately the bruising had been on his leg and no-one had seen it. But he had learned a lesson from the fall, and realised that, were he to fall on his head and be unconscious, or fall down a whole flight of stairs and break a leg, he might never be found.

At ground floor level the staircase ended near the locked door. He had to walk round to the back of the tower to gain access through another door to the steps that led down into the basement and cellar passages. It was even darker here, and the air felt thick and damp. He had to duck his head a little, and he felt even more at risk of falling. There were three flights of stairs down, and at the bottom he had to turn into the narrow passage that led underneath the Central Wing of the hospital. He had often wondered what lay on the other side of the walls. He assumed the foundations of the building were filled in with rubble and earth, so that there would be little to see, but there was no chink anywhere along the passage through which he could check his hypothesis. The floor was damp, and at times when there had been heavy rain there might be puddles along the way. He was careful on those occasions to have a rag handy with which to wipe his shoes. A set of wet footprints coming out of the storage cupboard might cause any sharp-eyed observer to ask questions.

As often happened, while he walked in the darkness back towards the hospital corridors, he seemed to hear the cries of victims, shrieking in words he could not understand. The dying people came out of the darkness towards him, and he felt that their hands were clutching at his arms and legs as he brushed past them. He thought that if he stopped and turned around he would be confronted by their fear and their rage and be overwhelmed by their terrifying numbers. He hurried along the last section of the bleak corridor, the torch shaking in his hand so that the shadows leaped and lunged at him. He almost broke into a run, and arrived at the end of the passage in a sweat of anxiety, before climbing up the final flights.

The doorway at the top of these stairs was very low. He had to stoop to get through. He stood still and tried to calm himself for a few moments. He turned the light on in the cupboard, put the torch in an old bag that lay in the corner and rolled the bag into a bundle which he replaced in the corner. He unlocked the cupboard door quietly – he had oiled it often to achieve a silent smoothness in the mechanism that was probably unique in the entire hospital – and opened it so that he could haul the trolley out once more. The upper wards he only visited on three afternoons a week. On the other two weekday afternoons he went to the secure wards, which meant hauling the trolley out of the building and along the pathway outside to the separate building which housed those wards. He called in at the shop to take some of the remaining newspapers – he did not sell many on afternoon rounds – and to replenish his supply of sweets and biscuits. Then he pushed the trolley through the Central Wing and into the open reception area.

Halfway along the hall leading to the East Wing a lift had been installed within a closely meshed wire cage. It was used by workmen with equipment or machines, by nurses and orderlies moving bed-bound patients, and by him, needing to move the trolley to the wards which led off the three upper corridors. The patients in these wards were often very long-term inmates, chronically ill and not able to respond sufficiently to the new drugs that were, to his observation, making other patients' lives better. Many were geriatric, whose bodies and memories were failing. They did not read much, though they listened to radio programmes that were in some wards relayed over loudspeakers so that all the patients could listen. In some other wards the patients, or the Friends of Black Roding, had managed to purchase televisions, which the patients were allowed to watch in the evenings. The superintendent, whom Richard sometimes saw or passed on his round, was very insistent that patients should be dressed during the day and should be engaged in meaningful activities. Watching television was not, according to the superintendent, such an activity. Richard tried to avoid entering wards while the superintendent was there. Winstanley had warned him that the superintendent had an eagle eye for anything out of order.

When visiting these upper wards Richard had mostly to approach the nurses' counters. The behaviour and even the dress of the patients could be so erratic that it was not considered appropriate for the trolley to be wheeled along the wards to catch the individual patients' eyes. Rather, the nurses would go along the wards to ask the patients if anything was needed, and return to Richard with the coins needed for the purchases. This meant that Richard had to wait at the counters, where nurses would often try to engage him in conversation. He felt uncomfortable at such moments, and often had to recall his mantra before replying: walk slowly, avoid eye contact, pause before speaking. In Ward 18, for example, the staff nurse asked him what was in the newspapers today.

"I – I – I don't know," Richard stuttered out.

"Yes you do. I saw the lady in the shop give you a newspaper. So you could read about everything." She said this without any hostility. It was just a nurse-to-patient exchange, an encouragement to reveal a little more of himself. She had obviously been in or near the shop as he finished his morning round and wanted to draw him out. But it made Richard sweat again, and he felt a shiver of fear run down his back.

"No… I didn't…" his alarm was obvious.

"Don't worry, Richard," the nurse said, making light of it, "I won't reveal your little perk."

"No, no, it's not – it's not that…"

She patted Richard's arm. "I'm sorry," she said, "I didn't mean to upset you. Just wanted to talk." And she smiled in apology.

Richard too was upset, but not for the reasons the nurse imagined. He longed to reveal the truth, to tell her today's news, to discuss the prominent political and civil events of the day with another adult. But he did not dare let his guard slip, for fear of the consequences. And so he felt ashamed of his deceit and was reminded again of its cause. If he was not careful he would become dizzy in his anxiety, so he leant on the trolley as he waited for the nurse to come back with the patients' orders, his head down to avoid eye contact with the staff nurse. He hoped she was not noticing his deep breathing as he calmed himself down.

By mid-afternoon Richard's round was complete. He took the trolley back to the ground floor in the lift, pushed it back to its storage cupboard in the Central Wing, removed the last few newspapers to return them to the shop and locked the cupboard. He briefly visited the shop to put the papers on the counter and, with his head bowed, to mutter a goodbye to Mrs Dearing. Then, starting to dread the return of thoughts which being busy through the afternoon had mostly banished, he walked slowly back to Ward 44.

CHAPTER FOUR

Ruth had kept walking onward, beyond the nurses' quarters, and the driveway had turned left. It was still hard to see anything, but she sensed that the third building she was seeking was now somewhere off to her right. The driveway then opened into a much larger tarmac space, and Ruth could see that cars were parked on her left. There was a large sign indicating that Reception and Central Administration were indeed to her right. Visitors were advised to park further on, the immediate car park being designated for medical staff. But Ruth was able to walk across the final stretch of car park to what she realised was a substantial stone staircase leading up to two heavy wooden doors. The old country house entrance had evidently not been altered, and remained the main point of access to what were clearly substantial buildings. As Ruth approached the doors she saw that, much as in a large church or cathedral, a smaller doorway had been cut into the left door. She turned the metal ring that served as a handle, pushed hard on the door and it swung open. She climbed over the foot of the main door and looked in.

Although she was prepared to see a large space beyond the door, the scale of it still surprised her.

The entrance hall was as tall as the building and as wide as the main wings that stretched out right and left. It was clear that it had been built to impress, for looking up Ruth could see all the way into a tower that soared above the doors she had just entered. A large chandelier was centrally placed and cast just sufficient light for the staff and patients who were criss-crossing the hall. There were some doctors, recognisable in white medical coats, and nurses, also recognisable in their deep blue uniforms. They moved with a sense of direction or purpose. Others in civilian clothes were more varied. Some were walking in twos or threes with that same sense of purpose, but some were slow or virtually at a halt, and Ruth recognised the uncontrolled shaking of a few patients. For all of them the scale and magnificence of the buildings, which had arrested her, had clearly ceased to impress and had rather become just one more part of their daily routine.

A long wooden bar hugged one of the corners of the hall and provided space for several desks, and each had a member of staff seated behind the bar, some with patients in small queues waiting for their attention. A wide hallway stretched ahead of Ruth, with a stone staircase leading up to the floor above. Beyond the staircase she could see more imposing buildings, though not clearly. Inside the hall it seemed to be as cold as outside, and many of the patients passing Ruth had big coats on. The walls were of dark stone, and a draught seemed to emanate from deep within the right wing of the building and to sweep down across the central hall and into the left wing. Ruth shivered as it passed. She walked across to the desk marked Reception, where a woman was busy marking up a pile of papers with a pencil. She looked up.

"Hello," she said. "Doctor Appleton? The porters phoned to say you'd be arriving. I'm sorry we hadn't realised you were arriving by foot."

"I don't drive," Ruth said, "so I had no alternative. And my transfer happened very quickly. No-one told me to arrange transport." Ruth tried hard to keep her exasperation out of her voice, but couldn't force herself to smile.

"The superintendent asked to see you when you arrived. His office is down the central corridor past the stairs, towards the chapel. But I think he's likely to be still on rounds at the moment. He's often delayed doing rounds. His secretary is in the office adjoining his, so if you knock on that Mrs Rogers will tell you where to wait." She pointed around the corner to indicate the route Ruth should take.

"Oh, my case," said Ruth, "the porters were going to bring it down."

"They'll be bringing the post down soon, I imagine, so they'll probably load it on the trolley. I'll keep it here for you for later. You'll no doubt want to look around. But you won't see much outside, I'm afraid. The smog is here to stay."

"Smog?" asked Ruth. "I've heard of that, I think."

"Yes. Around London the fog seems to mix with coal smoke. It's a horrible combination. Smoke and fog – smog – that's what it's called."

"And why is it so cold in the building?"

"The heating isn't going on until the first of November, or even the fifteenth if admin can manage it. So you have to do this." The woman pulled back the top of her heavy woollen cardigan to reveal another thick jumper beneath. "Just more money-saving!"

Ruth went in search of the superintendent's office, turning around the corner into the large central corridor and looking at the office doors as she passed the staircase. The superintendent's office was easily found, but as Ruth went beyond it to find the secretary her eye was taken by a splash of colour in a large room opposite. Ruth crossed the corridor and realised it was a chapel, indeed a good-sized chapel, with seating for a congregation of perhaps a hundred. But Ruth was looking beyond the seats to the spectacular window behind the altar. Even though the light was gloomy Ruth could see that the blues, reds and greens of the glass were brilliant, and that the whole window represented the Lord casting out demons. He was a central figure, blessing the afflicted represented by three tormented figures on this left, while the exorcised were represented by three calm disciples to his right. For a short time Ruth could not look anywhere but at this window. Although she had lost her own faith, or whatever faith her mother had tried to inculcate in her, she could see that this window had been made and positioned there by someone in the full belief that the work of the hospital was divinely inspired. For a moment she was tempted to sit, but then thought that she really should see the superintendent's secretary.

Ruth walked across the corridor and knocked on the door of Mrs Rogers' office. "Come in," the voice beyond the door called. The office was small but seemed well-organised. Mrs Rogers was ensconced behind a desk on which sat a large typewriter, and there were two tiers of document trays, one on either side of the typewriter. Behind Mrs Rogers was a wall devoted almost entirely to shelves of box files, and Ruth could see that each box file was neatly marked up with its contents: 'Board Meetings' was one complete row; other sets were marked as 'Letters' and 'Memoranda', each box containing the start and end dates of the correspondence they contained. A door obviously led through to the superintendent's office. Mrs Rogers was trim and efficient in everything, her clothes clearly pressed and her greying hair tied in a bun so that not a hair looked out of place. She seemed to be nearing the end of a lengthy typing session, because piles of newly typed letters lay in the trays to one side of her on the desk, with paperclips attached to the files of correspondence, while a much smaller pile of papers and files was in the document tray on her other side. She looked at Ruth as she entered, but did not speak, refocusing on the letter she was typing. Ruth therefore greeted her.

"Mrs Rogers, I'm Doctor Appleton," Ruth said. "I'm starting today." Mrs Rogers raised a finger as if to ask for silence while she completed the typing of the letter, pushing the carriage of the typewriter into position twice and typing a few strokes, and then pulling the letter and a carbon copy out of the machine. She put these down and looked up again at Ruth.

"Good afternoon, Doctor," Mrs Rogers said. "Forgive me just finishing that letter. It's easier not to get distracted halfway through. I hope you've had a good trip out here. Was it difficult in the fog?"

"I came by train," Ruth replied. "That bit wasn't difficult, but it got a bit harder when I was on my own. I hadn't expected it to be so bad. Nor so long a walk."

"The hospital is in a difficult location, I'm afraid. Please sit down a minute while I find your papers for the superintendent. Can I get you a tea or coffee?"

"Tea, please." Ruth was grateful to find this oasis of civility after her journey. She slumped as she sat in a chair that faced Mrs Rogers across the office. On a small table in the corner Mrs Rogers had a kettle, cups and other necessities for refreshments. She looked in the teapot, tutted to herself and left the office, returning a minute or two later, still dusting the pot clean with a cloth. While she busied herself, Ruth looked out of the window that stood opposite the doorway. But it was still impossible to see anything other than the smog. She realised, however, that Mrs Rogers had a small heater in the corner behind her desk, and that it was warmer in this office than in the corridor. She stood up, took her coat off and placed it behind her.

"Sorry, Doctor, I have to keep my room warmer. I couldn't type if it was as cold in here as out there. My fingers just wouldn't move."

"It's a comfort here, at least," Ruth said. "Will the superintendent be long?"

Mrs Rogers chose not to answer this at first, and brooded over the pot until she decided that the tea was sufficiently brewed. She poured Ruth a cup, handed it to her and proffered a small jug of milk. Finally she said, "Well, he does get immersed in what's happening on the wards. He's very enthusiastic about the changes he's trying to implement, so he spends a lot of time on his rounds. It's always difficult to say when he'll be finished."

"Does he run some wards, then?" Ruth was surprised by this.

"Yes, he runs one Admissions Ward," Mrs Rogers said, "but he also visits other wards where he is trying to get the firms to change things. That's what he's doing now." Although Ruth had not used this jargon in her training, she knew that in the large hospitals the doctors' team on a set of wards was often called a firm.

"You make it sound as if the firms are independent."

Mrs Rogers laughed. "Independent," she echoed Ruth, "yes, that's probably a good description of some of them, and the cause of more than a few of the superintendent's grey hairs." She grimaced a little when she had said this, as if she had been a little too indiscreet. "But I shouldn't be nattering on like this. The superintendent asked for you to wait in his office, so let's sit you down in there." She pointed to the doorway into the office beyond. Ruth stood up, holding her cup and saucer. "Yes, take that through and I'll bring your coat." She opened the door, ushered Ruth through and followed with Ruth's coat.

The superintendent's office was as disorderly and chaotic as Mrs Rogers' office was organised and efficient. A large desk was piled with files that threatened at any moment to topple over. The bookcase behind it was full of books, the bottom layer on each shelf fairly straight and upright, but on each layer further books had been stacked sideways so that it looked almost impossible to extract a book without commencing an avalanche. Personal belongings – various coats, hats, golf clubs and balls, three attaché cases – were scattered on an old sofa, and newspapers and journals were littered across a low table and the two armchairs that were grouped in front of a large marble fireplace. But unlike Mrs Rogers' office, there was no source of heat. The superintendent obviously did not do himself any favours, thought Ruth.

Across the whole wall on Ruth's left was a list, or a series of lists, which seemed to contain essential information about all fifty-two of Black Roding's wards, written on whiteboards that could be amended as that information changed. Ruth could not help but look closely at these boards. Each ward had a number and a name, and a location in the building. They were listed as female, male or mixed. Ruth drew in her breath. She had never worked on a mixed ward and felt instinctively that the atmosphere and ways of working must be different in one. There were two Admissions Units, with the names of the doctors attached to each, the firms that Mrs Rogers had just been talking of. Then there were wards dedicated to particular conditions – neuroses, psychoses, schizophrenics – with descriptions such as 'Chronic', 'Acute' or 'Severe'. Five secure wards were listed last of the fifty-two and coloured in a light yellow to distinguish them from the others. Again, each ward had the names of the doctors who controlled that ward. Ruth was drawn to the list, and she put her tea down in order to read it better. Behind her Mrs Rogers said, "The hospital is so large that one can't learn all that information, and it changes so often. But the superintendent often needs it, if he's called to a ward, or there's an emergency, or he's on the phone. So it's the most up-to-date information about which doctors are working where, and what numbers and kinds of patients they might have." His office might not look efficient, thought Ruth, but she could see that the superintendent knew what was needed to keep tabs on this enormous institution. She carried on her scrutiny as Mrs Rogers retreated to her own office. What must it be like to be in charge of so many patients, doctors, nurses, social workers and support staff? And all of them, in their own ways, responsible for so many patients and their problems. It made Ruth feel dizzy just to think of the enormity of it.

When her consultant had told the other doctors that Ruth was leaving to work at Black Roding for a while, the registrar had laughed. He was an unpleasant man, whom Ruth had had to tolerate but could never like, and he seemed to know how to unsettle Ruth. "You'll never cope there," he said to her afterwards when they were alone. "All the socialist claptrap you hear about that place. Letting the patients run the asylum. You'll hate it." Ruth couldn't pretend that she wasn't a little scared about working in this hospital.

As she scanned the list further, Ruth realised that the notes attached to each ward, written in a smaller script, contained information that was more varied. There was mention of group meetings on some wards, but by no means all. Nurse-led meetings also featured in some wards, as did small-group meetings and one-to-one therapy, and several carried the additional description of 'geriatric'. There was information about the condition of the ward's buildings, the number of beds, and finally information that seemed more difficult to interpret, using abbreviations that defied Ruth to work out. They were clearly personal to the superintendent. But if he was suddenly summoned to a ward, reading across the entries would remind him of all the information he needed, and prepare him for whatever awaited on the ward.

One thing escaped Ruth, however, as she completed reading the list for the second time. However hard she looked through the names of doctors, she could not find 'Dr Ruth Appleton' anywhere on the list. On that matter it was as foggy inside as it was outside. She sat down, therefore, to await the superintendent.

CHAPTER FIVE

Ruth's thoughts went back to the first time she had felt afraid. She was five years old and living with her mother in their small terraced house. She had a vague memory of her father, who had left for the war in the Far East when she was two. The worst effects of the war had not visited their small town – the bombers had always flown overhead searching for more metropolitan or more industrialised targets. But her father's absence had often cropped up in her mother's conversations with visitors. "I'm afraid for him," she would say whenever the topic came up in conversation. Gradually it had seemed to wear her down with worry, until one day two policemen came to the front door.

"Dear God, no!" her mother had shouted as she saw the helmeted profiles of the two visitors framed in the glass windows of the front door. She could hardly open the door, as grief started to overwhelm her. The two officers hardly needed to say anything. Everyone knew, it seemed, why two constables would visit the house of a woman whose husband was away at the front, because several neighbours were already visible behind the two men, leaving their own houses to bring the support they knew would be needed.

"I'm sorry, Mrs Appleton, we've had a message from the War Office and there was no-one else who could deliver it. Your husband's been killed in action, and the government has sent its sympathies to you at this moment of loss." It was the older of the two who spoke, and he tendered towards her mother a telegram. But Ruth's mother did not take it. She fell down where she was, standing in the doorway, landing on her knees and bending over in tears. Ruth, behind her, could not hear the policeman clearly, but she quickly realised that her mother's fears had indeed come true. And she cried with her mother, and for her mother, and she shivered as her mother shivered. And she was afraid, afraid of the unknown cause of her mother's grief, and afraid of her own lack of understanding. That's what she associated fear with – losing control over her situation, her position, her way forward. And in her reverie she understood, briefly, why she was afraid here in the superintendent's office. But her self-analysis was only momentary because, just as she had remembered kneeling down next to her mother and crying out "What's wrong?", her thoughts were interrupted by noises in the next office.

Ruth heard the superintendent before she saw him. He arrived in his secretary's room in a storm of oaths. "Bloody man!" She heard a Scottish lilt in the exclamation. "Never listens to what I say! And that flaming bevy of nurses. A regular coven, they are, when they get together. Why don't they just bloody well get on with the job and stop wittering?"

Ruth could hear Mrs Rogers' emollient voice but could not make out the words she was using to calm her superior. No doubt the superintendent had just experienced the independence of other doctors and nurses that she and Mrs Rogers had talked of just a few minutes earlier. "Well, why didn't you tell me?" She heard the question asked of Mrs Rogers. Then the superintendent came into his own office. "Dr Appleton," he said, "I must apologise if the first words you heard from the leader of this hospital were so violent. I did not know you were here."

The phrase 'pocket battleship' came to Ruth's mind as she stood in front of the superintendent, Dr Paul Verity. He was a small man, indeed smaller than her, with thin ginger-red hair fading into grey. He was in his fifties, an age when many administrators might withdraw into routine tasks and avoid change and conflict. But he exuded an energy that Ruth had seldom experienced, except perhaps among the most driven of academics in her college. His eyes were sharp and inquisitive, and his interest was keen. His shoulders were broad and his stance upright, almost military. His white coat was pristine, and the creases left by a hot iron on the sleeves were still sharp. In driving Black Roding forward, it seemed to Ruth, he must be at the vanguard of the fleet, not bringing up the rear.

Ruth was shaken by the oaths and already felt in awe of someone who could command so large an institution. She cautiously shook his hand, noting the firm grip and the steady eye contact of the superintendent.

"Don't worry," she said. "Ward rounds always…" she didn't quite know how to finish, so left the idea incomplete.

"Yes indeed. They can have a very bad effect on me. A lay person would no doubt think, well, he's the superintendent, so what he says must go. If he's off on a ward round he's no doubt telling all the doctors what to do." A small smile crossed his lips at the thought. "But the reality is different, and every firm has its own ways, and every consultant their own ideas, and every ward sister their own opinions. And so the lay person would be wrong. The superintendent has a lot of discussions on his ward round, but the only thing he can order is a cup of tea." The last words were uttered in a raised voice, and Mrs Rogers could be heard rising from her seat and starting to bustle around the office next door.

"Please sit down, Doctor; may I call you Ruth? I have to engage in some therapy myself." Ruth sat and watched the superintendent cross the room. He picked up one of the golf clubs and took a handful of golf balls from the sofa. He rolled one across the rug that covered part of the floor, where it stopped short of the carpet edge, and, placing the other balls at his feet, he proceeded to address each one with the club and then to stroke the ball across towards the first, which now constituted a target. "Like all educated Scots, I play golf. It is our nation's exercise in humility, to be unable to exert control over so small and uncomplicated an item as a golf ball. We have to learn from the humbling experience of failing to direct its trajectory. And I will only putt this ball straight and true if I am calm and fully in control of my emotions. So I will strike a few putts while you tell me how you came to be a psychiatrist." And while he criss-crossed the carpet in following his putts, Ruth had to concentrate much harder than she would have expected to in order to explain her own history, and to avoid revealing how distracting, even annoying, she found his behaviour.

"Where would you like me to start?" she asked, uncertain of the rules of this interview.

"Where does it begin?" he replied sharply.

Ruth had experienced oral examinations during her student days, *viva voce* they were called, or *vivas* for short. You were tested on your academic knowledge, but the rumours suggested that you were also tested on your ability to stay focussed, keep cool, hold your position and not give way unnecessarily. Even your body language was evaluated, they said. And the examiners would try to distract you. Was this what was happening to her? Certainly she felt anxious, just as in a *viva*. Wasn't it enough that she was here? That she had agreed to this transfer? Best go back to the beginning, she decided reluctantly.

"At school, I suppose. I was lucky. At the grammar school they employed specialist science teachers, even a couple of men, so that we girls could study Chemistry and Physics. And I was interested in these subjects." Ruth paused. The superintendent did not say anything, but he too paused, as if awaiting the continuation of Ruth's account before he struck another ball. "And I was good at them," she blurted out, feeling embarrassed about applauding her own achievements.

The superintendent looked up from his putting stance and scrutinised Ruth's face before looking down again at the ball at his feet. "Go on," he said.

"So I decided to try to study something scientific, and to go to university. At school they suggested Medicine, and I liked the idea of being a doctor."

Ruth paused again. She resented being subjected to this testing, which she regarded as unnecessary and intrusive. Any summary of her career and progress would have to touch on difficult areas where she still felt disappointment in herself, and the pain of the criticism she had received from others. But although her inquisitor still seemed occupied in his putting, she knew he was expecting some explanation of her abandonment of a purely medical career. People didn't just switch, as she had done, without good reason. Most psychiatrists had made a decision at some point, at some particular moment, to move into this separate branch of medicine, or they had experienced that decision being made for them. One of her tutors, for example, had been a medical officer during the war and was put in charge of a unit for distressed soldiers. He had never gone back to general medicine. And so she had to fill the vacuum with words that would explain her detour from the conventional career path.

"The scientific part was good, but the work on the wards was very demanding, and sometimes it upset me." Ruth stopped to take a breath or two. "But I was able to switch into psychiatry on the course that I was following. And the work seemed to be becoming more scientific, more medical, and so I was able to qualify through my course and my experience as a trainee." The final phrase came out with a gasp, as if she had been holding her breath while navigating carefully through the rocks and rapids of her past.

Still the superintendent putted. Then he spoke. "There, three in a row. I must have calmed down." He replaced the club and balls in their original positions on the sofa. "And what about your training?"

"Oh, that's been in small, secure institutions. Long-term patients transferred from other units. I've never worked in any hospital as big as Black Roding. Mostly psychotic patients in my last year, and patients were treated with drugs and ECT. And individual therapy sessions, monitored by senior physicians at first and then one-to-one in the past six months, but always with attendants present. There were some risks." Ruth stopped, unsure if more information was needed. The superintendent waited for a few seconds and then spoke.

"A very good summary. Matches what I'd heard about you. I spoke to your superintendent. I've known him a good few years, and he said you were one of the best scientists to cross his path. He said you were just about ready for what I'm about to ask you to do, and I trust his judgement.

But I am going to ask a lot of you. You'll meet a much greater range of patients here than you have before, and many more problems than you've encountered in your training."

Ruth had remained seated but now she became conscious of the awkward position she had adopted while summarising her career. She felt a pain in her back where she had held a twisted and awkward posture, and tried now to straighten herself without flinching. The superintendent spoke again.

"I dare say you've heard all kinds of things about Black Roding. And I won't deny that what you've probably heard has some truth in it. But let me try to give you my perspective on it, and then I'll explain your job."

The superintendent seemed to drop the pitch of his voice as he spoke, but it seemed to Ruth that his speech was rehearsed, his standard introduction to a prospective initiate.

"Black Roding is the wrong institution, in the wrong place, in the wrong buildings, and often doing the wrong work in the wrong way." Ruth could not help but react, and he must have noticed her startled look. "Yes, it's a shocking thing for a superintendent to say, isn't it? And I don't say it lightly. The Victorians and the Edwardians may have been excellent at all sorts of things, but building appropriate asylums, locating them in accessible places, developing good therapies, ensuring patients returned to life outside the asylum – they failed on all these counts. And here we are left with the consequences."

Mrs Rogers came in with a steaming cup of tea. As the superintendent took it, he asked her when someone would be available to give Ruth a tour of the buildings. "Not until four o'clock," was her reply.

"That won't do," he said, looking at his watch. "She can't sit around until then. I'll get someone on the ward to do it. Cancel whoever's been booked." Mrs Rogers accepted the instruction without demur. Then the superintendent continued, "You won't have seen much of the buildings as you arrived. The fog is very thick today. But it is essentially a very large country house, with a long facade and three wings, and onto that footprint the Victorians built lots of additional extensions as wards, so that the number of wards ran out of control. It's too big, too cold, too unwieldy and too forbidding a place to make anyone feel comfortable. So the buildings do not provide a proper mental health hospital. And they thought that this rural, or semi-rural, location would benefit the inmates. And the grounds are good for walking in and raising the spirits. I'll grant them that. But it makes it almost impossible for these unfortunate people to get to anywhere else, or for them to get jobs, or for their families to visit them. It just increases their isolation from the world. So the location isn't right. And then they and those who followed them used all kinds of treatment that didn't work – hydrotherapy, laxatives, isolation cells, rest cures, prolonged sleep and induced comas, morphine, bromides. And even when these treatments alleviated symptoms, which on some occasions they did, they often had terrible side effects. So the treatments have not been effective ones. But the asylum still grew larger and larger, and the number of long-term patients increased proportionately, until just ten years ago, when I came as superintendent, there were over two thousand two hundred patients locked up in here. And I do mean locked up – every single ward. And very few of the patients were getting better. So the whole place needed sorting out. And we are doing our best, and I hope the hospital is a much better place than it was ten years ago. But some things don't change. Doctors are over-worked, nurses are under pressure as a result, and the sudden death of a consultant leaves us without the resources to cope. And that is the prelude to your joining us."

The superintendent paused and drained the cup of tea.

Ruth asked, "So, what has changed?"

"Ten years ago this was a terrible place, with some of the worst wards in the kingdom. Places where even I feared to enter because the patients might simply attack me. And where some of the nursing staff were as dangerous as the patients. When you walked in you felt as if you'd entered a nightmare – the female patients dressed only in smocks, their hair unkempt, their behaviour completely unrestrained. A fight would break out, and the immediate response of some staff was to join in. Such brawls, and injuries, were an everyday occurrence. We've changed all that. First, some drugs have started to work, and to work quite well, in alleviating the symptoms of whole groups of patients. We've unlocked most of the locked doors and opened up the whole hospital. And we have managed to place some patients into hostels and other residential units, so that they can live without being permanently incarcerated here. Our numbers are down to eighteen hundred, and they need to fall further. After all, the minister said three years ago that he was going to shut us down. And in time we probably will shut down, but not yet. There's nowhere for most of these patients to go at present."

The superintendent waited for any question from Ruth, but she remained silent. He therefore continued, "There are ten consultant-led firms at Black Roding, of which one is the Secure Block and one is the other Admissions Unit, which my deputy runs. Sir Reginald Winstanley ran one of the firms until he died unexpectedly of a heart attack three weeks ago. In that firm there are five wards, two hundred patients, two registrar posts – two senior house officers, that is – and whatever junior house officers might be on their rotations. One registrar post was already unfilled because of lack of finance, so the whole firm is left with one registrar acting as consultant now. A good man, David Peters, but his wife is having a difficult pregnancy with extreme nausea. I looked across the whole hospital to find someone I could transfer, but I could not juggle things any further. There was no-one I could move without causing similar problems elsewhere. And the other house officer in the firm hasn't got enough service to act as registrar. So that's when I got on the telephone, and your superintendent said that he could spare you and that you were good enough to meet this responsibility."

He turned to look closely at Ruth, as if perhaps he knew that she had not leapt at this opportunity, but rather had not felt able to refuse it. She nodded her head in acknowledgement of the superintendent and said guardedly, "I wasn't sure about such a big change, but there was an opportunity to see other people at work, yes."

The superintendent again scrutinised Ruth for a moment before he resumed his speech. "So, you'll be acting registrar of Firm 9, which runs Wards 43 to 47, out on the West Wing of the hospital. There'll be David Peters as acting consultant, and John Sutton is the other house officer. You'll be one or two doctors down on a full team, I'm afraid, but that is now becoming the norm rather than the exception. Almost every firm is short of trained doctors. If I can find another house officer, I will give him or her to you as a priority. But I need you to try to do more than just run these wards." Here he looked at Ruth, as if trying to determine what impact his words had already had on her. *What now?* wondered Ruth.

"First of all, I have to ask you to review the patients and determine whether there are any who could be transferred to hostels or units outside the hospital. Sir Reginald always seemed to resist doing this, and it has not been done properly for some years. I think that you, coming from outside the hospital, are best placed to do this. On the basis of work on previous wards, there ought to be about twenty who can be considered immediately for such transfers, so bear that number in mind. Second, I am asking David Peters, as consultant, to manage the merger of Wards 43 and 47. Ward 43 is in the basement, one of four basement wards that are the most dreary and inappropriate of our wards. I've been waiting five years to start closing them, and consultants have been resisting – bits of their empires, no doubt. But that has got to change, and there's no better time than now. David and you can agree how much you'll be involved, given the reviews I've asked you to undertake."

Ruth was thinking hard. In her previous work a patient review took a week to prepare, involved a meeting of all the staff relevant to the patient and required detailed paperwork afterwards. It was a major task. Two hundred patients, to be reviewed in the six months of her placement! She knew she couldn't do it.

"That's impossible!" she protested. "I can't review all those patients in that time! There's too much work involved. It takes a week for one. I can't do two hundred proper reviews in the time I've got."

"I don't agree," the superintendent replied. "These patients have been waiting far too long already. Winstanley would never do it, and his stubborn attitude has done a great deal of harm. The reviews should be brief and done quickly, and agreed with David. If he then has any problems, he can bring them to me. But I expect the recommendations for transfer to start to come within a fortnight."

"I'll have to cut all kinds of corners to do that!" Ruth did not want to give way on this, even though she sensed that the superintendent would not change his mind. She prided herself on the thoroughness she had acquired during her training and did not want to abandon it.

"If need be, cut the corners. I'm not interested in all the frills. Just make sure you do cover all the essentials. Perhaps it's time I took you to the wards and got someone there to show you around. Then you might see what I'm talking about. Come on." And with that the superintendent stood up and ushered Ruth out into the corridor.

CHAPTER SIX

The superintendent's normal walking pace was much faster than Ruth's, so she felt as if she had to hurry. He had set off down the Central Wing, and as he passed any staff they greeted him briefly. One engaged him in conversation, so Ruth was able to draw alongside him. He looked around. "Cream paint!" he exclaimed to her as if in triumph, and waved his hands to indicate the walls, which were indeed painted cream. "It took me five years to stop the Board using the brown and purple paints they'd been using here for decades! You'll still see them on some of the wards, though! They're on a ten-year cycle for painting!"

The superintendent continued down the corridor even as he spoke, so that anyone in the corridor could hear him. As he passed each point along the corridor he waved an arm and shouted the room's purpose, but he gave Ruth no opportunity to see inside. "Patients' dining room," he called out, "for the patients not taking food on the ward." A smell of over-boiled cabbage caught Ruth's nostril. Then he went on, calling out "staff dining room" and "doctors' dining room" as he progressed. He stopped for a moment. "You'll be taking your meals here, of course. There are no cooking facilities in the individual doctors' rooms. Breakfast at seven, lunch at twelve thirty and dinner at seven. Someone is on kitchen duty during the night, so if you are on duty then you can get something here." He waited, as if expecting Ruth to say something, but she groaned inwardly and said nothing. Institutional meals were a grim prospect. Her previous accommodation had had its own small kitchen. An unrelenting diet of cabbage and carrots no doubt awaited her. And she was starting to resent the lack of choice she appeared to have over her own domestic arrangements. All in all, things seemed as bad as she had feared they might be. "Oh, I left out the theatre, which we passed on the other side of the corridor."

"Theatre?" Ruth asked in astonishment, looking back to see if there was any sign on the corridor of so remarkable a venue. But all she could see were two sets of doors without handles, both sets firmly closed. And the superintendent was not minded to tell her more, because he had already set off again at the same brisk pace that seemed to characterise everything he did. Again he waved an arm as he passed the various services provided by the hospital.

"The post office, open every morning, and the hospital bank, open Monday, Wednesday and Friday mornings; the hospital's shop, selling newspapers, sweets, toiletries, and so on; the library, open Tuesday and Thursday mornings; the purser's office; the social services suite; the head of occupational therapy; the chaplain's office." Ruth had been told in advance of the variety of services provided in this isolated community, but even so the idea of a hospital containing a bank was a surprise. At least she'd be able to get some money out of her account without travelling miles to do so – the only good news she had received all day!

Beyond where they stood was another staircase, with metal banisters and handrails. "All the administration offices are up there – the ones the patients don't need to get to – Personnel, Wages, Records, Rotas, Outpatients' Administration, the Boardroom, Buildings' Maintenance, the Porters' Room, and so on. We don't need to go there now, but you should report there later, or tomorrow. Start at Personnel and they'll tell you what to do. We'll go to the West Wing by the outside path."

At the end of the corridor were two tall wooden doors and, just as in the main entrance, a smaller door had been cut into one of the two. The superintendent opened this and stepped out into the fog. Ruth followed. While the hospital itself was hardly warm, here the chill gripped each exposed part of Ruth – her hands, her face and neck – and made her shiver. The superintendent appeared not to notice either the cold or Ruth's reaction to it. There was a tarmac path that led away from the building for five yards or so, at which point it linked to a wider path that appeared to go in both directions.

"This is the perimeter path," the superintendent said, "which runs around the whole building and gives a second access point to the other wings and to the wards that have been built off them. We're going to go right to the West Wing, but if you turned left you would come to the East Wing, and then beyond it the Secure Block, and beyond that the doctors' flats and houses. As we go along you might see the water tower, which originally fed water into the whole hospital. It isn't used now because there's enough pressure in the mains system. It's never been knocked down. And it gave the minister an interesting little point in his speech about closing us down." As they walked along the path Ruth peered into the murk, but she could not make out even a single brick of the redundant building.

After walking for perhaps two or three minutes more, there was another intersection on the path, and the superintendent turned right along it. "We're going in the same kind of back door at the end of the West Wing that the Central Wing has, and we'll be right where Firm 9 is based. So this is where you'll be working."

As she entered the building again, Ruth was reminded of things the superintendent had already said. The five wards at the end of the West Wing were certainly depressing. If you weren't a depressive when you were admitted, Ruth thought as she walked around the area, you probably would be one after a day or two. And the superintendent was right about the paint as well – brown walls and purple woodwork throughout.

They first went upstairs to Ward 43, which the superintendent said was a chronic ward, but a quick glance around showed Ruth that it was really a female geriatric ward. Most of the patients were not dressed in day clothing, but remained in nightwear and dressing gowns. Some were in bed, and others were seated near their beds. One or two were reading, but for the most part the patients were unoccupied, staring into space or obsessively fidgeting. The individual beds had flimsy curtains on rails that surrounded them, as in a general hospital, and bedside cabinets and chairs. There were some tables and chairs in the middle of the ward. The heavy brown velveteen curtains covering the windows were still drawn, making the area dark and shadowy. Two nurses were standing at a desk near the entrance door, but the appearance of the superintendent broke up their conversation. One walked down the ward as if to resume some task, while the more senior greeted the two doctors. Ruth was briefly introduced, but the superintendent was more intent on making some comments.

"There should be more activities going on, Nurse, and there should be more patients in their day clothes. And why are those curtains still drawn when it's almost the afternoon? Doctor Appleton will be checking these things in the future." He turned and walked out, but before she left Ruth sensed the hostility of the nurse towards her, now that she had been introduced as the superintendent's watchdog.

Outside the ward the superintendent waited for Ruth. He spoke quietly to her. "I don't know if David has spoken to anyone on the ward yet, but this is the ward I want him to merge with 47, the basement ward. And you can see, it's not going to be easy, when the nurses can't even do the most simple of things like open the curtains. We're going to have to change the layout, and build some partitions, if we're going to make it a mixed ward."

Ruth was taken aback. "A mixed ward?" She had raised her voice in horror. "But surely those patients aren't used to a mixed ward. They look as if they've grown used to a female-only environment."

"And that's why some of them have been here twenty-five years, Doctor. How can we possibly say we're preparing them to return to life outside the hospital if we separate them in this way? Do you think the local homes for the elderly will just deal with one sex? Of course they won't." Ruth noted the subtle but significant change from Ruth to Doctor in the superintendent's words to her. "The ward needs reorganising into three areas: one for male sleeping, one for female sleeping and one for communal activities. And the staff and patients need to be prepared for the changes. And that means getting far more of them dressed. At the moment we're allowing them to act as if they are in a general hospital and are unwell or sick. That costs a lot of money. But when you review them you'll find that some of them should never have been admitted here, and others are now no more ill than thousands, or millions maybe, of other females living in the community. I may not be able to move them on, but I must stop the circumstances that institutionalised women like these in the first place. It's not going to happen again."

"But isn't it going to distress these patients?"

"Yes, it probably is. But I have to balance that against the needs of many other patients, both now and in the future. And in the end that means shutting down these geriatric wards. That's what a superintendent has to do."

Ward 44 was next. This was listed as a mixed ward of neurotic patients. Here Ruth could see the kind of partitioning that was planned for Ward 43. Immediately on entry a more private space had been created to the right by a wooden partition across the ward, with a door into this dormitory space. A general area had been created in front of the nurses' desk, and further down the ward another partition created a second dormitory. The patients were seated in the general area, some women involved in handicrafts, some knitting, and a group of men playing cards. They were mostly middle-aged and older, but not what Ruth would characterise as geriatric, or in need of care. They were dressed in a mixture of hospital-issue and personal clothing. The walls and curtains were the same as in Ward 43, and by now Ruth could understand why the superintendent objected to the colour scheme, which seemed to dull the senses and deaden the atmosphere. The nurses were engaged with the patients, however, and one was laughing with the group of women who were knitting. The mood was more positive than in the ward opposite, Ruth felt.

"The average severe neurosis lasts around five to six years," said the superintendent. "Yet the average stay of these patients at Black Roding is already eleven years. That can't be right, Doctor; some of these patients must already be cured, without us having done anything! Yet Winstanley hadn't moved a single patient out of here in the past twelve months, and his average exit rate in my time was only one and a half per annum. This is one ward you must focus on. I'm convinced there are patients here who can look after themselves much more. That's why the review has got to be done quickly."

"And if they are institutionalised? What then?"

"Try to break it. We've got one or two patients' flats to help prepare patients for life outside the hospital, preparing meals, cleaning the bathroom, and so on. Use them, but you'll have to find a nurse to help supervise it, especially at first." The superintendent beckoned one of the nurses over. "Sister O'Sullivan, this is Doctor Appleton, who will be joining the firm from tomorrow. Help her to get to know the patients. She's got a lot to learn from you." The nurse smiled at Ruth, who tried to smile back. She did not like the suggestion that she needed the nurse's help, nor that she had a lot to learn from her, but chose not to vent her opinion in front of the nurse.

Once outside the ward, however, Ruth decided to speak up. "Doctor Verity, I'm not used to suggestions that the nurses know more than me. Why did you say that?"

"Because it's probably true, Doctor. You have got a lot to learn. And if you don't learn it from one of the top-class nurses here, which Sister O'Sullivan certainly is, you'll learn something worse from other staff, who are not all top-class. And I mean all the staff – porters, administrators, orderlies, attendants, nurses and doctors. There are good and bad among them all, and you need to know that and discriminate between them."

Inwardly Ruth seethed. Outwardly she stayed silent; at least that would not betray her feelings.

Wards 45 and 46 were on the ground floor. But the superintendent took Ruth first to the doctors' offices that were in the corridor leading to the wards. Here, David Peters and John Sutton were talking together in the largest office. The superintendent interrupted them to introduce

Ruth, and the doctors shook hands. David Peters was, thought Ruth, a man who must always have seemed middle-aged. His hair was already receding above a moon-shaped face, and the small knot in his tie and the white collar attached to his shirt made him seem well over forty rather than the thirty-something-years-old that he probably was. John Sutton, by contrast, looked like a teenager rather than a doctor. His black hair was long, overhanging his collar edge, and his tie was askew. Ruth thought they looked like a schoolmaster and schoolboy, discussing an essay, when the superintendent interrupted their conversation. Their greeting was friendly, however.

"I shall leave you here, then," the superintendent said. "Mr Peters can tell you about the rest. And here's the key to your room. It's on the West Wing corridor, so you'll be close at hand." He handed Ruth a key attached to a ring and fob, on which was written *DR 7*. "Doctor's Room 7. And for this week I want you to observe one of the Admissions Units during the mornings, and to work on these wards during the afternoons. My deputy runs the other Admissions Unit, and I want you to see what we're trying to do by observing there. Any problems, ask Mrs Rogers." And with that he asked David Peters to walk away with him, and they started to converse as they went.

Ruth was left, feeling slightly foolish, with John Sutton. If that conversation and walk with the superintendent had been a *viva*, she felt she had probably failed, but she couldn't quite say why.

CHAPTER SEVEN

As soon as Richard entered Ward 44 the nurses called out to him. "Richard, the doctors would like to see you. They've a job for you."

He waited for a few seconds and took a few breaths. He looked around as if he were confused by the message. "What is it?" he asked, and again paused before continuing; "I've only just got back."

"Don't know, but they've got the new doctor with them. Go and see what's wanted."

The nurses were used to Richard's hesitant ways, and to having to encourage him. He knew that any refusal on his part might draw more unwanted attention to him and he was keen to see the new doctor as well, though he was not really sure why. So he turned back and went down the stairs to the doctors' room. As he approached he could hear them talking, because the door was slightly open. He stood by the doorway as quietly as he could and waited, interested to overhear the conversation with the newcomer, who seemed to be doing most of the talking because Richard was a little surprised to hear a female voice within the room. There were only a few female doctors in the hospital. And there were very few young female doctors, which the newcomer seemed by her voice to be.

The woman's voice was a little raised, Richard realised, as if she were exasperated.

"But do you really think that we, or rather I, can review all these patients? And start making proposals within two weeks? That isn't medicine, it's..." there was a pause while the doctor cast around for something to complete her assertion, "it's a production line, that's what it brings to mind, doesn't it?" Then there was a silence.

Richard could sense the two other doctors thinking about how to reply, made uncertain by this challenge. He himself had overheard many doctors holding conversations in the course of his time in the hospital, because a majority of them were so accustomed to his presence with the newspaper trolley in their wards that they took no notice of him. But he had rarely heard so strongly voiced a challenge to other doctors as this, and the fact that it was the new doctor who was making the challenge intrigued him. He held back to hear how the conversation developed.

After a pause, he heard Dr Peters reply, "I understand the point you're making, but Dr Verity obviously thinks that this firm has been avoiding doing its proper work for some time, and that it's in the patients' interest to change that. You've maybe been conducting reviews in a place where there's already a routine, and where patients aren't disadvantaged as our patients may be. But the superintendent is right. Sir Reginald wouldn't see eye-to-eye with the superintendent, so he didn't do things as he was asked to. But I can't refuse, and I think we should at least try."

"So what do you think, then? How could we actually do it?" the new doctor asked.

"We should try some obvious and straightforward ways to get some of the reviews going. Maybe pick some obvious cases where we couldn't recommend transfer, and confirm those decisions, while we get the nurses to help us identify the more obvious cases where we could."

"And do you agree?" This was obviously addressed to the third doctor. There was a brief silence before an answer came.

"I don't see any alternative. If we refuse, I expect the superintendent will break the firm up and get others to do it anyway. And send us off to who knows where." That was Doctor Sutton. Richard recognised his rather nervous voice, as if he were slightly afraid to have a view one way or the other.

Richard was aware that the three doctors had all stopped talking. For a moment he wondered if they were aware of his presence outside the room, but no-one came to the door, so he guessed they were waiting for the new doctor to make up her mind, and she was taking her time in doing so. Richard had been in many such conversations when he had himself worked in the years before entering the asylum; one person with a strong opinion encountering two or more who disagreed. The one person would weigh up whether to stick to his own view or bow to the greater weight, experience or knowledge behind the others' views. He could understand the tension among them as they waited. Finally she spoke.

"All right, then, I'll agree to start that way at least. I'll draw up a survey form for the nursing staff to complete on each patient. I'll ask them to start at the two extremes – those most dependent on the hospital, the staff and the treatments, and those least dependent. Then I'll confirm the reasons why those in the first group can't be considered, and I'll meet with each patient in the second group. Then I'll talk over with you two how we might move them forward, and involve other staff. I assume we'd need to involve social workers, occupational therapists and some of the external welfare services. I'll need help in knowing where to find all these people. I don't suppose it's going to be easy. And I'm really not sure that it's properly professional to move at such a speed, but I don't want to make a stand over it."

"Thanks, Ruth," Dr Peters said. Richard could hear the relief in his voice. "No, it won't be easy. Those kinds of staff within Black Roding haven't been much used on these wards, so it will be hard to drag them away from their work elsewhere. And the superintendent said to me today that we have to start ward general meetings next week, once you've spent a week with the Admissions Unit. It's another thing that Winstanley would never agree to do. I understand why the superintendent wants us to start them, because almost every other firm in the hospital does. But it's going to be another big change for everyone here."

Richard understood what Dr Peters meant. He often saw ward general meetings taking place as he did his trolley rounds, but he usually tried to avoid entering wards if the meetings were still going on. They were meetings of all the patients and staff, usually organised by a doctor, at which patients could raise and discuss any issues they wanted to. The issues could be everyday ones, or they could be awkward problems that were hard to resolve. The doctors and nurses could raise matters as well, and then the staff met separately afterwards to continue their discussions. That was when Richard would return to the wards. And he would see and hear the results if something had been controversial, or there had been any ill feeling. Twice he had stopped patients arguing after such meetings, and in the best way he could had reported it to the staff. Clearly his own ward was going to face changes, and some patients were going to be transferred. A shiver of shock ran through his body as he realised that this could include him. Without Winstanley to prevent it, the doctors might want to move him on. With some trepidation, therefore, he knocked gently on the door, muttering a reminder to himself to pause before he did anything.

"Yes, who is it?" Dr Peters called from inside the room. Richard did not respond. "Come in!" Dr Peters shouted more loudly. Still Richard remained unmoving, silent. He heard a movement by one of those inside towards the door, and the door swung open. It was the new doctor who had been standing nearest to the door. Dr Peters peered around her and saw Richard. "Come in, Richard, come in. We've got a task for you."

The new doctor moved aside to let Richard into the room. He looked down at his shoes. Dr Peters proceeded. "Richard, this is Dr Appleton, the new doctor we've been waiting for. She just arrived today and doesn't know her way around. Doctor Sutton and I can't leave the wards to show her around, but no-one knows the whole hospital better than you, given that you go all around it twice a day. So we thought that you could just walk her around the main parts, so that she gets her bearings. Richard is a trustee, Doctor Appleton. He has special privileges in return for the work he does with the newspaper trolley. And he could pick up your suitcase at Reception as well."

While all this was said, Richard kept his eyes down and did not respond. But Dr Peters seemed to be expecting an answer, so he grunted an assent, although inwardly he was terrified by the thought of showing this new doctor around. She might be making decisions about him, decisions that could unravel the slender threads by which he felt he was clinging to a rock face. This was not good.

CHAPTER EIGHT

"Well, Richard, where should we start?" Ruth looked at the patient, but he did not meet her look, nor did he reply. "The superintendent brought me here via the perimeter path. Perhaps you could take me back to Reception through the building?" She smiled encouragingly, and Richard raised his arm a little as if to point the way forward, and set off in a trudge. Ruth quickly caught him up and walked alongside him. "I've never worked in so big a place as this. What can you tell me about it?" she asked.

Richard hesitated. He was going to have to make some conversation, he realised. If he didn't, this doctor might start analysing him immediately. But he did not know how much he should talk. Finally he spoke, "Old country house. It's an old country house with lots of wards built on the wings, and lots of patients, lots of them." Richard tried to let his voice drop a tone as he finished talking, so that his speech did not sound as if it was inviting the doctor to carry on the conversation. But the tactic did not work.

"Do you visit all the wards on your trolley round, Richard? And do you see all the patients?"

"Not in the secure wards. Too dangerous. I have to stay outside and talk to the nurses. But I go in the other wards. Sell newspapers, magazines, sweets, to any patients."

"That's a very responsible job. So do you get to know all the patients?"

"No. Lots of them don't speak to me. Some just hold out the money. I just know some, know what they want."

They had turned into the long ground-floor corridor that, Ruth guessed, ran the whole length of the West Wing of the hospital. Other patients, nurses, orderlies and just one or two doctors were walking along the corridor or standing outside the entrances to the wards talking to one another. Richard walked through or past them with his head down, while Ruth looked with interest at each person they passed.

"What about the staff, Richard. Do you know them?"

"Some of them talk to me. Some buy newspapers. Some buy stuff for the patients, if they know they need something."

"You do a good job, then. You're helping everyone." Ruth smiled at Richard, who saw the smile but dared not meet her eyes fully for fear that he might smile back at her.

As they walked they passed the entrances to many other wards, or to staircases that led up – or in one case down – to other wards. Ruth asked Richard if he knew how the wards were organised, but he would not answer her. He had quite a good knowledge of the groupings of mental weaknesses and illnesses that characterised some of the wards, but he did not want to appear observant or in any way able to analyse what he saw. "I think they're all ill… in the head," he muttered, grateful that Ruth did not probe this further.

At the end of the wing they turned right, in the direction of the reception hall that Ruth had first entered. There were still wards on either side of the corridor, using the rooms of the original house on the front facade, and other rooms that had been built to match them on the opposite side of the corridor. At least that was what Ruth surmised when she peered in through the swinging doorways that provided access and noted the bricked-in windows that had once allowed light and air into the corridor. And as a consequence the corridor was gloomy and ill-lit, and everywhere the odour of diluted disinfectant hung in the air and seemed to invade her nostrils and mouth with its sour taste. Perhaps it was just that it was Monday and the corridors were cleaned on that day. If not, it was never going to be a pleasant experience even to walk from one point in this vast complex to another. She thought of asking Richard, but guessed she'd just get another non-answer. She wondered already what was wrong with him, and why he was in the hospital, when he seemed capable of doing a full job and apparently doing it efficiently. But his responses seemed unsocial, and this was in keeping with many patients whose worst symptoms were controlled by drugs. Without the drugs, problems could quickly arise, and so many patients were held in hospital only to ensure that the drugs were taken. That much she knew from her training and observation. Nonetheless, she would look up Richard's file among the first that she would review, since it would perhaps reveal why he, and possibly others, had to be kept at Black Roding.

The corridor finally gave way to the reception hall, and here there was a little more light from the windows on both the ground floor level and the level above. But there was no sunlight – through the windows all that was visible was the same curtain of fog that had made her arrival so difficult. Richard paused, as if awaiting direction from the doctor, looking down at the floor.

"Show me some of the rooms off the central corridor, please, Richard. The superintendent rushed past them very quickly." So Richard led the way down the corridor, halting outside the chapel. He obviously wondered if Ruth was going to look in there. "I've seen the chapel, Richard. And the window in there. It's spectacular. I've never seen anything like it."

Richard tried not to show his appreciation of the doctor's good taste. He himself often sat for short periods in front of the window, although he felt no religious sentiments or beliefs. Somehow the power of belief that had inspired the window could calm him, giving a sense of separation from his surroundings that he only otherwise achieved when looking out from the water tower. He knew that some patients, and some of the orderlies and other staff, made fun of the window, but he would never join in their insults. The window was a point of beauty in an otherwise very bleak world.

"Show me the dining rooms, please," the doctor asked him. "I didn't get a chance to see what they are like."

Richard walked further down the corridor before stopping in the front of two battered doors on his right. "This is the canteen for patients," he said, keeping it as succinct as he could.

"Which patients? How would a patient know if they are to eat here?"

Richard paused. He did not want to get into any detailed discussion for fear of revealing himself too much. Eventually he dug in his pocket and showed Ruth his exeat, the grubby and dog-eared cardboard pass that allowed him out of the ward and into the hospital at large. He passed it over to Ruth, who read it with interest. It contained his name, date of birth, and date of admission almost thirteen years previously. Richard saw that the doctor was a little taken aback by that.

"What does it say about meals, though?" she asked.

"It's yellow," he replied.

"Yellow. What's the significance of yellow?" She looked at him, and he raised his eyes only to her waist.

"Second highest. Only a red card is better. You can walk out of the front gate with a red card. Other cards are green, blue and purple."

"So the card tells you, and tells others, what you are allowed to do?"

"Yes. They're on a…" Richard stopped himself. He had almost used the word 'spectrum', because he had long ago realised that the colour coding of the passes matched the spectrum of colours in light. The reply had almost come freely from him because he was engaged in this discussion with a new young doctor who did not know or understand the systems that governed every aspect of his life. He had not had such a conversation, with someone who was genuinely interested, for a long time. He gritted his teeth together to stop himself proceeding. Ruth had stopped, waiting for him to complete his sentence.

"On a what?" she asked as gently as she could.

"A, er, a list, which the superintendent has."

"Oh, right. I thought you were going to say something else." Richard sensed that she was looking at him quizzically, so he quickly changed the subject. "Patients' dining room," he said, gesturing towards the double doors.

Ruth looked at each of the dining rooms in turn. The patients' room was large with shabby furniture, and the pervasive smell of boiled cabbage and disinfectant. In the room for nurses and administrative staff there were individual tables with white and blue laminate tops, and utility chairs. The doctors' dining room held smaller tables than in the nurses' canteen, with white tablecloths on each, and wooden chairs with red-cushioned seats. To one side of the room there were armchairs and coffee tables, each with a glass ashtray in the middle. *The doctors obviously do better than the nurses and admin*, Ruth thought. Richard was now pointing to doors on the other side of the corridor.

"This is the theatre," he said.

Ruth looked at the doors with interest. "Oh yes, the superintendent mentioned that. Show me what it's like."

Ruth opened a door, but the room was dark inside, and she had to grope to find the light switches. A row of lights at her end of a large open room came on, enough to let her see everything there – and yes, there was a stage at the far end of this room, elevated above floor level, with heavy black curtains drawn across. There were chairs and tables stacked against the walls, which were painted brown. There were no windows, no natural source of light. To her left Ruth saw a boxed space, with a door, and a shutter closed over what was evidently a hatch, and outside the servery were two stacks of wooden crates, in which were empty beer bottles. Ruth had never in any of her training hospitals seen alcohol in an area accessed by patients. She was still looking at the crates when Richard came in.

"What happens here, Richard?" Ruth asked.

How to answer? thought Richard. He chose the single word strategy. "Shows," he said bluntly.

Ruth waited for any elaboration, but none came. "Shows?" she echoed.

"Dances, singing, plays. On a Saturday night. Lots of the patients come, and nurses. Even some doctors."

Ruth had heard that hospitals such as Black Roding were big enough to engage in entertainments for patients. With two thousand or more inmates, there was scope, and even a need, to provide such facilities. But she herself had never been to such an event. And the consumption of alcohol still amazed her.

"And do the patients drink alcohol?" Ruth pointed at the crates. "Surely that's not allowed?"

One of Richard's duties as an orderly was helping to look after the small bar when it was being used. He thought it a good facility for patients who otherwise experienced very little to distract from their illnesses. He didn't like the implicit criticism in Ruth's questioning. "Yes, but it's just bottles of beer. The superintendent agrees. On a Saturday night when there's a dance, or when there's a show on another night, the patients' social club is allowed to serve alcohol. There have to be doctors or nurses, and attendants or orderlies, to make sure no-one is served drinks they can't cope with." Richard had given his longest speech of the tour, and with some animus. He'd also looked directly at Ruth. He went red as he realised he'd broken all three parts of his mantra. Inside he was annoyed with himself for doing so and angry with her for causing this rupture.

"But it's hardly medicinal!" Ruth commented, more to herself than to him. But she was studying him quite closely, and with interest. She had clearly seen the change in him.

"Patients with red cards can go into local pubs," Richard offered in defence of the bar. He had heard the superintendent offer this explanation at a Saturday dance himself. "And it's always supervised by staff."

"Even so," Ruth responded, but still talking as if debating with herself about this new phenomenon, rather than talking to Richard. "A patient who goes into a pub is making their own decision, but here it's the hospital's decision. And aren't the staff compromised? What if something goes wrong?"

"The patients need some relief from their illnesses," Richard protested, and his protest seemed to bring Ruth back from her reflections.

"Yes, you're probably right," she said, almost apologetically. But she had noted the vehemence of Richard's reply, and the way his speech had changed. And the psychiatrist in her had noticed his ability to empathise with other patients. "Can you tell me any more?" but he just shrugged. He had already said far too much. "Let's just go and get my case, shall we?" And this time Ruth led the way back to the reception desk to reclaim her possessions.

Before they left the reception hall, however, Ruth looked down the eastward corridor. It was as gloomy as its counterpart to the west, and reminded Ruth of the dark mystery of a London Underground tunnel, inviting you on a subterranean journey to a different part of the city. "So, is it the same down that way? Is it identical to the West Wing?" she asked.

Richard paused, gave himself time to think how best to answer. There were indeed wards laid out in much the same way as in the corridors they had already walked, but the treatment rooms and operating theatres lay at the far end of the East Wing, in an area which Richard's trolley round never entered. He himself had been in the treatment rooms, and he did not like to think about those times. He pointed down the dark corridor, saying "Just wards", and then indicating with his hand that the corridor at the end held "More wards", before showing that further down the corridor were "Treatment rooms" and "Operating theatres".

The new doctor continued to look down the corridor, and then she turned to him. "No need to go down there, then," she said. "Let's go back to the ward." She walked off, leading the way.

Richard had to make an effort not to show relief that his ordeal was over. He picked the suitcase up and followed her, thinking over what he had said and how he had said it, fearing that he might have betrayed himself.

CHAPTER NINE

Ruth was vexed. Nothing seemed to be going right, and she hardly knew with whom she should be more annoyed – herself or others. Her room, for example, had turned out to be the very worst in which she had ever had to spend the night. When she unlocked the door, a damp, musty smell had immediately hit her. There was an old iron bedstead with a grubby mattress, no bed linen, and the light bulb hung bare from the wire in the middle of the ceiling. There was no window, and so no natural light or outside air at all. It was clearly an emergency overnight room for a doctor obliged to stay because a patient might be in crisis. It could not be considered suitable long-stay accommodation. But it had been too late to seek assistance from anyone on the administrative wing, so Ruth had used some bed linen from the ward stores and left her case still packed on the floor. Just under the light switch a previous occupant of the room had written on the wall the Latin words '*Nusquam insanius*', which Ruth remembered from her Classics lessons at grammar school to mean 'Nowhere more insane', or perhaps 'Nowhere more unhealthy'. And remembering those Classics lessons, Ruth had thought of the Spartans, whom her teacher had praised for deliberately eschewing all luxury in pursuit of ideal manliness. Spartan certainly described her room, she thought, but the unknown scribbler had probably described it more accurately. The very air of the room was hostile to health. She had spent an uncomfortable and mostly sleepless night.

But it was not just the room. Dinner and its aftermath had also been an ordeal. She had entered the doctors' dining room at the correct time, but it had been almost deserted. Two doctors were seated at a table, but there was no place for a third, so Ruth had taken a seat at another small table. Eventually a member of the catering staff had approached her and taken an order for cottage pie and vegetables, and Ruth had regretted not having a book or magazine to read. She had been almost relieved when another doctor took the other place at her table. He was in his thirties, Ruth guessed, a face and body already becoming fat, with beads of sweat on his forehead and upper lip. "Oliver Smythe," he had said as he took the seat, pointing to himself. "You must be new. I've not seen you in here before." Ruth had introduced herself, and for a while had exchanged pleasantries. Smythe was a registrar, she discovered, who appeared to have worked in a surprisingly high number of the large asylums across the whole London area. She later thought, as she lay awake in her room, that this excessive mobility should have been a warning to her. But she had thought nothing of it and had accepted his hospitality when he ordered some drinks to accompany the meal. She had also agreed to his suggestion that he make her coffee in his rooms, only to be shocked when, instead of the coffee, he had made an immediate pass at her. She had had to push him away and make a bolt for it. How stupidly bloody naive, she had thought to herself, to go to his rooms just because her own was so desolate. And now she would have to face him regularly, and she thought she knew the kind of insulting label he would attach to her when he told the other doctors of his failed conquest. "Prick-teaser," he would say, and they would look at her with a mixture of contempt and scorn on hearing of the escapade.

In the morning she had taken breakfast quickly, checking that Smythe was not in the dining room before she entered. Then she had taken her white coat out of her case, conscious that it was creased and that she had no iron with which to smooth it out. It was her mother's last gift to her, bought for her first period of training in psychiatry. Ruth had kept it as a special coat, using it only rarely, and more generally using the coats supplied by whichever institution she happened to be working in. But it seemed appropriate to wear it today, when Ruth felt her confidence waning after a poor night's sleep and that awful incident with Smythe.

She headed for the Admissions Unit, where she was due to spend four mornings in order to understand better the hospital's systems and methods, as instructed by the superintendent. She was the first doctor to arrive at Ward 1, and the ward immediately seemed noisy. It was divided in three, just as the superintendent seemed to wish, with dormitory areas to either end of the ward and the communal areas in the middle. A patient was arguing with another two patients, a man and a woman, in the seating area, but no nursing staff were in the communal area. Ruth looked into the men's dormitory area and saw that two nurses and two orderlies were talking to a large-framed man whose voice was raised in agitation. He was seated on his bed and shaking violently. Ruth moved forward slowly and asked the nearer of the two nurses if she should do anything to help. "No," the nurse had replied quietly. "He was admitted just yesterday, but he's finding the no-drugs regime very difficult." Ruth raised her eyebrows, quite taken aback. If a patient had been prescribed drugs regularly prior to admission, the sudden withdrawal of the drugs could provoke extreme reactions. But she could not ask questions when the staff were so occupied.

She went back to the communal area, where one or two more patients were gathering. The area looked extremely untidy. Old magazines were strewn on the tables, but some had fallen on the floor. Cups and saucers remained on the tables where patients had made themselves tea or coffee using the urn that stood on a table by the wall. Scraps of paper, and what looked like clumps of dirt, were lying on the floor. And if anything, the argument between patients was becoming louder. There were still no nursing staff visible, nor other doctors, so she went into the women's area. There, a mother was being assisted by two nurses in breastfeeding her baby, and for a moment Ruth was so surprised that she simply looked at the group, as if perhaps the scene would change and there would no longer be a tiny infant at the centre of their attention. She had never encountered a nursing mother in an asylum. She had never had to take any responsibility for a baby, except as a trainee house doctor on the maternity unit of the general hospital where she had initially trained. Black Roding was certainly full of surprises.

One of the nurses noticed her, and Ruth opened her arms with her hands pointing back at herself, as if to ask if further assistance was needed. Once again, the gesticulated reply was no, so Ruth withdrew, wondering if she ought to intervene in the argument which still continued. Just as she had decided that, yes, she should make some intervention, a doctor, whom Ruth assumed from the cut of his suit was the deputy superintendent, and another male doctor and a staff nurse came into the ward.

"Mr Brook," the staff nurse immediately called over to the patient who was arguing with the other two. "Not like that! If you want to raise an issue, do it in the general meeting, not directly with the others. You know that."

The patient stopped and turned towards the staff nurse. He was clearly angry, and for a moment seemed about to shout at the staff nurse, but he thought better of it and muttered to himself, "No-one will do anything even if I do raise it."

"Perhaps, Mr Brook, you and the other patients could gather in the chairs we need. The other nurses must still be busy, so we could do with help with the chairs." The staff nurse was obviously accustomed to defusing situations, and Ruth respected the firm confidence with which she spoke. Could she be as confident, she wondered, in this new and unusual place?

The deputy superintendent and the other doctor came over to Ruth. He was a tall and rather intimidating person, it seemed to Ruth from his approach, and he did not wear a white coat.

"Doctor Appleton?" he inquired. "I'm Mark Jennings, the deputy superintendent. Dr Verity said you'd be coming today. This is Kenneth Brown, my registrar. And over there is Staff Nurse Holly." Ruth shook the deputy superintendent's hand, but Kenneth Brown, a thin man whose jaw and cheekbones seemed to stretch his facial skin into a tight grimace, stayed distant, simply nodding his acknowledgement of her. He, like Ruth, was wearing a white coat. He did not smile, and he looked to Ruth to be rather old still to be a registrar. "We're going to start with the general meeting, and then we'll hold a staff meeting," Mark Jennings continued. "You'll attend both, though you may want to just listen at these first meetings."

"I think the nurses in both the men's area and the women's area are held up," Ruth suggested.

"Why, do you know?"

"A recent admission in the men's area, I think, who's finding it hard without drugs, and a woman breastfeeding in the women's area." Ruth tried hard not to allow her voice to express any surprise or criticism, but Mark Jennings seemed sensitive to even the slightest variation in tone.

"Not things you've experienced before, perhaps?" he asked.

"Well, no, they've come as a bit of a surprise, I must admit. But so have some other things. Black Roding is different to anywhere I've worked before." For a few moments Ruth met the gaze of the deputy superintendent, before looking aside.

"We can probably explain them, if we can find time, Doctor, but I think for the moment you'll have to accept them as given, whether that's patients without drugs or patients with babies." He turned away, but Ruth thought she heard him say softly to the registrar, "Not sure she's going to manage."

Ruth was not sure if she should respond. It seemed better to avoid a confrontation, so she helped to push and pull the chairs, which the patients were leaving in somewhat random places, into a more organised circle consisting of at least thirty chairs, Ruth estimated. This was certainly going to be a new experience.

As the circle of chairs was being formed, an orderly in a blue uniform came into the ward, almost running in his obvious haste. "Mr Jennings, Mr Jennings," he was urgent in his demand for attention.

"What is it, man? Spit it out," he said.

"Serious incident in the secure wards, Mr Jennings. And the superintendent is at a meeting in London, so he can't be called. His secretary said to get you."

"How serious? We were about to hold a meeting."

"Very serious. Two patients and two staff hurt because there was a fight. And one of the patients had a concealed weapon. And it's causing other patients to get upset."

"Right, then. We'll go with you straight away. Kenneth, you'd better come with me. Dr Appleton, you'll be the most senior doctor here, so you'll have to chair the meeting."

"But I've never even been to a general meeting like this, never mind chaired one!" Ruth protested.

"Patricia Holly will have to guide you. She'll do most of the talking. But a doctor has to chair the general meeting, not a nurse, so there's no alternative. I'm sorry, but in an emergency you'll have to cope." And with that the deputy superintendent, the registrar and the orderly all left the ward in a rush.

Ruth looked at the staff nurse. She took a deep breath in, paused to gather her thoughts just a little, and then said, "I really don't know the order of these general meetings. They were never held anywhere I've worked. What should I do?"

"Just introduce yourself to everyone, then hand over to me. If anything goes wrong, and if we can't correct it, call the meeting to an end. We must hold the meeting, though, because otherwise the patients will lose their sense of the order of the day. The routine is important."

"Don't be surprised if I call an end to it pretty soon, though." Ruth tried to smile as she said it but felt that the smile must have been sickly at best. "Sit next to me so I can call for help quietly."

Gradually the members of the meeting gathered. There were more female patients than males, several nurses and some other staff, and the patients who had been attended to by the nurses, who were the last to appear. The man, Ruth noticed, had a nurse on either side, and an orderly hovered a little way behind him, no doubt as an additional form of security. The woman had left her baby behind. "He's sleeping now," she said as she took her seat next to Ruth. The patients who had been arguing with the man, now known to Ruth as Mr Brook, were seated next to one another, and Mr Brook had taken a seat some way away from them.

Conscious of her white coat, and several people's obvious interest in her, Ruth felt suddenly and unexpectedly isolated. The young mother seemed to be looking quite intensely at Ruth, and this added to Ruth's discomfort.

"OK, everyone," Ruth heard the nervousness in her own voice, "the other doctors have been called away for a time, so I'll be chairing the meeting until they return. Staff Nurse Holly will be leading the discussion. I'm Doctor Appleton, and I'm new to the hospital. My usual responsibilities are in some of the wards out on the West Wing, but I will be here during this week to see how the Admissions Ward works. I'm sure I'll learn a lot about the hospital from you while I'm here." Ruth turned to Staff Nurse Holly and invited her to continue the meeting.

Ruth was surprised by the confidence with which the staff nurse commenced. "Could I just start by saying to Mr Weinberg..." and here she turned to the burly man who had been identified as the new patient, "that as a new patient in the hospital you have been asked to come off any drugs for your first weeks in the Admissions Ward. We know that this is difficult, and all the patients and staff will try to help you, and it does not necessarily mean that you will not be given drugs later. We just want to make a fresh start and make sure that any drugs, and the doses, are indeed the right ones. And only if we check this on admission can we be sure of doing this properly." She stopped, and there was a silence. Ruth felt that the staff nurse was hoping that someone would respond, and wondered if anyone would.

Mr Weinberg himself looked as if he might say something, but he was hesitant. One of the nurses, almost whispering, asked him, "Do you want to say something?" but he shook his head. Finally, one of the patients almost directly opposite spoke up. She was a small, middle-aged woman.

"I came in three weeks ago," she said, "and they stopped my pills. It was horrible, and I was very angry. I couldn't sleep properly, but it has got a little better. I suppose it's good for us, but I want to go back on my medicine soon."

The staff nurse seemed satisfied with this half-hearted endorsement of the policy, and continued, "We were talking last Friday about strong feelings and where they might come from. About how we might be repeating feelings that we'd had when we were children, and how we might not have been able to tell anyone about those feelings. And so we still have the feelings; and when something happens to us, those feelings rise up again. Does anyone want to say anything about feelings like this?" She managed to say this to everyone, not looking at one particular person at any time, and inviting replies by the openness and confidence with which she spoke. But again there was a silence, and Ruth noticed that the staff did not try to fill the silence. It was as if they were using it to encourage the patients to vocalise their thoughts. She found herself waiting with some anticipation.

"I've got some strong feelings," Mr Brook suddenly said. "It's about those two." He pointed to the two patients with whom he had been arguing. "They're always canoodling. Hugging and snogging one another. I don't think it's right in a hospital. We're supposed to be getting better, not running a marriage bureau."

Ruth realised she had gasped. Two or three people looked around, and others laughed, either at the bitter joke Mr Brook had made or at Ruth's reaction. His attack had shocked Ruth, but no-one else seemed surprised. She leant forward and pulled at one of her shoes, as if straightening the leather, to cover her own embarrassment. The baby-less patient still looked at her even when the discussion resumed.

At first, one or two other patients expressed some agreement with Mr Brook. One woman asked, "Whatever will happen next with them?", and another said, "It is difficult being ill, and it makes it harder when two people don't seem ill at all, and just seem to be having a good time."

Ruth looked around the circle to see if anyone wanted to reply to these comments. The woman next to her continued to look at her, and Ruth made a conscious effort not to return the stare. None of the staff spoke. One or two of the patients shifted in their seats a little. Then one countered, "Perhaps if people meet each other, and like each other, it's a comfort. I mean, in a place like this, where you're worried, being with someone could be good."

Ruth thought with instant chagrin of Smythe and the encouragement she must have given him by agreeing to go to his rooms, and why she had suddenly been so grateful for even a degree of companionship that it had affected her judgement and allowed him to think she was interested in him. She could agree with what this patient said.

Mr Brook took the matter up again. "I don't mind them being together, but they're doing things that should be done in private, and there isn't anywhere private here. Why should we have to see them kissing and touching one another? And what's next?"

The staff nurse hesitated, and then decided to say something. "It is unusual, Mr Brook, for two people to meet in a hospital ward, but it isn't unknown. People may meet each other in all sorts of unexpected places. If you went for a walk in the park, you might see courting couples there. And that's a public place. Can you think what you want to do about these strong feelings?"

"Yes," he protested, "I want them to stop." One or two patients laughed. Others had already lost concentration and were looking away. "Will you stop them?" Mr Brook was almost shouting at the staff nurse.

"No, Mr Brook, I don't think we can stop them seeing each other and meeting one another. Does anyone have a suggestion about how to resolve this?"

Up to this point the two patients accused by Mr Brook had said nothing, but they had watched and listened to the proceedings with keen interest once Mr Brook had intervened. Now they looked at one another. The man leant forward and whispered something to the woman. She shook her head. Then she spoke to him, and he paused to consider what she had said before nodding his agreement. She pointed to him, and then to the circle, most of whom by now were watching this dumb show. The man looked around the circle and spoke hesitantly. "I don't normally talk to this many people. But me and Vera agree that we'll only cuddle up to one another outside the ward. We'll go in the grounds, or the canteen, or somewhere else. Then no-one here needs to get on their high horse about us." He looked directly at Mr Brook as he said this.

"I ain't on no bleeding high horse," Mr Brook muttered. "I just think there's a right way of acting."

"Thank you, Vera and Stanley," the staff nurse cut in. "That seems a very good compromise. It may be hard to keep to what you've agreed." She looked at the couple.

"Then tell us if we don't. No, not him, you – the nurses – you tell us if we don't keep our word."

"OK, Stanley, we will. And do you agree, Mr Brook?"

He agreed, somewhat reluctantly. "I suppose I have to," he muttered. No-one responded.

The staff nurse commented on the whole event, however. "One of the things that can affect any of us," she said, "is not dealing with our strong feelings, or not having them dealt with by the others around us. We have the feelings, and they affect us a lot. But the feelings don't go anywhere, and they don't change. We just hide them away inside us, and then later on they burst out when we don't expect them to. I wonder if anyone else has experienced this."

As Ruth was to discover, the entreaty to a general meeting for individuals to present their feelings or experiences for discussion often led to silence. The staff nurse accepted this. She sat still, looked at an indeterminate point somewhere in the middle of the circle and waited. Some of the patients couldn't help but fidget – some shook regularly, perhaps because of the withdrawal of drugs, Ruth thought. One or two coughed and looked around at others as if expecting that one of them, rather than themselves, should be the first to speak. But no-one volunteered. Then one of the nurses spoke. She had a soft Irish accent.

"I had something like that happen when my mother died. I was only thirteen years old, and she had cancer. No-one told me what was wrong, or that she was dying. I didn't know right up to the last moment, so it was a complete shock when it happened. I tried not to let anyone see how upset I was, or how angry I was that no-one had told me. I suppose it was the way people did that in Ireland, but it hurt me. And I didn't let anyone know until I was in my first hospital. The senior nurse on the ward reminded me of my mother, and I kept getting angry at her for what seemed to be no reason. Then she took me aside and sat me down, asked me about what might be upsetting me. I blurted out about my ma, and she realised what had happened. She arranged for me to speak to a nun who worked in the hospital. She helped me to say what I felt about Ma's death, and why I was so angry with her and with my da. That night I cried for hours. Then it started to feel better."

Ruth was astonished by the nurse's self-revelation. She had never experienced professional staff revealing their own psychological state or previous traumas in front of patients. Somehow it seemed to her to be wrong. As professionals, the doctors and nurses should be keeping a distance, as she had always been taught. They should not be revealing their own problems, present or past, and they should not be talking about their own personal feelings. And Ruth expected others to think the same as her. She looked around the circle at the nurses and other staff, but none of them seemed perturbed by what the nurse had said. And then at the patients – surely they wouldn't expect the professional staff to be talking as though they too had mental health problems? But while some of the patients were looking at the nurse, it seemed to be in expectation that she had something more to say. They too did not seem startled to hear a nurse talk of her own suppression of feelings.

"Thank you for telling us that, Nurse Coughlan," the staff nurse said. "What you said could be very interesting to others who are here. Nurse Coughlan's mother died when she was young, and she couldn't tell anyone about her feelings. Has anyone had something similar happen to them?"

This time the silence was broken. A middle-aged woman sitting a few chairs to Ruth's left said quietly, and without meeting anyone's gaze, "I have. My mum died when I was fourteen. And I was the oldest of seven. I had to leave school and work in the house, even though I wanted a job." The woman broke off. She looked around the circle as if worried about the reaction to what she was saying. The staff nurse gave the woman a little smile and nodded, and the woman decided to continue. "I was going to be a secretary, and I was already learning shorthand and typing, but my dad said I was needed to get the others dressed and off to school, and then the house cleaned and dinner cooked for them when they came home. So I never got a job, and I had to become a mum to my younger sisters and brothers, and they were all able to go off and get jobs. But by then it was too late for me, and the war was over, and there were no jobs for a woman like me. I could never tell anyone about how I felt." And with that, the woman started to weep.

The circle of onlookers did not move, although Ruth sensed that several of them sympathised with the woman. The staff nurse waited, saying nothing. Ruth herself was tempted to stand up and console the woman, or to ask that someone else did, but she did not fully understand the rules of the general meeting, or how nurses and doctors were expected to act, so she too waited. And then Vera shuffled in her seat, hesitated, and decided that she would stand up. She went over to the woman and put one arm around her shoulder.

"Do you want to go back to your bed?" Vera asked the woman, turning to the staff nurse as if to check that this would be accepted. The staff nurse nodded. Vera encouraged the woman to stand, and helped her to walk away through the door into the women's dormitory. The nurses still did not move, although Ruth felt that they should. It should be the nurses who looked after the woman. Weren't there enormous risks in allowing another patient, another patient with mental health problems, to be alone talking with a patient at a vulnerable moment, unseen by the professionals. It would never have been allowed in the institutions in which she had worked, and she found it offensive that it was allowed here. She almost intervened to ask the nurses to follow the two women, but she held back. There were senior doctors, and their views and procedures, to consider here, even if they were not present.

Ruth was aware that throughout these exchanges the woman next to her had continued to look at her, whether by glancing to and fro between Ruth and the patients and staff nurse when they were speaking, or by staring at her for longer periods. She felt uncomfortable but did not think it wise to meet the stares. So she rather self-consciously looked anywhere but at the woman, even when someone on her side of Ruth was talking. Now there was a cry from the women's dormitory area, the unmistakeable cry of a baby. "Now they've fucking well woken him up by going in there," the woman said to the whole circle. She got up angrily and walked off to find her child again. One of the nurses, one whom

Ruth thought had probably been helping the mother when she had first looked in the dormitory, made to stand up and follow. But she noticed the staff nurse raise just one finger in warning, and the nurse sat down again. An uncomfortable silence came down on the circle, but the staff nurse again let the silence hold. The crying from the dormitory continued, and became louder as the woman must have picked up the baby and started to walk back towards the communal area. She appeared in the doorway, stopped and asked with a touch of anger in her voice, "Should I come back or should I stay in here?"

"What would you like to do?" asked the staff nurse.

"Well, I didn't want to be here in the first place, not with young Jimmy anyway. So I don't know. What's best?"

"Take your place if you feel OK with that."

And so, still rather surly, the woman sat down with the child. The staff nurse waited for a few moments, before resuming, "Perhaps we've lost the moment for talking any further about strong feelings now, but I would like to ask that the smaller groups have a discussion about it later today or tomorrow. It is a very important part of our work that we should talk about such things. And it could be very important for any patient who has had that experience to talk about it, so if someone in your group takes it up please listen and say what you think about it, and how that patient might now deal with the feelings. Now, does anyone want to raise any matters or concerns that they have?"

In the next few minutes there were some complaints about the food that was available in the ward. The staff nurse said that these would be relayed to the catering administrators but that the doctors and nurses could not do anything directly about this. One patient said he was worried that if he stayed in the hospital much longer he would lose his job. His sister had told him that his workmates had come to visit her, and warned her about this. The occupational therapist – it was she who was sitting on the other side of the woman and child – said that she would talk to the patient after the meeting, and then would talk to his employer about keeping his job open. One patient complained that other patients weren't helping with the cleaning, which again surprised Ruth. In her experience nurses and nursing staff tidied up and kept beds clean, and cleaners regularly cleaned the wards. In her last placement the cleaners had been on the ward every day before her. These complaints seemed banal to her, and she wondered why the staff nurse did not cut them off.

Just as the meeting seemed to be coming to an end, one of the female patients sitting opposite Ruth and the woman with the baby – whose cries had died down, and who was sitting fairly contentedly on his mother's lap – spoke for the first time. "Excuse me," she said apologetically, "but I don't know whether I should raise this or not. It's not really a complaint. It's just that I feel very troubled about something, and you said that we should raise any concerns."

The staff nurse turned to the woman. "I think you should say what you want to raise."

The woman looked worried. "Well, I've brought up two youngsters myself, and I don't think I would have wanted to bring a baby in with me, if I had one now. I don't think it's a proper place for a baby." The woman's voice tailed off towards the end of her short speech.

The woman with the baby stiffened and reacted immediately. "What business is it of yours? It was me that didn't want to come in here; but when they said I should, I said I wanted the baby with me. If you don't like it, you know what you can do."

While some of the patients were cowed by the aggressive response of the woman, one or two still felt the need to make a point. One said, "The baby crying keeps me awake!" while another said, "The nurses don't have time for us because they're always helping with the baby."

Ruth turned to look at the woman, who immediately turned on her. "And what are you looking at, you fucking stuck-up cow? Don't look down your nose at me. What are you doing here anyway? Couldn't get a boyfriend, eh? Not married? Bloody spinster, that's what you're going to be! Bloody spinster in the loony bin!"

Ruth was taken completely aback by the woman's anger, and by her words. She stood up, thinking that she should move away from the woman, but couldn't move any further. No-one, even at school where there had been some bullying, had ever spoken to her in such a way. Not even some of the violent and dangerous patients in her most recent hospital had ever done this. Their aggression was general, not particularly focussed on her. The whole circle of patients and staff had fallen silent, and even those who had been distracted or bored during the meeting were now turned towards Ruth and the woman. But no-one said anything. And Ruth could only protest, "I haven't said or done anything to you! How on earth could you think and say those things?" She felt that she herself was close to tears. Something about the woman's words had sliced through the layers of professional confidence and medical knowledge with which she normally protected herself, as if the woman had touched an inner fear of her own, and in doing so had brought that fear into life. "You shouldn't talk to me like that. It isn't right!" she said, recognising in her tone of voice how lame her protest was.

"Course I can," said the woman. "We can say what we think and feel in these meetings, that's what I was told. And sitting here watching you, you looked at all of us as if you were superior to us. But you wouldn't have been transferred here if you were a married woman, and you ain't wearing a ring, so I reckon I'm right, and you're a spinster! And you're stuck-up!"

Ruth looked around the circle. She did not know what to do. The staff nurse was watching, sitting slightly forward in her seat, as if tense but a little unsure how to act. Ruth hesitated, and wondered if she should resume her position in the chair. It seemed an act of weakness just to sit down and accept the woman's insults. For a few moments no-one did anything, but then the baby started to cry, and the woman stood up and took him back into the dormitory area. This time one of the nurses did silently follow her. There was a period of quiet, and then some of the patients started to stir.

"OK," said the staff nurse, "I think the general meeting is over. The staff will now meet in the conference room. Nurses Mayes and Wilkins will remain on the ward. A topic for discussion in small groups later on will be 'dealing with strong feelings'. I believe there are some one-to-one sessions for individual patients later on, and we'll check those are scheduled after the staff meeting. Thank you, everyone, for attending and contributing."

Ruth thought that she too should have said something formal to mark the end of the meeting, but she felt that her voice would betray her emotions. The patients, with the nurses' help, started to take the chairs back to their original positions, either around the tables in the communal area or near patients' beds in the dormitory areas. Some dumped them in the middle of the floor and walked away, and the nurses picked them up and put them in their allotted places. Some patients left the ward, while others gathered around the tables, sat down or stood on their own. Ruth was still shocked and upset by the verbal attack on her, and sat trying to re-compose herself. She was starting to grow angry that no-one appeared in any way bothered about it. No-one had spoken up in her defence, and now no-one was speaking to her to express any sorrow or to give consolation. Was it normal to treat a doctor like this? And especially a new doctor, such as her, on her first day in the ward? It offended Ruth's sense of how she should be treated, and she felt embarrassed and humiliated by the attack. And the fact that the attack had touched on some of Ruth's own sensitivities about herself, and her position, seemed to make it worse. Although she felt quite shaken, within herself she was becoming determined that she would let her colleagues know that she was not impressed by what had happened. Finally she gave up her chair as one of the nurses sought to put it back in its place by a table. She realised that the deputy superintendent and his registrar had returned to the ward. Ruth tried to regain her composure. She would not give vent to her feelings here, where there were still some patients picking up chairs, and others starting to sit at the tables.

"I hope the meeting went well today," the deputy superintendent said. "We managed to sort things out on the secure wards. Not quite the full emergency we feared, but enough to need our attention for a while. We'll hold the review meeting in a few minutes' time. The conference room is outside the ward, turn right and go back down the corridor. First door on the right. There should be an urn on to make a drink." Ruth took this as her cue to leave the ward, and turned to one of the nurses nearby to ask where the nearest staff ladies' toilet was. Once directed, she hurried there to compose herself before the staff meeting.

CHAPTER TEN

Richard had been distressed even when he woke up. As he'd lain in bed the night before, all he could think was that he might have betrayed himself, and the thirteen years of effort involved in concealing himself in the hospital. He'd learned to put up with the humiliation of living in a communal ward, observed by nurses and orderlies all the time, and changing the way he looked and spoke to everyone he met. He'd kept his past entirely secret; and as far as he knew, only Winstanley had been even partially aware of the reasons why he was there. He'd learned how to act like other patients, and how to present himself as someone suffering sufficient mental distress to justify his continuing stay at Black Roding. Winstanley had not treated him badly, except when he had prescribed the shock therapy, or some of the drugs he had prescribed for him in the early years. And Winstanley had coached him in some of the ways in which to act, helping him with his disguise. And yet all that effort, the physical energy that was so curiously expended in slowing himself down and presenting himself as a shy and uncommunicative inmate, had been put aside because he had engaged in conversation with the newcomer. Richard was still cross with himself, and with her, as he had finally fallen asleep.

These thoughts immediately resurfaced as he woke and dressed. He was late and had to avoid shaving and miss breakfast in order to start his rounds on time. Mrs Jones commented on his rather dishevelled appearance. But even while he loaded the newspapers and replenished the toiletries and sweets on the trolley, all he could really think of was the possibility that he would be discovered. And if that happened, what would follow? He had been warned of the importance of maintaining secrecy. There had been threats that if he were revealed he would be arrested, put on trial and imprisoned. A long period of labour in prison had been mentioned. He'd been told stories of what might happen to someone like him in a prison, reports of prisoners assaulted and attacked, and of living in fear that any day, at any time, other prisoners would be waiting for him somewhere away from the wardens – a toilet block, the showers, on a stairway. The asylum was definitely better than that. And he had jeopardised his safety by his foolishness, by forgetting his status and answering Doctor Appleton's questions and challenges too forthrightly. Would she have realised? She clearly didn't understand Black Roding, but she seemed to him to be a thoughtful and intelligent doctor, and sensitive to his responses.

And before a prison sentence, Richard thought, there would be the humiliation of a public trial. He had gone to the Old Bailey one day when a trial was on. He had sat in the public gallery and tried to imagine what it was like as a prisoner. To be brought in by van from a remand gaol and kept in the cells below the court. To hear all the activity of the massive court complex above you, and the guards outside your door talking together and laughing at each other's jokes. Perhaps there would be an uncomfortable meeting with your lawyers in a tiny interview room, men who – unlike you – had taken breakfast with their families and travelled into London by train from their suburban homes. They were free, free to chat together with their adversaries in the robing room, free to walk out at the end of the day in court. Then to be summoned from the cells and led up the internal stairs to the dock, seeing first of all the judge – a grim spectacle in his long wig and gown – in front of you, then the wigged barristers in the wooden benches below the judge. To turn and see the jury on one side, looking at you with deep interest and suspicion, and the journalists on the other side, taking pens from their jackets and preparing their notepads. And behind you other interested members of the public, just like him on this particular day. Richard thought it would be hard even to stand up at such a moment, and he shuddered at the thought that he might face this ordeal, and that his actions thirteen years previously could still bring him a long-term sentence. Fifteen years' imprisonment had been the sentence in the case that he had visited. He wondered again if the prisoner on that day had recognised him sitting in the public benches as he turned to scrutinise the scene, blinking a little as he emerged from the dark recesses beneath the dock. He hadn't had that much contact with him over the years, and none in the previous year and a half. But he had always known that there were rumours about him, and his actions, going back some ten years. And he had consciously tried to avoid him because of those rumours. His own actions, and his own motives, had been very different to those of that prisoner.

Suddenly Richard stopped and looked up from his thoughts. He had been trudging along the corridor, but realised that, deep in his anxiety, he had walked past two corridors that led to wards he should have visited. He retraced the steps he had not noticed himself taking and tried to concentrate on his job. The nurses found him distracted, though, when he came to their counters and desks, because he could not recover the masking act with which he normally approached them. "Are you all right, Richard?" one asked him, and he half-nodded and half-shook his head, so that she was unsure how to react and watched him with some puzzlement as he retreated down the corridor, dragging the trolley in his haste to avoid her questions.

As he continued, Richard's thoughts turned to the cell in which he had been held and the interview room in which he had been questioned. The rooms were cold and bare, much like the asylum, and Richard could remember that he had been crying in fear in the cell when he was pulled out to the interview. Shoved down on a wooden chair in front of the table at which his inquisitor sat facing him, he had not at first raised his eyes to meet the cold stare of the man. When he had finally looked up, the look of scorn and contempt made him feel cold, and he felt more lonely at that moment than ever in his life before. He could not remember all the questions, or how he had answered them, but he could recall the final allegations and threats. Richard had been caught cottaging in a notorious gentlemen's toilets, and there was a witness who would swear that he had been importuned by Richard. No good denying it – the matter was as clear as day. He was unmarried, had been suspected before, and now he would face charges if he did not co-operate. Left on his own he had tied together his tie and his shoelaces and attached them to his belt, with which he formed a noose. He'd put the noose around his neck and moved his chair beneath the electric cable that held the bare bulb that illuminated the room. He had kicked the chair away but the electric cable had not held, and he had collapsed on the floor. He had been kicked several times before the guards had come in and a straitjacket had been found, and Richard could still feel the sharp prickle of the coarse cloth around his neck where it doubled around him to hold his arms in. Then doctors had been sent for, and a sedative put him to sleep.

Richard had not relived these moments for some years. They were some of the worst experiences of his life, ones that he tried to keep from ever entering his head. He knew why they had come back to him now. Because of Winstanley's death, and the arrival of Ruth Appleton, any day he might be returned to just such another stark room, and would be looking across a flimsy table at another questioner or, more probably, the very same one.

While these memories and thoughts were reoccurring to him, he had pushed the trolley from the western corridor into the main corridor that led into the reception hall. His progress had become slow, and his path had not been straight, so that patients and staff had had to swerve to avoid the trolley hitting them. "Careful, there," one nurse had said, but Richard had not even noticed her. His legs seemed to be both growing heavy and becoming stiff, and it was hard to lift his feet off the floor, as if he were walking, or shuffling, up a steep hill. His arms felt weak, and for the first time in many years the trolley was difficult to push. He was trembling at the thought of what might happen to him, his fear overtaking any other thoughts. His heartbeat was racing faster, and his breathing was shallow, but he could not control the panic rising inside him. He came to a halt in the reception area, holding the push-bar of the trolley weakly to support himself but unable to move otherwise. He was crying silently, and tears ran down his face to the corners of his mouth, but he was unable to wipe them away. He bowed his head forward, and one or two teardrops fell to the floor at his feet. A passing nurse stopped, looked at Richard and called for help.

CHAPTER ELEVEN

THE STAFF TOILET WAS A DINGY SET OF CUBICLES, SMELLING OF disinfectant and without any natural light, as if it were an afterthought that had been fitted into an unused corner of the building. Ruth locked herself in one of the cubicles and sat down on the toilet seat to take some deep breaths. She dabbed beneath her eyes with the hard toilet paper. She never wore make-up to work, so any tears could not mark her face, but she would be red-eyed if she didn't stop. She opened the cubicle door and filled a handbasin with warm water. She lapped the water over her face with her hands. Then she wiped her hands and pushed her face into the hand towel hanging from a roller in the corner. She took out the small brush that she always kept in a pocket and raked it quickly through her hair. She felt calmer but still hurt and humiliated, and she knew that her anger and fear were mingling just beneath the surface of things. Checking her appearance in the mirror first, she left the convenience and went to look for the conference room.

In the room the doctors and nurses, and the other staff, were already gathering, and most had taken a seat around the four tables that had been pushed together in the middle of the room. The occupational health worker had made a pot of tea and was busy distributing it in chipped white cups and saucers. Ruth took one of the remaining seats and thanked the tea-maker when she put a cup of rather weak tea down in front of her. The deputy superintendent had taken a seat in the middle of the short side of the grouped tables and was preparing to preside over the meeting. Patricia Holly was on one side of him, and the registrar Michael Brown on the other.

"Let's make a start, shall we?" the deputy superintendent said. "Staff Nurse, could you do the first briefing?"

The first briefing included matters of information about patients, possible new admissions, decisions about existing patients and their further treatment in the hospital, and routine tasks. The staff listened, and some people took notes of matters obviously affecting them. The deputy superintendent then said that Mr Brown would lead the review of the general meeting since Doctor Appleton was not familiar with this part of their procedures. This review, as always, would follow the sequence of the meeting, and so Patricia Holly started to discuss Mr Weinberg, the new admission. Mr Brown reminded everyone that Mr Weinberg had been treated with drugs by his local doctor and had reached a high dosage before the doctor had considered an admission to Black Roding. Weinberg's admission was therefore after a period of two years of depression; he was single and had little family contact. He had been unemployed for eighteen months, and the doctors were considering employing a drug treatment for the depression but would need to decide on a drug or various drugs, and the ideal dosage, only after Weinberg had been weaned off his current dependence. The nurses who had been talking to him reported that he had felt particularly nervous before the meeting and had begged them to get him some drugs so that he could cope. They thought that once the meeting had started, and another patient had supported him by retelling her own history of admission, he had done well to stay. They were concerned about moments when he might again feel vulnerable, such as before a small meeting or before sleeping. The registrar asked what was known of his previous routines, and one of the nurses repeated from memory that he had been relatively housebound and had only walked to the local shops or the doctor's surgery.

"I think we should make sure he is tired this evening," said the staff nurse. "If the fog lifts this afternoon, could we get him and a few other patients to take a walk in the grounds for an hour or so? Attending the meetings is one thing to sort out, by persuading him again, but the no-drugs policy means that it would be better not to give him a sedative tonight because he can't sleep. If the fog doesn't lift, could someone at least walk him around the corridors?"

The staff nurse next raised the opening discussion of strong feelings, and the case of Vera and Stanley, and Mr Brook's opposition to their relationship. To Ruth's surprise, one of the nurses was the first to contribute. She said that Mr Brook had previously expressed antagonism about the relationship in a small meeting, and the meeting had not been able to resolve the matter. He had particularly said that he disliked the two people "getting physical" in front of other patients. Would he wake up one morning – or worse, be woken in the middle of the night – to find them sharing a bed in the dormitory? The nurse laughed nervously as she repeated this. The registrar asked if anyone else wanted to contribute regarding Mr Brook.

The social worker continued the discussion. She was aware that Mr Brook had been known to medical and social services for many years, going back to his childhood. He had had a violent relationship with his stepfather after his mother's second marriage and had spent part of his childhood in an orphanage. Could his feelings about that time be influencing his reaction to the couple? Ruth was puzzled that no-one was questioning the appropriateness of the relationship. While it might be the case that Mr Brook's reactions were based in his own history, she nonetheless was intrigued about the hospital's policy on the two patients. She was sure that such a relationship would have been discouraged elsewhere, but did not want to express this view to the meeting. So, when there was a pause she asked, in as neutral a voice as she could manage, "What is the view of the couple and their new relationship? Does that carry any risks for the two of them?"

The deputy superintendent seemed to raise an eyebrow at Ruth's question, and looked at her briefly but said nothing. One of the auxiliary nurses did interrupt, however.

"It has worried me. They have been snogging one another – sorry, there's no other way of saying it, really – a bit like teenagers, as if they've never had a relationship before, and in full view of the other patients and staff. Mr Brook isn't the only patient to complain. He's just been more persistent. The two of them haven't joined in other ward activities for the past week or so. It seems OK at the moment, but what if they are like teenagers and fall out as quickly as they've fallen for each other?" She looked around the group sheepishly. Perhaps, Ruth thought, the speech was longer than her normal contribution to the conversation.

The meeting was silent, as if no-one knew how to take this forward. The staff nurse looked at the doctors as if enquiring of them how to proceed. The deputy superintendent leaned forward a little in his chair.

"A development in a patient's life, especially in their social life, while they are in the Admissions Ward is quite rare," he said. "Usually we just see the changes that arise from their adjustment to the hospital, so a developing relationship gives us a potentially rich opportunity to learn about them. Their behaviour has been somewhat open and indiscreet, although it seems to have stopped short of being offensive to everyone, or of carrying a risk of pregnancy. So it is best for us to allow it to continue for the moment. After all, there was a clear desire to find a compromise, and certainly in Vera's case history that does not seem to have been something she could always do. But there are risks. Both these people have had failed relationships, and that has led to some extreme emotional reactions. Failed relationships may in part have led them to be admitted here."

"So is the risk acceptable?" Ruth had blurted it out without thinking, as if it was a one-to-one discussion between two professionals that others would never overhear. The words seemed almost to come from someone else, so unexpected even to her was her challenge.

The deputy superintendent seemed taken aback and took a moment to take stock of the situation before replying. "If it happened on a long-stay ward, we might have to consider separating the couple by transferring one of them, to limit their time together and make physical contact more difficult, it's true. And, Doctor Appleton, you have been on such long-stay wards, I think, where the risks would suggest such an action would be appropriate. But we cannot easily transfer patients out of an Admissions Ward. In Stanley's case we're only one week away from a decision about whether or not to keep him in the hospital, and Vera can't be that long behind him. If we transferred one of them to the other Admissions Ward, the team there would almost have to start again. So, for the moment we must monitor the patients, and I suggest we add some one-to-one meetings to allow discussion of their personal feelings. In those one-to-ones we should if possible discuss with them the risks if the relationship were at this moment in their lives to deepen or become a physical one."

Ruth felt quashed. The reference to her previous work seemed to be an implicit reference to her relative inexperience, a form of putting her in her place for not having worked in a hospital like Black Roding before. She had to acknowledge that the deputy superintendent's decision, even if she did not agree with it, was a considered one that the other staff could understand. But Ruth had been trained to reduce risks when she considered patients, not to run risks almost deliberately. She sensed that a chasm existed between her views and those of the deputy superintendent – and perhaps between her views and the policies and practices of the whole hospital.

"Nurse Coughlan," the staff nurse said, turning to the nurse who had added to the discussion at that point of the general meeting, "do you want to add anything to what you said?"

The nurse looked slightly embarrassed that the matter was being raised in front of the deputy superintendent. She stammered her reply at first, "N – N – no, n-no, thank you. I j-just felt that it was relevant."

"It was," the staff nurse said, "and you seemed to follow the principle of waiting to see if one of the patients wanted to say something at that time. We can use our own personal experiences if there is something relevant to share, and it is intended to bridge rather than reinforce the gap that exists between patients and staff."

The deputy superintendent reinforced this view by saying, "It's important that we show that any of us can be vulnerable – to psychiatric distress, that is."

Ruth stayed silent. It would have been all too easy to develop her different view of this. She believed that a proper distance should be maintained between medical staff and patients. How, otherwise, could they be objective and scientific in their treatment of the patients? They should not get emotionally involved in or with their patients' problems but should discuss them dispassionately. Patients should not be told that the medical staff also had psychiatric problems. That would only discourage them. But if she were to say these things now, it would surely make her future relationship with the deputy superintendent impossible.

One of the other nurses spoke up in response to the deputy superintendent. "It did get Mrs Baker to speak about something, didn't it, even though it upset her? We haven't been able to get her to speak up in the general meeting before, so it was a new step."

The occupational health officer looked up from the notebook she had jotted in during the meeting. "I took a note of what she said. I wondered if I should have a word with her about getting her some training – in typing and commercial work – and seeing if there's anywhere she could visit to look at some work. Would that cut across any treatment she's going to have? And will she be allowed an exeat for work?"

"No and yes, I think," the registrar said. "No decision has been made about her treatment yet. She is likely to need to be admitted to a ward, but perhaps a work placement alongside that would be appropriate when the time comes. So carry on. But someone needs to talk to Mrs Baker today. The nursing staff should arrange that."

The staff nurse then said, "I know we'll need to talk about Sarah and her baby, but could we just check where we are on the cleaning of the ward? It seems to crop up again and again, and there were complaints during the meeting about it. I wonder what a newcomer like Doctor Appleton thinks of the cleanliness of the ward." She turned towards Ruth as she said this. Ruth had a sense that this might be a dangerous point, but she could hardly duck the issue when she had been so directly asked.

"How do you mean, what I think of the cleanliness?"

"Well, do you think the ward is as clean as it should be?"

The deputy superintendent coughed loudly and deliberately at this moment. He did not seem happy with the turn in the conversation, but he did not intervene. The staff nurse looked at Ruth.

"Well," said Ruth, "I suppose that by comparison with the last ward I was on, which was in a specialist and relatively new facility, this ward is not as clean as that ward was. Perhaps it's harder here."

"No, it isn't," Nurse Coughlan said. "At least it shouldn't be, if we nurses were allowed to get on with our jobs and make sure the ward is clean. But it's the doctors who keep stopping us and trying to get the patients to clean the ward. That's why it's not as clean as it should be."

Ruth realised too late that she had stumbled, or rather been led unwittingly, into a contentious difference of view among the staff, and clearly the nurses felt strongly about it because several of them nodded or vocalised their agreement with Nurse Coughlan's words.

"I didn't... didn't know anything about previous decisions," protested Ruth. "I was just asked my opinion on the cleanliness of the ward."

"You should think before you speak, then," another nurse said angrily. "It's something we feel very strongly about!" Once again the other nurses clearly agreed and did not seem prepared to accept Ruth's protest.

Ruth did not know what else she could say to placate the nurses. She looked at the staff nurse, the registrar and the deputy superintendent in turn. Only the deputy superintendent seemed prepared to join in the conversation. He looked at Ruth and then at the staff nurse.

"I'm not sure it's right to ask a new doctor for her opinion on a matter on which we already aren't agreed. We know that as trained nurses in hospitals you would be accustomed to accepting responsibility for the cleanliness of your wards. But that is principally because the patients in conventional hospitals are vulnerable to poor hygiene, or to clutter not being cleared away, or to spillages not cleaned up. But our patients are not generally physically ill, although many are not well-fed or particularly clean. They have come directly from their homes and may return there very soon. If we allow them to cease to take responsibility for their own surroundings, we may be doing them and their families a great disservice. And so there is a different balance between tidiness and cleanliness, on the one hand, and personal responsibility and involvement on the other, a kind of compromise that you as nurses are asked to accept. It is actually good if patients complain about the cleaning of the ward, because it means that it matters to them. Now we need to get the patients to encourage one another in cleaning and tidying and not fall out among ourselves."

The deputy superintendent's speech seemed final to everyone, although it was clear that some nurses would still have liked to discuss the policy further. Ruth wondered if the staff nurse had not raised the matter deliberately, using as a convenience the fact that patients had raised the matter in the general meeting and taking advantage of her own inexperience of the ward to expose a difference of view among the staff. If so, she had walked straight into the trap.

"And now Sarah and her baby," the staff nurse said. "Has she still been finding it difficult?"

"Yes," said the nurse who had been with the young woman before the general meeting had started. "She's still breastfeeding with supplements, but the baby seems to want more and yet refuses other foods. Sarah becomes frustrated that the baby isn't satisfied, and angry. She thinks she's failing, and the depression she's been suffering isn't lifting; if anything, it's getting worse."

The social worker raised her hand to indicate that she wanted to follow that up, and said, "The admission certificate indicated that the baby was at some risk but that Sarah could not be admitted without him because of the feeding. We still need to monitor both of them very closely, during both day and night, and if necessary move Sarah away from the baby for some rest – for both of them – if her anger seems likely to move beyond the verbal tantrums we've seen. Can I ask what she's been like in small meetings?"

"Either very quiet or seeking attention," replied the nurse. "Much as we saw at the end of the meeting." Ruth felt her shoulders tense. The attack by the young woman Sarah had angered her more than anything else she had encountered in the past twenty-four hours.

"I thought that what she said to Doctor Appleton was possibly very revealing," the social worker said.

"Revealing," Ruth repeated, "revealing of what?"

"Well, of her reaction to you. Of all the people in the meeting whom she could have attacked, she went for you."

"Because I was an easy target, sitting next to her and chairing the meeting. And because there isn't the respectful relationship that I've had in other hospitals. We should be discouraging patients from attacking staff verbally."

"I disagree," the social worker said. "We have to try to learn from what she does. It doesn't just happen. She does things for a reason, even if it's hard to understand."

"But how can we treat her if she has no respect for us, if she's prepared to be so insulting and so aggressive? How do we engage with her if she hates us?" Of course, Ruth knew that by 'we' and 'us' she really meant 'I' and 'me'. It was Ruth who had suffered the attack and felt the sharp tongue the woman had employed against her. And within herself, Ruth was a little afraid that the woman's insults might just reveal something of what others thought about her, or, in her worst moments, what she thought about herself. So, for Ruth it felt important to attack what the young woman had done. "She should be stopped when she attacks someone like that!"

"I don't think she attacked you because you are a doctor. She attacked you, I think, because she saw you as being like her, a young woman, but different to her, in that you don't have a baby. She insulted you over these issues – not being married, not being a mother. And these are the very issues that she's finding it hard to cope with. I think it was a form of jealousy, if you like, that led to her attack on you. And perhaps that's where her treatment should begin."

As with other aspects of Black Roding, Ruth was not at all accustomed to social workers advising doctors on the treatment of patients. Social workers, in her view, were for close support and sometimes counselling of patients in transition, especially if they were leaving the hospital. But their work was to follow things up after the patient had been treated or while the patient was being treated, not to anticipate the treatment or to give advice on it. To her way of thinking, no-one at Black Roding seemed to stay within the confines of their proper roles, except perhaps the superintendent and his deputy, and as a consequence disorder and chaos – as she had experienced during the general meeting – seemed to be the inevitable consequence.

"Surely there's a need to reduce her aggression first?" Ruth half-said and half-asked. "We can't get into treatments for her deep disorder unless we can first reduce the antagonism. Letting her just give vent to her feelings in this way risks embedding them in her behaviour and her strategies for dealing with us. There must be a response that says, No, if you want treatment there must be a recognition that your behaviour makes that impossible. You must change that behaviour if we are to treat you. If we just let it go, and especially if other patients see it being let go, we look incapable and unprofessional, and they will imitate the behaviour."

The social worker said nothing in reply, but raised her eyebrows as if to dismiss Ruth's view. Ruth, angered by the gesture, went on, "You must see that her behaviour is in danger of undermining me, a new doctor. Other patients should see an active response when a patient acts like this, otherwise my position as doctor and my expertise are discredited in their eyes!"

Ruth knew that her assertions were aimed not so much at the social worker as at the staff nurse, whom she held responsible for allowing the attack to be made and to go unchecked. But the staff nurse did not respond.

Again the social worker refused to engage with Ruth, looking away towards the deputy superintendent. "I can't accept being abused by a patient without any response!" Ruth was almost shouting, and her comment was again aimed at more than just the social worker. She was angry that none of the hierarchy of staff nurse, registrar or deputy superintendent was picking up her objections or offering an apology. "Or is this how doctors are treated here?" Ruth shook her head to demonstrate her disbelief.

"No, Doctor," the staff nurse was finally goaded into replying. "It's not how doctors are treated here, not generally. But in this case Sarah is a patient whom everyone has been finding difficult, and she has refused to reveal anything of her thoughts or feelings in a genuine way. What she said to you was in some way typical of how she has responded to other staff, but more extreme and certainly more instantaneous. I suppose we all thought she was revealing something potentially important because it came so instantly, something Christine has already been wondering about. When a patient is revealing something, even if it is in this extreme but not physical way, that is not by our procedures a time to silence or to browbeat her. Please don't think we were being unsympathetic to you. No-one likes seeing and hearing a colleague attacked. But we must follow our agreed procedures."

Ruth was tempted to mutter that she had certainly never agreed to such procedures, but she held back. She breathed deeply and exhaled deliberately through her nostrils, snorted really, allowing the gesture to express her disagreement and frustration. She looked away from the staff nurse and then down at her feet. After a few silent moments, in which Ruth's anger and its effect on the meeting dissipated somewhat, the registrar intervened.

"I would like someone to speak to Sarah. I'd do it myself but I think it might be better if it were a female member of staff," he said. He paused as if to consider his own words. "Yes, I think a female member of staff should try to gently probe why she thinks she had this outburst. I'd do it but I think she would think I was intervening on Doctor Appleton's side. Does anyone think they could take on this delicate task? It will be delicate – and if it starts to go wrong, the person doing the probing should stop."

The registrar looked around the group. The social worker also looked around the group. When no-one volunteered immediately, she said, "I'll try it. I've got to speak with her about some domestic arrangements anyway, so I'll try to come round to it in the course of that discussion."

The registrar then called a close to the meeting and most participants went off to resume their duties. Ruth helped to gather in the empty cups and saucers, the activity allowing her to avoid continuing the conversation with anyone. And when she had done that, she decided to go and introduce herself to some of the patients who had not spoken in the meeting, and to keep her anger to herself. But the deputy superintendent had other ideas. He too had waited as the others left.

"Doctor Appleton," he said in a stern voice, "you clearly don't like all that you've seen and experienced going on here. That's understandable. Not all hospitals are the same, and not all doctors are the same. But you need to give us a chance to explain and to show you how our procedures work. If you start by criticising them in public, people will not find it easy to work with you."

"I've never asked anyone to find me easy to work with. I'm more interested in what it's right for a doctor to do, and to do that. And I'm not persuaded by what I've experienced that the hospital's procedures are all good ones. I certainly don't believe that patients should be able to treat doctors and nurses in an aggressive or violent way. There must be some consequence, some response. I don't like being attacked."

"You've not been physically attacked. A patient has used some strong personal abuse. That's not good, but it's not a physical attack. In part, it's your job to study what the patient does and not allow the personal abuse to affect you. If you do let it get to you, you won't be able to work here for long."

Ruth refused to say anything more. She looked angrily at the deputy superintendent, but he too would not be drawn further. They might have been left in a silent standoff, if an orderly had not come into the room. The man did not wait to be asked to speak but addressed the deputy superintendent immediately.

"Doctor, you're needed in Reception. A patient has been taken ill there."

"Who is it? Do you know what ward they're from?" asked the deputy superintendent.

"I don't know which ward, but it's the trustee who runs the patients' trolley. He's very upset, and no-one can get him to move."

Ruth was grateful for this opportunity to withdraw from the awkward discussion with her superior. "I'll go. He's my patient. I've met him already." She left the room as quickly as she could, followed by the orderly.

CHAPTER TWELVE

Richard was still standing by the trolley when Ruth and the orderly arrived. The nurse who had originally stopped was there, talking to him, but Richard was clutching the trolley's handle and not listening. He was taking short breaths, and Ruth could hear his breathing as she approached.

"What happened?" Ruth asked the nurse first, drawing her aside while the orderly stood by Richard.

"I don't know," the nurse said, "he was just standing here when I came by, and I've not been able to persuade him to move since. He was breathing very fast and holding on to the trolley. Someone said he had been pushing the trolley very erratically. He won't really speak to me. What will you do?"

"Try to get him to sit down and check him out. If there's no other sign, it might just be a panic attack. If we try to move him physically he might resist and become even more upset." Ruth turned to the orderly. "Could you get a chair for him to sit on?" she asked. He went away to find one while Ruth approached Richard. He was looking down at the floor, effectively holding himself up by the handle of the trolley, Ruth judged. She did not want to move him until a chair was available.

"Richard, it's Doctor Appleton. Can you hear me?" Ruth spoke quietly, her voice not much more than a whisper. He turned his head a little, but his body shrank away from her.

"Leave me be," he muttered angrily.

"I'm not trying to move you, Richard. I've sent for a chair for you to sit down, but it isn't here yet. I don't want to upset you."

"I don't want to move, I want to stay here." Richard seemed to say this through clenched teeth.

"I'm not going to move you. I'm just going to get you to sit down in a minute."

"No, that's not it. I don't want to move."

Ruth was puzzled. She had anticipated a patient in some shock who might not be able to articulate his feelings, as was common in a panic attack. But he was making his feelings clear. She still needed to eliminate any other possible causes of Richard's condition, which was the principal reason in seeking to sit him down. But Richard seemed to know what he wanted, or rather what he didn't want.

"OK, Richard, we'll just wait for the chair to come." Ruth turned to the nurse. "Could you try to take his pulse? I know it's not the best circumstance, but I need to start checking him physically. I think it is a panic attack, but I still need to make sure."

The nurse moved to Richard's side, took out the small fob watch from her top pocket and put her fingers on Richard's wrist. "Just over one hundred," she said after a while.

"It's high, but not too high, I think. I haven't even seen his file yet." Ruth was speaking half to the nurse, half to herself. "I should still listen to his chest, but not till I've got him sitting down." She moved nearer to him again, again trying to speak as quietly as she could. "Are you in any pain, Richard? Does it hurt anywhere?"

He turned a little towards her and spoke in a strained tone. "In my chest… a bit, in my chest."

The orderly came up to them carrying a wooden chair. Ruth motioned to him to put it behind Richard. She put her hands on his shoulders, feeling him tense at her touch. She moved her hands towards his armpits, as if to support him. "Richard, we need you to sit down, to let go of the trolley and sit down. Can you do that?"

Richard shook his head. "Don't want to sit down. Want to get on and do my work."

"No, Richard, you can't at the moment. I need to check you over. Just try to let go of the trolley." Ruth tried to move the man's arms upwards, encouraging him to let the handle go. Although she could still feel his tension, his arms did move, and his fingers slowly unfurled from the handle. "Ease yourself backwards," Ruth said, motioning with her head to the orderly to help him as well. She felt Richard give up the effort needed to stand up, and she and the orderly had to hold him tight as he sank backwards, his knees seeming suddenly to give way. The nurse stepped in to move the trolley away a little. "That's good, Richard, that's good," Ruth said. "Try to breathe in deeply, through your nose if you can." He was still panting and Ruth needed to listen to his chest. Unlike some doctors in an asylum, who would only keep a stethoscope in their office, Ruth always carried hers in her pocket. It was one of the new lightweight ones, an expensive acquisition but necessary for a doctor, Ruth believed. She brought her own hand to her forehead, to check if her hand would suffice to check the man's temperature. Sometimes her fingers were cold and no use as a guide. But her hand felt the same temperature as her own forehead, so she told Richard that she was just checking his temperature and placed her hand on his head. It was slightly hotter than her hand. He was not running a high temperature.

"I just need to check your chest, Richard, and then we'll wait for you to feel better," She raised his jumper up to the level of his shoulders. "Could you just hold his jumper up?" she asked the nurse. She obliged, and Ruth leaned forward to undo some of the buttons on Richard's chest. Instinctively he tried to stop her from doing so. "It's all right, it's all right," she said, again dropping her voice to a near whisper. He moved his hands away, resigned to the indignity of a public examination. Ruth quickly undid three buttons of his shirt, put the stethoscope to her ears and the chestpiece on Richard's chest. She listened, moved the chestpiece three or four times and then turned to the nurse. "I think it is just a panic attack. His breathing is okay, although he has been hyperventilating; and his heart and chest sound all right, even if the pulse is a little high. We need to get him back to the ward in a few minutes. Could you find us a wheelchair, do you think?" And turning to the orderly she said, "He's doing well. But he can't finish that trolley round. Could you take it back to the shop?"

Richard looked up at her for the first time since she had arrived. "Need to finish the round," he said, and tried to stand.

"No, that would not be a good idea. You seem fine to me now, but we need to watch over you for a while. Then tomorrow you might be able to do your rounds."

"I don't want to leave. Can't leave. Need to stay here and do my rounds."

"Not today." Ruth managed to combine a firmness of tone with the quiet of her whispered words. And she held his shoulders to stop him from making any further effort to stand up. "There would be too much of a risk."

Richard again looked up at her. "Risk?" he queried. "Why a risk?"

"Of you having another attack like the one you've just had. That's all." Richard said nothing more, and Ruth too stopped speaking, simply watching the way in which he recovered.

The nurse brought a very old-looking wheelchair, its frame scratched and the wheel hubs rusting. "It was all I could borrow," she said. "It should just about do."

"Let's hope so. Richard, could we move you into this wheelchair, to get you back to the ward?" He nodded. He had recovered enough to resume his taciturn approach. Taking one arm each, the nurse and Ruth helped him to raise himself from the chair and ease down into the wheelchair.

"Shall I take him back to the ward?" the nurse asked.

"No, I'll wheel him back. I'm due to go there anyway."

"Really, is that okay? Doctors don't usually wheel patients anywhere. Wouldn't it be better if I got an orderly to take him back?" The nurse was genuinely surprised.

"It'll be fine," Ruth said. "I'm used to helping to move patients. Thanks for your help, and for waiting with him." Ruth turned to Richard and squatted down to talk to him, again employing a quiet tone. "You seem ready to go back to the ward. I'll wheel you there now."

Richard said nothing, so Ruth took hold of the two handles and turned the wheelchair towards the corridor. As she started to push the chair she saw the superintendent approaching her. He was in a coat and scarf and had obviously just arrived in the reception area. Ruth's spirits sank a little. No doubt she was about to be told that she'd done something else wrong.

"Good afternoon, Doctor," Paul Verity said.

"Good afternoon. This patient just had a panic attack."

"I thought so, when I saw you dealing with him."

"You were watching?" Ruth could not keep the anxious tone from her voice.

"Yes. There was no need for me to intervene. You did everything very well and correctly. Believing a patient is having a panic attack can disguise the possibility of a cardiac problem, but you checked for that. And the lowered voice was exactly the right way to approach him. My friend, your superintendent, was right. You are a good scientist. But you've also learned some good strategies for dealing with crises."

"Yes, there were plenty of crises where I worked before."

"Keep up the good work, then," and with that the superintendent turned away. And Ruth, her spirits raised for the first time since her arrival at Black Roding, pushed Richard towards his ward.

CHAPTER THIRTEEN

The nursing staff were surprised to find one of their doctors wheeling an inmate back into the ward. One smiled, while the other asked Ruth what had happened. Ruth explained the panic attack that Richard had apparently had, and asked them to let him lie on his bed for a while, and to monitor him, calling for her if there was any concern. She intended to work in the doctors' office. She explained to Richard what she wanted him to do. He was reluctant, asking again if he could go back and complete the round, but Ruth forbade it. She did not want him to be upset again. He was silent, and reluctantly went to his bed and sat on it.

"That's the best I can do for him at the moment," Ruth said to the nurses, "but don't let him wander off." And in a lowered voice she told them, "His symptoms all suggest a panic attack, and he should be fine. But I had to check there was nothing wrong with his heart because there are similar symptoms. I thought he was fine, but we need to watch him for that reason as well."

Ruth went down to the doctors' office. Neither of her colleagues was there. Ruth would have liked to have asked them a little more about Richard, but evidently that would have to wait. She needed to draft a survey form for the nursing staff to provide her with essential information about all the patients, and to find someone who would type it up and get copies made. She started to prepare the outline of the form, asking the nurses questions about each patient's ability to communicate, to understand their situation, to talk about their own feelings, to wash, dress and feed themselves, to occupy their time constructively, to control their reactions to others, to contribute to cleaning up and tidying the ward and their personal space and belongings, to engage with staff and other patients and, if it was known, to deal with strangers and newcomers. She also asked about their visitors, their use of the hospital's facilities, and whether they engaged in any of the manual tasks for which patients were paid small sums of money. This information, put alongside the patients' medical records, should allow her to identify patients who were most suitable, and least suitable, for transfer away from Black Roding. Satisfied with the draft document, she went to see how Richard was. He appeared to be sleeping, lying on his back with a raised pillow, because his eyes were shut and he was breathing slowly and regularly. So she found out from the nurses where she had to go to get her form typed and printed and said that she would also call in on the personnel department to complete any administration with them.

Ruth decided to take the shorter route in the open air to the Central Wing of the hospital. A weak sunlight had started to penetrate the fog, which was lifting. The path was visible running alongside the building towards the central point of the complex, which was still shrouded in mist. She saw the base of the water tower, a square building of red brick, with small windows and a picket fence set a few yards from each wall. A 'No Admission' notice was hanging on the fence, and the door into the building had been crudely barred with two wooden planks. Ruth could not see the top but could see that the brickwork extended to several storeys in height. It must have been some ingenious Victorian engineering to pump water up to that height in order then to generate the downward pressure to provide running water inside the building. Thinking of it reminded Ruth of the experiments in her school Physics lessons, checking pressures and seeing how water could be retained and released by vacuums. Happy days, they had been, when she and her friend Angela, who was her partner for these practicals, had set up the equipment, run the experiments, called out measurements to one another and then sat down to see if their figures provided an answer, or a graph, which the Physics teacher could praise. They would laugh if their experiments went wrong, and they laughed even more loudly when the demonstrations provided by the teacher went wrong. She was so occupied by these thoughts that she almost missed the turning for the central block, but a variety of signposts, not visible a day earlier, did catch her attention, and she paused to look at them. 'West Wing' pointed back down the path, accompanied by 'Car Parks by External Route'. Along the path into the Central Wing the signpost indicated that the 'Administration', 'Reception', 'Canteens' and 'Car Parks by Internal Route' lay through the door which Ruth could now see. And the third signpost indicated that the 'East Wing', 'Treatment Rooms', 'Operating Theatres' and 'Secure Wards' lay further along the path. Ruth had not asked to see the secure wards on her tour, but Richard had reacted to the mention of the treatment rooms. She wondered if he had been treated there and what the treatment had been. Soon, she hoped, she would be able to find out.

She went up to the administrative floor of the hospital. Here she had to check signs on the doors to find the one marked 'Personnel', and she went inside to find a female clerk working at great piles of paper on her desk in what must have been the dustiest of all rooms in the hospital. "Yes, can I help you?" the woman asked.

"I'm Doctor Appleton, I started here yesterday on a six-month placement. The superintendent said I should report to you."

"We were expecting you yesterday," the woman said in an accusing tone. "Why did you not report here yesterday?"

"I wasn't told to. The superintendent said today would be all right."

"Oh, the superintendent told you," the woman said. "There are systems, you know, systems we have to run. And one of those systems says that you have to sign your contract and all the other documents on the day you start. Everyone knows that that's the system for starting, including the superintendent."

Ruth could take no more of this. "Yes, I'm sure you've got lots of good systems, but you don't seem to have one for telling people before they start what they are supposed to do on their first day. I wasn't even told how to get to Black Roding, let alone to report to you. And as I said, the superintendent—"

"Well, I suppose we'd better do what the superintendent says. Doctor Appleton, you said; yes, I think there's a set of documents in the tray over there for you." The woman stood up and retrieved a large brown envelope from a table in the corner of the room. Ruth noticed that the room was surprisingly warm, and saw that behind the desk there was a small electric fire, the bars glowing orange. The woman noticed Ruth's discovery. "I have to keep the room warm or I wouldn't be able to do my work." Ruth tried not to give any reaction, though she was noticing that some staff found their own ways around problems. "Well, anyway, here are your papers. You'll need to read them and sign them, and bring them back tomorrow. There's also a map of the hospital, a list of local buses and instructions about what to do if you're ill. Where are you living?"

"In a doctor's room at the moment, near Ward 44. It's not very nice."

"Not our department, I'm afraid. You'll have to talk to the buildings people along the corridor." And with that the woman resumed her clerical work and ignored Ruth.

Ruth felt like blowing any dust that had gathered on the large brown envelope into the woman's eyes but resisted the temptation. "Well, I'll be going along, then," she said, but the clerk did not even raise her eyes as she left the office.

Along the corridor Ruth next found the general administrative office, where the nurses on Ward 44 had suggested she should take her survey form for typing. But while the office was much cleaner and more organised than the personnel office, its occupants were not more helpful. "I'm sorry, it will take a week at least," the office manager said. "We've got all the typing for nine consultant teams coming through the office at the moment because we're so short of staff. There's a huge backlog."

"But I really need it done as soon as possible. The superintendent has only given me two weeks to get a big job done, and I can't start without this. Is there nothing you can do to hurry it along?"

"Not really," she said, though in the rejection Ruth sensed some sympathy. Ruth would have expected the office manager to be of middle age, but she was quite a young woman, probably in her early thirties, with long hair in a modern style that Ruth momentarily envied. "The typing has to be done on a special skin that gets fitted to the machine, so it takes some time. If you make a mistake it has to be corrected before you can go on, so that also takes time."

"I haven't got time, that's the problem."

"I am sorry. Only if the deputy superintendent told me to do so could I get it done any earlier."

Ruth did not want at this moment to go looking for the deputy superintendent. She waited, hoping the office manager would relent. But the office manager too was waiting, hoping Ruth would relent. An idea occurred to Ruth during this standoff. "Could I do it? I learned to type at school. There's an old typewriter in the doctors' office which I think is still used for typing small notices."

"That would be most unusual. I've never heard of a doctor typing a form like this. You have to remove the ribbon from the typewriter to type directly on to the skin. I didn't think doctors did things like that."

"I did it at school, it's one of the things they taught us, but not for some time."

"And then you have to load the skin in the typewriter and type the form exactly as you want it to be, doing all the layout." The doubt of the office manager was evident in her tone of voice.

"Could you give me a 'skin' – was that what you called it? – and just show me how to load it in the machine? And I'll bring it back to you tomorrow all typed up."

The office manager hesitated. "As I say, it's most unusual. I wouldn't want it getting out that we were giving out these skins right and left. It's very easy to ruin them. And the typists would be upset if they thought I was giving their work to the doctors, and the doctors might be upset if they thought they had to do this work instead of the typists. You see all the difficulties?"

"Yes, but I'd be saving my own skin, you see." The manager smiled at Ruth's joke, even if it was a poor one.

"If I give you one of the skins, you must bring it back only to me. Don't give it to anyone else. I'll run the copies off at the end of the day when the typists have gone home. So you could collect them at about six o'clock. Would that do?"

Ruth was grateful for the offer. "Yes. I'll work on typing it up this evening. And I'll bring it tomorrow on my way to the Admissions Unit. At what time are you in?"

"Around half past eight usually. Will that fit your timing?"

"Yes, it will. You'd better show me what I have to do."

The office manager fetched one of the reproduction skins on which Ruth would have to type her form. She showed her where on the form the space was, into which the letters would have to be cut. She warned her not to fold or roll the skin up, so she found an old paper carrier bag just big enough to cover the skin if Ruth held both the top of the skin and the carrier handles simultaneously. Then, the office manager said, no-one would notice the unusual sight of a doctor who was about to do her own typing. She smiled as she said this, as if the thought itself amused her. She also put into the bag a small bottle of red-coloured liquid, explaining that it would be needed for any corrections, and the liquid had to be brushed carefully over any errors and allowed to set before the correction was made.

"I'm Frances Avery, by the way," she said as she handed over the bag. "Do come back if you need some other help from us."

"Ruth Appleton," Ruth replied. "I'm only on a short-term placement. That's why I'm in a hurry, I suppose. I'll hand over the completed typing in the morning, I hope."

She left the office, but as she went along the corridor she realised she had made one mistake. She could not now go and ask about alternative accommodation while holding the Gestetner skin, so that would have to wait until another day. She returned to the West Wing and to the doctors' office, again using the back path which was now being warmed by the autumn sun. Some patients were walking along the path, and one or two had walked down onto the grass lawns. The grounds were vast, stretching across two great lawns divided by flower beds, with trees edging the boundaries. There were some wooden benches lined up on the lawns in such a way that patients could sit and take the sun. The water tower was now fully revealed, and Ruth could see its tiled and pointed roof. It was a distinctive building, Ruth thought, and it was no surprise that the minister had commented on it in his famous speech about the asylums. But his speech did not really show an understanding of how big the task was of closing a place like Black Roding. Its inmates, both the patients and the staff, were caught in a system so large and complex that even the slightest change of procedure appeared to have ramifications that were unthinkable. Here she was, after all, almost smuggling in secrecy a necessary tool for an administrative task. And the office manager had only agreed to allow her to take it if they made a secret pact about its use.

Ruth first checked with the nurses about Richard, who was now reading. He had stopped protesting about not being able to do his work and appeared to have accepted that he could not resume duties until the next day. His pulse rate had come down, and he had no chest pain. So Ruth was content to leave him for the present. She enquired about some other patients and told the nurses that she had some work to do in the doctors' room. She also learned that David Peters had left early to help his wife, and John Sutton was going round the other wards until he finished for the day. Ruth already knew that she was on late duty, so she expected to be in the wards until nine or ten o'clock. That seemed plenty of time in which to complete her typing.

When Ruth looked at the typing machine in the doctors' room, however, she was not so optimistic. It was an ancient manual typewriter, with a heavy carriage that required pushing across at the end of each line. The black typing ribbon was concealed by a metal cover that she would have to remove, and looking at the cumbersome machine made her realise that it was over twelve years since she had attended her last Commerce lesson, the compulsory class which the headmistress had insisted every girl should attend so that they could "always get a job, anywhere in the country". Yes, she had typed up brief notes and memoranda while training, but she hadn't done anything like laying out a detailed page for years. And she had never used a Gestetner skin, although she had seen office workers using the printing machines. It couldn't be that hard, could it? Not once she got the skin into the typewriter, she persuaded herself.

That task, however, was not so easy. The ribbon cover would not yield to Ruth's exploratory tugs, and when she looked more closely she realised that the cover was held in place by two screws, the heads being visible but placed awkwardly within the frame of the machine. Ruth had to turn the typewriter around completely to see them, straining to slide the heavy machine in a half-circle while retaining the soft baize sheet on which it stood. She looked in all the drawers in the office but could see neither a screwdriver nor any other similar implement. She had to ask the nurses in the ward. They looked at her in surprise. "A screwdriver? Well, that's the first time in all my years as a nurse that a doctor has asked for a screwdriver," one of them joked.

The other nurse said, "No, we wouldn't have one. The caretakers or buildings staff would provide those if they were ever needed. But I think Richard may have one. He has a toolbox in his tallboy that he uses when he does some metalwork in the machine rooms."

"Does he?" Ruth was interested to learn this of her patient. "I'll go and ask him." Ruth's view was that it was useful to speak to patients in a normal situation such as this, when something was needed, because then it was sometimes possible to see how they acted in ordinary circumstances. So she asked if he did indeed have such a thing as a screwdriver, as the nurses had suggested. He looked a little shocked by the question. He hesitated before replying, and then mumbled, "Yes," and stood up. He opened the tallboy and fumbled in the bottom, beneath the clothes that were hanging from the rail. He did not take out the box he was evidently opening, nor did he let Ruth see the box itself, but he soon came up with a small screwdriver with a thin blade. He held it up towards Ruth.

"Yes, that will be good," she said. "Thank you. Do you do a lot of metalwork?"

Richard's eyes betrayed his disappointment that she was learning things about him. "Some," he said, muttering his answer.

"Would you show me some of your work sometime?" Ruth asked.

"It's all… er… all gone," Richard managed to blurt out.

"Oh, that's a shame. I'd have liked to have seen it. What do you make?"

But Richard was not to be drawn. He shrugged his shoulders and turned back to his book, trying to ignore Ruth. She, taking her cue from him, turned back to the nurses' counter. "He's still a mystery to me," she said, showing them the screwdriver. "Look at this, for example. I don't know much about tools, but this looks and feels like an expensive one, as if it might be part of a set. But he won't talk to me about himself at all."

That's Richard for you," said one of the nurses. "He's always like that. He does do good metalwork though. One or two patients have got things he's given them."

"Really? Well, I must try to tackle the typewriter," Ruth said, brandishing the screwdriver. She went off to the doctors' room. She heard one of the nurses say, "It's hard to know who's insane and who isn't, don't you think?"

Ruth managed, after much fiddling with the screwdriver which kept losing contact with the small screw heads, to loosen the typewriter cover and then remove it. She put the cover on another desk, along with the screws. Then she addressed the problem of the ribbon, which ran between two spools. One spool clicked out very easily, but the catch on the other was jammed tight, and Ruth wondered how long it had been since the typewriter ribbon was changed. Finally, risking breaking the machine in order to remove the ribbon, she forced the screwdriver blade behind the catch and levered it open. She removed the spool but smudged her hand against the ribbon, and when she brushed her hair back she smeared her left cheek with the black ink. She decided it would be easier to type onto the skin without the cover back on, so she fed the skin through the rollers of the typewriter, grateful at least that the machine had several rollers so that the skin was held taut across the point where the keys would strike.

Ruth compared the size of the area to be typed on, helpfully marked out with lines, with the form she wanted to convert from her handwritten draft into a formal-looking survey document. She would need to top and tail it with some information for the nurses, and she needed to leave some spaces. She remembered that this was the kind of exercise she and her schoolmates had done at school. Her teacher would say, "You can't expect these busy businessmen to lay their handwritten drafts out neatly for you. You have to convert their scrawl into a proper-looking letter, or table, or whatever the draft is. So you need to do your sums first and plan the margins and the spaces, and know how many lines you are going to use and how many to leave empty. Until you've done your sums, don't even touch the typewriter."

But while Ruth could work out the layout of her form, she had not realised how her typing skills had declined since her schooldays. Within seconds she had made her first mistake. "Damn," she muttered, reaching for the bottle of correcting fluid and reading the instructions on the back of the bottle. She dabbed the liquid over her error and waited for it to dry. But almost as soon as she had resumed, she made another mistake. "Bloody hell!" she exclaimed. "What's happened to me?" Once again she had to pause while the red fluid dried, and the Gestetner skin started to look like a wounded hide. She became so embroiled in her task that she did not notice John Sutton standing in the doorway watching her, not knowing quite what to say about a doctor senior to him doing a task such as typing. "Bloody, bloody hell!" Ruth almost shouted as she made a third mistake and the keys on the typewriter jammed together.

"Steady up, Ruth," John Sutton said, startling her. "The nurses will hear you, or the patients will."

Ruth turned towards him. The black streak of ink across her face, and her cheeks reddened in frustration at being caught swearing at the typewriter, made him laugh. But she did not realise the cause of his humour and was angry at her junior. "Don't bloody well tell me what to do," she said. "It's bad enough that I have to do this, without being told off by you!"

He was taken aback by the venom in her speech. He held his hands up in a gesture of submission and walked away from the office towards the nurses' station. Shortly afterwards Ruth heard laughter from the ensuing conversation, and she fumed to think that she was the subject of her colleagues' jokes. In her vexation she made yet another mistake and once again had to pause in her task while the correcting fluid dried. The red stains were all too vivid as reminders of her poor typing. She thought she would be better to calm down a little by going to get a drink on the ward before resuming, so she too walked down the corridor towards the nurses' station. The two nurses were both still there, and they looked at her with interest as she approached. One of them tried to restrain herself but could not, and she laughed at Ruth's appearance.

"What are you laughing at?" Ruth asked. "What is it?"

The nurse said nothing but pointed to her own cheek by way of response.

"What do you mean?" again demanded Ruth.

"You've got ink on your face," the other nurse intervened, "and it's just very unusual to see a doctor looking like you."

Ruth looked down at her hands and saw that there were several patches of ink on her fingers and on the palm of her right hand. In her concentration on trying to type accurately she had not noticed the black stains before and had not realised that she might have streaked her cheek with the ink. She hurried away back down the corridor in search of a sink and mirror. She felt slightly humiliated, and angry with herself, with her colleague who should not have been making jokes about her, and with the nurses who were obviously talking about her. Sure enough, one glance in a mirror revealed the black smear, and it took a lot of washing to remove the ink, which had dried on her skin. Ruth did not go in further search of a drink but returned to the doctors' room and to her task, shutting the door to discourage John Sutton from entering. She told herself to slow down and type more deliberately, and she looked at the letter keys more often than her old Commerce teacher would have allowed as she completed her task. It took her two hours, however, and when she finished she had to stretch her legs and ease her back left and right to relieve the stiffness that had accumulated. She undid the Gestetner skin from the clamp that held it on the rollers and gingerly lifted the skin onto an empty portion of the table. The lower half of the skin was less stained in red, although she had made one or two mistakes. She felt she had made a fairly good job of the layout, although she knew she would only be sure of that when the office manager ran the copies off the next day. She fixed the spools and the ribbon back in place, carefully threading the ribbon through the metal holders that stretched it across the roller. Then she replaced the cover and refastened the screws. When she looked at the clock above the door, she realised that the afternoon and part of the evening had already passed and she would soon have to go for a meal.

She left the office and walked into the ward. The nurses had changed as the evening shift started, so Ruth did not face any embarrassment. She discovered that John Sutton had gone off duty. She felt foolish that her outburst had perhaps alienated him from her and resolved to apologise the next day. And she was still holding the screwdriver she had borrowed. She looked again at the smooth wooden handle of the tool and the shining steel shaft and circular grip that held the handle and shaft together. On this grip she saw the words 'American Screw Company' engraved. For some reason, and Ruth did not know why she thought it, she believed that the tool was an expensive and specialist piece of equipment, quite unlike those which her mother had kept at home.

Ruth went along the ward and into the men's dormitory area. Richard was sitting by his bed, still reading, and was absorbed in the book. Ruth watched him for a few moments. He was sitting completely still and seemed to read quickly, scanning the lines without moving his head, and to shift the pages at very regular intervals. Ruth watched as the pages were turned three or four times. If asked, she'd have said that he was an accomplished reader. He suddenly became aware of her presence nearby and looked up. He was startled, as if he had forgotten about the borrowed tool.

"I'm sorry, Richard," Ruth said. "I didn't want to disturb you, but I needed to return this." She held up the small screwdriver and held it out towards him. "It did the trick perfectly. It felt really well balanced in my hand. I'm normally useless with something like this, but I was able to do a very fiddly job. Thank you."

Richard said nothing. He took the small tool and put it on the bed. He was angry that yet again he had allowed this new doctor to discover something about him, however small. He moved his eyes back towards his book. But even that carried some risks, he realised, and he shut the book and placed it on the bed next to the screwdriver.

"Oh, I have disturbed your reading. You can't carry on," she half-questioned, half stated the fact.

"Need the toilet," Richard muttered as he stood up and, remembering to walk slowly, shuffled off towards the communal area. Ruth watched him leave, frustrated that she had interrupted his enjoyment of the book. It was a large tome, and she thought it was a library book. She turned to see if Richard had indeed left the dormitory area. Satisfied that no-one was watching her, Ruth picked up the book. It was by Winston Churchill, *Triumph and Tragedy*, and the back cover indicated that it was the last in a series that Churchill had written immediately after the war. Inside the cover was a library slip that revealed it belonged to the county library and was on loan to the hospital. Ruth shut the book and put it back on the bed. She would have liked to have seen the toolbox from which the screwdriver came, but it seemed too intrusive to open the tallboy and pry inside it.

In the doctors' office Ruth picked up the Gestetner skin to look over it again. She could see no errors but was unsure if the many corrections would work in the printing machine. But she would have to wait to find that out and, realising the time, she went off to the doctors' dining room to eat. As she walked along the corridors, she hoped she would avoid Smythe this evening.

CHAPTER FOURTEEN

I do not know if anyone other than me will ever read this. If they do, then something has happened, but I do not know what it will be. I am scared, I know that. So scared about what might happen that yesterday I could not move, standing in Reception with my trolley. A panic attack, they said. And who should come to help me but the new doctor? Every time she talks to me I think she is discovering new things about me, asking about why I do this, or think that, or have such a thing as an American screwdriver. And my every effort to put her off seems only to lead her to ask more questions, and so to find out more. I cannot blame her. The doctors' conversation I overheard tells me that she has to review every patient, and quickly, because that is what the superintendent has told her to do. And unlike the other doctors, she was never told by Winstanley to leave me alone, to let just him treat me. And so she asks me questions. And she observes things that the other doctors, or nurses, have never asked me about. The screwdriver, for example: no-one has asked me about those tools in all the years I have been here. Yet she holds it for a few minutes, and immediately she knows it's different. And she's right. A full set of ASC tools in a metal box, given to me by the others I'd worked with on the project. The most skilled set of engineers I'll ever meet. "Better than all those limey tools," they said at the little ceremony they'd arranged. And they were too, a set of fine tools that I've used again and again. And no-one ever questioned me about them until now.

I'm scared because I don't know what I said when I was having that attack in Reception. I don't know if I said anything about the project, or about why Winstanley agreed to me being here, or about what I have done. And I don't know what she'll find out when she asks the nurses about me, or looks up my records. I don't even know what Winstanley put in my hospital records, so I don't know how I will answer any questions in ways that match the records.

I dreamed last night of that dark room. I smelt again the foul stink of it, no windows, not decorated for years, the smell of my own sweat joining that of others who'd been there before me. I was crying again, just as I was then, and ready to punch him in the face if he came in again. And I saw my hands fumbling to connect my makeshift noose to the wire from the light. I remembered in my dream how long it took to tie the knot, to get it to hold. Twice the knot unravelled, and everything seemed to become wet as I wiped my eyes and brushed the sweat off my forehead. The moisture passed from my fingers onto the leather of the laces, and they slipped through my fingers. Finally I tied a knot that held and put the noose I had made out of my belt over my head. I was up on the chair but I hesitated, couldn't do it at first. Then my knee shook violently and the chair toppled forward, and I felt again the weight of my body on the belt, which cut instantly into my neck. And, just as it did thirteen years ago, I felt the light give way, the wire pulling out of the ceiling, and I crashed down onto the floor. And that's when I awoke, just as he was kicking me, calling me a stupid *fucking idiot as he did so. But I also recalled what happened next - the guards rushing in, tugging at the belt around my neck, pulling me up into a sitting position, shouting for more assistance and a doctor. Then the guards pulled him away and ushered him out of the room. But I can still feel that kick. I hadn't had anyone hit or kick me since I was a boy play-fighting with other boys. And then I turned back to the floor and wrapped my arms around my head.*

Richard had written for much longer than he had intended. He did not have time to read over it, certainly. He had to get back to work. Doctor Sutton had examined him and let him resume his duties that morning. Doctor Appleton was in the Admissions Unit so could not re-examine him. But Richard was sure she would soon be back, questioning him in her well-intentioned way. He'd hoped that writing about his feelings and dreams would help him. He'd heard that other patients had been urged to do this by their doctors. And the dream about the interview room was a recurrent nightmare. But now he wrote more in the hope that in the future someone other than him would read the journal and understand. But he did not want that day to be soon.

He hurried down the stairs and along the tunnel towards the main building. In his rush he almost slipped on a damp patch in the tunnel and had to put his hand on the floor to check his fall. He was frightened by this and stopped in the dank blackness to regain his composure, before reaching the cupboard and his newspaper trolley without any more difficulty. He pulled the trolley out into the corridor and moved off. If his lateness was mentioned, he would apologise. If not, he would stay silent on the matter.

CHAPTER FIFTEEN

"He tried to kill himself. Did you know that?" Ruth was talking to her two colleagues. She had spent an uneventful morning in the Admissions Unit after handing in the results of her typing. There had not been a general meeting, and the deputy superintendent was not there. Ruth had spoken to Mrs Baker at some length, having been unable to do so the previous day. She was surprised at the ease with which the woman spoke to her in a one-to-one situation sitting in the ward. Such conversations had not been a characteristic of her previous work, where the interviews were usually held in rooms that were clinically clean but hostile to personal conversation. The woman had even been sympathetic towards her; indeed she had apologised for the way another patient had treated Ruth, which Ruth had noted in her records as a very positive feature. Ruth had also attended a small-group meeting which one of the nurses was leading. The conversation, which included the topic of strong feelings as had been requested, was desultory at best. Ruth was still unsure about the meetings. Some patients seemed overwhelmed by the prospect of speaking in front of others.

In the afternoon Ruth had persuaded John Sutton first to accept her apology for being angry the previous day and then to walk around two of the wards and introduce her to both patients and staff. Ruth had taken all the records for the patients and scanned each set for the crucial information about background, symptoms, diagnoses and treatments. The superintendent had been right about the questionable nature of some of the admissions. One woman had been admitted by her family because there was a risk of her becoming pregnant, and Ruth could not find any clear diagnosis of a psychiatric disorder. Another woman had become depressed when her parents died and she was left homeless, but again Ruth thought that some different decisions prior to admission might have spared her the fifteen years she had already spent in three different wards being treated for three different disorders. Ruth knew that there was research questioning the accuracy of psychiatric diagnoses. This patient's records would undoubtedly have confirmed the research. John Sutton had explained that Winstanley had simply instructed him as to what to do for each patient and had not allowed him to look back at patients' initial records. He was as surprised as she was by what they were learning. And David Peters was likely to be in much the same position, despite his seniority. Winstanley had continued to treat him as a junior in terms of diagnosis and treatment, so he too had been confined to maintaining treatments and attempting to improve patients' mental health as best he could. The review of all the patients, he could see, might lead to some significant changes in patients' treatments. He was pleased it was going to happen.

Finally Ruth had turned to Richard's records. He, of course, had not been present when Ruth and John Sutton had toured Ward 44. So Ruth had brought his records, along with those of any other patients not on their wards, to look at in the doctors' room. And the first thing she had noticed was Winstanley's early recording of Richard's attempted suicide.

"I did know that," David Peters said. "Winstanley told me when I started, and he said it was the reason Richard was here: he could not be trusted outside the hospital not to make another attempt, and so he was never to be given an exeat to leave the hospital. Does the record say why he wanted to kill himself?"

"No," said Ruth, who was skimming through the documents. "There's less information about him than about any of the patients whose records I've looked at this afternoon. No address, no nearest of kin, no details prior to his admission, a lot of brief notes around every six months after that. There's a record of him being treated – oh, he had ECT, around three years after admission."

"I didn't know that," said David. "Does it say why?"

"No, nothing like an explanation. Just a record of start date, treatment dates and end date."

"I thought that two clinicians had to sign off an instruction for ECT, but that may not have applied ten years ago. Let me see."

Ruth handed him the records. She was thinking about Richard's reaction when she had asked him what lay down the eastern corridor and wing while they had been touring the building. David looked through the previous entries and then the entry about the shock treatment. He looked baffled.

"All I can say is that the date is about a month before the superintendent started here. Perhaps he changed the rules. In all my time here there should be two signatures in the records."

"You'd expect some explanation in the records, wouldn't you?" Ruth asked.

"Yes, I would. This looks almost like a deliberate attempt to minimise the information." David was looking further on in the records. "But there is one thing. All the six-monthly entries seem to have three other initials alongside them. They're initials I don't recognise. It looks like 'SFO', doesn't it?"

Ruth took the records back. The most recent entry was in July. Sure enough, the initials SFO were in the margin, written in Winstanley's handwriting, along with the date, and the written entry simply said, 'No change in conditions'. As she looked back she saw that this was pretty much the same wording for all the entries, and the entries themselves were made mostly in July and December of each year, each time with the mysterious SFO and Winstanley's signature. Only when she traced back to the entry about shock therapy did she find an entry that differed. She was puzzled because even at his most concise Winstanley had at least recorded treatments and changes in the other patients' records. And the necessary details about the patients had always been on the record forms, even if his handwriting was poor.

"Look, do you mind if I try to talk to him tomorrow? I'll be giving out the survey forms on all the wards, and I'd like to do the same with John as I've done today and cover the other wards. But perhaps tomorrow after his trolley rounds I could talk to Richard and see if he can give me any of the missing information, or if he has a record of it himself somewhere."

"No, I don't mind. Did you say you'd managed to get the survey forms done? How on earth did you do that?"

John Sutton looked at Ruth and smiled. Ruth could not be angry with him this time. She turned back to David and said, "Let's just say that I'm finding my way around the hospital, shall we?"

David looked questioningly at her, and then at John who feigned ignorance, and said, "Well, I'm impressed. I've never got any significant typing back in less than a week. You must tell me the secret some time."

"It's just a little know-how," Ruth said, and she put a finger to her lips to warn John not to reveal more. She looked at her watch. "I must go and pick up the forms. I'll see you both tomorrow." And she left the doctors' room to go to the administrative offices, again taking the outdoor route. It was twilight. The October sun had set, but there remained a pink glow in the sky as she came out of the door. The grounds were quiet, astonishingly so given that within the walls of the buildings were over two thousand people. Some golden brown leaves had fallen from the trees around the grounds. Ruth kicked at them with some pleasure, enjoying the soft feel of the leaves against her shoe and the swishing sound as she disturbed them. The meeting she had just had with her colleagues was the most positive one since her arrival in the asylum, and what had seemed a daunting, even impossible, task now appeared a little easier if she could maintain the support of the other two doctors. As she entered the building it felt colder inside than outside where the October sun had warmed the air. Ruth shivered as she mounted the stairs. The admin corridor was quiet, with some staff locking their doors and leaving. It was nearing six o'clock and Ruth guessed that most of the staff finished at half past five, so no-one would come up here to visit the offices at this time.

Inside the administrative office Ruth could hear the noise of machinery. She knocked loudly on the door, fearing that the machinery might prevent her being heard. After a few seconds the noise stopped and then the door opened and Frances Avery looked out at her.

"It is you," she said in a conspiratorial whisper. "I just had to check. I wouldn't like anyone to know that I was doing this running-off. Come in." She led Ruth into a side room where the Gestetner machine was sited. The machine was turned on but the mechanism had obviously been halted when Ruth had knocked on the door. The skin that Ruth had prepared was flattened against the drum, and on one side of the machine a small pile of clean paper waited to be fed in. On the other side a larger pile of printed paper had accumulated. "I'm almost finished," Frances said in her ordinary voice. "No need to whisper now. I'll have these ready in just a few minutes." She turned the machine on and the printing resumed. She lifted the pile of printed paper and looked around the office. Seeing a brown box resting on a shelf, she dropped the papers in and brought them over to Ruth. "That's what the forms look like. I can see that you must have done some typing at school. The layout was very good; our typists couldn't have done it better. But there are one or two points where the correcting fluid has affected the printing, so it's a little too light."

"I could remember how to do layout," Ruth said, "but my fingers couldn't recall how to do the typing. I should have practised beforehand." She looked at the form. As she skimmed down it she could see that some of the printing was faint on the upper half of the form but still legible, and the form seemed to contain all the essential information she would need. "This looks fine for what I've got to do. Thank you for staying behind to do it for me. I managed to surprise my consultant by promising it would be done."

"Well, just don't tell him how you managed it. By the way, I'll keep the skin when I take it off the machine, in case you need some more." Frances turned to the machine, looked at the counter on the side and said, "There. Two hundred and ten copies. That should do it." She turned the machine off, picked up the last copies and dropped them into the box. She then turned back to the machine and started to undo the clip that held the skin on the drum. "How are you finding Black Roding?" The question was light and conversational.

Ruth tried to match Frances's tone. "Oh. It's different to anywhere else I've worked. It's far bigger. I'm still getting used to it."

"It can be a frightening place. Whenever I tell someone around my home that I work here, they look at me as if *I* am mad as well as the patients. People only talk about Black Roding and its patients as a place that terrifies them, and someone coming in to work here can be affected by that."

"It's not the patients' fault they have a mental disorder or illness," Ruth said. "What's unusual is having such a large mental hospital out here on the edge of London, and what's hard to adjust to is that Black Roding seems to have a different set of rules and procedures to those I'm used to. So I have to adjust accordingly, for example, getting this work done. I've never been under such pressure to do the work, and yet I have to get you to bend or break the rules to help me." Ruth realised that Frances's politeness and helpfulness were drawing her in to a more confidential discussion than she would have liked, so she stopped talking. Frances seemed to notice.

"Oh, don't worry. I wouldn't repeat anything you said. But there are some advantages to Black Roding being so large."

"Such as?"

"The facilities we offer patients, the range of psychiatrists here, the additional things that are put on... like this coming Saturday, and the Different Registers."

"I'm sorry," Ruth said, "I don't know what you mean by that. The Different Registers?" Ruth's surprise was all too evident.

"I see you didn't know. The Different Registers are a group who play all the latest pop songs. They perform in the theatre on the second Saturday of the month. Lots of patients go along, and some of the nurses and staff.

They're pretty good, actually. Made some recordings themselves but never broke into the pop charts. They play between eight and ten thirty, with a break in the middle, and people seem to enjoy themselves. They'll be playing this coming Saturday. It's just admission at the door, so you could come along if you aren't working. I'll be going, along with some of the office staff. And some of the nurses will be there. And a lot of patients – and you'll see some of them in different circumstances to usual."

"I don't know, it's not really my kind of thing, you know."

"It's a good way to get to know people, especially if you're new. Why not think about it and see how you feel on the night? But I must go now. If I don't leave soon I'll be late home." She smiled and turned away from Ruth.

"Thanks again," Ruth called at her disappearing back. She lifted the box and walked out of the office, putting the box down to shut the door and deciding that it would be easier, if longer, to stay indoors as she walked back to the West Wing.

CHAPTER SIXTEEN

It seemed to Richard that he had just sat down after his rounds and picked up his book, when Doctor Appleton came and interrupted him. He was tired and felt irritated by her arrival, but he remembered in time to suppress his reaction and tried to look at her blankly. "What?" he muttered.

"I said I'm sorry to interrupt your reading again, Richard, but I need to talk to you for just a few minutes."

Richard motioned to the bed as a place for Ruth to sit. She did so, and opened a pad she had brought with her. She also had a pen in her hand. Richard tried to look at the page of the open book he had been reading, but he could not focus on the words and looked up again.

"Sorry," she again said. "I'll try to be quick and then you can read again. It's just that as a new doctor I've been looking at all the patients' records in the files." Ruth paused to check that Richard was following her. It was, she had already decided, particularly difficult at times to read his facial reactions. "Your records are missing some details that we should really have, so I thought I'd better see if you can remember some things from the past."

It was the last thing Richard wanted to do. He tried to make sure that Ruth could not see his disappointment and fear. "What?" he repeated. "What is it?"

"Can you remember a time before you came to Black Roding? You've been here a long time, but you must have lived and worked somewhere else before here. Can you remember?"

He could indeed, but he did not want to do so. He shook his head.

"Did you work, Richard? Did you go somewhere to work every day?"

Ruth waited. Sometimes a person's memory would refuse to recall certain events or periods of time, and trying to bring them to the fore again could be traumatic. She had tried to find an area of life which might not be so disturbing and had therefore avoided initially asking about Richard's family. But from Richard's first reaction, it was not going to be easy to discover anything. He remained silent. "I know that you have a set of tools, probably very good ones. Did you perhaps work with your hands?"

While Richard seemed impassive, his thoughts were jumping from one idea to another. What should he tell her? She was obviously determined to find out as much as possible. How could he tell her enough to satisfy her, without revealing too much? Should he lie and invent a past? Would she be able to check out what he said and catch him lying? And what did she know already? What would Winstanley have put in his records? He could still remember that first meeting with the consultant. "I understand you want to recover from some bad experiences and feelings," he had said. "So I'm happy that you are coming here to get over things." But how much did Winstanley know? What would he have been told? It was impossible to decide what to tell this doctor when there was so much he did not know himself.

"Can you remember where the tools came from?"

He could. He could remember the small ceremony. Lofty had been speaking. "We didn't think you were up to much when you first arrived. You looked such a young, scrawny runt that hadn't eaten for years. But, boy, you showed us. We were mistaken, and we couldn't have done things so easily and so quickly without you. So we hope that this gift will be a reminder of our thanks. And that you get better soon."

"Friends," Richard mumbled, "good friends." He did not know whether this would help him, but he felt he had to say something.

"Friends," Ruth repeated. She was trying to stay neutral in voice, not to let any keenness on her part put him off. "Friends from where?"

"Work. I was at work."

"Where was that? Was it in a factory?"

A factory, thought Richard, a place where things are made. "Yes, a kind of factory," he said slowly, as if he were remembering. "Making things. We were making things."

"What kind of things? What were you making?"

That he would not answer, and he shuddered slightly. "Just things. Some small things, and some big things, I think."

Ruth noted the shudder and wondered if she had made a mistake and this unknown workplace was after all the cause of his distress. "What about your birthday, can you remember your birthday?"

He could remember this but simply didn't know whether or not to tell her. He nodded his head but made no reply. "When is your birthday?

"Eighth of July. Eighth of July." This was the case.

"And what year? What year were you born in?"

"I think, nineteen twenty-two." This was not the case.

"Are you sure? Are you sure it was that year?"

"I think so."

"And where were you born? Do you know that?"

This was becoming too difficult, Richard thought. If he answered this, she might be able to trace his life through his birth records. He shook his head.

"And can you remember going to school?"

He certainly could: the redbrick grammar school that had been a long bus ride away from his home; the frightening first day; the academic success he had enjoyed; the sports he had not played so well, lacking co-ordination; the scholarship to go to university; the congratulations of the headmaster. Again he shook his head at Ruth and looked up at her to gauge her reactions. But it was hard to judge them because she was not showing any particular response beyond the next question. "Good school, I think. It was good," he said.

"What was its name, Richard? Can you remember what it was called?"

Richard shook his head.

Ruth felt that she had no choice now but to try asking questions about his family. "Did your parents take you there? Did you go with them?" she asked.

Again Richard shook his head. This was true, they had never accompanied him. Not even on his first day. But then, he wouldn't have wanted them to. School and home did not mix in his mind: they were separate lives, not just separate places.

"Can you remember your mother, Richard, even if she didn't take you there?"

Richard nodded. "Nice mother, kind to me. Looked after me."

"What was her name? Can you remember that?"

Richard paused. Was it better to answer or not? He could not decide at first but decided eventually that he should. "Victoria. Vicky. Short for Victoria," he said, hoping that his tone of voice would indicate uncertainty.

"And your father. What about his name?"

"Edward. Teddy."

"And where did they live?"

Richard shook his head. "No. Don't know."

Finally, Ruth thought she should ask about his illness. "Before you came here, you were ill. Can you remember that time?"

He could, all too well. Tying that noose and kicking the chair away. Lying on the floor, crying. The kick in the ribs as he lay there. "Very ill, in my head. It was bad," was all he could think of to say.

Ruth tried her last gambit. "Richard, do the letters S, F and O mean anything to you? S, F, O?"

Richard looked up sharply. How had she got those initials? "No," he said loudly. "No. Please leave me alone."

"All right. I will now. I'm sorry to have disturbed you. You can carry on reading now." She stood up and left him. But he could not read now. Not when those letters had been read out to him.

Ruth went to the doctors' room. John Sutton was there. He looked up as Ruth entered. "Well, any luck there? I saw you talking to Richard," he said.

"No. I didn't find out much. But do you believe in intuition?"

John looked up. "Intuition? Why?"

"Because my intuition says that he can remember more than he's prepared to tell. And he knows what those mysterious letters mean, S, F, O, but he won't tell me. But why he wanted to kill himself, and why he was admitted here, I can't guess."

Back in the ward, Richard was emptying the contents of the boxes in his tallboy onto his bed. Somewhere, he knew, he had a card with the telephone number. S, F, O. It was time to take some action. Winstanley – writing those letters in his records – had betrayed him, so it was time now.

CHAPTER SEVENTEEN

The card which contained the telephone number Richard needed was now in his pocket. He had found it the previous night after searching the box in which he kept documents he had been given during his hospital stay. All previous documents – his passport, birth certificate, driving licence, bank statements – had been taken from him before he even reached Black Roding. "You are not to reveal anything about your past," he had been told, "so you don't need any of these documents. They might give you away." But he had kept new documents such as library cards, ward exeats, the formal notification of his shock therapy treatment. He had stopped in his search when he found that one. He knew he must have reacted when Doctor Appleton asked him about the East Wing. And he assumed that his treatment was recorded in the files through which she was searching.

Winstanley had persuaded him that the shock treatment was necessary. He had told him that he was deeply depressed and that it was a routine treatment for depressions such as his. Many other patients had experienced it without damage. And it would prove to everyone that Richard was genuinely a mental health patient, needing the highest level of treatment. Richard had accepted it, but as the date of his first treatment approached he had grown more troubled about it. Other patients talked about the nastiness of the experience, the unsympathetic approach of the orderlies and the confusion and dazed feelings experienced in the aftermath.

The day of the treatment had been an ordeal. Denied any breakfast and forced to attend early for the clinic, Richard had become more and more distressed. He had waited, lying down on a trolley, while other patients were wheeled into the therapy room, and he had heard the click as each trolley was manoeuvred into position. The noise of the machine could be heard during the short periods of treatment for each patient, a frightening electrical whirring that was like no other machine he had ever heard or witnessed. He had started to shake before the treatment, and the orderlies had strapped him down hard in the trolley. Then he too had been wheeled in and heard the click as his trolley was connected to the machine. An electrode had been attached to each temple and a black rubber mouthpiece fitted between his teeth. The taste of the rubber was nauseating, and the smell of rubber – even now, after ten years – still made him gag. Finally, after the loud instruction to keep still, Richard thought he had felt the very first moment of the shocks, before the convulsions took over and he was unconscious of them. He woke up some minutes later and felt very weak, and it took him the rest of the day to recover. And his treatments had continued for three months, months he could hardly remember other than the treatment itself. Richard wondered if it had really been necessary, or whether Winstanley was simply testing his determination, or punishing him on another's instructions.

He had carried the card with him during the morning. All through his round he had wondered whether making this call was the right action. He did not want to stir things up, which he knew his telephone call would do. He feared the likely reaction. But the doctors were going to release some patients from the hospital. And who better to release than a trustee such as himself, who worked regularly around the hospital, was trusted with money and was left to his own devices so much? And if he were released? He had been allowed to enter the asylum on the strict condition that he was not to return to ordinary life. He knew what awaited him on release.

He had planned what to do. He would call the telephone number and try to speak directly to him. He hated conversations with him, not being able to forget what had happened in the interview room. He had put up with the six-monthly three-way conversations involving Winstanley, and the pompous euphemisms for what he, Richard, had done and for what was happening to him here. "Indiscretions" he had called Richard's offences, and "voluntary treatment" was used to describe his incarceration.

As his morning round came to an end, he gave up the inner debate. He knew the call had to be made. But he still put off doing so until he had a drink in the canteen and a slice of bread. When he stood up he felt dizzy and thought for a moment that he might be about to have another panic attack. He took several deep breaths and felt better, so he left the canteen and walked down the corridor to the point near the chapel where the two public telephones were. They were not inside the red boxes that one saw on the streets outside the asylum. Instead, the telephones and the money boxes used for the calls were attached to brown boards on the wall, and there was nothing to stop a patient being overheard when making a call. Richard looked up and down the corridor. There was no-one he recognised as being attached to his ward, no-one who might drop into a subsequent conversation that they had seen Richard in the unusual act of making a telephone call.

Richard took the card bearing the telephone number out of his pocket. It was faded but otherwise unblemished, having lain in Richard's box for a long time. The telephone number was in a London district, and Richard expected his call to be answered by a private secretary. He took the necessary coins out of his pocket, pushed them into the coin slot and dialled the numbers. He heard the telephone ringing at the other end, three, four times, and then a female voice answered. Richard pushed Button A and heard the coins slide down inside the machine.

"Good afternoon. Sir Francis Oates' private office. What can I do for you?" Richard heard the crisp pronunciation of the personal secretary.

"Speak to Sir Francis." Richard kept his words as brief as possible in case anyone was nearby and listening.

"I am sorry," the crisp voice said, "Sir Francis is on leave. He'll be back on Monday. Can I take a message?"

"Yes." Richard stopped himself, turned around and checked both sides of the corridor again. "Tell him… Richard Simms called… Winstanley has died."

"I see. Is that all the message?" The woman spoke as if she was called every day with cryptic messages.

"Yes. He'll understand it." Richard put the telephone down clumsily. He breathed deeply to steady himself and set off towards the Friends of Black Roding for his afternoon round.

CHAPTER EIGHTEEN

In the only large room available to them, Ruth, David and John were holding a meeting of the senior nurses from the five wards. There were twelve or so nurses there, varying in age from thirty to over sixty. The room was in Ruth's view completely inappropriate for such a meeting. It was next to the basement ward and without any natural light. It was sometimes used for the patients of the basement ward to sit in, and had several old armchairs, each of them leaking stuffing. The dirty brown paint, which reminded Ruth of the superintendent's pet hate, was peeling in places on the walls, and there was no shade on the bare electric bulb that illuminated the room.

"I apologise that we have to use this room. It's really not right for such a meeting, but it's the only confidential place we have that's big enough, and we will have to use it from next week for more regular meetings." David was obviously embarrassed by the surroundings. "I wanted to give you all details of some of the changes the superintendent wants us to make, now that the doctors' team has been increased. I know you've heard something about these as we've been talking to you and your colleagues on the wards, but this seemed the best way to make sure everyone has the same, correct information. Is that okay?" Ruth looked at the nurses. They were displaying a number of reactions to David's words. Some had their arms folded and were clearly tense and worried about the changes to be announced. Others were more relaxed, and one was even smiling. That was Sister O'Sullivan, Margaret O'Sullivan as Ruth now knew. She was nodding in response to David's last question. Ruth remembered that she had been especially praised by the superintendent.

"First," David was speaking again, "we are going to start the ward general meetings which the rest of the hospital has been holding for some years. Sir Reginald did not really like this policy, and he never agreed to it, but we think it has a lot to offer the patients on our wards, so we will be starting them from next week."

"Good!" Margaret O'Sullivan could not contain her pleasure on hearing the news. "It's about time some of the patients had the chance to speak for themselves." She said this more to her colleagues than to the doctors, because one or two had clearly dissented from her initial exclamation.

"Why?" Ruth recognised the challenger as the nurse in charge of Ward 43. She herself had not visited the ward as much as she had done on Ward 44. David had said that he would supervise the ward because of the changes that were planned for it, so she had only visited during evening sessions and when she and John had been looking at patient records. "Why?" again the sharp voice queried. "Aren't things perfectly all right as they are? Why do we have to follow the superintendent's fads? Sir Reginald's regime was fine."

"I think the superintendent is expecting to see more discharges and more patients being moved to other places than we've managed in recent years. But Doctor Appleton will talk about that in a while. The point is, we have to try to make the wards more like therapeutic communities and less like conventional hospital wards. We're expected to introduce therapeutic ideas into the ward general meetings, but also to allow the patients to speak about whatever they want to raise and to look for ways to solve their own and others' problems in a therapeutic way. I'm sure everyone is in agreement with that."

Ruth thought that David had handled the objection fairly well. The nurse couldn't easily object to the possibility of more therapy, since that was how David had put the idea, although she was conscious of her own doubts about the meetings. However, she was unsure about being introduced as the doctor responsible for discharging patients. That might prove even harder to manage than ward general meetings.

"So, from next Monday we'll be holding ward general meetings in each of the wards. We'll be holding one a week in each ward for the first two weeks, and then trying to move to two meetings a week. But next week we'll start with Ward 43 on Monday, 44 on Tuesday, 45 on Wednesday, 46 on Thursday, and 47 on Friday. All the doctors will attend these meetings, and I'll chair the first meetings. After that, we'll divide that responsibility among ourselves. As you know, senior nurses are asked to play a role in leading the discussion and responding to what patients are saying. And all staff are free to contribute." Ruth again looked at the nurses. If anything, their non-verbal and verbal communication had become more extreme. Margaret O'Sullivan was nodding her agreement vigorously, but some others were looking angrily at one another, puffing out their cheeks and talking in low mutters to one another.

David continued, after allowing a moment for the nurses' reactions to die down. "After each ward general meeting the staff will have a meeting in this room. I've asked admin to provide an urn and cups and so on from Monday, and I hope we can get the room redecorated and better furnished in time. At the staff meeting we will review the ward general meeting, following the order in which different things have been raised and discussed during the meeting. You will need to leave skeleton staffing in the ward, and we may need to use nurses from other wards if you are short of staff on any particular day. Once again, each member of staff may contribute to the meeting. It is not just for doctors or senior nurses to contribute."

Again, David paused for reactions. Another nurse, whom Ruth recognised as working in the basement ward, asked sharply, "What if they don't want to? What then?" and she turned to her immediate colleague, who nodded her agreement.

"I hope that in time they will. The meetings will be very new to some of the staff, but others, including some of you, have worked on wards that have been holding these meetings before you came here. So it's not new for everybody, and I would ask that those with experience of them encourage the others, and of course encourage the patients. Please don't let any anxiety of yours cross over to the patients. It will worry them if we seem worried."

Ruth agreed with this. She too had misgivings about the meetings, but her first week on the ward had shown her that things had not been done properly for some years. So some sort of shake-up was needed. Ruth herself might have wanted the nurses to undertake their work more efficiently, to free her to concentrate more on diagnosis and treatment therapy, as she had been accustomed to previously, but that had not been what the superintendent had demanded. David was now responsible as consultant, and she had to back him up if these changes were to be put into place. She was nodding her own agreement, therefore, but not as vigorously as Margaret O'Sullivan.

"Finally, on the issue of meetings, you will know that in most wards the programme of meetings includes small-group meetings led by nurses. We will introduce these but not immediately. We want to hold some meetings with the nursing staff on each ward before we make decisions about small-group meetings. On some wards they might start in around four weeks' time, but for the moment you need to concentrate just on the general meetings and the staff meetings. Could I ask you to inform staff and patients about the meetings, and to ask patients to assemble for the meetings at nine o'clock? They should not be going off to the workshops, to the shop or offices, or for treatments during the hour between nine and ten on each ward's day. Now Doctor Appleton will talk about the review she is conducting and the survey forms she's given out."

Ruth did not want to say anything wrongly in this brief talk. She tried to pitch her voice in the best way, loud but not too loud, clear and calm. "Thank you, Doctor Peters, I'll try to be brief. The second thing the superintendent has asked us to do is to hold a review of all the patients, and he asked me – perhaps because I'm a newcomer – to take the lead on this. What's more, the superintendent said that we should bring him the first results very quickly. As a newcomer, I couldn't undertake the reviews that are required without finding out more about the patients. So I devised a survey form and I've taken copies of that form to each of the wards. Where possible, I've spoken to you about the forms, but since I have been in the Admissions Unit every morning some of you were not in your wards when I came round."

"No, I wasn't." Ruth was interrupted by the nurse from Ward 43. "And I wasn't happy that you left the forms with my junior. It should have been me they were given to."

Ruth was unsure how to respond, so she hesitated. Fortunately for her, Margaret O'Sullivan was the first to intervene. "How can it matter who is given the form first? We have to take responsibility for them, and the doctors are only trying to do what's best for the patients and what the superintendent has told them to do. Let's just get on with it and not get all fussy about how it reached us." There was a murmur of agreement among most of the others.

The nurse who had objected was left fuming, but Ruth was grateful that her first week at Black Roding came to an end without any more conflict.

CHAPTER NINETEEN

Saturday morning had been frustrating for Ruth. She had decided to use her day off to go into a nearby suburb where, she had been told, there was a removals firm which could bring some of her possessions from Buckinghamshire. Never mind that she had still not managed to talk to the administrators about her accommodation, she would need to bring more clothes, books and some other possessions to Black Roding at some point. So it seemed sensible to make contact with the removals firm, and at least it would mean she left the hospital for a while. But breakfast had been served slowly, with the waiter telling that the kitchen staff had all been delayed by the fog that had returned. Ruth had walked down the driveway once more in that fog, again keeping to the side of the road. The fog was cold and damp, but Ruth felt that it would lift as the sun's rays penetrated, as it had done in preceding days, and there was the prospect of a fine day later.

The porters had been at their most curmudgeonly when she had asked for the gate to be opened. "Could you wait until there's a vehicle, please?"

one had asked. "Then we won't have to open them twice." But after ten minutes of silence on the driveway, they had to relent, and one of them led Ruth out to the gate. "Bloody nuisance," Ruth thought she heard him mutter as she left, but she decided it wasn't worth responding.

She retraced the steps she had taken in the fog just a few days ago. The fog was indeed lifting and she could see the suburban driveways and front gardens that had been invisible on Monday. The houses were still hard to make out, but no doubt they would be as neat and ordered as the gardens. The work and nature of Black Roding Hospital seemed incongruous alongside these respectable dwellings, just as many of the hospital's inmates would never be able to live in the expensive houses. The Underground station was quiet when Ruth reached it, but the ticket-seller quickly supplied a return ticket and advised her to hurry to the platform since the train was due. But Ruth was too late, and even as she arrived on the platform the doors of the train were slamming shut. Ruth pulled her coat around her against the cold, considered sitting on the bench on the platform but found it was still wet with the heavy dew that had descended with the fog, and stood with her back against the railings that bordered the platform. The next train took fifteen minutes to arrive, by which time Ruth was wondering if she should have stayed at the hospital, but she knew that with no-one to talk to, and no work to be done, she would have felt her loneliness more keenly and more gloomily.

The train was at least warm, and Ruth sat directly above a heater to revive herself. And it delivered her to the suburb, just three stops away, where the shops, and the removals firm, were located. She had a note of the number of the shop she wanted, but it took her a few minutes to find a number on any of the shops immediately next to the station. Then she looked in the windows as she made her way towards the address. The street was not yet crowded, but she sensed that the series of clothes shops, bakers, butchers, greengrocers, and the department store that dominated one part of the road, were likely to attract a larger number as the morning drew on.

The removals firm was situated near the end of the High Street, and its premises consisted of a small front office behind which Ruth thought there were probably storage spaces. She entered and stood by the counter, but there was no-one behind it. The boards on the floor were bare and the wood was rough, while the counter looked as if it had been there when Victoria was on the throne. Ruth tried to peer around the doorway that led into the rear of the premises but she could not stretch forward sufficiently. "Hello," she called out, "hello, is anyone in?" *Too timid*, she thought, *no-one will hear that*. So she shouted the same words, craning forwards to try to maximise the volume of her shout.

"All right, all right," a young voice called back. "Keep yer hair on!" The clerk shuffled forward, a small, spotty youth with hair heavily greased and combed rigidly across his head. "I ain't deaf. No need to shout like that."

"But you didn't hear me when I just called," Ruth protested.

"How do you know? I was right at the back of the building. I wasn't expecting anyone to start shouting."

Ruth waited for the clerk's anger to subside and then asked if she could talk about the removal she needed. He nodded his agreement, and she began, "I need to ask you about a small removal. It isn't a full household or anything like that, but a couple of rooms of furniture and my clothes. I've just moved down here from Buckinghamshire to start work, and I think I'll need to move my stuff in a couple of weeks' time."

"Just a van, then," the clerk replied, "unless any of the furniture is very large. A big wardrobe or something like that."

"No, it's just a settee, a small table, four chairs and a bed. And some clothes."

"How big's the bed? Is it a double?" He seemed to sneer as he asked this, and Ruth felt angry. Why did even such straightforward tasks as this lead to her being insulted or humiliated?

"It's just a bed frame, with a single mattress." The look of scorn was still on his face. "It should all fit in a van, I think, unless it's a very small van."

"Where are we going to move it, then?"

"Oh, from a place called The Victoria Centre to Black Roding Hospital, or somewhere near the hospital. I don't know yet where they are going to put me."

"Why, what are you, one of the loonies? Who's putting you where?" he laughed. It was as if the mention of Black Roding gave the clerk licence to insult her, she thought.

"I'm one of the doctors, and they're patients, not… not… what you called them. And if you continue to insult me, I'll come in next week and complain to the manager here." She tried to stare him down, and his eyes did flinch a little. "Now, could we just get on with how the removal can be done?"

He seemed for a moment to be calculating the risk of insulting her again. Then he said, "If we get the two addresses, we'll send you an estimate next week. Then you need to telephone us, or come in, and confirm when you want the move to take place. We should be able to do it in a day. Here," he took a form from beneath the counter and placed it and a pen on the counter, "write the addresses here and your name there, and anything else you need to add, like a telephone number, and the manager'll write to you. I'll write down the stuff to be moved, but until we see it it's only an estimate. Will that do?"

Ruth refused to rise again to his surly tone, so she wrote the two addresses down and the telephone number of the hospital and which wards to ask for if they called her. She handed the form back to the clerk and turned and left the shop without any further conversation. She did not wish to lose her dignity in an argument with the clerk. His view of Black Roding was, after all, the common one among people who had never had any contact with a mental hospital, and she had already heard it in the hospital itself.

Ruth visited the department store and bought some underwear, and tights, which she preferred to stockings. If she did not get her clothes and went another week without discovering how to launder her clothes, there was a danger she would run out of both. It also reminded her that even if she could not get better accommodation from the hospital, she would still need to visit her lodgings to bring more clothes. The suitcase she had carried with her on the first day did not contain enough warm clothes to cope with the temperature of the hospital. And that reflection made her wonder again if she had been right to acquiesce in the transfer to Black

Roding and whether she was in the right profession at all. Having made her purchases, which she stuffed into the large black handbag she had brought with her, she decided to try to lift her spirits and to find lunch somewhere along the High Street.

The shops were becoming busier as more families arrived to visit the department store and the electrical shops, as well as the butchers and bakers. This last was giving out the warm smells of baking dough and glazed buns. Further down the street Ruth could see a public house, and she wandered towards it to see if it had a restaurant. But through the open doors was the loud noise of men talking and laughing, and the sickly sweet smell of beer told her even before she looked in that it would not be a good place for her to enter – too little chance of good food and too many prospects of being insulted. She looked past the public house and across the street and saw the familiar windows and sign of a Lyons Corner House. Not the best of food, she thought, but at least a meal that had not passed through the hospital kitchens and an environment in which she would not be stared at and commented on.

Ruth crossed the road and entered the restaurant. The brown trays stacked at the head of the server, the metallic counters that ran down the side of the extended room and the polished brown furniture were immediately familiar. Ruth's mother had regarded a visit to a Corner House a rare treat, perhaps no more than four or five times a year, but to be made particularly special by the purchase of delicacies to eat and drink that were never purchased elsewhere. And just as on those visits with her mother, the clientele here was almost exclusively women and children, in family groups and pairs of friends, or elderly mothers with their daughters. The conversation was more subdued than that of the public house and the laughter less raucous. Occasionally a child would call out, but even in the larger groups of children the general atmosphere of the Corner House seemed to impose its own rules of seated conversation and self-control.

Ruth picked up a tray, walked down the line to the hot food section and scanned the menu and the trays of food. She quickly rejected the liver and bacon, which seemed too similar to the regular diet at Black Roding, but the roast dinner offered a welcome alternative to the food she had been eating. She collected the plate and asked for some tea at the drinks counter, before paying at the till that guarded the end of the counters. Looking around she saw that there was a seat at a small table in a corner of the room, and she walked quickly to it for fear that someone else might take it first. She would feel more comfortable at the edge of the room, able to look around her.

She ate the food slowly, enjoying the meat and the hot gravy, and looked around at the other customers. When she had been with her mother, she had often looked around for someone she knew and taken a shared table. Often, Ruth had realised later, the other woman and family would be one like hers, widowed and fatherless, the loss caused usually by the war. Ruth's mother must have felt more able to converse with another such woman on equal terms; and even though Ruth could not remember a single word of the conversations, they must have been about the difficulties of life without a man, the paucity of a widow's pension, and bringing up children without a father. Her mother had done a good job, it must have been very hard, and Ruth regretted that she could not thank her for the self-sacrifice it had required. She had been happy, but now the solitary nature of her life outside the hospital ward had pushed aside that happiness.

Ruth picked up a newspaper that someone had left on the chair next to her. She browsed through it as she drank her tea. As a teenager her schoolteachers had encouraged her to read the newspapers every day, but the events of the world outside her immediate life did not interest her as much as they had done when she was younger, and she rarely read a newspaper now. The French had carried out an underground nuclear test, the Pope was visiting the United Nations and The Beatles had a new record out. Ruth read the stories but was not engaged by any of them. The 'pop' music phenomenon of the past three years had seemed to her to be of greater interest to those younger than her, whom the journalists had started calling 'teenagers'. Once she had finished her tea, she decided she would leave and make her way back to the hospital.

Outside the weather had improved greatly. The sun had driven any mist away, and the sky was blue. Ruth could feel the warmth on her skin, and she decided instantly that she would take the train only part of the way back. Lopping Tree Forest, an ancient woodland protected by long-enshrined statutes, lay between her and the hospital, and she thought it would be pleasant to walk in this sunshine and enjoy the autumn colour and fresh air. She hurried back to the station and took the shorter journey to the edge of the forest, and when she left the station she was surprised at how quickly the suburban housing stopped and the tangled bushes and branches of the woodland started at the roadside. A path veered away from the road and was clearly a much-used route for walkers, so she followed it. There were others strolling along the path, some walking dogs, or couples sharing a Saturday afternoon.

The way led through a sequence of more open ground, where the trees had been cleared, and thickets where the trunks of the trees were close to the path and the branches hung overhead, dark and slightly threatening. But even in the darkest parts, shafts of sunlight penetrated the gloom, and she could see dust motes dancing in the spotlights. Ruth unbuttoned her coat as the walk warmed her up, and she looked around at the trees. The leaves had mostly not browned and fallen yet; rather, they were just turning golden at the edge, so that the yellows and greens shimmered a little when they caught the sun. Several times Ruth stopped to enjoy the radiant warmth when a shaft of sunlight fell on the path, and a fallen trunk gave her the opportunity to sit and enjoy the pleasant feeling the sun gave her.

She walked on further, sensing that the direction of the sun, behind her and casting her shadow in front of her, meant that she was walking in the right direction. There were fewer walkers here, and she guessed she must have followed the path for a mile or so. Earlier on the path she could still hear the sound of cars on the road, but now she had not heard any vehicles for fifteen minutes or more. Provided her sense of direction was correct, she should carry on, and the path would come back to the road. She felt exhilarated by the pleasure of the walk. There were deer in the forest, she knew, but she did not expect to see any. They were shy creatures – perhaps rather like her, she recognised – and would remove themselves from any contact with walkers.

Some twenty minutes later Ruth felt the first uncertainty about her direction. The sun seemed to be brushing her left cheek as she walked, which meant she was walking in a more northerly direction than she required, and as it sank lower there was less warmth. She did not want to have to retrace all her steps, perhaps two miles or so, when she thought she really should have been coming near to the hospital. But she did not want to go forward much further if eventually she was going to be obliged to turn back. She tried to peer through the trees to her right, but she could not see any path or way which might lead in the direction she wanted. She resolved, therefore, to continue on the path for ten minutes more and to take any path that led off to the right, but then to turn back if there was no sign of a return towards a road and the hospital.

If anything, the path seemed to grow a little darker as she progressed. The trees around her were thickly bunched, and the branches heavily intertwined, so that the canopy of leaves was thick, and there were fewer shafts of penetrating sunlight. The whole area seemed more damp and cold, and sure enough a small pond next appeared on her left, its waters dark and still. The path hugged the banks of the pond and was for a little while more slippery and muddy, and she had to plot a way through the stickiest sections. As she came to the end of the pond, however, she could see that the path was wider, as if it were used more frequently, and some sand had been laid down to dry the mud.

She walked on and found a metal barrier across the path, a low bar that was pinned to two posts within the trees, and clambered over it. And within a few yards the path widened out into a dirty, half-gravelled car park. But there were no cars. The area was filled by motorbikes, leaning on stands and unattended. Beyond them was a refreshment stall and some twenty-five or so customers in threes and fours talking, or leaning on the long counter of the stall. Ruth recognised them by their leather jackets and jeans – they were Rockers, the members of one youth group who had clashed with another group of young people – Mods – at various seaside resorts just a year previously. And the motorbikes parked nearby were their favoured mode of transport. The car park was at the end of a tarmac road, but the road seemed to her not to run in the direction she wanted but rather to continue the northerly route the path had followed.

Ruth hesitated. The stories in the press about Rockers had not been complimentary, and here she was, a young woman in an isolated area, unsure of her directions. The kind weather and the pleasant walk had masked any potential danger, but she was reluctant to turn around and walk back. Surely the stallholder would give her directions, even if she faced some nasty jokes from the motorcyclists. She decided to approach the stall and the groups of men and ask the first one who caught her eye for directions to the hospital, or otherwise ask the stallholder.

The first group were involved in a discussion of one of the motorbikes, and the owner – she assumed – was showing the others a part of the mechanism beneath the saddle, so they ignored her completely. A whistle came from the second group once she had passed them, but it was a small leather-clad biker who turned at the sound of the whistle, eyed her up and down and then spoke.

"Watch out, Fred," he called to the stallholder. "Better get the china cups out. Miss la-di-dah wants a cup of tea." He adopted a false accent for the last phrase, as if mimicking her. But Ruth smiled at the joke and stopped in front of the youth.

"Perhaps you could help me instead of making jokes about me?" she challenged him.

"Well, that depends what help you want. I'd take you for a spin on the bike if you want." This to the three men he had been talking to before seeing her. They laughed at the crude gesture he made with his fist to accompany his words.

"No," she said, trying not to get flustered in front of the group, "no, I wondered if you could tell me the way to Black Roding. I seem to have lost my way, thinking that the path would come back to the road."

"Black Roding," he repeated, "Black Roding – that's for nutters, isn't it? What do you want there?"

"I work there," she protested, "but I only just started there. So I got lost by taking the path through the forest."

"You must be nuts then, working there, and walking through the forest when you don't know the way home." While the others laughed at her again, one of the group came up to the joker and spoke quietly to him. Ruth could not make out what he said.

"Might be your lucky day, lady, cos my mate here just reminded me that one of us works there. Hey, Michael," he called across to another group, "one of your workmates here can't find her way back to the loony bin."

Michael, it seemed, was among a group of older men. He looked to be about thirty years old, and his brown hair was combed back in the same quiff style as the younger men. He was wearing a heavy blue denim jacket, and his jeans showed stains of oil and grease, as if he had been working on his motorcycle. He had not shaven, and the stubble was visible but short, as if it were just the overnight growth he had not removed. He looked at the younger man who had called him, and then at Ruth, before coming across to them.

"What are you shouting about, Tich?" he asked, though he was still looking at Ruth.

"It's this lady here, says she works at Black Roding but can't find her way back there. Must be as mad as you!" He ducked away as he said this, as if fearing a riposte.

The man looked again at Ruth. "What's he on about?" he asked her.

"I'm sorry, I'm causing a nuisance. I was walking back to Black Roding, but I took a detour through the forest thinking the path would come back to the road. But it didn't, and I don't want to walk all the way back. So I just asked him for directions."

"And he called me because I work there."

Ruth could not stop herself asking, "As an engineer? Or what?"

"No," he smiled, looking down at the oil stains on his jeans, "no, as a nurse. They all laugh at me about it." He swept an arm around to point at the other bikers. "In the Secure Block." Ruth gasped at her own mistake. She understood. The Secure Block would need physically strong and self-confident nurses at times, and many nurses would not be able to meet the demands of working there. A strong young man would be a great asset, if he understood the other requirements of being a nurse.

"And you?" he asked. "Are you a nurse as well?"

Now it was her turn to smile at the assumption, and his turn to be surprised. "No… no…" she stuttered, "I'm one of the doctors. I was just transferred here. I work for Firm 9."

"There aren't many female doctors," he said, "so you can understand my mistake. I'm sorry. None of the doctors in the Secure Block are…" His voice trailed away as he spoke.

"That's all right. No-one ever expects…" She too found herself leaving her thoughts and words incomplete. "Look, is there a way to walk to the hospital from here? If not, I do need to be walking back."

"Yeah, sure there is. I'd offer to take you, but I don't think you're best dressed for going on the bike. So, follow the tarmac down to where it meets an ordinary road, turn right and follow that for about half a mile, and then take the third exit at the roundabout you come to. The hospital's a few hundred yards down that road."

"Thanks. Perhaps we'll bump into each other there."

"Sure, yes, in the corridor or somewhere." He turned to go back to his friends. Next time, she thought, she wouldn't listen to her inner fears and prejudices. That encounter had not been anywhere near as bad as she had anticipated.

She followed the biker's instructions and came to a road that ran through the forest. There was no pavement for pedestrians, but a well-worn path between the kerb and the first small trees was sufficient to avoid the cars which passed by at some speed. And within half a mile, as promised, the road came to a roundabout from which several roads led in different directions. Ruth crossed and took the road for Black Roding. She came to the gate just as the sun was reaching the tops of the trees and slipped through the gates as the porters were preparing to shut them for the night.

The first wispy silhouettes of mist were rising on the open spaces to her left and right as she walked along the now-familiar grassy side of the tarmac road. Ruth thought they were like the spirits of the many patients who had lived and died in the hospital, drawing in around their former home as night fell and separated the hospital from the world outside. The fog prevented both those inside and those outside the building from seeing clearly, just as the reputation of the hospital and its patients prevented outsiders from getting a clear view of these needy people. The clerk in the removals firm, and Tich and his biker friends at the refreshments stall in the forest, had little or no idea of the reality of the patients' lives. But Michael, one of the bikers, was a nurse in the hospital, and yet his friends revealed the same prejudices as the rest of the world. Ruth felt heartened by the afternoon walk in the forest, but the heavy wooden door and dark reception hall made her heart misgive just a little as she entered the building and headed for her room.

CHAPTER TWENTY

There was always some work to do before a dance. Tables and chairs had to be set out with the maximum possible number of seats clustered around the tables between the bar and the dance floor, which was an open space in front of the stage. And this had to be done while the group's musicians were bringing their equipment in, setting up the speakers and amplifiers, attaching the microphones and instruments and warming up. The glasses were all to be polished with the clean towels provided by the kitchen, and the bottles of beer removed from their crates and stacked up on the shelves.

Richard was happy to do these tasks, but the doctor supervising the dance this evening was Oliver Smythe, a bad-tempered registrar who criticised whatever Richard did as not meeting his requirements. "Why have you squashed all the tables and chairs together like that? Spread them out!" had been his first command when he appeared halfway through the preparations. Richard knew that the group playing at the dance, the Different Registers, was popular, and he expected a large crowd of patients, staff and even some outsiders who followed the band. So he knew that the dance floor needed to be as large as possible or people would complain. Chairs and tables would then have to be moved while the dance was underway. But the doctor's instructions had to be followed, and as a result Richard was still stacking bottles when the first guests arrived, paying their entrance fee to the two nurses who always kept the door for such events and asking him for their drinks. Richard knew that not stacking the bottles would delay him later, but it was too late to complete the task. *Blast the man*, he thought, *why does he need to be so arrogant?* It was not the first time he'd had that thought.

Ruth had gone to her room after returning to the hospital and found a note pinned to the door. 'Dear Doctor Appleton,' it had said, 'A group of staff are attending the dance tonight in the theatre. Would you like to join us? It should be a good evening. Frances Avery.' She would not normally have chosen to go to a dance. Since Peter had left her she had never again attended a dance. As a single woman it would be embarrassing and awkward to purchase drinks and sit on one's own, but if there was a group of staff with whom she could sit it would not be so difficult. Perhaps she would go. It would be good to be introduced to some other people, especially in a different context. She was a little intrigued to see how such a dance operated, particularly with the sale of alcohol. The clothes she had brought in her suitcase were hardly the most suitable, but there was a skirt and top that would do. So yes, she would go to the dance.

The theatre had become busy even before the group started playing. Richard had been serving drinks for half an hour without stopping, and he saw that there were now some people sitting at every table, although some chairs were still empty. Soon he would need to start collecting glasses and washing some of them, if he was not to run out later in the evening, but he could not leave the bar unattended when new guests were still arriving. He had tried to identify Doctor Smythe among the guests, to ask him to man the bar while he collected glasses and finished stocking up the bottles, but he could not see him. Perhaps he was looking a little flustered, because one of the people at the bar, a woman whom Richard recognised as a member of staff who regularly attended the dances, said, "Do you need a hand for a moment? You seem to have a bit of a rush on."

Richard muttered some thanks and said haltingly, "Glasses… collect the glasses."

"All right, I'll collect some," she said, and went with the tray Richard gave her. As Ruth came into the theatre, looking around a little nervously, Frances almost bumped into her.

"Oh, great, you came. Welcome to the dance," she said with a smile. "You can help me collect some glasses."

"Are you running the bar?" Ruth asked. "I thought you'd be…" she waved at the seated guests all around her.

"Yes, I am, but I'm just helping the barman. Here, you hold the tray and I'll grab some more glasses." Ruth grabbed hold of the tray and immediately had to balance it as the glasses started to slide towards one edge. Frances picked up three more empty glasses from the nearest table, and said, "There, take those back to the bar and then find me at that table over there." She pointed at one of the tables near the side wall of the theatre.

Ruth smiled at being caught with this task, but she edged her way successfully to the bar. "Excuse me, please," she almost implored those standing at the bar, and she was relieved to put the tray down on the bar. "There we are," she said to no-one in particular. The barman looked up at her, and Ruth saw that it was Richard, her patient, who was staring at her in surprise. And the man beside her turned around and also looked at her as if taken aback. It was Michael, the biker who only a few hours earlier had given her directions. Ruth looked from one to the other and smiled at their double astonishment. "Sorry, Richard, I didn't mean to surprise you. I was asked to bring the tray back. I didn't know you were running the bar tonight. Are you doing it on your own? Are you busy?" She knew she was firing too many questions at him, but somehow being again under the scrutiny of the motorcyclist had made her garrulous. She stopped herself asking anything more. He, uncertain what to do, looked at her a few moments longer, before he took the tray and turned away to the back of the bar area, where the sink was.

"Good evening… Doctor," Michael spoke mischievously, aping a formality that was unnecessary and pausing before naming her title.

"Good evening… Nurse," Ruth replied, imitating his pause. "I hadn't expected to meet you here."

"I always come to this group, the Different Registers. They're good, and their own songs are good, not just the versions of others' songs that they sing. But I could also say that I hadn't expected to meet you here?" This last, from the upward tone of the ending, was a question.

"One of the office staff, Frances, asked me to come. She left a note on my door."

"Frances, the office manager?"

"Yes, I met her last week when I needed some help."

"I'm at her table. In fact, I'm buying drinks for everyone. What do you want?"

Ruth had not thought about what she would drink. She had criticised the sale of alcohol in the hospital. "Just an orange, I think," she said hastily.

"Really? It's Saturday night. Time to relax."

"No, an orange will be fine."

Michael shrugged and turned towards Richard, who had deposited the empty glasses and was now serving customers again. He took Michael's order and started to serve up the drinks. Michael turned again to Ruth. "Would you take these first ones over to the table, and I'll bring the rest?"

Ruth took another tray, this time loaded with full glasses, and again threaded her way gingerly through the tables in the direction Frances had indicated. She had to reach the last table before the dance floor to discover Frances, who was seated with her back to the bar and did not see her until she reached the table. "What a miracle!" she exclaimed. "I give you a tray of empties, and you come back with them full."

"I bumped into Michael, and he was buying them."

"First names already?" Frances laughed.

Ruth laughed as well. "I met him earlier, in the forest."

"More and more intriguing! A forest rendezvous! Whatever next?"

"Stop it. I went for a walk and lost my way a little. He was there with his motorbike, and his friends."

"Well, he's a real Sir Galahad, helping out a damsel in distress!" This was said more loudly, because Michael was approaching the table with the second tray of drinks. He smiled at the remark, but gave out the drinks rather than respond. "Let me introduce you to everyone. Over here are Tricia and Kay, who also work in the admin offices, that's Sue from the Secure Block and her boyfriend Ian, Maggie and husband Bill – Maggie's a nurse on the East Wing – Rachel, John, Sarah and Emma, all nurses but I can't remember where they work, and Sir Galahad you already know. This is Ruth Appleton, a new doctor, and yes they get younger all the time, and this one's a woman!"

Ruth had seen the slight surprise in the group reaction to the word 'doctor' and recognised that the normal hierarchy of the hospital, and the expectation that a doctor would necessarily be male, lay behind it. But Frances had made a light joke about it and made her entry to the group much easier. She laughed with them, and when Frances pulled up a chair for her between herself and Michael she sat down. Michael pulled her drink over, and she took a sip. Frances smiled again. "You're staying temperate? Very wise, especially when you're out with all these drunkards."

The nurse called Rachel, who was on the other side of Frances, protested at the generalisation, claiming that only half the group were drunkards and that she was usually abstemious. "Not tonight, though, by the look of that gin and tonic," Frances retorted. And so Ruth recognised that among this group of hospital employees the mood was jovial and the tone of conversation light. She relaxed a little and waited to join in when she felt more familiar with the others. But another of the nurses, Emma, seated on the other side of Michael, leaned across and asked her how she had found things, starting new at the hospital.

"It's been a bit of a shock. I was in a small secure unit and suddenly got told I had to come here. I haven't worked in any place as large as this, with so much going on and so much to do."

"Where are you living?"

"In a doctor's room, near my firm, on the West Wing."

Emma wrinkled her nose at the news. "It's not good," Ruth acknowledged, "but it should be only temporary. I'm hoping they'll find me something better soon."

At this point the group started to play a loud number, and conversation became harder. It was almost necessary to shout, even to the people next to her. Michael asked her how she had come to be a psychiatrist at all, and she tried briefly, and loudly, to explain. And Frances chatted to her about the hospital generally. As office manager she knew exactly how many patients were in the hospital, how many doctors, nurses and orderlies, the size of the weekly food order, the cost of heating the buildings. Ruth listened to the figures, which emphasised again the vast scale of Black Roding.

"People call it a town on its own, and I know what they mean," Frances said. "It's so big it gets cut off – it doesn't get involved with the community around it because everything is brought into the hospital." Ruth could only just hear her above the music, but she was interested to hear someone else talking about the difficulties of size generated by Black Roding. Frances even sounded a little like the superintendent, being prepared to criticise things even though it was obvious she was also dedicated to the place.

As they talked Ruth realised there was a large glass on the table with some money in it. She asked Michael about it. "That's the kitty. Everyone pays in the same amount and we buy the drinks with it. If there's anything left over at the end of the evening, I take it away and bring it to the next dance. We just put in seven and six each earlier on."

"I should do the same," she said, reaching for her bag.

"But you're a guest tonight, and you're only drinking orange juice. That's not the same as these other drinks."

"Even so, I'd prefer to pay my way." Ruth took out the necessary coins from her purse. Michael held the glass out to her and she dropped the coins in.

"I'll get the next round in, then," Michael said. "How about helping me again?" He held out the tray on which Ruth had brought the first drinks to the table. She took it and followed him through the tables and chairs to the bar. "Want a different drink this time?" he asked.

Ruth thought for a moment. It was Saturday, she was on site where she had to work next day, the people she was with were all friendly – why not, then, have something stronger than orange? "All right, then, I'll try the beer you're drinking, to see what it's like."

They carried the drinks back and Ruth found herself in conversation with another nurse, Sarah, who had taken Michael's seat. "We don't normally find ourselves socialising with the doctors. Mostly they're older than you, and very few come to a dance like this, even the younger housemen. They've usually got their own friends back in London. Too stuck-up for the likes of us!"

"I chose earlier than many do, it's true. And I wasn't trained in London, so I don't have any friends there. So I came along to see what a dance is like here. It's certainly loud!" Somehow Sarah's response to her was not quite like that of the others. She seemed to sneer at Ruth's remarks and went back to her own seat.

Ruth looked at Frances, who had been listening. "Don't worry. She was going out with a doctor from London, but he gave her up. She hasn't forgiven him, or any other doctors, since. Too bitter about it." Ruth was taken aback at this reminder of her own past, and her face fell a little. "You OK?" Frances asked, seeing her reaction. Ruth nodded and reached for her glass to hide her reaction.

Too bitter?! If this Sarah was too bitter, was she also too bitter? Was it bitterness that had left her isolated and alone? She did not even have the group of friends that Sarah had. How had she reacted to being dumped by Peter? For a few moments Ruth tried to recall the period after he had given her up. Certainly she had not had anyone to turn to at the time because she had given all her free time in the previous years to being with him. She had been at a loose end when she was not working and had accepted doing additional hours to fill her time. She had become like an automaton, she thought, getting up, breakfasting, working, lunching, working, eating dinner, working again, and following that routine day after day. Successful in her work, yes, moderately, but happy, no. Perhaps others would have seen her as bitter about something, even if they did not know the cause. Just like this Sarah, letting the sharp feelings of loss and regret overtake her normal emotional condition but without a Frances to explain to others.

"Penny for them," she heard Michael's voice as the group stopped playing.

"What, sorry, what did you say?"

"Just that you seemed lost in thought."

"I was just remembering something. Sorry. I didn't mean to be rude."

"What do you think of the group, the Different Registers?"

"It's an unusual name. Why are they called that?"

"Two of them are students, I think, of languages or linguistics. That's where the words come from. They say it's because they can play different kinds of music."

"Do you know them?"

"Only from the dances here. I've talked to them during the intervals."

"I know nothing about pop music, so I don't necessarily know the songs they're singing unless I've heard them somewhere."

"So, do you like any other music?"

"My boyfriend used to take me to classical concerts, and that's the music I was taught at school."

"Used to…?"

Ruth felt her cheeks colour a little. "Oh, yes, we… we… broke up some time ago. So I don't really go to any concerts. I used to listen to the radio, but I've not got that with me now."

"Because you had to come here at short notice?"

"Yes. I left all my furniture and most of my possessions behind. At some time I shall have to try to collect them." Ruth felt she had revealed enough about herself, perhaps even more than she wanted, so she switched the conversation around. "What about you? Do you have your own place?"

"Yes, I've got a flat a couple of miles away, far enough to feel I'm away from the hospital and living in the real world. But I lived here for three years when I first started. Almost all the nurses have to do that, especially when they're just starting. But the nurses at least live together in the block. They're not in an isolated room like you."

They continued to talk for a while, and Michael again enlisted Ruth's help in carrying another round of drinks from the bar, and Ruth again chose to drink beer along with the others. Soon after they had sat down, Frances stood up and said, "Time for a dance, I think. Come on, Ruth, I'm sure you can dance."

Ruth tried to protest – "No, no, I'm not really a dancer, I don't dance" – but Frances would not accept her protests and took her by the hand to the dance floor. In truth Ruth did not dance in the modern way; she had been taught how to dance formally with a partner by the staff at her school, Ruth and her classmates acting as both male and female partners, giggling as they did so. But she had not danced in the hip-shaking arms-waving way that had become popular with the arrival of the new generation of popular musicians and groups. Not because she had deliberately chosen not to, but more simply because she had never been to a venue or event where such dancing went on. She was not refusing to dance, but she had never danced in this way. And rather naively, she thought as Frances dragged her to the dance floor, she had not anticipated being obliged to do so now, when she felt her professional position at Black Roding might be compromised if she made herself look foolish. But going along with Frances's enthusiasm seemed better than refusing, so she would have to do her best. "What should I do?" she muttered at Frances.

"Just copy me," Frances said quietly, as she started to twist and rock her upper body and stretch out her arms. Ruth did her best to imitate Frances's movements, and smiled nervously when Frances gave her a look of encouragement. She thought that her movements were awkward and clumsy and showed that she had never danced in this way before, but she quickly found that no-one among the dancers was paying her any particular attention, and the lights were sufficiently dark to mask her embarrassment, and she could start even to enjoy the movement of her body in time to the music. When the band finished that number, she did not retreat to the table but stayed on the dance floor to dance again. "You danced well," said Frances, "you should do it more often."

"I'm not sure I agree, but I'll try another."

"No, really, you were fine. Don't worry about it."

The music started again, and Ruth let her body sway a little more, as she saw Frances doing, and she moved her feet more quickly to match her swaying body and Frances's movements. The song was a popular one and more guests had come on to the dance floor, so there was less space between the dancers and Ruth was bumped once or twice by other dancers. As the song went on, Ruth saw that the young female patient, the one with a baby, had come in to the theatre and was also dancing. She had not yet seen Ruth, it seemed, but Ruth was a little anxious and Frances saw her face fall. "Everything all right?" she asked.

"Yes, but perhaps I'd better take a drink now. You carry on. I'll sit down."

Ruth returned to her seat and struck up a further conversation with Michael. A few minutes later the band announced that there would be a break, and Frances and the other members of the table returned from the dance floor. Michael surprised her by the interest he took in her, and by the intelligence of his questions. She had certainly misjudged him on first meeting. She helped him to bring more drinks to the table as the interval ended, and she carried on talking to him as the music re-started. Frances and some of the others again went off to dance, but Ruth at first declined. She felt happy talking to Michael, although she was perhaps not taking sufficient note of how much beer she was drinking.

For Richard it had been a busy evening. The popularity of this group had indeed drawn a large audience. Other events would not be so busy. The local Gilbert and Sullivan society, for example, would draw a good-sized audience but one not so large, nor so young and thirsty, as that drawn by the Different Registers. And so Richard had tried to collect the used glasses at every opportunity, and to wash them, but he had been falling behind. Whereas other doctors who supervised these events would join him in doing such tasks, Smythe would not. All he did was come to the bar and tell Richard that he had to do more to collect the glasses, and then slip away to the other side of the hall, where he sat watching the guests dancing. Richard would have been grateful if the office manager and his own doctor, Doctor Appleton, had come back to repeat their collection of glasses. But whenever Doctor Appleton had come to the bar she had been with one of the male nurses whom Richard knew from the Secure Block.

They had not offered any further help, so he had to start washing and drying glasses even when people were waiting at the bar, and often had to ask them to collect in some glasses so he could serve them what they wanted. He wondered if he could keep running the bar on such nights without more help, and how he might ask for such assistance without drawing attention to himself. So he decided to ask the office manager to repeat what she had done before, by presenting her with two trays and indicating that the glasses needed to be collected. He carried the trays under his arm and looked out for her. He recognised the back of her head where she was dancing. Coming up behind her, he tapped her arm and, when she turned towards him, pushed the trays towards her.

"What do you want? More glasses collected?" she asked him. He nodded. "OK, then, we'll collect them in. Come on, Ruth, you can help again."

Ruth was already watching her patient with interest. She stood up and went across to Frances and Richard. "You need our help again, Richard, is that it?" she said. Again he nodded and turned away immediately. Ruth smiled, both at Richard's departing stride and at Frances. "He never says much," she said quietly to Frances, "but he always seems able to get his meaning across."

They went three times back to the bar with trays full of glasses and saw that Richard would not be able to both wash the dirty glasses and serve the customers. "I think we'd better do the washing-up, don't you?" Frances said, opening the door into the serving area. Ruth followed, and as Frances filled the sink with water she looked around for a tea towel with which to dry the washed glasses. She caught Richard looking at them both, and he handed her two towels. Again Ruth noted the anticipatory ability of her patient as she turned towards the sink where Frances was busily swilling water around the washed glasses.

"Come on, you've got to keep up with me or I've nowhere to put the glasses," Frances joked. "I bet you didn't think when you were transferred here that you'd be doing the washing-up within a week."

Ruth hurriedly dried some glasses and looked around for the shelf on which to stack them. Once again Richard helped her by pointing to the shelves behind him, and she placed them carefully on the shelves. Within a few minutes she and Frances had replenished Richard's supplies, and they had also persuaded Michael, who came to the bar to purchase another round, to gather in any more used glasses. Just as Ruth was drying the last glass, she saw that Oliver Smythe was standing, red-faced, at the bar and staring at the two women.

"What the hell are you doing there?" he asked.

Ruth hardly knew what to say because she was not aware of what unspoken rule she had transgressed. "Just helping with the washing-up," she said almost apologetically. Frances was still swirling the last of the water in the sink as it emptied and had not heard Smythe's challenge.

"You need my permission to be behind the bar. You should have asked me."

"I didn't know that. Richard seemed not to have the time to get the washing-up done. We'd collected all these glasses, so…" Ruth's explanation was, she thought, obvious enough.

"But you should have asked *me*, not a patient. I'm the one in charge, not him."

Frances had just turned at this point and caught the last point of Smythe's anger.

"Well, if you were in charge, you'd have seen that he needed help, wouldn't you?" she said firmly. Ruth looked from Frances to Smythe. Frances's words were directly challenging, but she seemed to hold some authority, and Smythe had not immediately replied. He looked back at Ruth and spoke to her.

"One doctor should not be undermining another one," he said. "You surely understand that."

"I had no idea you were in charge. I just saw that Richard needed help." Ruth tried to sound as firm as her friend.

"But you knew that a doctor was in charge, and you should have asked me if you were going behind the bar."

Frances moved in front of Ruth. "No, Doctor," she said, "you should have been close to the bar and monitoring what was happening. One patient can't run the bar alone on a busy night like this. And you should know that."

Smythe breathed in deeply through his nose, looking angrily at first Frances and then Ruth, but he made no reply. Instead, with an audible puffing out of air, he turned and stalked off to his seat. "Jerk," Ruth heard Frances mutter to herself, before turning to Ruth. "What an unpleasant man he is," she said, just loudly enough for Ruth, but no-one else, to hear. "Come on, let's join the others."

"Let me just have a word with Richard. I need to reassure him, I think." Ruth turned towards him and saw that he had been watching the confrontation. "Just call us if you get too busy again, Richard. Don't worry about what Doctor Smythe said. Next time I'll check with him if we have to wash up." She smiled at him, trying to use good humour as part of her reassurance, but he did not smile back. It was not his way.

As Ruth returned to her seat, Frances asked, "We'll have another dance in a minute or two, shall we? And see if we can get Michael to risk the dance floor. That would be an achievement!"

Michael laughed at the suggestion. "No, dancing is most definitely not for me. I'm happy to listen and watch." And he still refused when Frances said that it was time to dance and took Ruth by the arm again. Ruth looked around for the young woman from the Admissions Unit, but she could not see her. Perhaps she had gone back to the unit. Ruth stopped thinking about her and once more tried to imitate Frances in her dancing. To her surprise, she was finding it enjoyable and did not feel as embarrassed as she had feared. Some of the group from their table joined them, so that there were five or six women dancing together. The others seemed no better at dancing than her, and Ruth relaxed and let her body enjoy the physical activity and the strong bass rhythms of the music, the volume of which seemed to have been turned up for the second half of the dance. They danced in this way for half an hour or so, during which time the band moved from playing their own songs to once again singing cover versions of popular hits. They were all lively songs, which made the dancing more and more energetic. Finally, Frances suggested they sit down for a drink, and the group returned to their table. Ruth, made thirsty by the vigour of the dancing, finished her drink quickly. Michael collected some more money to top up the shared kitty, and Ruth again helped him fetch new drinks.

If Ruth had reflected on the past few hours, she thought afterwards, disaster might have been avoided. She had eaten lunch but not an evening meal. She had drunk several large glasses of beer when she was unaccustomed to drinking much alcohol at all. She was dancing and making herself hot, which was making her more thirsty. But the pleasure of being in a group of friends, and of finding unexpected pleasure in the dancing, prevented her from such thoughts. Instead she accepted another drink and drank it quickly before Frances called them all to the dance floor again. Ruth found herself eager to join in the dance and now felt considerably less inhibited.

After two or three more energetic songs, however, the singer said they would be playing some slower numbers. Ruth thought that this was time to return to her seat; but before she could do so, a male patient appeared in front of her, with open arms, inviting her to dance with him. He was in his forties, Ruth guessed, but she could see no harm in accepting his invitation. Frances too had been selected for a dance by a man who looked more like an outsider. The other women returned to their seats. At first the man held her arms in an almost formal, ballroom-style grip, and Ruth allowed the man to lead her in gentle circles in time with the music. This seemed much like all the other couples on the dance floor, which was now filled with just pairs of dancers. But as the song progressed, Ruth found that the man was pressing more closely against her, and his grip was tightening. She could not push him away, or walk off, in the middle of the dance, so she resolved to stay until the song finished and then return immediately to her seat. By now, though, the man was holding her tightly to him, and Ruth suddenly realised that the man was becoming sexually aroused, and that his penis, beneath his clothing, was erect. She made to push him away, but he held her all the more tightly, and she stumbled backwards into another dancer.

The woman she had stumbled against swore immediately at her, and Ruth recognised the harsh tone of the young woman from the Admissions Unit. When she realised it was Ruth, she let go of her dance partner and pushed Ruth violently. Ruth, still held by the aroused patient, who would not give up his source of excitement easily, toppled forward with him; and as he fell backwards, so she fell on top of him and then to the side. With her arms pinned by the patient, she could not put out a hand to defend herself, and she hit her head on the floor and was momentarily stunned. The patient crawled a couple of steps away before attempting to stand up, as other dancers stopped to look at the fracas. The young woman stood near Ruth, sneering at her, but the violence of Ruth's fall had silenced her. The music continued for a while as more and more of the dancers ceased their slow dances to look on at Ruth and the others, and finally the band stopped playing as they realised an incident of some kind had occurred.

Ruth looked up from the floor. She could feel a bump on her forehead where it had struck the floor, and she could not at first work out what had happened. She was aware of the circle of onlookers, and then of Oliver Smythe, standing over her and shouting. "Doctor Appleton, how dare you act in this way? You're drunk! Get up and get out of here!"

Ruth could not move at first, however. The combined effect of the drink and the blow on her head certainly made her feel as if she might be intoxicated. Her legs did not seem willing to obey her need to stand up, and when she lifted her head off the floor she suddenly felt nauseated and had to let her head fall back.

"You're right," called out the young woman into whom Ruth had involuntarily bumped. "She was falling over on me, almost knocked me down. Can't hold her drink, I reckon."

Still, Ruth could not do anything more than lift her head a little. "Help me up, someone, please," she said quietly. "I've bumped my head." But with Smythe and the young woman standing over her, no-one could easily approach her. Some of the onlookers were laughing at her, while others just seemed puzzled.

Smythe was still standing over her, half-shouting, "Come on, Doctor Appleton, stand up!" when Frances shoved him aside.

"What happened, Ruth?" She knelt down next to her. "Are you OK?"

"I bumped my forehead, when I fell over. It was an accident… of a kind… I just fell over…"

Frances put an arm under her. "Can you stand? Can you get up?"

"Yes, if you hold me just to help me, I think I can." With her support Ruth managed to sit up, and then slowly to turn in order to lever herself up. Frances looked with concern at the bump rising on Ruth's forehead, and Michael, who had only just realised that an incident had occurred involving the two women, also burst into the circle.

"Get her away, will you, she's bringing all of us into disrepute," Smythe hissed at Frances, who hissed back, "Don't be ridiculous, man, she's been injured." Frances helped Ruth to stand, and Michael stepped in to take her arm. "Come and sit down for a minute," Frances said, and Michael held her elbow and forearm up, so bolstering her as she moved gingerly back towards the table.

Ruth sat down and slumped a little. Frances came back from the bar with a handkerchief soaked in water. She held this to the bump on Ruth's forehead. Ruth pulled back but Frances insisted on pressing the bump. "You hold it," she said, "tight against the bump. Then you can tell us what happened when you feel OK."

Ruth pressed the handkerchief against her forehead. The bump hurt, and Ruth could feel a broader headache coming on. She tried to think. She had been dancing… then the slow numbers started… then a patient asked her to dance… then he pulled her against his body, and she had realised he was becoming aroused… she'd felt his penis being held against her, and she'd reacted… But then it was all unclear in her mind what had happened and how exactly she had fallen on the floor.

"I think," Ruth paused. All around the table the others were looking at her, "I think it may have been the patient dancing with me." She stopped. She did not feel she could say more in front of so many people, people who did not really know her and whom she did not know. "Yes, I think it was him, but maybe another patient as well."

Frances looked at her uncertainly. "Perhaps you'd better go back to your room in a few minutes."

Sarah had been listening along with the others. "Perhaps you've just had too much to drink and you fell over. Why blame the patients for that?"

"No, no…" Ruth did not know what to say, "no, I'm not trying to blame anybody, I'm just saying what happened."

"Well, how could a patient cause that?" Sarah was scornful. "You fell over while you were dancing. How could he have caused that and not you as well?"

"Because he was using me to get aroused!" Ruth blurted out the truth she had tried not to make so explicit. But Sarah was not to be placated by that.

"So do lots of them when they dance with you. It's inevitable. They're locked up here without any companionship, and then they're allowed to come to a dance and get up close with somebody. We've all experienced that. Why make such a song and dance about it?"

"I wasn't! I just tried to move him away from me, that's all. But the woman behind me pushed me, and before I could stop myself we'd fallen over."

"But why did you have to cause all the problems? If you'd just left it until the dance finished, nothing would have happened. The man got a hard-on, he wasn't actually assaulting you. You know you're attending a dance in a mental asylum. What on earth did you expect?"

"I just wasn't expecting that, that's all." As Ruth was defending herself she was becoming more angry. She looked around the group and wondered if the others thought that Sarah had a point. She stood up, with a little difficulty, and said, "I'm going to leave now. I don't care what you think."

She bumped into a chair as she moved away, and Frances said, "I'll come with you."

"There's no need," she said, and walked away.

Frances hesitated and sat down, but Michael said, "It would be good if you did go with her. See she's all right." So Frances followed Ruth's path out of the door and along the corridor. For someone who had just had a nasty injury to the head, Frances thought, Ruth was still walking quickly. She did not call her, but tried just to keep the distance between them the same. Ruth walked through the reception hall and along the corridor leading to the West Wing. The corridor was quiet, and only a few nurses or orderlies were moving between the wards. Ruth turned down the West Wing corridor a few seconds ahead of Frances, but she was able to follow her as she hurried towards the far end. As she reached the end she turned up the stairs, and Frances thought it was quiet enough to call her with a muted greeting. But Ruth went on up the stairs, and Frances wondered if she would recognise the doctor's room. She ran the last few yards of the corridor to reach the stairs and hurried up them. Ruth's door was just shutting as she came to the top corridor, so she was able to knock on the door. "Ruth, it's me, Frances," she said.

"Go away. I don't want to talk to anyone," Ruth replied. Frances thought that Ruth had probably been crying. Her voice certainly sounded cracked, as if forcing out the words in between sobs.

"Just let me see that you are all right, please," Frances pleaded. There was a pause. Then the door opened, just a few inches. Ruth looked out at Frances, and yes, she had been crying. Frances pushed gently on the door to open it just a little more.

"We were worried about you."

"Really? Sarah didn't sound very worried."

"I told you, she's biased against doctors. Don't think that what she says goes for everyone." Frances was trying to look at Ruth's face. The bump seemed to have stopped swelling, but it was prominent on her forehead. "How are you feeling?" she motioned towards the bump. "Could I come in just to see?"

Ruth opened the door and drew back so that Frances could enter. She reached up to touch Ruth's forehead but not the bump. "Is it sore?" she asked.

Ruth shook her head. "No, it's not hurting now, unless I touch it. But it has given me a headache." She sat down on the bed. Frances looked around at the bleak room, then back at Ruth.

"This room would give me a headache. It's awful. What on earth are they thinking of, giving you this? Surely it's just an emergency room for overnight stays?"

"I don't know. It's the room the superintendent gave me. I haven't had time to check with admin. Thanks for your concern. I'm all right. I didn't anticipate what might happen, and I'm certainly not used to things here."

Frances realised she would have to leave soon if she was to get out of the hospital at the same time as her friends. It was better to go down the drive together with others, and to get some transport from outside the hospital grounds, whether a bus or a lift with someone picking others up, than to try to get home on her own.

"I'll see you next week. Call in at the office," she said, and left the room and walked to take the stairs down. Ruth sat back on the bed again. She wondered what the aftermath of the evening's incident would bring.

CHAPTER TWENTY-ONE

The first general meeting on Ward 43 on Monday had gone well. The nurses had all been briefed about taking part, and David had some general information and some notes that he intended to use to start the meeting and to prod the discussion if it wandered too far from purpose, or if it tailed away. Ruth and John Sutton had provided up-to-date notes on all the patients' treatments so that David could know the situation with anyone whose contribution became sensitive, and Ruth had also indicated those patients whom nurses had in their first survey returns identified as having the potential to be considered for alternative treatments and housing outside the hospital.

Ruth had spent the Sunday working on these notes for David and on the reviews that would be needed for the superintendent later in the week. She had not had much time to think over the events of Saturday evening, but when she did she had a sinking feeling in her stomach when she thought about how everyone – or almost everyone – had concluded that she was drunk. She doubted that the incident was over – somehow she expected there to be repercussions. The staff nurse who had objected so much in advance had clearly decided not to intervene during the first meeting. David had told the meeting that there were to be changes in the hospital and in the ward, particularly when the ward's consultant had died and he and Ruth had had to take charge. He explained that every patient was to be reviewed over a six-month period and that one or more of the doctors might be talking to them in one-to-one sessions as part of that review. He then explained the purpose of the general meetings, to allow patients to express concerns and anxieties, and to explore their own and other patients' conditions and how they might be helped to get better and to resume life away from the hospital. He had stopped there, and the patients had been silent at first. Then some had asked if that really meant that their illnesses might be discussed by everyone, but one of the nurses had said reassuringly that such a discussion could only go on if they agreed to it and that it was not that different to the discussions nurses and doctors often had with the patients themselves.

One patient, a pretty sharp one Ruth had thought, had asked if the reviews meant that Doctor Winstanley's opinions no longer counted. David had not replied immediately, so Ruth had thought it right to chip in that she was coming from outside the hospital and that the superintendent had asked her to review all the patients so that she got to know them and then make some suggestions about any changes that might be good. If any change in their treatment was to be considered, it would be discussed with them. That had caused some concern, and several of the patients had asked if their treatment was going to be changed. Ruth said no, any change would only be made when she had completed a review, and this had to be discussed with the patients. Another of the nurses had then spoken, saying that she had been physically ill some years previously and that the first treatments had not worked very well. She had still been ill when she was seen by another doctor. This doctor had realised that there were two illnesses at the same time and that she needed different treatment. In her case, the review process had worked out very well. Some of the patients had still said nothing, so David had asked everyone to think about what the nurse had said. Had anything like that happened to them? He allowed several minutes to pass in silence, and then one patient said yes, a doctor had not recognised the symptoms of a serious illness in her mother, and only when her mother had gone to a hospital had the illness been diagnosed. This seemed to reassure other patients a little, and then a woman suddenly said that she had disagreed with her doctor when he had first sent her to Black Roding. Ruth had leaned forward at that point, because the woman was another patient about whom Ruth was curious. The diagnosis on the woman's records did not seem to be supported by the nurses' accounts of her, and Ruth determined to go back to the original diagnosis with her, to see if she, rather than the doctor, had been right.

There had been some complaints from the patients. One indeed complained that the superintendent had come round insisting on patients being dressed, curtains being drawn back, all patients doing something useful. That must have been the message received by the nurse from her own visit with the superintendent, that the nurse had then communicated to the patients. She could not help smiling to herself – the staff nurse was trying to manipulate the patient to defend her own actions, or inaction rather. But David did not give way, and said that these policies on the part of the superintendent were important for all the patients and could not be changed. He allowed more discussion of complaints about the hospital's food, about the cold temperatures in the ward and especially in the bathrooms, and about patients' concerns about their treatments. He said it was good to be prepared to talk about their illnesses and their treatments in front of others, and reminded them that they probably spoke about these things with other patients, and certainly with the nurses and doctors, all the time. The meetings were an opportunity for everyone to focus on these things and to think about how to help people to get better. And he took the opportunity to say that those patients who got better would have the chance to move away from the hospital and to live elsewhere. But, as he had agreed with Ruth and John, he did not broach the topic of ward mergers and closures. That needed a lot more preparation and thought about how to introduce the idea, since the patients were likely to be opposed to such a change. And Ruth herself had said that she was concerned about how they would make that change and wanted to know the whole plan before they tried to introduce it.

Their intention had been to run the meeting for Ward 44 in just the same way as the one for Ward 43. Ruth had prepared similar notes, and she had observed that Richard had scored highly in the survey for the ability to take responsibility and organise himself but not so well for communication. He was one patient she would need to consider for moving on. On the Tuesday morning, however, David had telephoned the ward to say that his wife was badly ill and he could not leave her. When Ruth turned up at the ward half an hour before the meeting, it was not to give David some final support but to hear that she would have to chair the general meeting. She quickly called the nurses and John Sutton together to confirm that the meeting would go ahead, and then she retrieved the notes and outline of the meeting that David had left on his desk. She mentally rehearsed the sequence of the meeting and looked over David's outline to confirm what should be said and when she should introduce each important issue. Then she went to the communal area in the ward where the nurses and patients were gathering chairs for the meeting and saw that, unlike the previous day's meeting when they had not attended, there were both an occupational therapist and a social worker waiting. She spoke to each of them to confirm their names and to remind them that this was to be the very first general meeting held on the ward, so not to be surprised by the patients' unfamiliarity or lack of preparedness to take part.

The patients were slow to gather together, and Ruth allowed the nurses to encourage them rather than chivvy them along. There was uncertainty on their part at the innovation, and several of them looked tense and worried before the meeting started. Ruth reminded herself to speak slowly and clearly, and to avoid looking too directly at individual patients – two points she had learned from David's example. And then she opened the meeting, introducing herself again and explaining David's absence and the two new faces from the hospital. She said how good it had been to come to the ward when she first visited the area, and then explained, in the simplest terms she could find, what was involved in the meeting and in the parallel work of the individual patients' reviews. Then she paused for questions, and there were some. Why had there not been meetings before? Could they really talk about anything? What if someone did not want to talk about their illness? Why was a review necessary? Might she be changing patients' medication? Could they ask her if they felt that something had gone wrong before? Sister O'Sullivan had said in advance of the meeting that she had spoken to many of the patients and had encouraged them to raise any matters or questions that they wanted, and had even got some to memorise their questions. Ruth was grateful for her preparations, because the discussion proceeded well, and without many pauses. She, John Sutton and other staff were able to answer the questions and keep the patients reassured.

Ruth then steered the discussion on to the wider issues that patients might want to raise. Just as she had previously experienced, many of the patients wanted to complain about the food, but others were more positive, and two asked about how they could learn some new skills for work outside the hospital. The difference in the patients' responses created by Sister O'Sullivan, when compared with those of the patients in Ward 43 the previous day, was again obvious to Ruth, and she felt guilty that she had objected when the superintendent had suggested that this nurse had much to teach her. He had been right. She had used her good relationship with them, and the trust they had in her, to talk to them about what they could gain from the general meetings.

Throughout all this, however, Richard had kept his silence. He understood well enough the implications of the reviews, and of the changes that Ruth was talking about. He had heard the conversation of the doctors when Doctor Appleton had first joined the team. And he knew from the conversation he had already had with her that she was uncertain about him and that she realised there was something unusual about him. He had not helped his cause with her by not following his usual rules at times when she had caught him off guard, and he was sure she had taken note on those occasions that he was not talking like an ordinary inmate of the hospital. At what he guessed was near the end of the meeting, she introduced the fact that patients who recovered from their illness or whose mental health was restored would be able to return to their homes or to other accommodation outside the hospital. He decided he should ask at least one question – all the others seemed to have taken part, and he did not like to stand out as different.

"Please, Doctor, I... I..." he stuttered deliberately.

"Yes, Richard, what do you want to ask?" She smiled at him as she always did, and waited for him to respond.

"I... er... I have no home now. Only here. Nowhere else." There were some sighs of agreement. No doubt Richard was not the only long-stay patient who had given up his accommodation on entry.

"We could not just put patients out of the hospital without considering their housing," the occupational therapist intervened. "If someone was recommended to leave the hospital we would have to liaise with other organisations about where they would live."

Ruth was sitting between Richard and the entrance to the ward. She noticed that Richard, who would usually look downwards when he was in a conversation, was actually looking over her shoulder at something, or someone, and he was looking worried. His mouth had fallen slightly open. When he did not respond to the occupational therapist, the staff and some of the patients looked at him and, seeing his reaction, they too looked past Ruth. Silence fell over the whole group, causing Ruth herself to turn around.

A stranger had entered the ward, a late middle-aged man in a smart black overcoat, a red scarf tied around his neck and a charcoal-grey trilby hat in his hand. His hair was silver-grey and combed back. His shoes were highly polished, and he looked well-manicured, his soft hands holding two black leather gloves. When he spoke it was with what Ruth thought of as an Oxbridge accent, an almost affected pronunciation of his vowels that, together with his clothing and appearance, made him completely alien to the hospital. Before he spoke he surveyed the whole group, as if checking whether the young woman who had turned towards him could really be the person in charge. Satisfied that she must indeed be the leading doctor present, he addressed her.

"Why did no-one tell us Winstanley was dead?" Some of the staff gasped at the abrupt nature of his question and his rudely brusque manner. Ruth was startled and did not reply. Again he asked, "I said, why did no-one call us? We should have been told."

Ruth replied this time. "I'm sorry, I don't know who you are or why anyone should have communicated the news to you. But we are just finishing a meeting and cannot deal with you for a few minutes. Would you mind waiting outside the ward?"

The man hesitated, seeming to be on the edge of an angry retort. But he smiled – not, Ruth thought, in a pleasant way – and turned away. "I'll be in the corridor," he said loudly as he left.

Rut turned back to the meeting. The patients settled down fairly easily, and Ruth looked at her notes to remind herself how she should bring the meeting to an end. Then she looked at Richard. He seemed frozen in the same attitude he had adopted when this stranger had first appeared.

"Richard," she said, "do you know that man?" He did not even notice her talking to him. "Richard," she tried to raise the volume of her voice without seeming sharp, "Richard," again she called, and he looked at her, "do you know him?" She pointed back over her shoulder. But still he did not answer. "OK. Let's end our meeting at this point. We'll be holding the next general meeting on Tuesday next week. But the nursing staff will be asking you to think about whether you want to bring something to my attention while I am reviewing all of your situations." Ruth said all this loudly, clearly meaning everyone to hear it. But her eyes were fixed on Richard, who was starting to look rather as he had done when she was called to him in the reception hall the previous week. "Doctor Sutton," she said this quietly to call him to her, "would you keep an eye on Richard while I see the gentleman who just arrived? I want to find out why he had this effect on him. Please check his pulse and his blood pressure, and monitor his breathing. And call me if there is anything unusual. I'll be back as soon as possible."

John Sutton did just as she had asked, and quietly got one of the nurses to help him while the others were replacing the chairs in the communal area or returning them to bedsides in the dormitory areas. Ruth left the ward and found the man in the corridor outside. He was talking to another man, a squat, broad-shouldered fellow wearing a kind of uniform

– blue serge jacket and trousers – and holding a peaked cap. They ended their conversation and the silver-haired man spoke to her.

"Good morning," he said, in a tone that indicated he did not mean the greeting at all. "Are you really in charge here? You seem so young to be in charge."

Ruth bridled inwardly but determined not to show her anger. "Good morning. Yes, I am in charge. I'm Doctor Appleton, registrar for the ward, and the consultant is not in today. Can I ask who you are and why you've come here today?"

"I am Sir Francis Oates, a civil servant. I only just learned that Winstanley was dead. We should have been told that earlier. I've come here because we have an interest in one of Winstanley's patients, one of *your* patients now. Richard Simms is his name."

"And who exactly are the 'we' in this, and what is the interest in Richard?"

"Is there somewhere less public where we could discuss this?"

"In the doctors' room. We can go there now."

The man turned to his colleague. "Wait for me outside," he instructed. "I'll be out shortly." The other man scowled at Ruth and walked away. Ruth found herself almost threatened just by the man's stare, and his colleague must have realised something of this. "He's a good driver, very loyal, but a bit of a bulldog. He doesn't like mental hospitals, something which I'm sure you've found in others." The man smiled at her, though Ruth thought that the smile was almost as threatening as the other man's scowl. She led him to the doctors' room and he sat down in one of the chairs. "I work in a rather discreet part of Her Majesty's government," he started his explanation as if it were a well-rehearsed phrase. "I can't tell you much about it. But Richard Simms also worked for the government when he… when he sadly had a breakdown and tried to commit suicide. We arranged with Winstanley that he would be admitted here for treatment, and I've reviewed that situation regularly with Winstanley. Did the records not tell you this?"

"No. The records were too concise for that, and there was nothing about his history before admission except that he had tried to kill himself.

And there was nothing about you." *Except for your initials all over Richard's records*, Ruth thought. "Can you tell me more?"

"No, not really. The nature of my work requires a great deal of discretion, and I am not in a position to tell you more. How is Simms? He didn't seem very well just now."

"I can't discuss details of a patient unless I know more about your relationship with him. I can talk with next of kin and family, but not with someone who worked with him thirteen years ago. There is not enough connection there."

"But Winstanley always did. I don't see why you can't. You're just a slip of a girl." The man's tone had changed, sharper, sterner, attempting to be more authoritative. But Ruth thought that it had changed because, in the battle of wills, at least for the moment she had the upper hand.

"I would need to know much more before I could discuss Richard with you. Perhaps Sir Reginald knew more and was able to talk with you because of that. Now, however young you think I am, I am the one with legal responsibility for Richard." Ruth tried to maintain a professional tone. She did not like being patronised and was determined to find out more if she could. But the man seemed to be thinking about his strategy in the light of her unhelpfulness.

"I can't tell you more at present," he eventually said. "But I would like to speak with Simms."

"If Richard wants to meet you, he can. But, like you, I did not think that he was perfectly well just now, so I will need to check if he is able – and willing – to meet you. Would you wait outside again?"

"Why not here?" The man was becoming more angry. "I'm not just some ordinary visitor."

"Because there are confidential records in here. It is not just you who has to maintain confidentiality."

"Very well, but I need somewhere quiet to meet with Simms."

"We have a meeting room you can use for a short while. But the staff will need to meet in a while, so it can't be for long." Ruth waited for the civil servant to leave the room, before she too left. She found Richard sitting next to his bed.

John Sutton was just writing up some details on the sheet of paper kept at the foot of each patient's bed. He looked up as Ruth approached and quickly reported, "Richard's pulse and blood pressure were both up, and he seemed on the edge of another panic attack. But he's calmed down now, and things are returning to normal."

Ruth looked at Richard. Ideally she would not have wanted to upset him, but Sir Francis Oates' appearance had given her the first, and perhaps only, opportunity to find out more about him. She thought that she should at least ask Richard if he would meet the stranger, and was wondering if she could place someone in the room with them if he did agree. Then she might be able to learn more. She approached her patient and sat on the bed in order to speak to him at his level. "Richard, there's a man here, I think you saw him, who's asking to meet with you. He's a civil servant, Sir Francis Oates. Do you want to meet him?"

To her surprise, Richard groaned at the thought, and his head slumped down. She put her hand on his shoulder and said, "I'll tell him no, shall I? You don't seem ready to meet him at the moment."

"No!" Richard almost shouted, even though he was still looking at the floor. "No! Don't say that. I'll see him. I'll bloody well see him." His words, and his tone, alarmed Ruth.

"I don't think it's a good idea. You're obviously upset. Let me put him off."

"No! No!" Richard's vehemence made Ruth pull back. "I'll see him."

"All right, Richard, if that's what you want, I'll let you." Ruth stood up and whispered to John Sutton, "Get Sister O'Sullivan for me, quickly." She turned back to Richard. "I'll have to arrange for you to meet him in the meeting room, Richard. I'll just be a few minutes sorting it out."

Ruth left the dormitory area and met Sister O'Sullivan. "I'm sorry to ask you to do this, but I think it's necessary. Richard is going to meet with the man who interrupted the general meeting. But it is obviously upsetting him. I will only allow it if a nurse such as you is in the room. And here's the issue. I'm not asking you to eavesdrop on them, but this man's arrival is obviously upsetting Richard. If you were to hear anything, anything that might help me to find out what's going on, and what's upsetting him, I would be grateful. It's a little, er, unprofessional in one respect, but not in another. What do you think?"

The nurse considered the request for a moment. "Perhaps if I take my badges off, so I just look like the other nurses, and I take a magazine in to read while they are talking, would that do?"

Ruth nodded. "Yes, I don't want you to do anything wrong, but I am very keen to unravel the mystery of Richard."

She went back to find Sir Francis striding up and down the corridor impatiently. "Well?" he said. "I am busy, you know."

"Richard has not been very well. I can only allow you to meet him if a nurse sits in the room. Let me show you."

"I said I wanted the meeting to be confidential."

"No, I think you said you had to be confidential. But I can't allow a patient who is at risk to be unattended by a member of staff. It's a large room. You can stay at one end, and the nurse at the other."

Sir Francis was fuming. "Our conversation must be private. What you are saying is intolerable."

"It's the only way I can allow it. There is too much danger for my patient."

Ruth thought she was about to face the full force of the man's anger, but instead Sir Francis adopted an ameliorative tone. "Very well," he accepted, "but the conversation must be just for us."

"She can sit at the other end of the room."

Ruth led him to the meeting room and then went to fetch Richard and Sister O'Sullivan. Richard was pale and looked very worried. Ruth wondered at the effect on him of the civil servant's arrival. What could it mean? It justified, in her view, the slight deception about having a nurse in attendance. She ushered the two in to join Sir Francis, and then went to tell other staff that the debrief meeting would be in half an hour.

"What happened to the OT and the social worker?" she asked at the nurses' station, and was told that they had given up waiting and returned to their offices. "Call them and apologise, and see if they can come back for our meeting in half an hour, please," she asked. And she went to gather her thoughts about the general meeting and to prepare some notes for the staff discussion, while all the time wondering what was happening in the meeting between Richard and Sir Francis.

CHAPTER TWENTY-TWO

Richard was distressed at the thought of meeting with Sir Francis. He had expected such a meeting, and had even initiated events with his telephone call, but he loathed and feared the man so much that it made him feel sick just to be going into a room with him. He was surprised that Sister O'Sullivan was coming into the meeting room with him, and he was observant enough, despite his fears, to notice that she had removed the badges that marked out her status. But he judged that it could only be in his interest to have her present, since it might reduce Sir Francis's ability to threaten and frighten him. And he knew she was a very good nurse and trusted by the Superintendent, who had probably placed her there to counteract the worse effects of Sir Reginald. She went to the end of the room and sat down with her back half-turned towards them, opening a magazine she had brought with her.

Richard sat down and turned to face Sir Francis, though he looked down at the floor rather than looking at him. Sir Francis waited for Richard to raise his eyes; but since he refused, he spoke first. "Well,

Simms," he said in a quiet but threatening tone, "you called my office. Now I'm here. What's going on?"

Richard paused. He did not want to set aside his mantra, not with the nurse in the room. After a few seconds, still regarding the floor, he said, "Changes. Changes because Winstanley's dead. Saying they'll move patients out."

Sir Francis raised his voice. "Is this right, Nurse, what Simms has just told me, that patients are being moved out?"

Sister O'Sullivan stopped reading and pretended she hadn't heard. "I'm sorry, was that question put to me? I wasn't paying any attention. Sorry."

"Of course it was put to you! Are the doctors moving patients out of the hospital?"

"Well, I don't think that's how they'd put it. I think they're just reviewing all the patients."

"But might some of the patients be moved out as a result of these reviews?"

"That's always possible, if a patient has recovered their health sufficiently. So, yes, some patients might move to accommodation outside the hospital, or go home, and continue their treatment there."

The civil servant turned back to Richard. He waited a few moments. He heard the nurse pick up her magazine and start leafing through it again. "Is that what's worrying you," he asked Richard, "that you might be moved out?"

It was not exactly how Richard would have put it. But to say more now, when the nurse had actually been brought into the conversation and might be watching him, would be too dangerous. So he nodded, while still looking downwards.

Sir Francis leaned towards him, so that he was almost whispering in his ear. "You're right to be worried, Simms. I can't let you loose out there. You've got to stay here. If you leave here, we might have to do something about that. And you know what that would involve." The threat was obvious, and Richard groaned. He sensed that across the room the nurse had looked up again.

"I think Simms might still be feeling upset, Nurse," he heard Sir Francis say. "Perhaps I should leave him for today and come again another time."

"So quickly?" she asked. "Are you sure?" And to Richard she said, "Are you all right, Richard? Do you want to stop now?"

Richard nodded again. The others stood up, and he, slowly and deliberately, stood up and left the room without looking back at either of them. Sir Francis turned to the nurse and said, "I think I'd better see the doctor quickly before I leave."

CHAPTER TWENTY-THREE

Ruth did not manage to complete the notes she wanted to prepare. Within five minutes of sitting down at her desk to write them, she was surprised to be interrupted by Sir Francis again. This time, if anything, she thought he was even more brusque.

"Are you planning to move Simms out of the hospital?"

"We call him Richard here. And I already told you, I can't discuss his case unless I know more about your connection to him."

"He said there were changes going on and that you were moving patients out. He's clearly terrified. And it is not just me who has the interest in him, it's the government."

"Yes, but you never told me which part of government, nor who 'we' are." Ruth felt strongly, though she could not say why, even to herself, that she should not give way to this blustering. "I would be breaking my own oath if I started to discuss Richard with you at the moment."

Sir Francis, as he had already done twice, was again able quickly to appear calm and to try a different tactic. "Could we speak generally, then?"

Ruth acquiesced to this. "Is it the case that some patients are likely to be moved away from the hospital? Is there a policy that this happens after a review?"

"It is the case that any patient who has sufficiently recovered to be treated at some remove from the hospital, whether as an outpatient or within a different part of the health system, should be given the chance to move to that new location, including their own home. And we have to keep the patients under review to see if any have reached that position."

"But would they *have* to be moved? Don't they have a say?"

"Yes, if there is any doubt about their condition, we would not move forward. If they are anxious about a proposed change, we have to deal with that anxiety. But a final decision would be made on a case-by-case basis. The hospital is not allowed simply to keep people here if they've got better."

"But surely that's what places like this have been doing for a hundred years?"

"That's what's changing, Sir… Francis, was it? The government wants the number of people in mental health hospitals reduced. Surely you of all people know that?"

Ruth knew straight away that she had pushed things too far. The man drew closer to her, looked her in the eyes and said with a hiss, "Don't you dare get clever with me, Doctor. I could get you removed from here very quickly."

But Ruth was still prepared to brave it out with him, and replied, "And don't you dare get threatening with me. I could get you removed from here very quickly." And although she felt herself trembling, she reached for the telephone. "Shall I call for security? The orderlies pride themselves on how quickly they can get to any ward."

"No, that won't be necessary. You'll hear from me again." He turned sharply and strode out of the room. Ruth felt herself expel air – she hadn't realised she was holding her breath – and she trembled still as she put the telephone back on its black box.

Next, Sister O'Sullivan burst in. "I was waiting down the corridor till he left. What a horrible man!" Ruth gave her a questioning look. "He hardly spoke to Richard. Once Richard said that patients might be moved, he started asking me questions. And Richard seemed scared of him."

"Anything else?" asked Ruth.

"Oh yes, I thought that at the very start he said that Richard had called his office on the telephone. I couldn't be sure, but that's what it sounded like. But why would Richard call a man like that?"

"I don't know," Ruth answered, "but I think I'd better try to find out. It's probably time for the staff meeting, isn't it? I'll need to talk to Richard later. Thanks for doing that. I couldn't really ask anyone else, and I couldn't have done it myself." Ruth smiled at the nurse and gathered her papers together confidently, but inwardly she did not feel so assured.

CHAPTER TWENTY-FOUR

After Doctor Sutton had taken his pulse again, Richard had been allowed to go on his rounds. But Doctor Appleton had sent a message asking him to be back in the ward by three o'clock, so he had not taken his free newspaper from the shop, nor visited the water tower, but had resumed his round immediately after eating lunch and completed as much as possible before returning to Ward 44. The round, as it often did, distracted him from the worst of his thoughts, and a feeling of foreboding only grew within him as he pushed the trolley into its cupboard. For a short time he toyed with the idea of going to the water tower and missing his appointment with the doctor, but that seemed the worse of the two options. It would initiate a search for him and draw even more attention. So, very slowly, he locked the cupboard and made his way across the hospital.

Ruth was waiting in the doctors' room for Richard. John Sutton had agreed to spend some time on each of the other wards, leaving the room free for Ruth to meet Richard. She had previously visited the library and borrowed some books with a variety of photographic plates of life in England across recent decades. She had used photographs before in therapy when asking patients to think about their earlier lives. Now she wanted to use the illustrations to see if she could jog his memory. The little information she had – that he had worked for the government, that he seemed skilled in metalwork and had expensive and well-crafted tools in his tallboy, that he had had a happy childhood, that he read history books about the war, that a civil service grandee such as Sir Francis Oates was a regular visitor to the hospital concerning him – was very puzzling. And so she marked the illustrations that she thought might coincide with these snippets of information: scenes of social and family life from the 1920s and 1930s, pictures of schools and factories, wartime photographs of cities that had been bombed, photographs of government buildings, in short anything that might overlap with the little she knew of the life of this mysterious man.

Richard knocked on the door of the room at around a quarter past three. Ruth smiled a little when she noted the time. He was as reluctant to communicate as ever, it seemed. Ruth encouraged him to sit and tried to make some small conversation about the hospital before she came to the crux of the discussion.

"I saw how hard you worked on Saturday evening," she said first, to which he nodded his agreement. "Have you been a trustee for a long time?" was her next attempt.

Richard took his time mentally calculating. "Five years," he answered.

"And you've seen a lot of things change?" Again he nodded.

"Does it worry people, the patients, when things change?"

"Sometimes. Some changes are good."

"I wanted to show you some pictures in these books. They show some of the changes that have occurred in your lifetime. I wondered what you might think about them. Would you tell me?" For the third time Richard nodded his head.

Ruth opened the books at the earmarked pages. She showed Richard one or two, and then came to a picture of a family, at home, in the 1930s. "What do you think of this one?" she asked.

Richard looked at the picture. There was a man sitting in an armchair, puffing a pipe and reading a newspaper. A woman was pouring a cup of tea, and the tea things were on a tray on a table. Two children were in the room, a girl reading at the table, and a boy playing with toys on the floor. Richard studied it. He looked up at Ruth.

"Father, mother, children," he said, "like mine, but no sister. Train set like mine." He pointed to the boy playing on the floor. It was indeed a toy train set that he was playing with.

Ruth turned the page and again leafed through a few illustrations before coming to a picture of London during the Blitz. A bomb had fallen on a row of houses, and they were partially demolished and burned out. Bricks were lying in a pile against the remaining walls of the houses. People were looking at the damaged buildings, and one woman was crying – perhaps the house in front of the woman was hers, and perhaps there were family members buried under the rubble. But Richard would not look at the photograph once he realised what the content of the picture was. He turned over the page containing it. "I don't like the picture," he said. Ruth reassured him, and turned over several more pages. One was of an American Air Force bomber. Richard stopped her turning the page over while he looked a little longer at the picture, but he said nothing.

Ruth next opened the book containing pictures of several large government buildings. She showed all of them to Richard.

"Do any of these seem familiar to you? Did you ever work in a building like one of these?" Richard turned back to a picture of a large office block. "One like this, Richard?" He nodded. He did not want to utter the lie, but he did not want to reveal the truth, so had picked the building most unlike any place in which he had ever worked. He nodded again.

"Richard, the visitor today told me that you once worked for the government. Can you tell me anything about that?" At first he shook his head, then he thought for a while. He remembered what he had said before. "Factory," he said, "making things."

"What kind of things? Can you remember that?"

"Machines. Machines, I think."

"Machines that did what, Richard? Try hard to remember."

"Aeroplanes? Perhaps aeroplanes?" Richard was trying to provide information that would coincide with what he believed Doctor Appleton already knew. But the anxiety that this effort caused was great, and Ruth could see he was becoming upset.

"I'll stop there, Richard. I don't want to disturb you. Why don't you go back to the ward and rest for a while. It must be hard work pushing that trolley around all day."

Ruth took out his notes and jotted down some details of what had taken place during the day. She was just finishing these when the superintendent appeared in the doorway. "Busy?" he asked.

"Yes, extremely busy. Doing all the reviews you asked for, and struggling with some of them."

"I'm grateful for your work, but I didn't really come to see you about the reviews. Tell me about them in a minute. The fact is, I've received a complaint about you, from a colleague, about events last Saturday, and I thought I should talk to you about it. Are we likely to be interrupted here?"

Ruth already had the sinking feeling in her stomach that she was beginning to think was a daily experience at Black Roding. She had feared the superintendent coming to see her, or being summoned to see him, but she had forgotten all about it because of the unusual events of the day. Now, she thought, she must be in deep trouble if the superintendent had come all the way to talk just to her. She motioned to an empty chair. But the superintendent shut the door and remained standing.

"I've received a report that surprised me greatly. It suggests that you attended the dance held in the theatre on Saturday night and that you were drinking all evening. By the end of the evening you had consumed so much that you fell over on the dance floor, dragging a patient with you and knocking against others. And that Doctor Smythe, who made the complaint, had to ask you to leave the dance. I was greatly surprised by the report. But I've asked one or two other people whom Smythe mentioned, a patient in the Admissions Unit for example, and the report appears to have some foundation. Before I decide what to do next, I thought I should ask you what happened."

Ruth was hardly able to reply. The superintendent asked her to wait until she had collected herself and then give him her answer. She therefore breathed deeply and tried to look at him calmly.

"I was not drunk. I was dancing, with a patient. It seemed rude to refuse him. Because of the patient we both fell over – I couldn't help it. Doctor Smythe is quite wrong. And if the admission unit patient is the woman I think it is, she has already attacked me verbally during a meeting, something which your staff did nothing to stop. So the allegations are completely false."

"I'm pleased to hear that there is another side to the allegation. But you can understand my position. I was surprised to hear that you might have been drinking excessively."

"I did have a few drinks because I was with some other staff. I didn't think there might be any such consequences as Doctor Smythe has alleged. I was just socialising with some people I had met. They were attending the dance and I agreed to join them. But I was not drunk." Ruth looked at the superintendent with an air of defiance.

"Good. I'm glad you are ready to defend yourself. I'll look into it further. And on the other matter, how are the reviews coming on?" The superintendent changed the subject so quickly that Ruth found it hard to return to professional matters.

"Yes," Ruth dropped her voice a little, "yes, I am doing them. I hope to have the first reports with you by Friday. It's been difficult…" Ruth thought of raising the problems she was facing with Richard, but decided that now was not the best moment to trouble the superintendent more with her problems. "I just can't always understand—"

"What that idiot Winstanley was doing? I can agree with you there. I couldn't understand most of the decisions he made, or didn't make, and I transferred some of his patients to other wards if I thought he was doing them too much harm, but only occasionally. Most of the time I could only try to encourage him, because he had powerful friends and a strong reputation. If I told him what to do, he'd get on to the Board and they'd tell me to back off. So if you think there have been misdiagnoses, or other odd things, don't hesitate to put that in your reports. I'll look further into that other matter." And with that, he left her.

The strength of the superintendent's feelings, and the extreme criticism of the dead colleague, once again amazed Ruth. She had not experienced a senior manager who was so prepared to offer criticism of others, and while it surprised her she also could not help but agree with him. Winstanley, it was already clear to her, had kept his little empire almost as a sinecure while he devoted more attention to his private practice. In doing so, he had not devoted the necessary work to looking after the needs of the patients, and in particular to trying to heal them, to enable them to resume a more normal life. She too had been critical of what she was finding in the files and records of patients, and had determined, despite the pressures of time, that it was indeed necessary to consider alternative approaches to the treatment of some of the patients. But at every turn she seemed to face new difficulties, ones she had never experienced before. And now these accusations by Smythe were a further concern. Ruth turned back to Richard's file and finished her notes – *Although a small amount of information has been provided by this visit, it has raised more questions about Richard's background, original symptoms and diagnosis than it has answered. His responses to some visual stimuli from the last three decades were limited. I thought that some of the wartime photographs did elicit a slight response but he did not say anything. At present, although he meets the criteria to be considered for outpatient treatment, a final recommendation cannot be made without more information.*

Ruth signed the notes and closed the file. There were other patients whose needs she also had to consider.

CHAPTER TWENTY-FIVE

Since he could not now resume his trolley round, and Doctor Sutton had asked him not to do anything that might agitate himself, Richard had told the nurses that he was going to walk around the grounds for a while. But instead of doing so, he had made his way to the trolley cupboard and into the underground passage to the water tower.

Even as he made his way through the dark passage his mind was in a tumult. He needed to think about the events of the day, but he could not think clearly while he felt that one or other of those assailing him might return to question him further. He was frightened that Doctor Appleton might discover something more, something that would reveal his identity to her. Some of the photographs in those books seemed to have been deliberately chosen, as if she had gained some knowledge about him. She had put bookmarks in specific pages, so her choices were not random. And yet he respected her attempts to unravel the truth even while he dissembled. She was doing her job properly. And it seemed that Sir Francis Oates had not told her anything directly, otherwise she would not still have been putting the photographic illustrations before him. But Oates was a different matter.

He sat at his rudimentary desk and wrote in the exercise book that served as a journal:

> Oates. I saw him come into the ward because I was looking at Doctor Appleton and he came in right behind her. Just on seeing him I felt as if someone had taken hold of my heart with icy fingers and squeezed hard. I almost choked, and felt tears welling up in my eyes. Why does he bring that response from me? Why do I fear him so much, and loathe him as well? He hurt me, for certain, by kicking me, but there were bullies in the playground who did that. I would not fear them if they appeared in front of me now. But then I do not remember their blows, whereas I can feel still the ribs he bruised, the pain in my chest, as if I am again lying on the floor of that room. But he hurt much more than my body. He hurt me! He damaged me! He changed me through the fear of what he could do to me, what he said would happen to me if I went to prison. Do you know what the other prisoners do to a man like you? he asked. In the toilets, in the showers, in your cell when the warders are distracted? And no, I did not know. But he told me. The fists that would beat me, the feet that would kick me, and worse, worse, that I would be assaulted and raped by men who would take advantage of me and mock me for what I am. That they would bring tools or sticks and thrust them into me. And that is why I fear him now. Once he had told me all this, he left me in that room, knowing what I might do. Yes, I fear a man who can get me to try that, to try to end my life through the anticipation of what he said would happen, not the actual deed. And because I still fear him, I must do what he decides is to be done. He clearly does not want me to leave the hospital. He questioned Sister O'Sullivan the moment I said that patients were going to leave. And he must have gone to find out more from the doctors. But what will happen now? What has he agreed with the doctors? Doctor Appleton is still

asking me questions. She does not seem likely to stop. So what will happen next? Will she make a decision, or will it be Oates who tries to change the situation? I had hoped to make some sense of things, but I am as uncertain as when I sat down to write. I hope for my quiet life here to continue. But I cannot see what will happen.

Richard shut the exercise book and put down his pen. He turned and looked out of the open window across the hospital grounds, in which just one or two patients were walking around the paths, and further across the trees that formed a boundary of the grounds, and then further still across the landscape that stretched across the suburbs and towards the centre of London. It was, as ever, a view in which he could lose himself and all that troubled him, and could think of the millions of other people going about their lives without a thought of the grief that he and others in the hospital suffered. He imagined in vague terms a life in which other decisions had been taken, both by him and by others. It could have been one cut short by warfare, as had happened to a couple of his classmates called to fight far away from home and never returning. But it could also have been a successful life, in which his work, his abilities and his knowledge had been rewarded. He might indeed have been like one of those millions in the houses, flats, factories, offices, parks and shops that combined into one amorphous body stretching to the limits of his horizon. He knew the lines of Shakespeare that would next come to mind, from his boyhood playing of Antipholus of Syracuse:

*I to the world am like a drop of water
That in the ocean seeks another drop
Who, failing there to find his fellow forth,
Unseen, inquisitive, confounds himself.*

And he knew that he would recall the schoolmaster who himself could not remember which of the two sets of twins should be appearing in a scene, and who would grab the script from the schoolboy prompt who attended every rehearsal and bellow out, "Syracuse! Damn you, boys, it's Antipholus of Syracuse here, not of Ephesus. Where are you, Simms?"

And the boys, who had deliberately mistaken their cues, would rock their shoulders with mirth and giggles as they corrected the error.

And then the moment of relief would pass, and he would come back to the confines of the water tower and the asylum, and to the constraints of his self-chosen imprisonment. He stood up and walked to the door, preparing for the darkness of his route back to the uncertainty of his situation.

Chapter Twenty-Six

"No, he hasn't said that? That's completely wrong! How could he?"

Frances's outrage was immediate and frank. Ruth had not been able to see her on the day of the superintendent's visit. She had been working on the reviews which had to be discussed just two days later by the doctors and senior nurses, and any other staff they could persuade to attend. On the Wednesday, David Peters was still not in. His wife was reported to be "feeling better" and he hoped to be in on Thursday. Ruth had cancelled the first general meeting on Ward 45 because she did not think she could cope with any additional issues arising from such a meeting when they were so short-handed. She had also warned the staff on Wards 46 and 47 that their meetings might also be cancelled, depending on David's attendance. She had held a number of one-to-one sessions with patients whose future treatments might be transferred to outpatients, or to care and supervision by local general practitioners. She was optimistic that the doctors and nurses would be able to agree to four of the cases she had been reviewing, and it was the paperwork on these four that she had been preparing. So it was not until late on Wednesday afternoon that she had managed to visit the office to tell Frances of Smythe's complaint.

"The bastard!" she added, and immediately said, "Sorry, I'm not sure my language is appropriate. But he is one!" Ruth could not help laughing at her friend's outrage. "It's no laughing matter, Ruth. It could be very serious."

"I know. I couldn't help laughing. You were so angry! But I was upset when the superintendent told me. What do you think I should do?"

"Let's just talk about this somewhere quiet. Come into the office. The others have left already."

The office was cramped, and cluttered with metal filing cabinets and open shelves. Four people usually worked there, and Frances's desk was the only one without a typewriter set in the middle. But unlike the other offices Ruth had visited during the previous week, it was clean and quite well-ordered. Frances pulled a chair over for Ruth to sit on. She was obviously thinking about Ruth's last question.

"I don't want to know the details, at least not at the moment. But I know a little about Smythe, and I can guess a little more. So let me just speculate a little. Saturday night was not the first time he'd spoken to you. He'd had some previous conversations with you, treated you nicely, was the first person to make you feel welcome and human in what is a strange and often scary place when you first arrive, and he asked you to come to his rooms, for a drink or coffee, or to listen to some music." Ruth was astonished, but nodded at almost every point in Frances's speculative account. She felt foolish that her own part in the narrative was so predictable, but it was reassuring that someone else at Black Roding could so understand what had happened to her. "And then he made a pass of some kind at you, just when you had relaxed and were not expecting it." Frances stopped and looked at Ruth, who gave one more nod. "But that's my speculation. Did you tell the superintendent anything of what happened?"

"No!" Ruth gasped. "I couldn't possibly have told him. How could I? And what would he think of me then? It might just make things worse."

Frances thought for a while. Ruth thought that she was weighing up various arguments, including what she herself had just said. "Don't do anything," she said, "at least not for a few days. I think I may be able to do something, so give me until next Monday. If nothing has happened by then, we'll talk again."

"But what will you do?"

"I don't think I should answer that. If I did someone could claim that you put me up to what I intend to do. So it's best if you don't know."

Ruth was doubtful, and her face showed it. "Don't worry," said Frances, "I'm sure I can do something." She looked up at the clock on the wall. "There's a bus due in fifteen minutes. I can just make it. Come with me now to Reception, while I go to leave. You can get back to your wards from there." She said this as she started to put on her coat. They walked down the stairs and through the small stretch of corridor that led into the reception hall. Frances was hurrying due to the need to walk down the drive in time for her bus. She turned to Ruth and said, "I am still determined to do something. I don't think it can do you any harm if I do. So wait and see what happens." She gave Ruth a confident smile and hurried away even more quickly towards the door.

Ruth was left standing in the middle of the hall for a few moments, as she wondered what on earth Frances could do to help her. She could protest Ruth's innocence to the superintendent, but that might not work, and it did not seem to be something to be secret about. Just as she was about to turn towards the West Wing, a voice interrupted her thoughts.

"Hello. Everything OK?" It was Michael, the biker and nurse from the Secure Block. "You seemed lost in thought for a minute there."

Ruth felt embarrassed to be discovered so hesitantly standing in the middle of the hall. "Oh, yes, I was. I was so busy I couldn't think what was needed next."

He smiled and did not make a joke of her embarrassment. "And did you decide?"

"Yes – more work, more work. It's work that's keeping me busy. I was about to go back to it."

"How are you finding things?"

Ruth did not know how to answer. She could have spent an hour or more telling him about her experiences, but she hardly knew him. She did not want to be indiscreet and did not want to reveal what Smythe had alleged, so she thought it better to keep her counsel. "It's been a challenge, I must admit. There have been some interesting parts and some difficult ones. And while I'm at work there is a great deal to be done."

"And on your days off? Are you busy then?" Ruth was surprised by the question. It did not seem just a casual part of their conversation. No-one had asked her such a question for many months.

"Oh, I'm still sorting myself out really. I only brought one case with me, so I've got to move more things down from Princes Risborough."

"Where's that? I don't know it."

"It's in Buckinghamshire. I suppose it's about forty miles, but you have to go into the centre of London and then back out. It takes a lot of time."

"Not on a bike, it wouldn't. I could take you there." Ruth looked at him more closely. Was he just chatting her up, or more genuinely offering help? "I said you should try riding the bike when we met you at Harry's… no, sorry, you don't know Harry… at the tea stall by the forest. Seriously, I could take you there to pick some things up, if you wanted, but only what I can get into the side panniers and you can carry on your back. Would you like to do that?"

Ruth was torn. He was obviously expressing some interest in her, but after the disastrous incident with Smythe on her first night Ruth was reluctant to accept any offer from one of the male staff of Black Roding.

"Could I think about it a little, and work out if it would be worthwhile? It could help me with some necessities, but I also have to get some accommodation sorted out here and move my furniture."

"Sure, but when are we talking about? I can't do this weekend but I could the Sunday after. What about you?"

"Yes, I could on that Sunday."

"So, how will you let me know? We could drive there in an hour, by the way."

Ruth thought for a while. She had a great deal of work to complete. She needed to find out if David Peters was going to be in work during the next two days. She needed to call the meeting for Friday morning and then complete the paperwork to hand it over on Friday to the superintendent. Four reviews completed in a week! Her old colleagues would never have believed it. If David Peters was back he would hold the two general meetings, and there might be issues to follow up. But she would be working over the weekend and could do some follow-up work then.

"Yes, I could let you know in the next few days. After I've seen the superintendent this Friday." Her voice fell slightly. She had momentarily forgotten about Smythe's complaint. The superintendent would no doubt have something to say about that on Friday. "Could I call you on the ward, or should I come over?"

"Come to the main desk in the block and ask for me. And I won't take you if it's raining. The bike's difficult in the rain, and it's not at all nice for someone on the pillion. But if it's fine, I'll take you. You need to wrap up warm, though. Two pairs of trousers, one over the other. And three or four layers on top." He laughed. "I don't usually tell people what to wear, but the bike is cold, much colder than the day might seem. So even if the sun's out, still take my advice."

"Thank you." Ruth was again surprised by his thoughtfulness. She didn't mind if he was interested in her, which surprised her. "I'll come to the desk next week." She smiled at him and turned to walk back to her office and the work she still had to do.

CHAPTER TWENTY-SEVEN

David Peters did come in the next day, and Ruth found him reading the notes that she and John Sutton had prepared. He looked worried and exhausted, she thought, and he explained that his wife was still ill but he had found a friend who could stay in their house for the morning and who would call if more assistance were needed. She had not slept well for four nights, and he was clearly afraid that she might be about to have a miscarriage. He would have to go home in the afternoon. Ruth asked if he wanted to postpone the general meeting on Ward 46, but he said no, not when the staff, including Ruth and John, had done so much to prepare the way. He would use the notes but would try to avoid raising any issues that might give Ruth and John problems to sort out in the coming days, since he might have to take more time off duty.

Ruth felt sympathetic towards David and the wife she had not met. Pregnancies could sometimes become difficult in all kinds of ways, and it was easy to see the need for a woman to be allowed rest and given support. Providing that help was also difficult for husbands. But the pressure on her and John Sutton could become intolerable if David missed too much time. Doing everything that the superintendent wanted was likely to raise new problems, and time-consuming work was needed to correct Winstanley's inadequacies. She briefly summarised the visit of Sir Francis Oates and its effect upon Richard. She reminded David that these were the initials that had been placed on Richard's file, and told him that it had been suggested that Richard had worked for the government in some unrevealed way. The mystery around their patient was, if anything, greater, and she had not been able to elicit any more information. But Oates had been an unpleasant, and rather threatening, visitor. She did not think the issue was going to go away. David, however, was only half-listening to her account, evidently thinking of his wife and unborn baby. She did not, therefore, press him for any further advice about Richard.

The general meeting went much the same way as the one chaired by David on the first day of the week. He was clearly skilled in sequencing the information that he believed the patients had to receive, so that there was time for them to accept it little by little. And he was concentrating on the meeting and did not seem as distracted as he had been in the office. Once again the news about reviews and the possibility of transfer caused some anxiety, and patients responded with their concerns. But the two patients on the ward whom Ruth was considering for movement had already been informed of this in her one-to-one sessions, and their reactions suggested that they still accepted what she had put to them, even if they were nervous. She herself was referred to when the patients acknowledged that they were being considered for movement. But they said she had talked to them about several possible options, and at one point David made clear to her by his approving nod that he was more than satisfied with the preparatory work she had done.

David kept the meeting short. He then convened the staff meeting immediately afterwards. In the meeting room he apologised for the relative brevity of the meeting, but explained his own personal situation and asked staff to keep Ruth informed of any developments. He reviewed all the responses of the patients, and some of the nurses also spoke about the patients. Ruth asked that the social workers and occupational therapists attend the review meeting two days hence because two of the patients in the general meeting were to be reviewed. Towards the end of the meeting one of the nurses who had been left in the ward brought in a message for David just as another nurse asked a question. Was it right, she asked, for all the patients to be taking a sedative at night? She understood that some patients might need one, but Sir Reginald had prescribed sedatives for all of them. Ruth had seen this on the files of the patients she had been reviewing, and it had been one cause of concern that needed to be discussed, so she did not mind the matter being raised now.

David was still reading the message, so she stepped in. "It is true," she said to the whole meeting, "that it may be necessary to prescribe sedatives for a period of time to certain patients, but a blanket policy of prescribing them for all is not good. It means that even those who do not need them are receiving them, and it builds up a dependency that may prevent treatment outside the hospital. Given the reviews that are taking place, perhaps we should follow the principle of the Admissions Ward and remove the sedatives while we consider which patients should then receive them once we've looked at the results."

David stood up. "I'm sorry," he said, "but I've been called away. I suggest that you do what Doctor Appleton has suggested and we review the matter again next week." He looked worried, and Ruth went up to him. "It's my wife again. I may have to take her back to the hospital. I am sorry that this is happening so much."

"You can't help that," Ruth replied. "Your place is with her, no doubt about that, when things are so difficult. Don't worry. We've managed so far, so I'm sure we'll continue to do so."

"I'll call later to say whether or not I'll be in tomorrow."

"If you're not, I might still hold the general meeting. It's Ward 47. I won't say anything about the ward merger and closure, but I will cover all the ground you did today. And then I will have to hold the review meeting. Unless everyone has their say tomorrow, we can't really take the results to the superintendent. Now, you should go, and quickly."

Ruth wished she was as confident as she had suggested she was to him. She brought the meeting to a close by asking that the nursing staff talk about the general meeting with the patients, and that in their discussions they prompt the patients to raise issues which were important to them. She was indeed learning from Sister O'Sullivan, just as the superintendent had told her she should.

Ruth left the room with John Sutton. When they were out of the hearing of the other staff he asked her, "Did David say anything else? Will he be in tomorrow?"

"I don't know. He doesn't know himself, I think. That's the problem when a pregnancy gets very difficult. You don't know where you are from day to day, even from hour to hour. So we'll just have to carry on tomorrow even if he isn't in. You were preparing the notes for Ward 47. Are they ready?"

"Yes, almost. I'll have them finished by three o'clock."

"Well, none of the patients from 47 are up for our review tomorrow. In fact I'll be confirming three of them as still in need of long-term treatment, since they had the worst scores on the nurses' survey, so I will meet some of the superintendent's targets. But I don't trust all the nurses completely. I would not be surprised if word of the ward closure and merger with 43 hadn't got out somehow. If it has we'll have to deal with it, but there would be no point in pretending it isn't happening. David was considering telling them next week anyway. So, if the patients do know or suspect it, we'll just have to deal with the anxiety now instead of next week. Are you tired, with all the work you've been doing?"

"Yes, it's been tiring, especially all the extra note-summarising and preparing people for the general meetings. But at least..." He stopped mid-sentence and caused Ruth to look at him more closely.

"At least what?" she asked.

"Well, I feel that, unlike when I started and Winstanley was here, there's something happening, something positive for the patients. That the work may be worth something and achieve something. I don't know what exactly, because it's too soon to know. But when I started I felt I was asked to be here just to keep everything the same and to make sure everything was under control. And that was all Winstanley wanted. Now some of the patients might be able to move on. So I don't mind doing more work, staying up late writing up notes, having more one-to-one sessions, talking to the patients more, whatever is needed. It's more tiring, but it's more satisfying."

Ruth was silent. She did not really know what to say in response. Since she arrived she had been troubled by much of what she had been asked to do, and indeed had been critical of the superintendent and of the hospital She had found it hard to adjust to the enormity of Black Roding and had not endeared herself to everyone. But her junior, who had experienced the hospital for longer than she, had exactly the opposite perception and emotions, and was excited by what he was involved in. She recognised that she might have to take on board John's very different ideas and shift her stance somewhat. She thought again of the boards in the superintendent's office, with the scribbled details of every ward and the doctors working on them. What view would he now have of Firm 9, the wards on which she was working?

CHAPTER TWENTY-EIGHT

Richard had never gone all the way through the trees that were at the furthest boundary of the hospital's grounds. They were cultivated by the gardeners where they were at the fringe of the lawns and open grass so that one could penetrate any barrier they represented. He himself had sought shade there on hot summer days and had sat among them to read a book or newspaper. But he knew that the cultivation stopped after twenty or thirty yards, and a combination of thick, thorny bushes, saplings and older trees made it much harder to walk through. Beyond the thick growth must be the continuation of the high walls that ran down the two sides of the open parkland that patients used for their walks.

He had come here with a newspaper after his morning round, having eaten just a roll and a piece of cheese in the patients' canteen. He did not know why exactly, but he had thought during the previous evening, after all that had happened and was threatened, that he should seek out a means of escape from the hospital in case one was needed. He knew about the porters at the front gate, and he realised they were likely to know all the patients who had exeats allowing them to leave through the gates each day. Although he might be able to steal such an exeat from another patient, they would know him from seeing him so often around the hospital, and that he would not have an exeat that allowed him suddenly to leave the grounds for the first time. The stolen card was likely to be grubby and worn, not brand new as it would be if his status had suddenly changed.

If the front gate represented a problem, and the metal fencing and walls that ran along the front of the grounds also did not seem climbable, he had to find another way out. The stories and anecdotes of patients over the years had suggested that the asylum did not maintain the wall behind the trees well, since those responsible for security believed that the thick undergrowth would deter any patients who suddenly sought escape. So he had decided to walk the length of the undergrowth and to discover if any fox or badger runs might allow him to gain access to the rear wall of the hospital. The weather was in his favour. It was another clear day when the autumn sunshine had driven away the mists, and patients had been allowed to walk the grounds from mid-morning. He had walked quickly down the eastern path to near the forest's edge, and had then sat on a bench and studied what was happening around him, pretending to browse through the newspaper. There were only one or two patients who had walked down as far as he had done, and none of them were accompanied by nurses or orderlies. Within a few minutes he had judged it safe to walk into the trees and to reach the point where the thicker growth made it hard to walk further.

At first he was disappointed in his search. There was a path just visible in the scrub grass between the bushes, but it ran parallel to the undergrowth and not into it. He followed it, hoping that at some point it would turn into the thorns and brambles that limited him, but it went on in the same direction, never wavering to the left. Once or twice Richard approached the thickets, to see if there might be any way through. But even to approach the wall of brambles was to have thorns pulling at his sweater and trousers. He would not get five yards before he was forced to stop and untangle himself.

As he came to the western end of the animal track he realised that the gardeners and builders employed by the hospital had been doing some work on the wall. The flowers and small bushes that marked the boundary between the patients' path and the wall had been trampled down, and the brickwork had been repointed. The new mortar was still light grey, not weathered and moss-strewn as the eastern wall had been. And to take their work further, the men had cleared the undergrowth away from the wall as it stretched away towards the rear of the grounds. He was able to walk fifty or sixty yards down the cleared wall, and soon reached the point where the work had stopped. He looked at the wall. It was twelve feet high, and the brickwork and mortar were smooth and would not readily allow even a foothold, let alone somewhere to grip with his hands. He could not scale it. But just where the thicker growth started, one tree had grown more dominant than the saplings around it, and its third branch stretched towards the wall and overreached it. If he could climb the tree, he might be able to slide along the branch and drop onto the top of the wall. Provided that the wall was no higher on the other side, he could drop down by clinging to the top and easing his body down to a stretch, before letting go of his grip. The drop would be just four or five feet, he reckoned, no difficulty in his youth but probably still a challenge now.

He took hold of the trunk of the tree and looked for somewhere to put his first foot. Then he looked up and saw that the first branch was just within reach. By pulling himself up he managed to get sufficient purchase with his feet to scramble up so that he could reach the second branch. He hadn't climbed a tree since he was a boy, and then he had been several stone lighter and much more nimble. But once he had a grip on the second branch he was again able to find toe-grips on the rough bark of the tree and to haul himself up. And when the third branch was in contact with his stomach, and his arms were straight, he could lean forward and pull one of his legs to straddle the branch. And seated there, he was able to edge forwards, and he was sure that, if he wanted, he could get as far as the wall and slide off the branch onto the top of the wall. All he needed for the moment was to edge forwards, to try to check the length of the drop on the other side. So he simply slid along the branch in his awkward seated position. The branch bent downwards and creaked in protest at his weight, but it held up and did not crack. Richard looked up and down the wall. He could not see the drop immediately next to the wall, but the ground beyond the wall appeared to be on the same level as on the hospital side. So he edged back and then repeated in reverse the step-by-step route he had taken up the tree, dropping to the lower branches and then stretching down the trunk. But this time he slid down the trunk, scraping his knees and hands against the bark and falling down as he landed. He lay on the floor for a few moments, winded a little by the fall and making sure that the pain in his ankle which he had felt on landing was indeed passing. It was, but not completely, and he realised he must have turned his foot over as he landed, twisting the ankle sharply and spraining it. He stood up gingerly and felt the weight on his leg. It was bearable – nothing broken, then – but still hurt. And so he had to limp slightly as he returned to the hospital, and he had to brush himself down before he emerged from the trees. His clothes were dirty from the contact with the bark, and from falling on the ground, and his shoes were more scuffed than ever. He would have to put up with a swollen ankle while he completed his trolley round because to refuse to do the work would bring yet more attention to him.

CHAPTER TWENTY-NINE

It had taken Ruth at least half an hour to fall asleep every night in the barren doctor's emergency sleeping room she had been given. Each night she realised that another day had passed and she still had not done anything about changing the room, which made her feel depressed; and with that feeling taking over her she could not fall asleep easily even though she was tired. The hospital was physically demanding, just through its size and the necessity of climbing stairs to move from one ward to another. But emotionally and mentally she was often too anxious to fall asleep easily.

She had fallen asleep after a troubled half hour, but in the night she was woken by a hammering on her door. At first she did not realise what it was, and she let her head slip down on the pillow again. But two further loud raps on the door startled her, and she sat up.

"What is it?" she called from her bed.

"It's Ward 46, Doctor. We've got some hysteria on the ward."

The message was given loudly but not shouted. It was clearly urgent.

Ruth got up and unlocked the door. It was one of the nurses from the ward. "What's happening?" asked Ruth.

"It's because we didn't give any sedatives tonight. Some of the patients couldn't sleep. They started complaining, and woke up the others who had fallen asleep. Suddenly we had the whole ward crying out for sedatives, but we can't give them any unless you come and sign the order. Doctor Sutton signed the order stopping them after the meeting in the morning, when it was decided. We're worried it will spread to other wards, because some of the patients have got out of bed."

Ruth could hardly remember. She was still feeling dazed from being woken up. She had a vague memory of suggesting the withdrawal of a blanket regime of sedatives but could not recall what had happened after that. "Just let me get dressed. Get back to the ward. I'll be right behind you." The nurse turned and left hurriedly.

Ruth put on the same clothes she had discarded when coming to bed. She was all the time trying to recall what exactly had been decided. The fact that all the patients were receiving sedatives had been raised by a nurse. Yes, that had happened. Then she had said that a blanket policy was wrong and that the sedatives should be withdrawn. Yes, she had said that, but she had not followed it up with any further suggestions or amendments. And she had not made a final decision. But she could not recall whether or not such a decision had been made, and by whom. She was still pulling a jumper on as she left her room, and she ran part of the way towards the ward. At least it was nearby, she thought.

When she arrived the scene was chaotic. There were only two nurses on night duty on the ward, and they were both near the door of the ward, clearly positioned to stop any patients leaving. In front of both, some of the patients had gathered, and since the ward was all female it reminded Ruth instantly of the scene the superintendent had recalled being typical of the asylum years ago. The women were all in their nightdresses, mostly long cotton shifts that gave their shrieks and cries a ghostly aspect. Their hair was loose and unkempt, and some were indeed showing signs of hysteria, crying hysterically and shouting out their pleas for sedatives.

The nurses were struggling to contain the patients and were, step by step, moving backwards towards the door. Further down the ward she could see that other patients were near their beds, or sitting on the edge of beds, crying in a similar vein. It resembled a nightmare, and Ruth needed to take control and to subdue the feelings of the patients.

Ruth stood between the two nurses and faced the patients. "Go back to your beds," she said, but her voice could not be heard above their collected shrieks. "Please, go back to your beds," she said more loudly. But still there was no reaction, and the ten or twelve patients who were crowding them now pushed against them. They were next to the nurses' desk, the final point that guarded the ward. Beyond that the patients would be out in the corridor, patients in Ward 45 would hear them, and the hysteria could spread.

Ruth knew that under the counter of the nurses' desk was a handbell, which was used to signal meals and other key moments in the day. She shouted to the nurse who was nearest to the desk, "Get me the handbell!" and moved over to cover the gap left by the nurse.

The nurse walked quickly to the desk, looked underneath and grabbed the bell. She handed it to Ruth. The patients were almost at the door. Ruth shook the bell, violently at first, so that the peals caught everyone's attention, and then less vigorously as she realised that the cries had started to die down. The noise of the handbell distracted the patients, who were used to gathering for meals when it rang. They looked around for the food trolleys that would normally be in the ward when the bell was rung. Their cries became less loud, and one or two stopped pushing against Ruth and the nurses and turned back into the ward. She kept ringing the bell and pointed back into the ward. Now others followed the first patients in going back towards their beds. There was less pressure on the two nurses, so Ruth skirted around the whole group in the melee and went towards the centre of the ward. Gradually the patients there started to look at her, and those at the door followed her.

When she judged that the patients were sufficiently quiet, and were for the most part looking at her as the source of this untimely pealing, she stopped shaking the bell.

"All right, everyone!" She tried to project her voice so that it was not a shout, but just authoritative. "All right. We will give out some sedatives in a minute. But we need everyone who wants a sedative to be seated in the chair by their bed, so please go to the chairs by your beds."

The two nurses quickly grasped what Ruth was attempting to achieve and ushered the patients towards their beds. They spoke to individual patients, encouraging them with the promise of the sedatives. Ruth stopped one of the nurses and said, "Get the right sedatives from the drugs cupboard. I'll keep getting them back to their beds." The nurse turned back, because the drugs cupboard was near the entrance to the ward. The other nurse had moved further into the ward, while Ruth stayed nearer to the door, in case any of the patients nearest to the door should suddenly decide to leave their bed again. But the promise of sedatives seemed to be working, and the nurse had reached the far end of the ward.

Ruth helped the nurse to start to issue them, and as she worked her way down the ward she signed an instruction for each patient to restore the sedatives, at least for the interim. It took a while to reassure the patients that everything was in order and that there would not be any more sudden changes. Some of them took longer to actually swallow the drugs than she would have thought possible, so that at least an hour must have passed from her being woken to the three of them completing the drugs round and quietening the last remaining patients.

"I am sorry we didn't anticipate that," Ruth said to the nurses.

"It was a bit drastic, wasn't it? Stopping all the sedatives, all at one time?" one of them asked.

"Yes, with hindsight it was. But even now you can see that not all the patients need a sedative."

"We'll have to tell Sister, you know, when the day team comes on duty."

"Yes. Do tell her. I'll come and see her myself if I have time." Inwardly Ruth groaned. Another member of the hospital to whom she would have to give an account of her actions. And it would help if she could remember how the final decision had been taken, but she did not want to ask the nurses. That might create even more problems. She would need to ask John Sutton what he could remember and why he had signed off the changes to the drugs. Wondering if now she would be able to get back to sleep, Ruth looked at the clock. It was half past two. If she couldn't sleep, she thought, she would just get back up and carry on with all the paperwork piled up in the tray on her desk.

CHAPTER THIRTY

Ruth had managed a couple of hours more sleep but, awake by half past six, she had dressed again and visited each of the wards before going to breakfast. Ward 46 was quiet after the group hysteria of the night, and Ruth confirmed that she would come back to see the ward sister later in the day. In Ward 47 the staff were preparing for the general meeting and were encouraging the patients to wake, wash, get dressed and have breakfast so that they would be ready.

In Ward 44, however, she was asked to read over a note on Richard's file, to the effect that the nurses had noticed that he was limping badly the evening before and that his clothes were mud-stained and dirty. He had told them reluctantly that he had fallen while walking in the grounds and that he had completed his afternoon round with the injury. But they did not think that the staining on his clothes could have been the result of just a fall, and his shoes were badly scuffed, much more so than usual. He had never presented in a similar state to the best of their knowledge. They were therefore concerned that he might have been involved in some kind of fracas out on the grounds, although nobody had reported a brawl. Ruth knew that inevitably patients were sometimes involved in fights, but the more serious attacks were usually confined to the Secure Block. She had not heard or read any suggestion that Richard might be involved in aggression. It would surprise her if he had been violent, given his usual symptoms and demeanour, but then as a psychiatrist nothing should really surprise her. Patients were capable of all kinds of strange things. Nonetheless it added to her interest in the patient, who seemed capable of surprising the staff at every turn.

In the doctors' room she turned her attention to the general meeting scheduled for Ward 47. The patients there were among the most uncommunicative in her care. They had often been moved into the basement ward when doctors and nurses on other wards gave up hope of recovery, and the patients were more institutionalised and more dependent on drugs than on the other wards. Ruth had not found a single patient whom the survey identified as immediately worth considering for transfer, but she wanted to know more about some of them because she strongly suspected they had been the victims of misdiagnoses. The survey forms returned by the nurses did not always describe the patients in terms that matched their original diagnoses, and some of them, she thought, might improve if she could devote enough time to re-evaluating them. But she would need David to be in the hospital more; and changing treatments, which principally meant changing drugs, could cause dramatic and unanticipated consequences.

She had prepared notes on the patients for David, but had also provided a note about her initial thoughts about the patients as a whole. She was hoping that David would make it in for the general meeting because she was not looking forward to chairing it if he could not attend. The patients would need a lot of encouragement to participate, and there was a risk that the meeting could fall flat if the doctors and staff could not elicit sufficient responses. She was just checking all her notes when David Peters surprised her by entering the room.

"Hello, Ruth," he said. "I'm sorry I've not been in."

"How is everything?" Ruth asked, a little nervous of what his reply might reveal.

"It's still OK. There's not been a miscarriage. But it was a bit touch-and-go. I managed to find someone to stay with her today, but it looks as if the difficulties are going to continue. I'll have to see the superintendent about it today. It must be putting a great strain on you and John."

"If it's any comfort, I think John is enjoying the additional responsibilities. He was very enthusiastic yesterday, pleased that some changes are taking place to benefit patients. And I, well, I don't really have anything else to distract me, do I? So we have been getting on with things."

"And has everything been all right? Any problems?"

"I had one problem in the night. I don't remember how we made the decision so quickly, and I haven't seen John to check with him, but Ward 46 stopped all the sedatives last night. It was because of what we'd been talking about just when you had to leave the general meeting. But the patients didn't like their sedatives all being stopped simultaneously, and there was hysteria on the ward. I was called in at around one thirty, I would think, and it took us an hour to calm everyone down. I put them back on sedatives and said I'd go back to the ward today. Can you remember what was said in the meeting?"

"Hardly. I was so worried on receiving the note, I just wanted to get out. Let me think." David recounted for himself what had happened in the meeting. "One of the nurses said that all the patients were receiving sedatives. I remember that. Then you said that such a policy was probably wrong. Oh, and you mentioned the no-drugs policy in the Admissions Unit, where we try to start again with what drugs patients really need. And then the note came in and the meeting ended, at least for me. But in handing over to you, I might have said that the nurses should do whatever you tell them. Maybe that's how it came about, if the nurses thought I'd simply approved the policy by saying that. You'd better ask John what happened."

"Yes, I will. I know he signed off all the changes. But he must have thought the same as the nurses, that we had decided it. Not that I think it was such a bad idea, but it seems we would have been better talking to the patients about it. Live and learn, I guess," she finished with a sigh.

"Live and learn? How do you mean?"

"Well, the more I live here, the more I learn about how best to do things. But I seem to learn it too late – the damage is already done!"

"No, that's nonsense. We all have to learn about the patients and how best to treat them. And you must have had the superintendent tell you that he doesn't think that Black Roding does things in the best of ways. You know, when he starts to say, 'it was built in the wrong place, in the wrong way, and gave the wrong treatments…'"

Ruth laughed. She had not thought of David as having a sense of humour particularly, but his mimicry of the superintendent's voice, manner and emphases was undoubtedly accurate. "Yes, on my first day," she laughed again. "That's just what he said. He must say it to everybody."

"Yes, including the minister apparently, when he told him he was right to try to close us down, even though it would cost him his job. Well, that's what people say he said."

"Anyway, I'm glad you're back for this meeting. Ward 47 doesn't seem likely to give us a lot of people chattering during the meeting, and I was worried about it just fizzling out if I was chairing it. John and I prepared you some notes, and there's a general note you might want to read, though I suspect you would think the same as me anyway. I'm not sure that all the original diagnoses are correct, and I think that some of the treatments need urgent review. So there's plenty more work to be done. I'm going to go for some breakfast."

Ruth walked quickly through the corridors. She could not help herself wondering again about Richard. There were so many questions she couldn't answer. Apart from the fact that he had tried to commit suicide, that he appeared to have worked for the government and that an important government officer had visited the hospital at six-monthly intervals, she could say very little else with any certainty. What was wrong with him? Where had he come from? What family did he have; what doctor had referred him to the hospital and to Winstanley; what did he want to happen to him; was whatever trauma that had led to the suicide attempt now long past? And most important for her, what should she do about him? How could she find out any more? Perhaps, she thought, she should ask the superintendent for advice, even if it meant appearing a little incompetent, not up to the task, because the concerns about him were mounting.

She was walking down the central corridor as she was asking herself all these questions, and not taking much notice of those people also on the corridor with her. She realised, however, that the tall man in front of her, with the stooping gait and now a limp, was indeed Richard himself. He in his turn must be on the way to the patients' canteen before doing his rounds. His limp was quite pronounced, and Ruth walked around him and turned back to speak to him.

"Good morning, Richard. How are you?"

Richard looked startled, even frightened. He backed away from her.

"I'm sorry, Richard. I didn't mean to startle you. I wondered how you were. I heard you hurt your ankle."

"No," he blurted, "no, not badly hurt, not badly hurt." He looked around as if seeking a way to get away from her. She stood aside and let him walk on. He was still limping, but less than before. It seemed to be a conscious effort on his part, but the consequence was that he walked even more slowly than usual. She let him turn into the patients' canteen, and she herself went for breakfast.

The doctors' dining room was unusually busy. Ruth could see only a couple of empty seats, and she took one opposite someone reading *The Daily Telegraph*. She could not see the person at first, and had turned to look for the waiter, and it was only when she turned back to the table that she realised she had sat down opposite Oliver Smythe. His face reddened the moment he saw her, and she guessed that hers must have done so also. She did not know what she should do, but the looks on both their faces had attracted the notice of other doctors nearby. His eyes bore a hatred that Ruth did not remember ever experiencing before. They seemed intent on cutting into her, but she was not prepared to give way to him just because he looked at her in an evil way. He leaned forward, and hissed in a soft but malevolent whisper, "Fucking bitch!"

If she could have stood up then and left at that moment, she would have done, but her legs seemed for the moment to have disconnected from her body. She sat still and stared back at him. Then, in as clear a voice as she could muster, she said, "Really, Doctor, if you must use such language so early in the morning, perhaps you should breakfast in your room." And hoping that her legs would now obey her, she stood up and went to sit at the other empty seat on the other side of the room. But she saw the doctor sitting next to Smythe smiling to himself – perhaps he had heard Smythe's whispered oath after all.

CHAPTER THIRTY-ONE

The day went well for Ruth, or at least it had gone well until mid-afternoon. But now she would have to go to see the superintendent, and she was dreading what he might say about the original incident with Smythe. And what if Smythe had made some further complaint about her after the incident at breakfast?

David Peters had chaired both the morning meetings before he had to leave, telling Ruth that he was going to talk to the superintendent before he went home. The general meeting for Ward 47 had not been easy, as Ruth had anticipated. The patients, and some of the nurses, were very reluctant to join in the discussion at all, or indeed even to listen to it, and David had allowed several long pauses to develop while waiting to see if someone would break the silence. Ruth had noted, however, that there were two or three patients who did follow closely what was said, and who by the few words spoken indicated that they were not beyond hope. David had not broached the topic of merging wards, indeed he might even have been asking the superintendent how quickly he should proceed in the light of his wife's difficulties and their impact on his work. But he had asked if there was anything that patients felt strongly about, and that was the point at which some of the patients – just two or three – said that they hated being in the basement. And that was what Ruth had particularly noted. At the staff meeting the issue of the merger had not been raised. Ruth was not sure that the proposal had remained confidential, but she was grateful that the meeting did not become mired in conflict around that particular part of their planned work. There was enough to deal with as it was.

Then they had held the review meeting. David had asked Ruth to speak about each of the four patients she was recommending be moved, and to explain her reasons. She referred to the original diagnoses and treatments, to the length of stay of each patient and their family (or lack of family), and then explained her evaluation of the evidence from the survey of nurses and her own one-to-one discussions with the patients. She had concluded that one patient had been the victim of a misdiagnosis and that residential care was not needed, and that the other three patients had made sufficient progress for it to be worthwhile encouraging them to live outside the hospital but still be attached to the wards for outpatient care. They could self-administer the drugs they were taking, and they had some family or friends with whom there would be social contact. The nurses were invited to say anything they wanted to add, which several of them did, and then the occupational health officer and the social worker were invited to explain the implications of the recommended move. At her previous place of work, one such review would have taken up two hours, but here the whole process hardly lasted longer than that. Ruth's main concern was that one of the nurses had said that they – the nurses – had not understood how the surveys might be used and that she was concerned that other patients who were not ready to be moved would be moved on if the survey had been too positive. Ruth had tried to reassure her that it had to be based on a reconsideration of diagnosis, treatment and progress, but did not think she had been successful. She could see that the speed with which she was undertaking the reviews and making these recommendations was not allowing the nursing staff to understand the process. After years of inaction both patients and staff were held captive by the inertia that had characterised these wards. But the staff had seemed to accept that the first four recommendations were soundly based and were in the interests of the patients. And Ruth did not think that she was making any recommendations about these four that would have been different even if she had had more time to undertake the reviews.

Ruth signed the top sheets that would go with the recommendations for each of the patients and would mark her own professional commitment to them. They would only need now to be signed by the superintendent, since he had asked to be involved in these rather than the more normal practice of the consultant's signature being sufficient. She believed that in the circumstances she had done everything she could to conduct the reviews properly, but she still felt some misgivings about making such potentially life-changing recommendations when she had only been at the hospital for twelve days. But it was time to set her misgivings aside and take the papers to the superintendent.

Ruth walked as quickly as she could through the two corridors that brought her to the reception hall. Having completed the reviews, the last thing she wanted was to find that the superintendent had left the hospital early, for a meeting or some such commitment, and that he would not receive the outcomes of her work. The size and surroundings of the hall no longer caused her to pause as she entered from the corridor: she noticed that herself as she marched through. She went straight to Mrs Rogers' office, but was surprised on opening the door to find that what was normally a centre of orderliness and administrative efficiency had more the feel of a theatrical farce. The superintendent and Mrs Rogers were entering and exiting the office in a rush, locating some papers in the office and others in the superintendent's room beyond, and piling them on any spare space they could find. They hardly noticed her, until Mrs Rogers looked up after placing a number of files on one of the chairs near the door. She was flustered and rather red-faced, again quite unlike the appearance she had first presented when Ruth arrived at the hospital.

"Is everything all right?" Ruth asked.

"Oh, oh yes, it's all right. But we've suddenly got a lot to do. The superintendent has been asked to replace another superintendent on a government visit to the United States, and he's agreed to go. But he has to give a lecture during the trip. And he needs lots of papers. Which would be easy if they were papers from *this* office, but is not so easy because they're all in there." She pointed in the general direction of the superintendent's office.

"When does he leave?" Ruth asked, anxious that her reviews should still be processed despite this unexpected and chaotic scene. Mrs Rogers stopped. Ruth could hear in the office beyond that the superintendent was still searching through documents, perhaps even books.

"On Monday morning. But he has to prepare the lecture over the weekend and wants to take all the references away with him tonight. As you can see, it's a bit difficult to find everything. If it was just hospital papers, but it's all the academic references…"

Ruth hardly knew what to say. The world of international conferences was beyond her experience. The superintendent came into the office again and stopped when he realised Ruth was there.

"Oh yes," he said, "we do have some business to sort out, don't we, Doctor Appleton? You can see that we've been a little inconvenienced by agreeing to help the ministry out of a rather difficult situation. I have to stand in for another superintendent next week, so we're looking for a lot of things that are needed."

"Yes," Ruth said, "Mrs Rogers told me. It sounds… er… exciting, I suppose. To go to America, that is."

"It doesn't feel exciting at the moment. In fact it feels like far too much work, under intolerable pressure."

"Then why go?" Ruth could not help but ask; she was genuinely puzzled.

"A good question. Because, well, because it's the ministry that's asked me, and someone in my position can't easily say no to the ministry. They have plans for all the asylums, and I think the overall plans are right; but when the time comes for those damned civil servants to make crucial decisions about us, I want to be the superintendent who helped them out of a hole, not the one who left them further in it. They've promised that a superintendent will speak in Chicago, so I will do so, even if it means putting up with all the problems of conjuring a lecture out of nowhere in two days. Now, we had some business to sort out, didn't we?"

"Yes, I brought you the four reviews you wanted done by today." Ruth lifted the four bundles of paper attached to the patients' files that were the culmination of her work in the past fortnight. "You asked for them to be ready for today," she added.

"Yes, I did. And I will have to sign them tonight and leave them for you. Are you on tomorrow?" Ruth nodded to show that she was indeed working the next day. "I'll return them to the wards tonight. I can't have them hanging around or getting caught up with all this." He smiled at Ruth. "Well done. You've kept the deadline very well."

Ruth felt as if this word of congratulation was a cue for her to leave, but she did not want to wait for the superintendent's return from his transatlantic trip to know what was happening about the Smythe incident. "Isn't there something else?" she asked awkwardly.

"Is there?" he asked. He thought for a few moments and then seemed to realise what she meant. "Oh, Smythe. That's all over. He dropped the complaint. Yes. Said he'd obviously misunderstood the situation. So, there is no complaint, nothing for me to do or for you to worry about."

Ruth was astonished. She had so feared that the outcome would be bad for her that she had not imagined the complaint could be dropped so quickly. "Good," she managed to say. "I'm glad. I hope it was not too much trouble."

"No trouble at all, in the end. Though now I think of it, there is one other matter."

The exhilaration Ruth had briefly felt was dissipated immediately. "What?" She tried to keep the anxiety out of her voice. "What is it?"

"The ward sister from 46 reported a case of group hysteria in the night. It can happen from time to time, and it used to happen a very great deal. But she seemed to be suggesting that it was somehow your fault."

"No, no, it wasn't… or perhaps it was. I did play a part. It was a mistake."

"Well, that sounds like no, yes, someone else, and me! I'm confused. Tell me quickly what happened."

Why did everything go wrong for her? thought Ruth. But she had to reply. "I found out, in a staff meeting, that there was a blanket policy of sedatives for everyone. I suggested that we should consider doing what was done in the Admissions Unit, and withdraw the drugs, and then re-prescribe them only when we'd considered it all. But it was only a suggestion. The nurses thought we'd made it an instruction. And the sedatives were withdrawn without notice. So when some of the patients couldn't sleep, they woke others up and the hysteria started."

"So you saw it, then. It can be pretty frightening. That's what some of the wards were like all the time when we started to make changes." The superintendent stopped and looked at her. "Would you do it differently another time?"

"Yes. I'd not let a suggestion become an instruction without much more discussion and planning. I'd explain to the patients why the change was being brought in, and I'd ask for their co-operation. Maybe get some of the patients to do it voluntarily."

"But you wouldn't change your intention? You'd still want to end the blanket policy?"

Ruth bridled a little at the suggestion. "No, I would not change my intention. Ending the blanket policy is the right thing to do." Ruth gave the superintendent a challenging look. He for a moment did not reveal his thoughts. Then he smiled again.

"Good," he said. "If you'd said you would return to the blanket policy I'd have returned you to Buckinghamshire. But David said how well you were managing the work, and I think he's right. Your suggestion had a sound scientific basis, but it was always going to be difficult to implement without a lot of preparation. You've learned a lesson about the human side of it, but your medicine was completely right. The blanket policy, I take it, was Winstanley's? I hate to speak badly of the dead, but that man… Now, I must get on with all this. Thank you, Doctor."

He turned back to go into his room again, so Ruth thought it best to leave. It was only later that evening, as she again went through what had been said, that she remembered she had meant to ask the superintendent if he knew anything about Richard, her mysterious patient.

Ruth went straight from the superintendent's office to that of Frances and the administrative team upstairs. She was amazed that Smythe had backed off, just as Frances had suggested he would, and she wanted to ask what she knew about it. The office was noisy, with two typewriters clattering and the Gestetner machine humming as it churned out copies. Frances was seated at her desk and studying a set of papers, sometimes using a small calculating machine that sat on the desk. Ruth was able to watch the office at work for a time before Frances looked up and saw her. She smiled, completed a calculation she had started and scribbled something on a pad. Then she ushered Ruth out of the office and along the corridor to a bench seat that was obviously left for people who had to wait for an appointment in one of the offices. "There's no-one waiting now, it's Friday afternoon," she said. "How is everything?"

"It's surprisingly good," Ruth said. "The superintendent just praised my work." She waited for the effect of this to work on Frances, but she seemed unimpressed.

"I should think he should," Frances said. "He's a good judge."

"But more importantly, he told me that Smythe had dropped his complaint about me. Just dropped it, the whole thing, all over."

Frances tried to remain as cool over this news as she had been about the superintendent's praise. But she could not prevent the small suggestion of a smile passing across her lips. "Good," Frances said, "he's probably been a good judge there as well."

"Who? The superintendent or Smythe?" Ruth sensed that she was being played with a little.

"Why, both of them, I suppose."

"Come on, Frances, you know something, or you did something. What is it?"

"I did help to move things along a bit. I went to visit him in his rooms."

Ruth gasped. "No! You didn't? What, to talk about me?"

"Eventually," Frances still teased her with partial information.

"Tell me! Stop tormenting me!" Ruth too was feigning a false anger.

"I went to talk to him, I said, about the administration of the dances. He invited me in, offered me a drink, I took it but poured most of it into a pot plant. Then I took another drink and did the same, and a third. And then he made a pass at me!"

"Oh God! Just like with me! Except I... I..."

"You... what?"

"Well, I drank the wine."

"Yes, well, you weren't to know, were you?"

"What happened?"

"I poured his drink over his head." This was said in so matter-of-fact a tone that Ruth had to ask her to repeat it. "I poured his drink over him." Ruth's mouth fell open, and she did not immediately correct her gape. Frances continued, "I told him that I'd report him for molesting me while I was working. He started to protest and whinge, but then I told him that I knew he'd done exactly the same to another member of the hospital staff and that he'd then complained about her. I said that if he withdrew his complaint I would not report him, provided that I never again heard of him molesting a female member of staff. Oh God, Ruth, you should have seen him. He went white... except where the drink had run down his face. Then he got angry – accused me of conspiring against him – then he started whinging again. But the upshot was that I said that if I did not hear that the complaint had been withdrawn, I'd make my complaint against him. So, he must have thought about it and decided to withdraw."

"That explains it!" Ruth said. "That explains why he was so angry with me in the dining room this morning. He was poisonous, swearing at me openly."

"I guess you'll have to live with that. We've both made an enemy. But I think it's better than doing nothing. He had you on the back foot because we'd all been drinking and enjoying ourselves, I guess, and as the senior doctor in attendance at the dance he would have been listened to, even by the superintendent. Better not to have a disciplinary case brought against you, I think."

Ruth reflected on this for a few moments. In some ways she would have preferred to have cleared her name and reputation with the superintendent more openly, but she could understand the weight of Frances's argument. She had only been at the hospital a week. She had placed herself at risk by drinking alcohol which she was not accustomed to, and Smythe's motives had been so malevolent. But he would have wished her harm even if she had successfully defended herself, and this way there was indeed no disciplinary case on her record. So, on balance, she was grateful to Frances.

"Thank you," she said warmly, "thank you for beating him. He deserved it. And he hates me anyway, so that's unchanged. But now he hates you as well."

"I can live with that." Frances was confident in her tone. "Next time I'll pour a drink over him in public!" They both laughed at the thought. "Now," said Frances, "there's one more thing I must ask." Ruth could not think what more there was, and looked inquisitively at her. "Is it really true that you are going bike riding next weekend? On the back of Michael's motorbike?" Frances had returned to her stiff-lipped teasing tone.

Ruth laughed but could not stop the slight blush on her face. "Oh, yes, I was thinking of it. How did you know?"

"He asked me if I thought it was all right for him, a male nurse, to be driving you, a doctor, around on his bike. He didn't want you to be seen in a wrong way by anybody. He's conscious of the great divide between doctors and nurses in some matters and that what he suggested to you was definitely unusual. That's all."

"So, what did you say to him?"

"I said I thought it would be great for you to get your things without having to spend a whole day on trains. And I said I'd tell you—"

"What?" Ruth interrupted. "What were you going to tell me?"

"To wrap up warmly. The back of that bike is freezing cold. I know; he gave me a lift one day. You need at least two things on your legs, an inner layer as well as thick trousers, and then a windproof jacket. It's no accident they all wear leather, you know. He promised to borrow a jacket for you, and if you don't wear a helmet you should put something on your head. I think he'll have a helmet for you, though."

"I feel well looked-after," Ruth said, "though I didn't know he was going to tell you. He said to tell him next week, but perhaps I'll just go now."

"He was checking out the propriety of it, making sure he wasn't going to make you seem to be acting rashly. I told him it would be fine, especially since he was helping you out. Remember, though, wrap up warmly. The effect of the wind is really cold." Frances pretended to shiver as Ruth walked away.

Ruth chose to walk by the indoor route for most of the way to the Secure Block. It meant that she had to walk through the eastern corridor and then finally through the further parts of the East Wing where the treatment rooms were. There were few people moving through these areas – it being Friday afternoon, the treatments were coming to an end. The corridor was poorly lit, and the lights seemed to cast long shadows through the open spaces. She wondered how many people before her had hurried along in the half-gloom, and what it must have been like when there was no electric lighting. Either a fortune had had to be spent on candles to light the corridors, or people must have carried a candle or a lamp. That thought reminded her of *Northanger Abbey*, and reading the book in the classroom and at home when she was thirteen. She had been able to appreciate how the heroine had so misunderstood everything. She too had found the ways and customs of her school, and the labyrinthine nature of the school buildings, unnerving when she had entered the grammar school. She too had not at first understood the adults she had encountered, just as Catherine Morland had misunderstood some of the people she had encountered. And in her initial isolation her fancy might have led her to all kinds of false judgements, just as had happened to Catherine. For a moment Ruth wondered what Catherine might have been thinking if she had been hurrying through these darkening corridors. Anxiety, fright, fear? A dread anticipation of what lay beyond, perhaps? These were the emotions of many patients, after all. But Catherine would also have been fascinated by the possible discoveries beyond, whereas many of those patients would have known only dread.

Ruth thought again about Richard Simms. He, mysteriously, had experienced the treatment rooms, for the electrical shock therapy that was on his records. But why, exactly? Yes, he had attempted suicide, but the reasons behind that failed attempt were not on file. And yes, he was uncommunicative, but he did not display any symptoms of the severe depressions for which he might have been directed to shock therapy. And the civil servant had talked of him working for the government. But he had no occupation listed on his files, although he had an expensive and high-quality set of tools in his tallboy. If things were quiet next day, she thought, she would make another attempt to penetrate his defences, perhaps in a different way. After all, she really should include him in the next batch of patients to be reviewed, given his general self-sufficiency and his capacity for work.

By this time Ruth was walking past the final treatment rooms, which were quiet now. The last patients had left and the orderlies were cleaning the machines and the couches on which patients would lie for their treatments. Ruth momentarily stopped to look at the machines, shuddered a little at the thought of the treatments, and hurried on towards the end of the corridor and the doorway through which she could gain access to the pathway to the Secure Block. On the previous Saturday she had thought that the gathering wisps of mist were like the spirits of dead patients re-gathering around the asylum. Here, she felt that the pain and humiliation of these ghosts had somehow been absorbed by the walls, the floor and the ceiling, and her feet seemed to stick and be held back as she sought the quickest escape.

Outside it was becoming dark. The clouds seemed to have drawn down towards the grounds and the surrounding trees, bringing a descending gloom with them. The wind was not strong, but it had the sharp cold of the coming winter and she felt it instantly. If anything it hurried her along the path to try to seek some refuge. The Secure Block was flanked by trees, but the path turned through an opening and then led directly to the entrance. On either side of the path was a high fence with barbed wire, and Ruth assumed that the fence surrounded the remainder of the building so that there was just one entrance from the hospital grounds. The door was heavy, and it had an old metal knocker that must have dated from the hospital's origins as a country house. Servants' accommodation, perhaps. Ruth pushed it open with some difficulty and stepped inside. Here she encountered a long reception counter that barred the hallway, with a pair of double doors to her left that obviously provided access to the remainder of the building.

An orderly was at the desk, checking some documents. He was a thick-set, dark-haired fellow, probably in his forties, with a deep voice. "Hello," he rumbled, "a new face. I haven't seen you before. What can I do for you?"

Only as she went to answer him did she realise that she didn't know Michael's surname. She hadn't thought to ask him, or indeed to ask Frances for his full name, because she hadn't anticipated the situation when she went to see him. "Oh, yes," she stumbled in her speech. "I, er, I want to see, that is I came to see, one of the nurses."

The orderly could not resist making a joke of her request. "Yes, we've got a few of those here. Which nurse was it you particularly wanted?"

"I'm not sure. That is to say, I only know his first name. Michael. He asked me to call in with a message."

"Well, I can give him a message. What is it?"

"No, I have to give it to him personally. Could you call him?" Ruth silently cursed, foolish for not having asked for Michael's full name.

The orderly lifted a telephone that sat beneath the counter and dialled some numbers. He waited for an answer and then said, "Michael Radcliffe, please." Ruth gave a brief look acknowledging that Radcliffe must be the name, and waited. After a few moments the orderly again spoke into the phone. "Michael, there's a doctor here with a message for you." Ruth could hear the drone of Michael's reply in the earpiece of the telephone, but not what was said. "He'll be down in two minutes," the orderly said. "Wait here."

"Thanks," she muttered. It felt awkward standing in the stark reception area of the block, but she knew that this was how the security of the block had to be maintained. Many of the patients were either a risk to themselves or a potential danger to others, and only accredited staff should venture beyond the reception area. The orderly was staring at her, obviously surprised that a doctor should be bringing a confidential message to a nurse. There was nowhere to sit, nor anything other than the orderly to look at. And so, until Michael did appear two minutes later, they looked at one another.

Michael's appearance on the other side of the counter surprised Ruth. He was wearing a hospital cap, into which he had somehow swept his hair so that it was all concealed. He wore the white shirt and blue trousers of a male nurse, and his badges were shining on the pocket of the shirt. He did not look like the biker she had first met in the forest, or later at the dance. He grinned when he saw her.

"Perhaps I should have just telephoned over?" Ruth asked.

"No, no," he answered, "you can't rely on that. Sometimes we can't answer a call. And it's been a quite difficult shift today, but everything's quiet again now."

"Could we just…?" Ruth motioned to the door and then at the orderly, who was looking first at her and then at Michael. Michael moved round to the doors and slipped a catch on the other side, so he could join her. She led the way outside the block and immediately shivered in the cold. "Sorry, he just seemed too nosy," she said. "I came to ask if you would give me that lift up to Princes Risborough on Sunday week. I could do with collecting a few things. Though if it's as cold as this…"

"You must have been speaking to Frances," he said. "She's always telling me how cold the bike is, and I only gave her a lift on the back once."

"Yes, I was, but she was only giving me her best advice."

"It can be cold, it's true, but I was going to borrow a jacket for you. The thing is, I can put a couple of panniers on the back, and they shouldn't get in your way, but to carry anything else you'll have to put your things in a rucksack and carry that on your back. It will weigh down on your shoulders. Do you think that will be OK?"

"I hope so. I've nothing to judge it by. I've never ridden on the back of a bike. Do you think I can manage it?"

"Well, if not we'd just have to cram as much as possible in the panniers. I can't borrow a car that weekend. And I will only go if the weather is good. If it was raining, you'd have a miserable time. So you shouldn't worry too much. What time should I pick you up?"

Ruth suggested half past nine, which was agreed, and then felt slightly embarrassed at ending the conversation. "Thanks very much. Just outside

Reception, then, at half past nine Sunday week. Good." She half-turned, and then said, "I hardly recognised you in your uniform, Nurse. Very smart!" and so she left him laughing. He watched her turn away up the path before he returned to the end of his shift.

CHAPTER THIRTY-TWO

"Check, I think," Ruth said after moving the black knight. She looked to her opponent for confirmation. He seemed to study the whole board, as if ensuring his king was indeed in check. But he did not make any response except to move the piece to a safe place that was adjacent. Ruth's knight would be captured by a pawn if she moved it to check the white king again. She hesitated for a moment and then withdrew the knight to its previous position. She was not a great chess player and usually gave up trying to work out strategy beyond three moves. She knew she should have had a further move planned, and not a retreat, but she found the processing of multiple alternatives tiresome. But she had chosen both the game and her opponent carefully. "I know you play chess, Richard," she had boldly lied when she sat down at the table where he was reading, "so would you play a game with me? I'm in danger of forgetting how to play if I don't have a game every so often."

Richard had been uncertain how to reply. He had, on occasion, played games of chess with other patients when they had suggested it, but he had always been careful not to have it drawn to the attention of the staff. To refuse the request he might have to lie, claiming that he didn't play, and risk the doctor knowing that it was a lie. To accept the request meant revealing something he had kept hidden – for playing chess was considered a sign of intelligence and education – and in the process opening further questions about how, when and where he had learned to play. In the end he had shut his book, which Ruth had noted was still the Churchill tome on the Second World War, and accepted the challenge. He had allowed Ruth to set out the board and had deliberately made some errors early on, hoping that this would shorten his agony, but Doctor Appleton was either a poor, rusty player or she too was making some deliberate errors.

Ruth could not help feeling a slight exuberance in playing the game. She had planned to bluff Richard by asserting that she knew he played the game, and with interest she had watched him hesitate over whether to play or not. She was immediately sure that he could play, or he would have refused instantly, but she thought he had actually been calculating whether or not to agree. Other patients might accidentally dissemble through the conditions of their illness, or their lack of communication skills, but for just a moment or two she thought that Richards was dissembling quite deliberately, and it made her think over their previous encounters and conversations. His panic attack seemed genuine enough, but in some of their other conversations she wondered if they had not been playing an extended game of chess.

Richard played what she would have described as a defensive game, seeking only to swap pieces when necessary and otherwise defending his king behind a screen of other pieces. Once or twice she was able to move her pieces forward threateningly and make it possible for him to attack her, but he did not do so. He mostly paused before playing and looked at the whole board, but once or twice he seemed to forget himself and move a piece in accord with a pre-determined strategy. This game of chess was indeed a game of chess, she thought, and could not keep herself from smiling at her own confused metaphor. But her momentary pleasure was spoiled by a voice behind her, which she instantly recognised as belonging to Sir Francis Oates.

Her reaction was as nothing, however, compared with that of Richard. The colour seemed to drain from his face, and he groaned, even shuddered. Ruth did not turn around, but felt it right to continue to study her patient. She sensed that Sir Francis was approaching them, and she could hear his voice, but Richard half-rose and then sank down in his chair and put his head in his hands.

"Richard," she said, "Richard, is everything all right?"

Richard did not acknowledge the question, but managed to twist his body and his chair half-round so that he could get up and stumble away in the direction of the male sleeping area, and his bed. Ruth looked around for a nurse and motioned to her to follow Richard. Then Sir Francis was upon her.

"Did you not hear me?" he said angrily. "I need your urgent attention!"

"So does my patient, Sir Francis," she replied, making every effort not to become angry herself. "And I did not know you were coming again."

"And is this a new treatment, playing chess?" Sir Francis's sarcasm was all too clear. "Is this what you do all day?"

"No, it's what I do on a weekend shift to try to get to know a patient better. They're not like conventional hospital patients, where we can address their symptoms with operations and drugs and make them better. It takes time and patience."

"Yes, well, I have neither today. I want you to meet Doctor Markham. He's a consultant at a hospital in North London. A place called Botany Bay."

"Botany Bay?" Ruth exclaimed. "Wasn't that where we sent criminals in the nineteenth century?"

The man who had been standing near the nurses' station came forward when he heard Ruth's question. He was grey-haired, in his fifties, with a thin face. "That's a coincidence, Doctor. It's a mental hospital, and I'm a consultant there. That's why I'm here."

Ruth stood up and looked at both men. "I don't understand, but I think you'd better come to the doctors' room. We can't talk here. But I need to check something first."

She went into the men's dormitory and saw that the nurse was talking to Richard, who was sitting in the chair next to his bed. Satisfied that he was being monitored, she returned to the two men and led them out of the ward and into the doctors' room. She sat down, and the new doctor took a seat, but Sir Francis declined Ruth's offer of the third seat. He seemed still to be in a hurry.

"It's all arranged now," he said to Ruth. "Doctor Markham has a transfer and admission document to take Richard Simms to Botany Bay, and all you need do is sign your hospital's transfer form and we'll take Richard with us."

Ruth jumped up. "What?!" she cried. "What are you talking about? No-one's going to transfer Richard. Why on earth would we do that?"

"Because Botany Bay is a better place for him," said Markham. "Sir Francis has told me about his case and I'm confident we can offer him a more specialist facility."

Ruth turned her anger and astonishment on the consultant. "What kind of specialist facility? And how would you know? You haven't asked for any information. And you turn up on a Saturday asking to make a transfer in this way? I don't think it's right." She stopped, and there was silence between them. Markham did not seem to know what to say, and Sir Francis was obviously waiting to see what happened next. Ruth steadied herself and her voice and said, "It isn't right, is it? That's why you're here on a Saturday. You hoped to find a house officer in charge and to bluster him into agreeing the transfer. And once it was done, it would not be undone, would it?" She looked at Markham, and he squirmed slightly in his chair. "You bastard," she hissed at him. "You'd treat a patient like that, would you?"

"Mind your language, Miss Appleton. Doctor Markham agreed to a request from the government to place Simms in his hospital."

Ruth turned towards him. "You're no better, are you? You arranged for this to happen on a Saturday, no doubt. I suggest you both leave, now, before I have you escorted out of the hospital."

"I want to talk to Simms," Sir Francis insisted. "You must allow that. Then I'll leave." His anger was cold, and showed only in the metallic tone of his voice.

Ruth tried to be as steely as him. "Only if he'll speak to you. If he doesn't want to, you'll leave without speaking." Ruth left them without explanation and went back into the ward. "How is Richard?" she asked the nurse who had followed him into the dormitory.

"He calmed down, and I brought him his book."

"I may be about to upset him again, but I think I have to ask if he'll see this visitor. Stand by in case I need you again." Ruth approached him with regret. She did not want to upset him, and the appearance of Sir Francis in the ward, for the second time in a week, had clearly startled him. But he was entitled to any visit he wanted; and although she was confident that the superintendent would back her about her insistence on not transferring him, she knew that the hospital's policy had to be to allow any visit requested by a patient unless there was an obvious risk of harm. But although she feared the visit might upset him, she was not able to give any good reason for her fear, and she could not point to any harm that would arise. So she had to ask him.

He looked up as she came nearer. He looked at her without speaking. She half-crouched so as to address him at his own level, and spoke as gently as possible. "Richard, Sir Francis would like to talk with you, if you want to talk with him." He looked as if he wanted anything but to agree, but he nonetheless started to stand up. "Do you want to?" she asked again. He nodded slowly; and as he stood, his head seemed more bowed than ever, his stoop more weary. "Let's get it done quickly, shall we?" Ruth suggested, trying to sound brisk and confident, although she felt anything but those emotions.

She led the way to the doctors' room and ushered Richard in. She had already thought of her next play in this menacing game. "He can't stay," she said, pointing at Markham. "He's here on false grounds, and I'll report him if he tries to attend a patient's visit without mine or the patient's permission."

Sir Francis stepped closer towards her, and for one moment she thought he might even hit her, but as he had done on previous occasions he regained his composure. "Wait in Reception for me, Markham. We'll sort this out later." Richard watched the exchange with interest. He had never seen anyone tell Sir Francis what was going to happen next. It was usually the civil servant who gave the orders. Doctor Markham left the room meekly, without a word, and Doctor Appleton, seemingly content that she had asserted who was in control, followed him out. But she might never have left if she had known what Sir Francis's first words would be.

"You are in a right bloody mess now, Simms, and it's down to you to do something about it."

CHAPTER THIRTY-THREE

"A WORKING PARTY? I HAVE TO GO OUT WITH A WORKING party?" Ruth was shocked when Dr Peters told her this on the following Monday afternoon.

"Yes. The hospital does get asked if the patients want to do some straightforward work in various tasks during the year, and patients are chosen according to their previous skills and their general condition. They have to be accompanied by nurses and a doctor. And since Richard Simms is going on the working party – he's been on it before and knows what needs doing – you became the selected doctor for the first day. Other doctors will do any other days. It will at least give you a chance to see Richard with others and in a situation outside the hospital, though you'll be expected to give a brief report on any patients who particularly strike you."

Ruth sulked at first and wouldn't even respond to this. Dr Peters waited for her annoyance to subside somewhat. Eventually she asked, "What is this working party? What's it supposed to do?"

"It's at a local cricket club, a rather unusual one. It's set in the forest. The ground was cleared in the nineteenth century for cricket to be played. There's a small pavilion, changing rooms and a groundsman's hut. It's all empty now that the season is finished. So the club pays the hospital for the whole premises to be cleaned, the outside painted, and the areas around the pitch cleared of undergrowth. The working party is eight patients, three nurses, and a doctor who must be at least a registrar. If the weather's good, it's a good break from the hospital for a few hours each day. But you will be expected to join in."

"And if the weather isn't good?" Ruth's final question was left unanswered.

So, on Tuesday morning Ruth, dressed in some of her oldest clothes, met the working party members in the vast foyer of the hospital. The nurses introduced themselves, and then the patients, to her. One introduced Richard, who was hovering on the edge of the group, looking away once he realised Ruth was accompanying the working party.

"Oh, I know Richard. He's on one of my wards, aren't you, Richard?" But he would not even meet her look, let alone reply. "It's how he is," she said quietly to the nurse. "He doesn't like to talk with me at all."

Their transport was an old, open lorry, with two benches down the sides of the open top. Between the benches was a pile of brooms, buckets, spades, forks, secateurs and grass cutters, tins of paint and brushes, brown overalls and two wooden ladders. There were also two cardboard boxes in which Ruth thought she could see sandwiches wrapped in greaseproof paper, and cartons of drink, with a few apples. Ruth looked in a little dismay at the pile.

"It's a real working party, then," she muttered to the nurse who had tried to introduce Richard to her.

"Yes, it is. I went on it three years ago and I asked to go on it again. It's a good change from the hospital, and you see the patients in a new light. We all join in, you know."

The lorry trundled along the road out of the hospital and turned towards the forest. It passed the last suburban houses and reached one of the roads that cut through the forest, then followed it for around a quarter of a mile. Then it stopped alongside a track that led into the forest.

The nurse told Ruth, "The lorry can't go down the track. It's only good enough for a small tractor. So we have to walk from here and carry the equipment." It took a while for the patients to unload all the equipment, and a little while longer for the nurses to allocate the equipment sufficiently for everything to be transported. Ruth found herself carrying one of the food boxes perched on her outstretched arms, and in each hand a fork and a spade. The others were similarly overloaded.

Ruth brought up the rear as they strolled along the track. The forest had only just started to die back. The grass was still long, there were trees that were changing colour, and there were small streams that meandered across the forest floor and joined a ditch that ran parallel to their track. The leafy trees made a general gloom that seemed to crowd in upon them as they walked. Two hundred yards in, though, Ruth saw a patch of light ahead, and the track seemed to widen as they grew nearer to the light. Then she encountered one of the most surprising sights she could recall. The trees receded to reveal a circle of grass around a hundred and fifty yards across. The grass was emerald green and obviously manicured by regular cutting. The contrast between this open field and the forest could hardly have been greater – the one dark, irregular, naturally wild and with a brooding sense of danger, and the other neat and light, a source of sport and pleasure, a cultivated oasis. Across the field she could see the cluster of low white buildings that was to be their main centre of work, and the others ahead of her were already depositing their loads near the largest of the three wooden structures.

When she reached the group, the nurses were already trying to allocate the tasks ahead of them. Richard, she noted, was donning a pair of overalls, having volunteered to paint the buildings' exteriors in the white paint they had carried down. He seemed to have recovered from the leg injury.

She said to one of the nurses, "I'd like to work close to him (pointing out Richard) at some point, but maybe this afternoon rather than now. So perhaps I'll do some of the undergrowth work this morning."

So, Ruth, one of the nurses and three of the patients started to clear back the edges of the forest which threatened the cultivated grass on every quarter. They cut back small bushes, dug up seedlings that threatened to turn into trees if left alone, and cleared a zone of about two yards between the grass and the forest itself. This, one of the patients said, was what he had done four years earlier, when he had just become a patient at the hospital. He was a stout middle-aged man, his hair receding a little. Ruth asked him if he thought his stay in the hospital would last much longer – a safer way of approaching his problems than by directly questioning him about them, she thought. He confessed that he didn't know, that he was getting treatment and that it seemed slowly to be helping him, but he was aware that others in his ward had been in the hospital longer than he.

"Would you like to leave and get back into working?" Ruth made bold to ask.

He seemed uncertain. He thought for a few minutes about her question. "I would," he answered, "if I was sure I was over it." Ruth thought that when she returned to the hospital she should check with this patient's ward to find out more about him. If she was expected to make a report on him, it was better to be informed than ignorant. More work, she thought to herself, piling on the mounds of paper she feared would already await her when this working party had finished its task.

Towards noon the late autumn sun had risen sufficiently to clear the trees that surrounded the pitch, and Ruth's group felt its rays warming their backs as they worked. Some late insects hovered around them, bees searching for any last blooms that might yield a harvest. Ruth kept thinking of a poem she had read, and even memorised, at school, but the precise words eluded her. Innis-something, she thought it was, a poem of the imagination, as her teacher had described it, the poet imagining himself somewhere else but in his mundane urban life, and becoming one with nature in that imagination. Working away at the undergrowth, feeling muscles that had hardly been used in months starting to protest now at the physical work, discarding one jumper as the heat of the sun and her labours made her sense the sweat forming on her back, Ruth thought she could understand the poet's imaginings, even if she couldn't exactly remember the words of his poem.

By lunchtime, Ruth's group had worked their way around a quarter of the perimeter of the cricket pitch. Behind them they had left a trail of scratched and torn-up ground on which the forest could recommence its invasion in the coming spring. They joined the remainder of the work party and Ruth had her first chance to see the buildings more closely. They were made of wooden slats neatly fitted each into another and painted over with white. Inside they were empty, the cricketers having removed the trestle tables and chairs that no doubt allowed them to eat tea or store their clothing while the game was on. The floors were bare boards, and the roofs above were red tiles which overhung the buildings so that there was no need for gutters or drains. The rest of the working party had started by washing down the wooden walls outside and had already commenced to paint them. Richard was still brushing away when Ruth came up for her sandwich, though he stopped when one of the nurses called them all in to eat. Some of them sat on the grass, which was now dry, while they ate. Ruth stood looking at the smallest of the buildings, the groundsman's hut, she assumed, which had no door, just a rectangular opening. As she ate her sandwich she thought again of the poem. Wasn't there a hut in the poem? No, not a hut, a cabin. And the place was Innisfree, *The Lake Isle of Innisfree*. As she remembered the words, she started to recite them without realising she was speaking aloud:

"I will arise and go now," she said tentatively, "and go to Innisfree, And a small cabin build there," (she was growing more confident in her memory), "of clay and wattles made."

She paused. The slightly sing-song metre had brought her through the first two lines. Now she had to dig deeper to catch the next two.

"Nine bean-rows will I have there, a hive for the honey-bee, And live alone in the bee-loud glade."

She stopped. She couldn't recall the next verse, though she could remember that the final verse had something about the "deep heart's core". But a man's voice picked up her recital behind her. She was startled but did not turn around. The voice spoke unerringly.

"And I shall have some peace there, for peace comes dropping slow, Dropping from the veils of the morning to where the cricket sings; There midnight's all a glimmer, and noon a purple glow, And evening full of the linnet's wings."

Ruth turned around. As she had guessed, it was Richard who had picked up her words, as if suddenly untroubled, and recited them word-perfect. He too must have memorised them as a child, but somehow the words of that verse appeared to have special meaning for him. He was not aware of where he was, nor of his interlocutor, but appeared momentarily to be in a trance of past memory. Ruth waited. So did he. Then he seemed to become aware of her and looked around him. Two of the nurses had been listening to their recital. "That's lovely," one of them said. Richard looked first abashed and then mortified. He turned and walked away. Ruth watched him pick up a piece of fruit from the box and enter the main building to eat it. She walked over to the two nurses. "Well," she said, "that was revealing, and yet even more mysterious," though neither of them really seemed to understand her.

For the afternoon Ruth joined the group working on the buildings. Painting the wooden walls was a fairly straightforward task, she found, but she needed strength in her arms to keep raising them high above her head to reach the higher boards. The fresh paint brought a pleasing brightness to the areas they had already done, and by three o'clock, when they started to pack up, they had painted three walls of the largest building, the pavilion. The group clearing the undergrowth had not quite reached halfway around the pitch, but several piles of the cleared branches and bushes showed where they had completed their work. It was agreed that they would burn these piles the next day if it continued to be fine. It seemed there was a hose and a water supply behind the groundsman's hut that could be employed if any fire were to risk breaking beyond their control.

Ruth felt tired as she climbed onto the flat back of the lorry. Her arms and her back ached, and her legs were weary. She noticed Richard sitting not quite opposite her. He seemed to show no emotion, no weariness, no painful muscles. Yet he had painted the whole time they had been at the cricket pitch, and it was mostly down to his efforts that Ruth could predict the whole job might be over in another day and a half. He didn't talk to anyone, he looked down at the floor the whole time of their homeward journey, and he seemed not to be paying any attention to anything at all. Ruth sighed. The enigma was no nearer resolution. If anything, it looked even more difficult to unravel.

CHAPTER THIRTY-FOUR

"What do you look like?" John Sutton asked, laughing as he said it. "Let's see: the Scarecrow in *The Wizard of Oz*? No... A turkey at Christmas? An over-stuffed teddy bear?"

Ruth looked down at her clothing. She had three layers of jumpers on and tights, some tight trousers, and some looser ones on top. Even in the relative cold of an early Sunday morning in the wards, she felt hot, and she knew she was not walking or standing naturally.

"I'm going on a motorbike in a few minutes. I was warned to dress up."

"But will you be able to get *on* the bike?" John asked, still teasingly.

"Of course I will. Now, let me just remind you of what happened last week with Richard."

She had explained, as well as she could, what had occurred with Sir Francis Oates and his accompanying psychiatrist to both David and John during the week that had passed. David had wondered about informing the deputy superintendent, but Ruth had not wanted him to do so. She was not confident in him in the way she was starting to be about the superintendent. "Leave it a while, and let's see if anything more happens. I'm still puzzled about why this Sir Francis is going to such great lengths with regard to Richard."

To John Sutton, therefore, she now said, "Tell anyone who comes in to remove him that I expressly forbade anything because the patient was too distressed. Don't let anyone get him out of the hospital."

"You're sure you're not over-dramatising this?" John asked. "If he worked for the government maybe they just feel responsible for him."

"Maybe, but if so, why all the secrecy? Why turn up on a Saturday with a consultant from another hospital? Why not just ask formally, going to the superintendent? No, something's going on, and we don't know what it is. Perhaps nothing will happen today at all."

"Well, good luck getting on that motorbike," he returned to his earlier joke.

"And good luck to you if Sir Francis and another of his friends turn up!" She made light of the situation, although one part of her could not help thinking that she should be staying on the wards in case anything happened. She walked out into the weak sunshine that was penetrating the last mists in the grounds. It was twenty-five past nine, and Michael was sitting on his motorbike which he had propped up on its stand. He was wearing a black leather jacket, and his helmet was in his hands, and on the floor next to him was a rucksack, a helmet and another black leather jacket. Like John Sutton, he could not help smiling as Ruth waddled towards him.

"I think Frances has been warning you too much! You'll never get the jacket on with all those jumpers."

"What should I do, then?"

"Leave a couple of them in Reception. The leather jacket will keep the draught off you."

Ruth went back to the reception desk, pulling off the biggest jumper as she went, and then another as she stood by the desk. "Could I leave these jumpers here until this evening?" she asked. "I'll pick them up then." Even the clerk at the desk smiled at her, but she agreed to keep the clothing, and Ruth returned to Michael. She pulled on the jacket and zipped it up. It fitted her closely, and Michael said that it would do. He got on the bike, kicked the stand up and then kicked down on the starting lever, revving the engine with his right hand as it came to life. Ruth saw that he had put two panniers on the machine, and she picked up the rucksack and struggled to get it positioned on her back. Michael leaned across, pulled the bag into position and told her to tighten the shoulder straps. Then she put the helmet on. Finally Michael indicated that she should get on the saddle behind him. It was easier said than done. When Ruth first raised her leg she also bent forward, and the weight of the helmet caused her to lose her balance. She had to put her hand down on the ground to prevent the indignity of falling completely over.

"Come closer to the bike and lean on my shoulder!" Michael shouted. "Then put your leg over the saddle." Ruth felt foolish to be so instructed, but she found he was right. With her left hand on his shoulder she did not lean forward but was able to swing her leg across the saddle. Then she transferred her weight and sat down rather bumpily. The rucksack tugged her slightly further backwards. She rested her feet on the two pedals that he had pressed down for a pillion rider. Michael did nothing.

"What are we waiting for?!" Ruth shouted over the noise of the engine.

"For you!" he shouted back. "You can't sit back. You'd fall off. You have to take hold of me, around my waist, and lean forwards."

She had not anticipated the physical proximity of a driver and a pillion rider. She had not expected to make such close contact with him so soon, even though she should have been aware of its possibility. "I'm sorry. I didn't realise." She shifted her position, put her arms around him and leaned forward. He surprised her by letting go of the handlebars and taking her hands in his. He pulled her arms even more close to his body and overlapped her hands, so that she could clutch herself. Now she was so close to him, she found she had to rest her head on his back. And only then did he engage the clutch with his left hand and let the bike start to move forward. The bike accelerated, and Ruth felt the effect of the increasing speed pulling her body backwards. She tightened the grip of one hand on the other and felt the effect of the acceleration in her stomach and on the parts of her face exposed to the sudden draught. It took her breath away, and she was frightened, for a moment, and then exhilarated. They seemed to be going down the drive of the hospital at a very fast speed, but she wondered if that was the effect of feeling so near to the ground and so vulnerable, not as she would feel in a car. Then Michael slowed the machine as they approached the main gate, which was open, with one of the porters standing outside the lodge watching vehicles and people going in and out. He waved at the porter, but he did not wave back.

Michael stopped at the junction with the road, and said, "I think it's about an hour to get there. We'll go there and pick up your stuff, then you can decide how soon you want to come back." He gave her no time to reply but turned towards Lopping Tree Forest and the main road that ran on its other side.

Ruth had to learn how to be a pillion rider as they made the journey up to Princes Risborough. Although Michael seemed to be driving quickly, she later realised that the first part of the journey had been made at relatively low speeds. As they reached a bend, Michael would lean the machine inwards, and he himself would lean towards the ground. She discovered that she too had to lean, and within a few minutes she was peering around his shoulder and anticipating the direction of the next bend. This was not easy, however, because the draught made her eyes water, and she had to spend some time sheltered behind him to let them recover. Once or twice he had to stop at junctions, and he put both feet down to steady the bike while she kept her feet on the pedals.

There was little traffic as they went through the forest, but the main road was busier. Michael kept pace with the cars, and he had evidently planned a route because he did not stop to look at signposts or to consult a map. They crossed through several towns as they made their way northwestwards, slowing as they passed through the busiest areas. Once in the lanes of Buckinghamshire, Michael went faster, as if he was more confident in his passenger, and Ruth got the greater sense of the thrill to be gained from riding a bike. She also felt assured by Michael's closeness, surprising herself by the comfort she found in it. Towards the end she did start to feel colder. Her legs were slightly numbed by retaining the one position on the bike, and her hands were definitely chilled by exposure to the full force of the draught caused by the higher speeds at which Michael had driven. Only when they were close to Princes Risborough did Michael slow, and shout back, "You need to direct me from here."

"Don't go into the town. There's a traffic light just before the town. Turn left there and it's about half a mile down that road." Ruth still had to shout, even though she was leaning against him. Michael followed her instructions and soon she was able to let go of her left hand and indicate where he should turn in. He drove along a tarmac driveway and pulled up in front of a large old house. "This is it," she said, and he turned the ignition off. The engine roar died, and Ruth was able to move back a little.

"You have to get off first," he said, but she was finding it hard to do so. Her legs had become very stiff, and she had to pull at her right knee to move it upwards. She shifted her body in a leftward direction, hoping that her trailing leg would follow, but instead the forward momentum carried her head first towards the ground. Michael tried to prevent her falling but could not quite manage it. She fell in an undignified heap on the floor but could only laugh at herself. He moved the bike a couple of yards, propped it on its stand and came back to her. She took his hand and sat up.

"Sorry! My legs don't seem to obey me. I couldn't get off the bike any other way."

"You should have leaned on me again. Come on, try to stand now." She took both his extended hands, and he, rather than she, pulled her up to a standing position. "It was a long drive for your first ride on the back," he said. "I guess your legs aren't used to being stuck in that one position. What happens now?" He looked around. The house did not reveal its identity – it could have been any large detached house in the country.

"This is the original house. It's used for accommodation. The asylum is beyond the trees and is all fenced off. The house isn't in the secure area. As soon as I can walk, I'll take you in and we can get my stuff. It's very straightforward, but…"

He looked at her when she paused. "But what?"

"Well, could we just wait a while before we drive back? I enjoyed the drive but I don't think I could just get back on the bike too soon."

He laughed, and Ruth thought she liked his laugh. "Yes, of course, especially as the ride back will be a bit harder. You'll have the rucksack full then, and it will pull you backwards a little." He undid the two panniers and showed her that he could take them into the house for her to fill with clothes or other necessities.

Ruth reached for the keys which she had carefully tucked into the pocket of her outer trousers. She led the way to the front door and opened it. Inside it was warm and well-lit. There was a large hallway, and several doors, each with their own lock, which obviously led into apartments within the building. "My rooms are upstairs," she said, and again led the way up. On the first landing there were more apartment doors, but her rooms were under the roof up a further flight. They climbed the stairs and Ruth opened a door on the left. There was an identical door to the right.

"Not like your accommodation at Black Roding, I'm guessing," he commented.

No, indeed not, she thought. In fact her first weeks at Black Roding had made her realise how good the accommodation here had been. The apartment had a small kitchen, a bathroom, bedroom and living room, each room opening off a central passageway that was lit by a window at the far end. It had been cleverly designed to maximise the available space, so that the bathroom and bedroom at the back had sloping walls where they met the roof. But it was self-contained and had allowed her to escape from the pressures of work. It was a little outside the town but close enough for her to purchase things from the shops. And her hours had been regular and the workload much lighter than in her new role at Black Roding. For a moment she felt a nostalgia for her old position, but then she set that aside. The challenges of her new role were great, and she felt involved in a way that had never occurred here.

Michael had put the panniers down in the passage between the rooms and had then taken a seat in the living room. Ruth struggled with the rucksack on her back and finally shook it off, placing it next to the panniers. She looked into the living room. "I could make us a hot drink but there's no milk."

"You got some instant coffee? I'd have that black," he replied. She entered the kitchen, filled the kettle and put it on the first ring of the hob. The familiarity of the apartment was coming back to her, and she opened the cupboard, took out two large cups and the tin of coffee powder, and spooned the powder into the cups. The apartment was warm because the central heating applied to the whole building, not to each apartment. While the kettle heated the water, she went back to the living room.

"Thanks for bringing me here today. I'll fill the bags in a few minutes. It's mostly my warm clothes and another coat that I need to pack."

"If you don't mind my asking, why did you leave this apartment, and a good job in a secure hospital, which I assume was slightly dangerous but not very challenging, for Black Roding? It's even warm here, and you're not living here." He seemed genuinely curious. And she did not find the answer very easily, even though it had been in her mind ever since they pulled up outside the house.

"I don't quite know. They don't lay out a single career path for you as a doctor, or as a psychiatrist, especially once you're fully qualified, and so I thought the move was part of a progression I should make, though I couldn't tell why."

"But this apartment, for example. You'd have to be a consultant, and an established one at that, to get anything like this at Black Roding. The nurses often have to share rooms, and the single doctors' apartments are mostly nothing like this. Why leave it?"

"Partly I felt I had to. My consultant made clear that I would be making a mistake if I didn't. And partly I felt that I wanted to work somewhere like Black Roding, just to see what it was like."

"And what is it like? I mean, how have you found it as a place to work as a psychiatrist?"

"It's much more difficult than working here. The range of patients, the size of the place, the responsibilities, the pressures to do things. It's been like transferring to another world. And there's been added difficulty…" Her voice trailed away. Michael raised his eyebrows as if to question her further. "No, leave it, I'll tell you another time. Let's just say that I've had to learn a lot more, and not just about psychiatry, in a short space of time."

She wondered how to change the subject. "What about you? How did you come to be at Black Roding?"

"Me? My mother was a nurse, and I wanted to do what she did. She kept saying no, boys didn't do nursing, but I pestered her and pestered her until she agreed. There weren't many male nurses where I trained," he laughed, as if remembering some hitherto forgotten aspect of that period of his life. Again Ruth was aware that she liked his laugh. It seemed both genuine and self-deprecating. Not what she would have expected when she first met him, was it really just two weeks ago? "And after training, it was suggested to me that I would get along more quickly as a male psychiatric nurse, where there were shortages of men but a real need for physical strength at times. So I did some more training and came to Black Roding, and after a couple of years they asked me to work in the Secure Block. I guess I'm somehow attuned to it, the work, and not put off by some of the bad stuff that happens."

"It's not what I would have thought when I met you last week, in the forest. I thought you were just one of those… er…" She did not like to finish her own sentence.

"Rockers? Yes, I look like one because I wear leather and ride a bike, but they're often stupid, and some have gone looking for trouble. All the stuff that went on, still goes on, at the resorts on Bank Holidays. But I only wear a leather jacket because it's the best thing on a bike, as you've found today. It's the most windproof and rainproof jacket; if they made one from some other material that was better, I'd wear that instead. It's all because I just love the bike. That's why you might mistake me for a Rocker, but I'm just a biker. It becomes like an addiction, riding the bike. How did you find it coming up here this morning?"

"It was strange. I hadn't thought about it in advance, except for Frances telling me to dress up. I didn't really know what I had to do, you know, to stay behind you, hold on, lean over at the right time, but I did enjoy the driving at speed, once my stomach had got used to it." She laughed, and he joined her in laughing. The sound of the kettle boiling in the kitchen interrupted their conversation, and she went to take it off the ring.

Once she had made and served the coffee to him, she indicated that she should pack the panniers and the rucksack. She took them into her bedroom and started to rummage in the drawers and the wardrobe, taking some items out but rejecting them for being too thin, and selecting thick clothes, warm underwear and a coat that could be folded and laid at the bottom of the rucksack. She also found some walking boots and put them in the rucksack, mindful that the forest on the doorstep of Black Roding must become muddy over the winter. To her surprise, she was already anticipating meeting Michael there again. She picked up some books, although they were heavy, and put them in the panniers. She would have liked to have packed more, but the space available dictated the quantity of clothing she could bring, and she was conscious that she had to wear the rucksack all the way back.

"There's much more that I would like to bring, but I think that's all I can manage on my back. And the panniers are full."

"Do you have some gloves? I noticed your hands were cold as we drove up, so I guess you'd be warmer if you had some."

Again Ruth noticed his thoughtfulness. "Yes, you're right. My hands did feel cold. I'll find some gloves." She went back to the bedroom and found a woollen pair, but they were rather thin. Deeper in a drawer she found a pair that had a lining inside, which she thought would offer more protection. "Would these do?" she asked him when she returned to the living room.

"I guess so. I've got leather ones I use back at home, but I didn't think to bring them today. If they're the thickest you've got, that's it. Use them. But let's stay here a little and you can warm up fully before we go back."

They drank their coffees and made some polite conversation, as Ruth would have described it, about the area around Princes Risborough. Michael had visited it once or twice on biking trips, and he described areas that the bikers loved most – hilly, forested areas where there were fast bends and challenging roads, and open, flat areas with straight roads where they could test the speed of their bikes. Ruth could not fully grasp the urge for speed, but she could see that it meant something to him. She suggested that the scenery would be important for her, but he said that it was secondary for a biker, only to be appreciated during the intervals between driving or when they were deliberately going slowly. After twenty minutes she said she was ready to make the journey back, and they gathered the panniers and rucksack, picked up their helmets, locked the apartment up and went down the stairs.

"There's a bit of fast road we could use on the way back," he said, "if you wanted to feel what going a little faster is like." Ruth hesitated. He was not pressing her to agree, but she was a little nervous at the thought of travelling faster than they already had.

"I don't know," she said. "Do you think I'll be all right with the rucksack on my back?"

"Shall we wait and see? If you say okay in a few minutes, I'll go by the fast road, but if not we'll take the same route back that we used to get here."

Ruth accepted this. Michael zipped up his jacket and donned his helmet. "Get on the bike first and then put the helmet on," he told her, and sure enough this was easier. She held the helmet in one hand, leaned on his shoulder and straddled the bike with her leg much more easily than she had done in the grounds of Black Roding. She put on the helmet and did it up, and then put her gloves on. Finally, holding on with her arms around him as she had learned to do, she raised her thumb to tell him to start. On the initial movement of the bike she felt the rucksack pull her back, but then her shoulders took the weight and it was easier to stay leaning forward. Once again she started to peer around Michael to anticipate the corners. And she found herself quite enjoying the sense of control that this anticipation brought, even though the wind made her eyes water. When Michael slowed and shouted at her that they were approaching the decision point, she raised her thumb again, with a slight thrill of anticipation.

The greater speed came with a rush of air that caused her to gasp. She had been looking forward as they joined the trunk road, and Michael accelerated immediately. The added force of the wind struck her, and she had to redouble the grip of one hand on another, pulling herself even closer to him. She kept her head behind his body, but she was able to see the fields to the side of the road rushing by, and they swept past a car going in the same direction as them. Involuntarily she let a high half-scream out but tried to clamp her mouth shut to stifle it. Michael increased the speed a little more and then reduced the throttle so that the speed remained constant. She had never experienced such a sensation of speed. No doubt she had been driven at a similar speed at some time in a car, but it would not have had the same impact. Her legs could feel the wind, and she had to press her knees in to prevent them being blown out and backwards. And at times her arms were buffeted also, as a sort of turbulence seemed to circulate just in front of Michael. And then the speed of the bike reduced, and she felt able to look around him to see what the road was like. They were approaching a roundabout, and Michael indicated to her that they would turn off the road at this point. She was relieved, but she knew she would also remember the physical assault and the emotional thrill for a long time.

The journey back to the hospital should have taken another forty-five minutes, she reckoned; but as they came near to Black Roding, she realised that Michael was taking a detour of some kind. He left the road that would have led back to the asylum, and turned into Lopping Tree Forest. "Get a drink," he shouted back at her, "at Fred's kiosk." She realised that he meant to stop at the clearing where she had met him and his friends just over a week previously. In one way that seemed a good idea, because the ride had made them both cold and a hot drink would be welcome. But Ruth was not quite sure how he would introduce her to any of his friends, and she felt more than a little self-conscious to be seen in a leather jacket and the bulky clothing on her legs. It was too late to prevent such a meeting, so she accepted that she might feel some embarrassment. She had, after all, been able to get the additional clothing that she needed, and that might have taken the whole day and several rail journeys otherwise. So some joking at her expense, as was likely to occur, was an acceptable price to pay.

Michael pulled into the parking area that the bikers used. There were seven or eight bikes already parked there, and their owners were in two groups near the counter from which Fred served the drinks, sandwiches and hot rolls that were his trade. There were also some more elderly people, who must have been walking in the forest, sitting at the rudimentary tables and folding seats which Fred put out each day for his customers. Ruth realised that Tich was one of the group of bikers, so some rude, and possibly lewd, comments were inevitable. When Michael stopped the bike she dismounted with more ease than before, although her legs once again felt stiff. He said that she should leave the rucksack by the bike – no-one would take it from there. So she tugged it off and left it by the back wheel of the bike, which he had propped up.

"Tea or coffee?" he asked. "Though you may not be able to tell the difference. Not even Fred himself can sometimes."

She asked for tea, and he walked towards the counter. Tich separated himself from the group he was with and approached them. "What's this, a new girlfriend, Michael? You didn't say anything about her! Where's she come from?" He looked from Michael to Ruth, and then back to Michael. Then again at Ruth. "One minute, don't I know you from somewhere? You weren't dressed like that though. Leather jacket and extra trousers. Where do I know you from?"

"Lay off, Tich," Michael growled, "this is a colleague, the one who asked the way a couple of weeks ago. That's where you know her from."

"You're a quick mover, then," he mocked Michael, "giving her directions one day, and next thing she's on your saddle."

"Careful, Tich, no crude jokes now. She's a doctor, and just needed help to pick some things up."

"Oh, Michael," Tich said, kneeling down on one knee and raising his voice to a falsetto, "you are the answer to a damsel's distress, you are my knight in shining armour. I'll let my hair down and you can climb up and rescue me."

Ruth could not help laughing. She doubted that the others, including Michael, could follow what Tich was saying, and the absurdity of Tich's humour appealed to her. But Michael again surprised her.

"Bugger off, Rumpelstiltskin! She's no Rapunzel."

Tich was silenced. Michael laughed and ordered the two drinks. Ruth had to ask, "How did you know those names? It doesn't come automatically with being a biker, does it?"

"My mum again. She used to insist on reading us stories every night, even when I was evacuated. She asked the people in Somerset to read from a big book which she sent down with me. I could hardly carry the case, you know. Well, I was very young."

"I stayed with my mum through the war. But there weren't so many raids where we lived," she recalled. "Was it hard?"

"Yes and no. It was a very good place to grow up, but it affected my education. You know, I sometimes think that I would have liked to have been a doctor, but I hadn't got enough education to get a scholarship when I came back to London."

"When do you think that?" she asked.

"Usually when I'm in the middle of a struggle with a patient in the Secure Block." She was not sure if he was joking or not. "Especially if I don't duck fast enough and get a black eye. You don't see many doctors with a black eye, but if you work where I do you'll see nurses with one regularly."

Ruth joined him at the counter and was silent for a while. It was true that she, unlike many children of her time, had received a consistent education. The junior school she had attended had been kept going by the female teachers, and her secondary education, likewise, had been overseen by the female staff of her grammar school. She had not suffered any period of disruption, or any period without a school at all which some evacuees had experienced after their moves. They had helped farmers to run their farms, or they had run semi-wild across the countryside, but it was true that such children would not have been able to take and pass the kind of scholarship examination she had taken. The schoolteachers had prepared her for the preceding two years on the kinds of questions that were asked. "I'm sorry," she said softly.

"What was that?" he asked as he moved a cup on the counter towards her.

"Oh, I said I'm sorry that your schooling suffered. It wasn't fair, was it, what happened then?"

"No, but I can't do anything about it. It's just one of those things that one regrets from time to time. I could wish I was a doctor like you, really responsible for healing people and not just caring for them, even though that's important too."

It was surprising indeed to be having such a conversation in the forest clearing, drinking a cup of tea with a group of bikers, Ruth thought as she sipped the hot drink. But then Michael had already surprised her several times, and she had only met him fifteen days ago and been in conversation with him just four or five times.

Tich, who could not be suppressed for long, it seemed, came to join them at the counter and ordered a coffee. "You two look serious," he said. "What's happened? Ran over a cat or a dog on the bike?" That was to Michael. Then to her, "Lost your purse on a sharp bend? You wouldn't be the first. He's not a very good driver."

"No, we were just having an adult conversation about the war years… you know, before your time. Are you sure you're old enough to ride a bike?" Michael was clearly accustomed to Tich's banter. "And didn't you lose a helmet when it fell off because you hadn't tied it on hard enough?"

"That old thing? No, I was just fed up wearing it. Wanted to buy that new one that's sitting on my bike. Good way of getting rid of it!"

"Let's sit down," Michael said to her. "I'm feeling too old for conversation with this teenager." He motioned to one of the tables, and they took their cups and sat down.

"Blimey," said Tich, "you'll be drawing your old age pension next. Watch out, love, his arthritis might stop him ever standing up again." She laughed again. Tich's humour was shallow, yes, but it was quick and not bitter. She enjoyed listening to the jesting, partly because it was not a form of conversation she had often been in.

"He's very quick with his remarks," she said as they sat down.

"Tich, yes, it's a form of self-defence really, with him being the smallest bloke you'll ever see trying to manhandle a bike. But also…" His voice trailed away.

"But also?" she echoed.

"But also because he's had a particularly hard life. His dad was probably an American, who never came back from Europe for his mum. And his mum turned to drink as a consequence. He puts on that humour like a shield to protect himself. And we all put up with it because we all know it. He's settled down a lot compared to four years ago, and he's got a job at Ford's. So if you come to Fred's for a drink, you have to put up with his bad jokes."

"So, are you always here?" There was a lot she did not understand.

"No, not always, but we'll spend a bit of time here any Saturday or Sunday I'm not working. There's always someone to talk to, and we talk about bikes a lot. It keeps us out of pubs, I suppose; and we might agree to go for a drive somewhere."

"And you would just drive there and back?"

"Yes, that's the pleasure of a bike; it's good just being on it. You must have felt that, just a little at least?"

She had. Hitherto she had only ever thought of travel as functional – you go somewhere by bus, train or car for work, for shopping, to visit someone, to go on holiday. But you didn't travel just for the pleasure of the travel itself. Travel was really an evil, or at best an inconvenience, that you had to put up with in order to do something else. But when she thought of the drive back, and especially the fast section, she could understand that travelling on the bike brought quite different sensations to any she had had before.

"How quickly were we going, on that fast section we did on the way back?"

"Probably seventy to seventy-five miles an hour. The bike doesn't do much more than that with two people on. And I don't like to thrash it."

"And what speed could you go, if you drove at full speed?"

"A hundred and ten miles an hour, maybe a little more if it's downhill. It's a big engine. I've not ever pushed it to its maximum. Why do you ask?"

"I'd never even been on a motorbike in my life, let alone at that speed. It's just one more of the many new experiences I've had in the last three weeks. It's something I've never thought about before."

"Did you enjoy it?"

"Yes, in a strange way I think I did, though I was a bit scared as well."

"Everyone is at first. And I guess I still am, a little. In fact, if you're not a little bit scared you're probably becoming dangerous."

They finished their drinks, and Michael asked her if she would like to return to the asylum, or if he could provide her with some food back at his flat. Ruth had only to think for a moment of the food at Black Roding to accept his offer, although she had no idea what the food might be.

CHAPTER THIRTY-FIVE

Richard had not slept well for a week. What Oates had put to him had prevented all sleep. He was due to be released from the hospital, and nothing could be done to stop Doctor Appleton making that decision. He had tried everything he could to dissuade her, but she was determined. But Richard could not just be released. If he was in the outside world he would have to face up to what he had done all those years ago. There had to be consequences, and in his case that would mean being charged, and then being tried in a full court. Probably the Old Bailey, given the gravity of the charges he would face. All the evidence was still on his file, and Oates would have no alternative but to turn that evidence over to the prosecutors. The going rate was about twelve years for what Richard had done. Did he really want that? Now, after all he had sacrificed to stay out of court, and out of prison?

Oates had been relentless. He had said it all in one tone of voice, a dull, hard tone that Richard recognised meant that he would do exactly what he was stating. He had offered him no alternatives, no suggestion of mercy, no other way out of the dilemma. There was no other action that would allow him to stay in the hospital. He had to do as Oates was telling him.

After Oates had gone he had pretended to read his book. He thought he had fooled the staff into believing he was not upset by the visit. But within himself he felt physically sick. What he had done before in his life had hurt people, killed and maimed them, but it had been impersonal action, prepared in the workplace, in the hundreds and thousands of hours that he and others had spent working together. He had not had to assault anyone, not in the whole of the war in which millions of people had been maimed and killed, and in which he had played a terrible role, one that haunted him daily, and nightly. He had not been enlisted in any armed service, and so had not learned to fight hand-to-hand with weapons as many combatants had learned, nor to assault those whom he encountered. He had not fired a gun and had never seen one of his victims. The suggestion that he should directly assault her had made it impossible to think of anything else but the knowledge that he would hurt her, perhaps break a bone or harm her permanently. He could not think of himself doing it, could not imagine himself in the act. But nor could he think of himself coping with the consequences of not doing it. Surely he should be able to think some of it through to a different solution? But the enormity of what he would have to do simply overwhelmed his thoughts. To plan for the assault, to work out when, where and how to approach her, whether to use a weapon and, if so, what weapon – thoughts only of this dominated his mind to the exclusion of all else.

These same thoughts distracted him while he was on the working party. The clean-up of the cricket club had been something he had looked forward to, but his time there had been spoiled by the thought of what he had to do, and he had unthinkingly recited that poem! But a week had passed and he had not seen a good opportunity, or if he had his own hesitancy had prevailed, for example when they were both painting the wooden walls of the clubhouse.

He did not eat that Saturday evening. He left the ward as if to do so, but instead he walked the corridors slowly, head bowed, as he struggled with the evil that was corroding his spirit. He could not see how to strike a blow on the ward. She might avoid any blow that was aimed at her, and others might intervene to stop him. And somehow the thought of others witnessing what he was to do repulsed him. Rather, he thought, he would need to catch her unawares, perhaps coming up behind her in a corridor and letting her know it was he just at the last moment when, surprised, she could not avoid his attack. Then perhaps he would be able to control the force of the blow, although Oates had said that it must be "effective". The word had been like a stiletto blade slicing through his chest. It was a word that somehow encapsulated all that he had learned about Oates. He was effective. Look no further than the effect he had had on him, driving him to try to kill himself in just thirty-six hours. Or the way he had managed him over the years, the six-monthly visits, the veneer of politeness to Winstanley and even to him, at least until they were alone. And then another effective side of the man would appear, the bullying agent of government, seemingly able to control the processes of law and justice to fulfil his own strategic desires.

He returned to the ward, not wishing to draw attention to himself by an over-long absence, and once again pretended to read his book. Churchill! He doubted that the wartime leader, who made decisions that affected the lives, and deaths, of thousands of people, would have hesitated to save himself by the mere assault of a woman. He had fought in South Africa, hadn't he? And fought all his political career with a tenacity and a vigour that Richard knew that he lacked. Somehow the guilt he experienced daily did not seem to affect political leaders like Churchill. They could accommodate the evil that they committed as a necessary evil. But Richard could not, at least could not usually. But as he twisted in his bed, conscious of the rough texture of his blankets pricking his feet and arms, he knew he would have to accept the necessity of this deed. The shame it would bring him, the painful memories it would no doubt stir in the future, were outweighed by Oates' threats and his own fears.

He slept for only the last couple of hours of the night, and woke from a terrifying dream with a shout. He had been once again in the desert, at that familiar site, and another of the team was saying to him over and over again, "What have we done? What have we done?" *What did we do, indeed?* Richard thought, as he had thought many thousands of times in the intervening years. *We ended many people's worlds, even as we changed the universe. And my part in it was to help ensure it happened. What have I done? What have I done?*

He could only just bear to haul himself out of bed and try to follow his normal routine. He knew she was not very likely to cross his path today, and he would have to wait until Monday, or even beyond that, for the right opportunity. He went for breakfast but had little appetite for the toast and butter he usually ate. One of the patients who had sat down near him asked him for the food, if he didn't want it, and he handed over the plate. He sat staring into space until he realised that no-one was left in the canteen, and then he went to sit in the chapel. He picked up a hymnal and read over the words of the many hymns he had sung as a schoolboy. He had lost his faith finally and completely at some point after the desert scene he had recalled in his dream. He could not look on it as others had done, as opening a new science, a new understanding, harnessing a God-given power. That was how he had initially thought of it. But when he realised the enormity of what they had done, he felt that God had been destroyed, that they had ventured into the final territory in which he might remain concealed, and found it empty, filled only by the evil of men. But the beauty of the words in the hymns had always comforted him, even after he had returned to England. And they would have done so again but for the horror of what he knew he had to do.

He looked up from the hymnal and towards the stained-glass window of the chapel. The Lord casting out devils. He had sat in front of this window many times, especially when he was unhappy, admiring the colours, the outlining of the figures, the blocking of the figures emphasising the separation of disciples still afflicted from those who had been healed, with the figure of Jesus central to the setting. He had thought at times that he was like one of the afflicted, maddened by what had happened and what he had done, and at other times like one of the healed, comforted by having found a role within the hospital in which he could do some good, some service to the inmates. And now even that little comfort was at risk, and he knew he would be made mad if he were put on trial, found guilty, sentenced and imprisoned. The window brought him no release from his torment this time; it merely confirmed the horror of the choice he faced. He sat with his face in his hands for perhaps twenty minutes; but just as he had realised every time he had tried to think it through, Oates' logic was exact. Attack her and the whole future would be changed – he would not be discharged, there would be no accusations, charges, trial, and no imprisonment in one of the nation's most severe penal institutions, to be subjected to whatever the prisoners there cared to do to him. Just one blow would be enough. He could soften it somehow, reduce its impact on her, not hurt her too much, surely he could? Just the one blow itself would be enough, no need for more. So hit her in the stomach – it would wind her but not damage her. She would report it, and she would stop considering any possibility of discharging him. She was a scientist, he recognised that. She would want to keep him in the ward so that she could learn more about why he had done it, and she would not want to have him moved elsewhere. So there was only one way.

He stood up, left the chapel and walked down the central corridor and into the gardens, thinking that by walking he would occupy himself and curb the horror within. The weather was good enough to walk and keep warm, so he set himself the task of circumnavigating the grounds before lunch, but he still stuck to his mantra and walked slowly. He turned left and steered around the Secure Block, in order to walk down the side path that overlooked the lawns. There were a few other patients out, all of them walking. It was not warm enough just to sit on a bench. He avoided anyone's gaze as he walked, and tried to remember the words of the hymns he had been reading in the chapel, in an attempt to distract himself. When he was sure that no-one was near, he hummed the music too, and recalled when and where he had sung the hymns as a boy. Primary school, grammar school, church – his mother had taken him fairly regularly – trailing the Sally Army band through the streets at Christmastime, Sunday school, weddings, funerals. Many of the memories were good ones, and they cheered him a little. Nostalgia for his boyhood, and the innocence it had contained, swept over him. And he cried, silently cried, because of what life had done to him and what he had done in life.

The craving for some food cut through his sadness, reminding him that he had not eaten since breakfast the previous day. He finished his slow circumnavigation of the grounds, re-entered the building and walked down the central corridor to the canteen. The food was as unappetising as ever, but he took no notice of that, almost forcing himself to chew each morsel at length in order to spin out the time. Then he simply sat and stared into space for a while, until once again he realised he was the last patient left, and felt obliged to leave and return to his ward.

A few patients were involved in some craft activities, and one of the nurses was supervising them. Sister O'Sullivan was working on files at the nurses' station, and she tried to talk to him as he passed her, but he ignored her and walked into the dormitory area. He lay down on his bed and tried to sleep, but he found that this just brought thoughts of what he had to do back to the fore, because there was nothing else to think about. So he got up again and read his book, trying hard to concentrate on the meaning of each sentence. This was not his usual way of reading, but he found that if he read at his normal speed he would not take in the meaning but would return to his worst thoughts.

Gradually time passed, and he thought he should go for dinner in the canteen. Perhaps then he would finally be able to sleep and get some rest from these evil thoughts. He left the ward and went out into the corridor at a trudge. He kept his eyes down and refused to look up at anyone passing in the opposite direction. Not that there were many people on the corridor. He was early in leaving the ward, and other patients were more likely to follow in the next quarter of an hour. But no-one was heading in the direction of the wards on a late and quiet Saturday afternoon.

A woman passing him caught his attention, and he heard her say suddenly, "Oh, good evening, Richard," when she was directly next to him. Richard walked on, and a few yards down the corridor he stopped and turned to look at the woman. She was not dressed like Doctor Appleton, since she was wearing a black leather jacket and bulky trousers. She was also carrying several bags. But her hair was Doctor Appleton's, he was sure, and her gait was also, even if affected a little by the bulky trousers. Richard looked back in the direction of the central corridor. There was no-one in sight. He moved a few steps in trail of the woman. He needed to be absolutely sure. But this was the best opportunity he would get; so although he had not planned it or expected it now, if it was her he would hit her.

"Doctor!" he called. No, that was still too soft. "Doctor!" he called more loudly.

She stopped and half-turned to look around. It was her! Then she smiled. "Richard," she said, "you called me. What is it?"

He approached her. She was holding a backpack and two motorcycle panniers, all of which protected her chest and stomach. No good striking a blow there. It would not be effective. No, he would have to strike her in the face.

"What is it? You've never stopped me in the corridor before. Is everything all right?" She was still smiling, with surprise and pleasure, as he came within reach.

CHAPTER THIRTY-SIX

Michael's flat was in a 1930s block about two miles from Black Roding. He told her that he had bought it with the legacy from his parents, who had died within nine months of one another five years previously. The block itself, one of three identical sets of apartments, looked as if it would be inhabited by elderly people, Ruth thought, and she wondered how he fitted in such a community. The paths were all swept clean, the late flowers still blooming in the beds, and the lawns were neatly trimmed and swept clean of falling leaves. There were only two or three cars parked in the spaces in front of the flats, and certainly no other motorcycles. Ruth could sense the net curtains twitching as she walked with him towards the central entrance, and she smiled to herself at the thought that those looking out would see a second leather-clad biker, whom they would judge much as she had judged him a week or two before.

The flat was rather shabby, and untidy in places. The kitchen still contained dishes and cups that needed washing, and newspapers and magazines were scattered on chairs and the small table in the living room. Through the open door of one bedroom, probably a spare room, she saw newspaper laid across the floor and the frame of a second motorcycle, and a number of engine parts were evidently being worked on from the tools and oil stains that surrounded them. Michael saw her looking at the machine. "An old scrambling bike," he explained. "I'm putting it back together again."

"Scrambling?" she asked, ignorant of the sport.

"I'll explain another time," he answered. "You might think me mad if I told you now what's involved."

He explained that he had some eggs and cheese and asked if she'd be happy with an omelette. She said that she was happy with any real, newly cooked food that didn't contain cabbage, carrots or lumpy mashed potatoes. She had enjoyed only one meal since starting at Black Roding, and that had been at Lyons Corner House a week ago. He told her that the hospital kitchens, after many arguments about food, sent filled rolls for the staff in the Secure Block to eat. They could not leave the block unstaffed at lunchtimes and so had to be supplied with food. But they had objected again and again to the meals that were sent over. And when the patients had discovered that the rolls were available, they too had asked for them, to the annoyance of the head cook.

"No such luck for us doctors. We're even expected to make polite conversation while they serve it to us!"

"With the likes of Doctor Smythe, I suppose. I heard what he was alleging about you at the dance, but Frances said she would sort it out. I take it she did?" He was momentarily alarmed that he might have crashed inadvertently into some unresolved matter, but Ruth smiled to reassure him.

"Yes, in what must be her own indomitable way. One could almost have felt sorry for him. Well, maybe not, but you know what I mean."

"I'd fear her even more than the superintendent."

"Would you fear him?"

"If I did something badly wrong, I would, but not if I was doing my job properly. He has a good reputation among the staff."

"And his deputy?" She tried not to let her curiosity show too much.

"No. His reputation is more of a toady. He does what the superintendent says, but not because he believes in it. He didn't get the job when the superintendent did, and he'd never miss the chance to show that he should have been chosen. People say he's not to be trusted. Any reason for your question?"

"No, I was just wondering," she lied, "just out of interest."

He turned back into the kitchen to get on with the cooking. "Put some records on," he said, pointing to a small Dansette record player that sat on the floor near the electricity socket. Some records were scattered on the floor around it, and behind it there was a rack of record sleeves. She had not invested in one of these, preferring to listen to concerts on the radio. But she had seen them in others' houses or apartments and knew roughly how they worked. She switched on the control at the front and lifted the lid. There were already some singles sitting on the turntable. She raised the metal arm that hung near the central spindle, lifted the records up the spindle and then dropped them on the small catch that held them. She turned the internal control to automatic and set the machine going. The first record dropped onto the turntable and she shut the lid. At first there was an empty, hollow sound as the needle tracked the outermost rings, and then the music sounded through the speaker. She sat on a faded two-seater settee that hugged the main wall of the room.

From the kitchen came noises of food preparation and cooking. First some vigorous whisking, presumably of the eggs, and then the sound of eggs being poured on hot butter in a frying pan. The first song on the record player was familiar to Ruth, a Rolling Stones song that had been prominent on radios all over the country during the summer. She listened to the song and could hear Michael singing the words in the kitchen – clearly it was a favourite. The record finished, and the record player made several clunking noises as a second record dropped onto the first and the needle again dropped onto the record. The song was not familiar to her, but she was struck by the words and by the aggressive, surly tone of the singer. The meaning of the verses was unclear to her, but clearly the singer, or was it the songwriter, was being critical of a woman:

"*Once upon a time you dressed so fine, You threw the bums a dime in your prime, didn't you? People'd call, say, 'Beware doll, you're bound to fall', You thought they were all kiddin' you,*" sang the unknown singer. But it was the chorus that caught her attention:

"*How does it feel?, How does it feel?, To be on your own, With no direction home, A complete unknown, Like a rolling stone?*"

The words seemed to describe much of her situation. She did not have a home, no family, few friends, although Michael and Frances had befriended her in the past two weeks. She was indeed like a rolling stone, forced to follow the effects of gravity downhill, but where was she headed? The song suggested that such loneliness, such shattering of illusion, was a bitter experience, and she could confirm that.

"*You used to ride on the chrome horse with your diplomat, Who carried on his shoulder a Siamese cat, Ain't it hard when you discover that, He really wasn't where it's at, After he took from you everything he could steal.*"

Peter had not taken anything from her, really, but he had led her up a cul-de-sac in which she had only been in his social world, and had not developed a world of her own to replace the parents who had died and the lack of siblings, relatives or other friends. When he left her, he left her entirely alone. And she had contributed to that loneliness by her choice to go to him all the time, rather than to oblige him also to come to her.

"What's this song?" she called to Michael. "And who's the singer?"

Michael imitated a gasp. "You don't know? You don't know Bob Dylan? Where have you been in recent years? That's his new single. It sounds very different to his previous songs. But how can you not know Bob Dylan?"

She asked herself the same question. The changes in popular music of the previous three years had been a kind of revolution, but she had identified it as a teenagers' revolution, not one in which she would or could be involved. Stories about the leading groups surfaced from time to time in the broadsheet newspapers she read, but she only read them intermittently. When popular music was on a television or radio, she usually turned it off. But something about the words of the song, and the contempt and aggression she felt were in the music, had struck her for perhaps the first time as having something to say about her.

"Could I play it again?" she asked.

"Sure, just lift the needle, put it back on its arm and then stop the turntable. Then start all over again." He was clearly preoccupied with the cooking because he did not turn round when answering her.

She listened again to the song. This time she felt she had misunderstood the song. Bob Dylan was pretending to address the woman who was the subject of the song, but really she felt that he was singing about himself. That the whole song was about feeling lonely, defeated, cynical about the motives of others. And yes, it echoed many of her feelings about her experiences.

Michael interrupted her thoughts by bringing in two plates with the omelettes on. He put them on the table and returned to the kitchen to bring in some bread and two mugs of tea.

"Sorry this is all I have. Maybe another time I'll cook a proper meal."

"This is fine," she answered. "I'm very grateful for what you've done today, it's been very helpful and saved me a long trip in and out of London."

The omelette was perhaps not as fine as her remark suggested. Some of the egg was still runny, while the skin was partly burned, but she would not have mentioned it. They ate in silence for a while, both evidently hungry after the day's trip. Then he asked, "So, you're not a lover of pop music, then? The Beatles, The Rolling Stones, The Kinks, none of it?"

"No. I was brought up to appreciate classical music, I suppose, through my school and learning to play an instrument. And so I never really listened to other music, and I thought the new groups and singers were all aimed at people, well, younger than me, if you follow me. So, no, I don't know anything about the groups, except what I read in the papers or hear on the news from time to time. But thinking about it, I've probably heard one or two songs by Bob Dylan before. But he didn't sound like he does on that record."

"No, it's different. He's changed things a lot. There's a whole album of new songs. But why the interest now, then?"

"Oh, I don't know… just something about the song struck me as interesting. The song seemed to be partly about me. But that sounds absurd. But like a rolling stone is how I feel things have been with me."

"I'm sorry," he muttered. Then he thought for a while before asking, "Is that the right word? Should I be sorry? Or are you feeling sorry for yourself when perhaps you shouldn't? You're a doctor, doing a very important job. You've got everything to look forward to. You're not really like a rolling stone, you're more like… a…" he hesitated, casting around for the right simile, "like the central cog in a watch. Without you the hospital, and its work, would just stop. It can't go on if you're not doing your work properly. And there have been a good number of doctors in that hospital who haven't done their work properly. You must have seen the evidence for that!"

"Yes, I have. But I still sometimes feel as if I'm not controlling my life. Other people, and the job itself, are controlling me. And sending me here was just another example of that."

"But there was a big job to do, I'm guessing, and you seem to have done the job well under pressure."

"How do you know that? What have you heard?"

"Just what people say. A new, young, female," he emphasised the word 'female', "doctor is bound to attract some talk. It's not the normal profile of a doctor at Black Roding. And the talk that I've heard says you're doing a very good job."

"But who has been talking about me? And who have you been talking to?" Her mock indignation wasn't entirely humorous. She did not like the thought that there was tittle-tattle in the hospital about her. In many ways she preferred to remain anonymous.

He looked at her a little inquisitively, as if trying to work out her reaction to what might have been an injudicious remark of his. How annoyed was she to hear that there had been talk about her?

"I shouldn't have said that, about people talking. I'd just heard people saying that the new doctor in Firm 9 was doing a good job in very difficult circumstances. I probably heard it from some other nurses. Something about the acting consultant having to take time off, was that it?"

"Yes, that is true. His wife is not very well. She's pregnant and things have not been progressing well. I suppose the nurses talk about things like that. After all, we doctors aren't so different. We gossip among ourselves."

They finished the meal and he asked if she would like to listen to some more records. She agreed, and he had played a few more singles, and one side of a long-player, when she saw the time and asked, "When should I go back to the hospital? Do you need to take me?"

"Perhaps now is a good time, before it gets much colder," he replied. He looked out of the window. "Also, it's going to get misty, I think. May be more fog later. So let's get going."

This meant putting on the jacket she had discarded when they had arrived at the flat. She was surprised to find that her arms were stiff, and it was an effort to pull them through the sleeves of the jacket. He helped her by pulling the sleeve down.

"A bit stiff? It'd be no surprise, first time on a bike and holding on in one position. Uses muscles you didn't know you had, or if you did you didn't know you hadn't been using them. You get used to it."

They went down to the bike with the bags that had accompanied their journey. He again helped her to pull on the rucksack, and strapped the two panniers to the bike. Ruth could sense the first wisps of mist rising even in this suburb. The fog would be worse even before they reached Black Roding. He got on the bike and kick-started the engine, before holding it upright so she could get on behind him. Even though she now knew how to get on easily, her legs and arms would not flex at all comfortably, and she groaned at every movement. She had only sat on the back of the bike, she thought, not been responsible for wrestling with the handlebars or keeping the machine upright. How could she hurt so much, then?

She gave Michael the thumbs-up sign to indicate she was ready, and he drove off. Within half a mile he was driving down a road that first fringed the forest and then ran through it. Sure enough, Ruth could see the fog closing in through the trees, its grey-white swirls edging onto the road. Although clinging on to Michael, she shuddered at the sight of it. The memory of her first day arriving at the hospital came back to her, the concealing shroud that enveloped the asylum, the long walk up the driveway, tracking the edge of the tarmac and always looking and listening for a vehicle, and her recollection of that terrible incident and the patient's death, forcing her to stop on the road and wonder what she should do. "Like a rolling stone," she muttered to herself, leading Michael to shout, "What was that?" and her to answer, "No, nothing. Don't worry." Like a rolling stone, she had certainly gained some momentum. The past three weeks had gone by astonishingly quickly. Now she was not walking through the thick fog but driving at speed to avoid its growing threat. Then she had felt completely alone, but now she had formed some friendships. Then she had been a junior doctor of some, but limited, experience. Now she was working for the benefit of two hundred patients and facing the responsibility thrust upon her by David's regular absences. Michael's words had been kind, and she was grateful for them. They raised her interest in the week to come, and in him.

When they reached the gates of the asylum, the porter was just shutting them after a car had left. Ruth had seen it pass them. He scowled when he realised he had to re-open at least one of them immediately, and Ruth thought that he scowled at her and Michael when he saw who they were. But Michael chose to drive rather quickly along the drive, trusting that he would see any oncoming vehicles despite the gloom that was encircling the asylum, and so she thought no more of it. He slowed as he neared the turn into the car park but manoeuvred the bike right up to the steps leading up to the main door. She dismounted, and he turned the engine off and stood the bike on its stand. She took off the helmet and made to take off the jacket.

"No, keep them a while," he said. "Perhaps you'll need them again." He smiled, and she smiled in agreement, before he reached over the bike to undo the panniers. "You'll need to take these as well as the rucksack. Can you manage it all?"

"Yes," she answered, "I'll put them over my arm and carry the helmet in this hand." She showed him how she could manage. "I think you should get home before this fog gets worse."

"Don't worry. I often have to drive in far worse, but I will go now. I'll see you around the hospital, no doubt."

He was still in his helmet, but she surprised herself by leaning towards him. "Yes, come over to Firm 9 one day when you've finished your shift, I'd like that." And she further surprised herself by leaning further forward and kissing him on the cheek, albeit awkwardly because of his helmet. "Thanks again," she said, as she pulled back. "See you in the week." And she turned to mount the steps and enter the hospital, treading carefully because she was holding both the helmet and the panniers, and was conscious of the rucksack on her back. As she reached the door she realised she would also have to pick up her jumpers at Reception. Well, those would have to drape across her other arm.

The receptionist was surprised by her appearance and looked with some disdain at her leather jacket. But Ruth simply smiled and asked for her jumpers without responding to the contemptuous look. She managed, just, to pick up the helmet once she had draped her jumpers over her arm; and, feeling very stiff and encumbered, she set off down the corridor towards her room.

The corridor was becoming dark, and as usual the caretaking staff were not turning on lights until it was completely dark outside. It was also quite empty, being a time of day, particularly a Sunday, when patients were not yet going for their evening meal, and staff were not changing shifts or moving between various locations within the hospital. She passed no-one before she reached the end of the corridor and had to turn left down the West Wing. There she saw a tall but bowed figure in the distance, and immediately recognised the man's gait as that of Richard Simms. Michael might have praised her work, she thought, but she had enjoyed no success with Richard. She still did not know who he really was, what had happened to him and what he was suffering from. It was absurd that there was so little information about him. Was it that the trauma he had suffered had drawn a curtain across his mind as obscuring as the grey fog that even now was drawing in on the hospital outside? Or was it that he did not want to confront whatever was the cause of the emotional trauma, and he himself was responsible for the uncertainty? He and the arrogant civil servant Sir Francis Oates. He too was part of that concealment, but what was it that was being concealed?

The distance between her and her patient gradually diminished. She could see that he was not looking up but was walking slowly by the corridor wall with head bowed. He had not seen her; even if he did, he might not recognise her. She was concealed behind and two pannier bags, her jumpers, the rucksack, and a helmet and leather jacket. As they came to cross paths, she gave him her customary greeting, "Good evening, Richard," but he ignored her, much as she had expected.

She walked on, not turning back in case it should discomfort him. She sensed, however, that he had stopped and perhaps turned around to look at her. Then she was surprised to hear him call out, "Doctor!" His voice was low, but he raised it and called again, "Doctor!" this time more loudly. She was instantly halted by this. It was a complete change of behaviour. She turned to look back at him, and she smiled.

"Richard," she said, "you called me. What is it?"

He approached her. He seemed to scan all her belongings as if reckoning up all that lay between him and her. This was so unusual for him, and he approached closer than she had ever seen him do to anyone.

"What is it?" she asked. "You've never stopped me in the corridor before. Is everything all right?" She was still smiling, with surprise and pleasure, when he smashed his fist into her face. She reeled backwards, overladen by her baggage, and fell down. Unable to employ her hands to break her fall, her head struck the floor and she instantly lost consciousness.

CHAPTER THIRTY-SEVEN

Richard Simms broke his mantra. He gasped at what he had done, and without thought he ran down the corridor to the rear entrance. He stopped at the door to look back. Doctor Appleton was still lying on the floor, not moving. There was no-one on the corridor, but he was sure someone would be along soon. He opened the door, went through and shut it behind him. There was no-one outside. The mist and gloom were gathering at the edge of the grounds, and soon they would blanket the building, firstly in grey and then the black of night. He took the path to the right, passing the building and hoping that no-one would be looking out of the wards on the ground floor and above. But most of the curtains were already drawn, the nursing staff using the thick curtains to try to keep in what little warmth there was in the wards. When he reached the turn in the path that led along the side of the West Wing he instead stepped straight forward onto the grass lawn that would take him to the side of the hospital's grounds.

He strode across the lawn to reach the gravel path that stretched the full length of the lawns to the wooded area he had explored just a few days previously. He had no plan in mind except to escape from what he had done. The sickening thud as her head hit the floor, and her immediate loss of consciousness, had frightened him as nothing had done since the interview room with Oates. Never mind that he had not intended to hurt her so much; he had struck her, in the face, when she was defenceless. And not the single blow to the stomach, winding her, as he had planned, but true to what Oates had insisted upon; he had been effective, and he could still feel on the knuckles of his hand the force of the blow he had landed. He stopped as he reached the shrubs and trees that bordered the grounds and the gravel path. Here it would be more difficult for anyone in the hospital or on the path to see him. He stopped to catch his breath and to try to focus his thoughts. He had to remember the location of the tree whose branches overhung the wall and the road beyond, and to find it in the mist and dark of the falling night. He had not anticipated the effects of the fog and of night when he had scouted the route, and he knew that it would not be easy. But he could not go back. He could not face what he had done, not now.

He tramped down the gravel path, stopping only once to wipe away the tears that ran down his face. But he had to pick his way very carefully once he reached the trees. He could only just make out the outline of the wall to guide his direction, and he needed to pass through the first clump of trees to reach the area cleared by the workmen. There were nettles and other ground weeds whose fingers seemed to wrap around his feet and ankles, and he stumbled several times. Twice he had to move away from the wall to skirt around thick bushes which he could not cross directly, and each time he was relieved to see the tall brick structure loom menacingly to his right as he rediscovered his route. Then his way was more clear, and he was able to walk along the path created by the workmen, and he saw overhead the thick branch that stretched towards and over the bricks, its far end disappearing in the dark.

He was now sufficiently calm to take a minute or two recalling how he had initially climbed up the trunk. He slid his hands up and down the bark, which was cold and damp. Its scabbed surface made him shiver. But he found the gnarls that had provided hand- and foot-holds on the previous occasion, and was able to haul himself up a little way and grab the first branch. The tree had not been as slippery as it was now, however, and in the dark it was certainly harder to find the hand-holds. His shoes slipped and his hands were scratched as he gripped the tree's surface. Once he had the branch in hand he was able to scramble and haul himself up. He straddled the branch first and then used the trunk to assist him in standing up. With a solid branch beneath him, he was able to step up to reach the next branch he needed, and to put one foot on it. Even so, he was trembling and still crying when he straddled the third and crucial branch.

He had not on his first venture along the branch gone quite as far as he needed in order to dangle his feet down onto the wall. He chose the same method as before, and with one leg on each side of the branch he used his hands to shift his body along it. The branch protested at his weight, just as it had done previously, and as he approached the wall it started to bend alarmingly. He stopped. He was not quite far enough to drop his feet onto the wall, but it seemed risky to maintain his present method of moving forward. He felt likely to fall by toppling forward if he continued. So he moved his left leg back and simultaneously leaned forward so that he could hold himself on the branch with just his hands and arms as he slowly pulled his leg back across the branch. Now he could slide sideways along the final two feet or so to be above the wall. The branch bowed still further, with a louder creak than before, as he moved, and hurried him in his movements. He let his feet further and further down and moved his right leg so that he could touch the top of the wall. His arms were extended, but he moved them quickly along the branch so that he could straighten himself and stand on the wall.

He was almost upright when the branch broke. It cracked some way back towards the trunk, and the part to which he was clinging gave way suddenly. He was pitched forward by the sudden loss of his support, and landed on the wall itself. The snapped branch was beneath him and it sprang back upwards, sliding him off the wall. He felt himself starting to topple, and scrambled with his hands to take hold of the wall. He managed to obtain some purchase with the fingers of his left hand, and used the momentary pause in his fall to re-grab the wall with his right hand also. His legs found no grip, however, and he was left facing the cold wall with his arms stretched above him. By fortune, it seemed, he was in exactly the position he had hoped to gain, and he took one deep breath before he let go. He crashed to the floor, and a sharp pain jagged through the ankle which he had hurt coming down the tree previously. He fell backwards onto the ground. It was grass around him, he could sense that. The tarmac path must be on the other side of the road. He needed to stand before anyone passing by noticed him and was suspicious, although here the mist was thickening and it was hard to see the other side of the road. He raised himself with some difficulty, leaning a hand on the wall while he waited for the pain in his ankle to subside. A quick glance up and down the road told him that no-one was there to see him. Once the pain reduced, he could go. But where to go, he had not yet decided.

CHAPTER THIRTY-EIGHT

Ruth awoke only gradually. She was immediately aware that her face hurt, around the right eye, and then that her head hurt also, further on the same side and above her hairline. She opened her eyes and found that they barely focussed on the ceiling above. She shifted the bedclothes with her right hand, finding them tight against her body, and freed her hand so that she could touch her head. Her fingers immediately encountered a large oval bump on the crown of her head, and she winced when her fingers explored it. Moving down they met the new swellings on her face, unfamiliar in shape and contour around the bruising. If anything, the bruising here was even more tender, although the pain seemed to run through her whole head. She moaned, an indistinguishable and soft complaint but enough to bring a nurse to the side of her bed. She felt her arm being placed back inside the sheets and the covers being retightened around her. She could sense the nurse bowing towards her. "Try to sleep," she said quietly, and Ruth obeyed.

The next time she stayed awake a little longer. The headache was still dulling her wits and making it hard to open her eyes, and her face and head still felt sore, but she managed to lift herself onto her elbows by forcing the tight bedclothes upwards. "Hold on a moment," a familiar voice said, "I'll help you."

"Frances," Ruth said in recognition of her friend, and opening her eyes. "What… what happened? What's gone on?"

Frances was trying to loosen the bedclothes and to provide her with another pillow. She did not answer her questions at first. Ruth had to hold her arm, and tighten her grip, and say again, "What's happened? Please tell me," before Frances sat down on a chair by the bed.

"You're in the Infirmary. Yes, the Infirmary, in a hospital, for goodness sake. Why couldn't they just call it Ward 53? Oh yes, I know the answer. Because in this ward you have to be physically sick. They wouldn't want to confuse you with one of the other patients."

Ruth tried to laugh at the absurdity of the reply, but she could not. The pain was too great, and she felt angry with Frances for not answering her more directly. "I know I'm not very well, but why am I not very well? What happened?"

"I'm sorry. I didn't mean to make a joke of the situation." Frances squeezed Ruth's arm in friendship. "You were knocked unconscious yesterday evening. They found you in the corridor. Your bags and coat were on the floor. One of the nurses recognised you or they might have thought you were an intruder. You weren't dressed like a doctor."

Again Ruth could not laugh at the joke, as she would once have done. "It's no laughing matter," she said as loudly as she dared given the pain that reverberated around her skull. "I was attacked. I know I was attacked."

"Stay as calm as possible, Ruth," Frances said quietly but very firmly, "or they'll throw me out for upsetting you. Everyone's saying that one of your patients must have attacked you. He's gone missing. No-one's seen him since yesterday. I only know all this because it was reported through admin. They're searching the grounds still now."

"Who was it?" Ruth asked weakly. She was finding it hard to concentrate on Frances, and her eyes were closing.

"A patient called Simms, Richard Simms." Frances's voice had become a whisper, or perhaps it was more that she could not hear her so well. Her eyes closed and she fell asleep again.

* * *

"I warned Verity that he was risking things bringing just a slip of a girl in as registrar when Peters was also having difficulties. But he wouldn't listen." The voice was that of Mark Jennings, the deputy superintendent, and Ruth had no intention of opening her eyes when she heard him. She had no idea of the time, but could vaguely recall that Frances had been at her bedside and must have left, and she could understand that the deputy superintendent was not aware she was conscious. The pain had not left her head, and she would have liked to have called a nurse and ask for a painkiller, but she thought it better to listen to the remainder of the conversation. It was one-sided, but she guessed that Kenneth Brown, the registrar who seemed to accompany the deputy superintendent everywhere, was probably the other person.

"I'll have to start arranging to transfer her back. We can't have incidents like this causing trouble, and she was obviously too opinionated and sure of herself. I'd better start checking around the other firms and see who could replace her. And I've got some high-up civil servant calling me and complaining about her as well, and that's something to do with this missing patient. What a damned mess she's created. If we're not careful we'll have to inform the police about it all, and that will cause some good publicity, won't it? And Verity's only been away one week!"

That was all she heard, except for the sounds of two people walking away from her bed. She tried to think, but anger overtook her. Not a word of concern for her, nor any interest in why and how it had happened. That all seemed to be resolved. It was her fault, and she would be held responsible. And Jennings wanted to sweep it all under the carpet. She would not allow herself to be treated in this way. But despite her anger, she felt very weak. She could not move her head upwards, and had to lie still. Soon she could not stay awake any longer, and her eyes again closed.

***

"Ruth, can you hear me?" It was a male voice, close to her ear, not loud but gently urging her attention. She groaned in response. "Ruth, perhaps you can wake up. See if you can open your eyes. I'd like to speak to you." It was Michael, she realised, and she opened her eyes a little and tried to focus on him. "I heard what happened," he said, "from Frances, but the deputy superintendent also came to see me. Can you understand me?"

She could. This time she wanted to stay awake longer. She nodded her head just a little; even this small movement made the pain in her head worse.

"Help me to sit up, will you?" she asked. "I can't seem to do it…"

He picked up a spare pillow, and then slipped an arm under her shoulder and across her back. He lifted her slowly, as if checking she could move her head as he took responsibility for her torso. Then he stuffed the pillow in behind her and pulled the pillow she already had in behind it, so that together they would support her. Then, surprisingly gently, he laid her back and removed his arm.

"That's all I can do. They don't want you to sit up. You took quite a blow, well, two blows."

Gradually she was recalling what had happened to her. She had seen Richard on the corridor, although she could not recall what had happened next. Then her conversation, such as it was, with Frances. Richard was missing, being searched for. And finally the one-sided conversation of the deputy superintendent. She looked at Michael.

"He blames me, you know. He said it was my fault. That I was too opinionated and too young. It's all my fault!" She was almost shouting in anger.

"Sssh, sssh," Michael said in response. "Don't shout. They'll throw me out if you do. I don't understand. How can it be your fault? A patient attacked you – it happens from time to time, even in the main hospital."

Ruth shut her eyes to gather the strength needed to speak, and to overcome the pain which seemed worse even than before. "It was my patient… who attacked me… my patient, and they think it's my fault. It wasn't." She stopped, because she was going to cry if she carried on, and she refused to cry.

"I still don't get it, but don't say anything more for a while, it's obviously hurting you." Michael had come close to her again and was urging her with the same firm tone with which he had awoken her. "Shut your eyes again, if it helps." She did, and again it helped her to reduce the pain and to focus. "I heard it was a patient called Richard Simms, who was missing from the ward when they found you last night. But the staff nurse on the ward said that it was really out of character, and unexpected, if he did it."

Her anger rose up again. "I want him put in the Secure Block. He's dangerous. I've only been trying to find out more about him, and to help him. But he has really hurt me." She freed her arm from the sheet, which was still drawn tightly over her. She touched the bump on her head again and recalled that she had done so earlier. It did not seem any larger, but it was still very sore. And so was the cheek beneath her right eye, and the lower part of her forehead above the eye. "He punched me here," she protested, "and I don't know why he did it. He needs to go in the Secure Block. It's not my fault."

"I understand why you're angry with him, though I still don't understand why you think you're being held to blame."

"I heard the deputy superintendent talking while I was asleep... I mean, when I awoke and he thought I was asleep. He wants to blame me, so the hospital isn't to blame. But it is. There's something odd about that patient, and he's obviously dangerous." It was all she could say. He was silent for a while. She concentrated on staying awake; she did not want to fall asleep again just because her eyes were shut. Despite the pain, she realised she cared about his reaction to the events. She wanted him to agree with her. Surely he would?

"It would be a right reaction to a violent attack," he said, "but they haven't found him yet. One of the porters, or perhaps an orderly, told Frances that they'd found a broken branch on a tree at the end of the grounds. The branch must have overhung the wall. But it's still so foggy outside that no-one knows where he might have gone. They may have told the police that someone's escaped who shouldn't. Though if the police are told about the attack, they'll probably come and talk to you, even if he isn't charged. It's what they have to do if a serious attack occurs." He ran out of things to say, and she was disappointed that he had not agreed with her.

"They need to lock him up when they find him. Don't you think so?"

"Yes, they do. But they need to find him first. Do you have any idea where he might have gone? The fog was thick last night, and it was cold. And although it cleared a bit today, it's coming down again. Where would he go, do you think?"

She found it hard to think compassionately of him. He had smashed his fist into her face and caused the blow to her head that had made her feel so much pain. At first she did not reply, but then a possible answer occurred to her. "The pavilion…" she blurted out. "The pavilion, in the forest. There's a shed there that's open."

Michael had not been able to understand her fully. "What was that? In the forest? Try to tell me again."

She had to take a couple of deep breaths first. "In the forest there's a sports field. It seems odd, but there is one. And it's got a pavilion, and a shed for storage. There was a work party there last week. And he was part of it. The shed's empty so it's not locked. That's all I can think of."

"I know the place. Perhaps I'll go there and take a look. But there is one thing I want to say…"

"What is it?" she asked, hoping that he would endorse her feelings about Richard.

"I know that you're very angry with him, and it's right to be angry when you've been attacked. And the deputy superintendent doesn't know anything, except how to try to undermine the superintendent. And what he said would make anyone angry as well. But I know that you want to understand things, what's happened to someone and why it's happened. And it's just that it's my experience, and what I've seen…"

"What is?" she asked sharply. This was not what she wanted to hear.

"Well, in many of the cases where I've seen violence from a patient, even experienced it myself, it's not been because they are violent in themselves. It's because being violent is the only way they know to make sure they stay here."

He stopped speaking. She was lying with her eyes closed. "What do you mean?" she asked.

"Just that, bizarre as it seems to us, they actually want to stay here. They're too scared of something out there, and the easiest way of making sure they stay here is to commit an act of violence. I'm not saying that that's what's happened here, but just asking that you consider it."

"No, Michael," she said without opening her eyes. "He attacked me, and he needs to be locked up and stopped from roaming around the hospital. He could do even more to someone else. Please leave me now." He left, but not without squeezing her arm in reassurance and telling her that he would return next day.

* * *

She woke again sometime later. This time a nurse came to her and offered her a drink of water and some painkillers. She was able to sit up a little more, and asked what time it was. "Nine o'clock," she answered, adding "at night. You've slept most of the day. But people have been in and out. Do you remember?"

"Yes, I think so," she said. "But my head hurts so much. I don't really know what I can remember and what I may have dreamed."

"The deputy superintendent wanted to talk to you but you were asleep. But you spoke with your friends."

Ruth finished the drink and rested her head back. She had spoken with her friends. And they were friends. They had been open and friendly to her, had helped her out, had distracted her from her loneliness and isolation, and engaged with her, made jokes with her. And yet neither of them wanted to share her anger at what had happened. No, that was not quite fair. Frances did not know what the deputy superintendent had said. But Michael did. And he knew that Richard Simms had attacked her, whereas Frances had just repeated what everyone thought. But still he had not fully backed her up. And why had he not? Because he believed that patients often committed violence in order to stay at Black Roding. Could that possibly be the case? She had to acknowledge that he could be right. She had, after all, been reviewing patients and moving on those who could be treated elsewhere and in different ways. Richard's past was a puzzle, but he was an obvious patient to consider for a move. And yet a very senior civil servant did not want him moved out of the asylum, indeed had even involved another doctor in trying to transfer him to another asylum and had spoken in private to Richard. But she had tried to help the man, had gone out of her way always to be kind to him and considerate. She had studied him as closely as she had studied anyone in the weeks she had been here. Friends? Who was a friend in this situation? And what did a friend do? And what should she do? Her last thought, before she fell asleep again, was that only she could condemn Richard Simms. No-one else had seen the assault, and the hospital staff had simply assumed that a missing patient must be the culprit.

CHAPTER THIRTY-NINE

It was cold in the shed. The fog penetrated the wooden slats and filled the air with icy water that condensed on his clothes and skin. Having dragged himself here with an injured ankle, limping the whole way, he now realised he could not drag himself away. His ankle had swollen in the night, and when he attempted to stand it had given way. He had not slept, and his head ached. He had cried during the night, but during the morning even his tears had given way to despair. Now he did not think he would survive another night, but he could not crawl any distance at all. The sports field was half a mile into the forest. He could see no more than five yards through the open doorway because of the fog. And he guessed that it would soon be evening, and then night. He would be even more exposed to the cold and the fog. At least, he thought, he would not be troubled anymore by the haunting dreams and the shame of what he had done and its effects. But he wished he had been able to resist Oates, and not hurt her. If he wished he could change anything, he wished that.

A noise outside the shed awoke him from the deathly sleep that had overtaken him. He listened with as much attention as he could muster. It was an engine, a vehicle of some kind. Here in the forest? It did not seem possible. Yet it seemed to be coming closer, and then its approach halted. But it sounded very close to the shed. Then a shout – "Richard! Are you in there?" – and a figure stood in the doorway. Instinctively he doubled up, thinking that such a visitor must be hostile. But no kick or blow fell on him. Rather, the intruder bent over him and spoke, "Richard. Is it Richard? I'm from the hospital, from Black Roding. Come to take you back. Can you straighten up, sit up? Let me see you a little."

He shifted his body so that he could straighten up. In the gloom he could hardly see the incomer, but he only wanted to know one thing. "Is she all right? Is she hurt? Is she OK?" he asked, and the other man said, "She's OK, Richard. I just left her. She suggested that I might find you here. It wasn't easy in the fog, but the path here is clear enough. And my motorbike is outside." Sure enough, Richard could hear the engine still running. "I'm Michael, a nurse from the hospital. I've seen you delivering things with your trolley to the Secure Block. Do you remember?"

Richard shook his head, but he doubted that Michael could see the gesture. "She's not dead?" he gasped out. "I thought I'd…"

"No, she's not dead. I left her spitting mad about you, though. You'll have to make it up to her, won't you?"

"I'm sorry, I'm sorry," he stuttered, before the tears of relief and sorrow overwhelmed him.

Michael waited for the emotion to die a little before asking, "Can you walk? Can you stand up?"

"Hurt ankle," Richard said slowly, remembering suddenly his mantra. "Can't walk."

"That's no problem, we've only got to get you to my bike. But you'll have to hold on then. It will be cold as well, and the fog is bad, but we'll get there."

Michael lifted the patient's body a little, encouraging him to bend his good leg and get the foot firmly on the ground. Then he supported him as he raised himself more fully, and helped to take the weight off the injured ankle. Clinging together, they made their way towards the motorbike and its shining headlight. Michael encouraged the other man to put his injured leg across the saddle and then to sit back, so that he could, awkwardly, get on in front. He pulled the man's arms around him, noticing how weak he was. "You've got to hold on tight, very tight!" he shouted, demonstrating by pulling the man's arms even more tightly around himself.

The most awkward part of the journey was the path out, which was not a regular one of sand or gravel, as some paths in the forest were. Rather, it was simply the timeworn route through the shrubs and trees that everyone used when going to the field. It was easily visible in daylight, but not in the fog and dark of night. The headlight only illuminated so much ground in front of the bike, and Michael tracked along the edge of the field until he thought he had found the right spot to enter the forest. To make sure, he circled around so that the light shone directly forward. He could see about five to ten yards, but it was enough to confirm that it was a path, and so he entered it, driving very slowly and cautiously to avoid the bumps and the holes that were inevitably part of so rough a route.

It took him fifteen minutes to manoeuvre the bike out of the forest and onto the road. But even there he did not feel able to add much speed to his journey, so thickly had the fog hidden the way forward. He relied on the little patch of ground he could see in the headlight, and on tracking the edge of the road, so that he always kept to the left of the carriageway. At least the roads were familiar, and he could recognise the road signs and markings as if they were old friends. Once, it was necessary to stop, as he felt his passenger's grip around him weaken. The man was obviously cold and in urgent need of water, food, warmth and comfort, but Michael knew he had to keep him on the bike. He pulled the man's arms roughly to tighten the grip, and shouted to him to pay attention to holding on.

At the hospital's gates he was halted for a moment. His bike had a horn, but it was faulty, and when he pressed the button only a tiny whistle emerged. He shouted several times, however, and one of the porters came out. "What is it?" he shouted at the motorbike.

"I've got the missing patient on the back. Let us in, and phone ahead. I need help in Reception when I get there, and a wheelchair."

There was help waiting, indeed it was waiting outside Reception in the car park. The deputy superintendent, his accompanying registrar, two orderlies with a wheelchair, and another porter were all there waiting.

"Put him in one of the old cells in the Secure Block," the deputy superintendent said.

"No!" Michael shouted angrily. "He won't last the night in one of those rooms. He's ill and very weak. He needs to go to the Infirmary!"

"But Doctor Appleton's there, blast you!" the deputy superintendent shouted back.

"Even so. Someone can watch him. But if you don't give him some heat, some drink and some food, he'll be dead. And how would you explain that?"

"Take him to the Infirmary, but I want him watched all night, by two men," the deputy superintendent said to the orderlies. Then he turned to Michael. "I'll deal with you later," he said quietly, preventing others from hearing. Michael briefly contemplated a response but decided against it. He watched the entourage enter the hospital, the two orderlies lifting the wheelchair and Richard up in order to mount the stairs, with the porter helping from behind. But instead of turning his bike around and driving off, he pushed it into a space between two parked vehicles, turned the engine off and pulled the bike up on its stand. Allowing a few minutes to pass, he took the same path into the hospital that the five men and their patient in the wheelchair had just taken.

The Infirmary was not far from Reception. It consisted of two rooms, one for male patients and one for females. Its use was supposed to be restricted to patients with contagious illnesses or serious injuries requiring rest. It was also used sometimes for patients needing respite from difficulties on the ward. But Ruth had been the only female in the Infirmary that day, and the nurse's attention had been taken by the new patient in the men's section when Michael opened the door of the ladies' section. He crossed the room to sit on the chair by her bed. She opened her eyes and turned her head to see who it was, but said nothing. She was still in pain, and angry with everyone in the hospital.

"I found him," he said. "Just as you said, in the shed by the pavilion. His ankle was injured, and he couldn't walk. Looked like he hadn't eaten or drunk anything since he ran away. He was almost collapsing when I drove him back."

Ruth looked at him. She tried to stay cold and determined. This was the man who had attacked her. "So? He's back now. Have they put him in the Secure Block?"

"No. He's too weak. He's in the other part of the Infirmary. Just over there." He pointed to the doorway through which the nurses could pass from the male room to the female.

"What?" She started to pull herself up. "He's here? He shouldn't be! He should be locked up."

"No, Ruth, they can't lock him up. He's half-dead, and if he'd spent one more night there he'd probably *be* dead. But here's the thing. When I said I was from the hospital, all he said was, 'Is she all right?' He was afraid he'd killed you, and he said, 'I'm sorry, I'm sorry.'"

Ruth was silent. She knew as well as Michael did – this was not the usual reaction of a patient who had committed a violent attack. He smiled, or at least tried to smile, and as he had done earlier just squeezed her arm. Then he left her to her thoughts and, if she could get any, her sleep.

CHAPTER FORTY

Ruth had a troubled night. She started to think through what Michael had said to her and all the implications, but she found it difficult. Whenever she came to think of Richard Simms, the memory of the sudden punch in her face would return and overwhelm her. She could remember nothing between then and waking in the Infirmary, but the thought that she had been physically assaulted made it hard for her to balance her professional, medical and scientific understanding of the situation against her personal sense of having been violated. She slept for a while, and on re-awakening tried again to think things through. And again she failed, feeling that the two sides of the question could not be weighed on the same balance. A further sleep passed, and she woke in the middle of the night. The nurse on duty spoke with her for a while, asking about what had happened and what she could remember, but Ruth did not tell her. She was still undecided about what to do. Finally she fell into a deeper sleep, only to be woken by the changeover of nurses and the arrival of breakfast. The pain in her head had subsided, although the bumps on her head and her face remained very tender. When she looked at herself in the mirror in the nearby bathroom, having been allowed to walk for the first time since the assault, she realised she was going to have the most awful of black eyes. Already her skin was changing colour, with purple and yellow streaks clearly visible.

Immediately she had returned to the Infirmary, she was visited by the deputy superintendent, and his shadow, the registrar. He allowed her to sit back on her bed before launching into his questions: What can you tell us about what happened? Where was Simms? What conversation took place? What did Simms do? What had happened between Simms and her previously? What had she done that might disturb him, a patient with an unblemished record from his time of admission? Why had she resisted what Sir Francis Oates, a highly respected and high-ranking civil servant, had proposed for Simms, which was only a transfer to another asylum, after all?

But she refused to answer most of the questions, saying either that she could not remember the incident, or that she had acted professionally throughout her management of Simms and would report on that when she returned to duty. She tried not to mention that she had only been doing what the superintendent had asked of her, or that David Peters knew about her work. Better, she thought, to refuse to engage with the man's questions until she had thought things through. He stumped off, with the registrar surprised by his sudden departure and trailing behind him. He gave Ruth a contemptuous glance as he shut the door.

Ruth asked if she could get dressed, and managed to negotiate that she could do so later in the day if she rested for a while longer. She could use the clothes that were in the bags she had been carrying, which she realised had been stored under her bed. Also there was the leather jacket that Michael had loaned to her. Michael. She had started to think well of him and to feel attracted to him. But he had not backed her when she thought he should have done. And he was urging her to think about his experience of violence in the asylum, and of its causes. At last she remembered the words of her mentor in psychiatry and what he had told her to do when she was uncertain – "However hard it is to do this, try to look at what is happening from the point of view of the patient. He or she is not seeing things, and not experiencing things, as you might do in their circumstances. You cannot explain their behaviour, or their thoughts and emotions, if you only see them as deviations from your norms. To them, their thoughts, their emotions and their actions are logical." It was as if he were in the room with her. That, for sure, was what she needed to do.

She asked the nurse for a pen and paper, and at the top wrote down what she knew of Richard's background – an obviously intelligent and educated man, brought to some unknown crisis in which he made an attempt on his own life, a voluntary patient for thirteen years in an asylum which the outside world abhorred and shunned but in which he had found a way to serve the patients, treated in some ways for his illness (unknown!) but in recent years not taking any drugs. This was a man for whom the word 'asylum' was invented, she thought, and wrote the word in capital letters beneath the description. Then she noted Winstanley's death, a necessary change of doctors, the arrival of a new doctor replacing Winstanley, the panic attack, changes in procedures, the reviews, the planned movement of patients from the firm's wards, the disturbing effects of Oates' visits to the ward, with their private conversations. This was a catalogue of threatening change, and she could see that for Richard Simms the asylum was no longer a place of refuge. She wrote the word again in capital letters beneath the list, and then she crossed it out. That, she felt, matched the patient's view. And that, she decided, lay behind the attack. Michael had been right, and she, upset by her personal involvement and pain, had been wrong.

She stood up and walked over to the window. The fog, just as it had done on her first days, had obscured everything from sight, but now the sun was penetrating the grey mists, albeit weakly and partially. She could see that it would drive away the curtains of cloud within an hour or two. And she could see more clearly in the room as well as outside. She had decided what she had to do.

Frances interrupted her thoughts by coming in to visit her. She hugged Ruth and then leaned back to look at her face. "That's not going to look very nice for a while, is it? Does it hurt a lot?" she asked.

"It's easing. It was worse yesterday, as was the pain in my head. But I'm feeling better, and I'm going to get dressed later on. But I've had quite a time, not just because of the pain."

"In what way? What more could there be?" Frances pulled her over to her bed, sat her on it with a gentle gliding push, and pulled a chair in front of her so that she too could sit down. "What's going on?" she asked.

"The deputy superintendent, that's what is going on. He blames me for what happened. He's going to transfer me back. I heard him say it while he thought I was sleeping."

"Oh God, that's unfair. What can we do about it? Can we contact the superintendent?"

"I doubt it. But I don't think I'll need to do that. I think he's misunderstood what happened. In fact I think everyone has. So this time you must leave it to me. Though I'm grateful for how you got me out of my problem with Smythe, I'll have to take care of this problem."

"What will you do?"

"Just tell them what really happened. But let me tell them first, and then I'll tell you. Could you do me one favour, though?"

Frances smiled as if she could guess what it was. "What do you want?"

"Could you tell Michael he was right, and that I'm going to tell the deputy superintendent some things that he won't want to hear? And that I'm glad he found Richard on the road outside, in the forest as he was driving home. Make sure you say that. And that I'm getting better. And…"

"And what?" Frances asked. She looked interested, slightly amused, and perhaps on the verge of making a sarcastic comment. Ruth hesitated. Could it really be just three weeks ago that she had walked down the driveway of the hospital in the fog, and now she was saying this?

"That I'm sorry… sorry for being so upset."

Frances did not make a sarcastic comment, but if ever a raised eyebrow replaced such a remark, hers did now. "Well, well, I will, but I really don't think you have to apologise for being upset. You'd just been half-killed by someone attacking you. You were unconscious and then given some drugs to help you sleep or to ease the pain, no doubt. Why should you have to apologise?"

"Well then, tell him I'm sorry for being wrong. Yes, that's better, for being wrong, when he was right." This time Frances simply looked at her. Only the look on her face asked a further question. "He'll understand, even if you don't. I'll explain it all later, I promise."

"I'm starting to wonder if you haven't been mixing with all these lunatics too long. Is it catching, this madness?"

Ruth laughed, then immediately regretted it; her skin around her right cheek objected strongly to a change in demeanour. "Ouch! Don't make me laugh."

"Well, at least I did," Frances smiled as she stood up, "and now I'll go and play Cupid, just as you asked." And before Ruth could object to that, she left the room.

Ruth waited for the nurse to come back into the room and told her that she thought she was starting to remember what had happened. She needed to tell the deputy superintendent urgently what she had remembered; and would the nurse call down and ask him to come up when he could so that she could relate what she had recalled? The nurse did so, and told Ruth he would be up to see her in about an hour's time. That gave her an interval to consider carefully all the possible implications of the information she would impart. But instead of writing these down to help her thinking, as she had done in considering Richard's view of things, she did this in her head, and she found that the decision she had made enabled her to focus more clearly. When the deputy superintendent arrived, he surprised her by being alone. She assumed that the registrar must be delayed in the Admissions Unit, but it did not matter as far as her announcement was concerned.

"I thought I should call you up because I was starting to remember what happened on Sunday evening, and it seemed important."

"Well, what happened, then?" his impatience was evident.

"There was an intruder."

The impatience on the face of the deputy superintendent was replaced with a look of astonishment, and then with anger. "What do you mean, an intruder?"

"I mean somebody had got inside the hospital who shouldn't have been there. He was trying all the doors on the corridor and didn't notice me coming along. I assumed he was looking for something to steal, so I called out to him."

"But how did you know it was an intruder?"

"Because he wasn't dressed in any uniform of the hospital, and he was trying any cupboard or office door on the corridor. I told you that already."

"Yes, and what happened then?"

"He ran up to me and demanded the bags that I was holding, and the leather jacket I was wearing. It was borrowed. Look, it's there under the bed."

He looked under the bed where she was pointing, and let out an exasperated sigh. "Yes, I can see it there. So he didn't get it?"

"No, because a patient came up behind me and when the intruder saw him coming he punched me. But the rest I don't know because I fell down and hit my head. But it was definitely the intruder who hit me."

"Are you sure about this, Doctor? Because everyone has assumed it was the patient who did it, Richard Simms, who disappeared from the hospital that same evening and was only found yesterday. Your patient, whom you had upset."

"No, I think it was Richard who came up behind me. I just caught a glimpse of him before the other man hit me."

"So, why did he disappear? Why did he leave the hospital grounds and run off?"

"I don't know. I was unconscious. Perhaps he chased after the intruder and followed him out by whatever route he took. Or perhaps he just panicked. He had a panic attack the first week I was here. You might recall, I had to leave the Admissions Unit."

"Yes, well, I'll check this with everyone else, including the male nurse who brought him back in. Right." The deputy superintendent looked almost embarrassed and seemed not to know what to say next. He said "Right" again, and then left her. She let out a deep breath – she hadn't realised she was holding her breath – and hoped that Frances had got her message to Michael before the deputy superintendent confronted him. But she was confident that he would not reveal where Richard had been, nor how he had known.

She lay down on the bed for a while and dozed just a little, until the nurse disturbed her rest with lunch. This was as unappetising as ever, but she felt hungry and ate it at the table in the corner of the room with a relish she had never previously shown the hospital's food. Then she crossed the Infirmary to her bed and pulled out the bags and other items that were under the bed. These included the helmet she had borrowed from Michael. *A pity I wasn't still wearing it when Richard hit me*, she thought, with a sudden fear about what she had done. She had lied to the deputy superintendent in order to allow a patient to remain relatively free within the asylum. She – and Michael – had better be right about him, and she had better get on with her review of him and deciding what to do before anyone else was hurt. She tried to set her worse fears aside and to concentrate on what next to do. She thought that, along with the clothes she had been wearing, those in the bags would allow her to get dressed. So she rummaged through them and gathered her outfit on top of the bed.

"Could I have a bath, do you think?" she asked the nurse, who turned her mouth down at the question.

"I'd have to supervise you if you did. Patients in the Infirmary have to be supervised, even if they're doctors, and especially if they have had a concussion. I'm sorry if it would be embarrassing." Now it was Ruth's turn to curl her lips downwards and shake her head. She had not been supervised in the bath since she was eight years old and her mother had had a new bath installed in one of the upstairs rooms. No need for the old tin bath in the front room, filled with water from the kettles and saucepans that her mother boiled up to heat the water.

"No, I'll leave it. I've nothing against you, but I just think I'll leave it until I'm discharged. Will that be tomorrow?"

"That depends on the doctor supervising you – Doctor Smythe."

"No it doesn't," Ruth raised her voice, until she realised that it was not the nurse's fault. "I'm not being treated, or diagnosed, or discharged by that man. Call him and tell him that. And call Doctor Peters, or Doctor Sutton, from Firm 9 and ask them to come and check me over."

The nurse was confused, and looked worried. "Can I really do that?"

she asked. "Tell a doctor that the patient won't let them treat her? I've never done that in my life before. What should I say?"

"Just what I told you. He'll understand." Ruth was furiously considering the possibility that Smythe had examined her while she was unconscious. The thought was appalling. But she could see why he might have been asked to do it. He was one of the doctors actually resident in the hospital, a senior, or relatively senior, doctor. The staff who found her on the corridor would not have known of their previous history. Nonetheless, the thought that he had touched her was repellent. "I'm going to get dressed," she said sharply, and then, thinking better of her treatment of the nurse, she apologised. "It's not your fault. I shouldn't take it out on you. I just wouldn't have wanted him to be treating me."

"I think I understand," the nurse replied. "I guess I was a little slow in following you." She smiled, and Ruth smiled back and then turned to gather her clothes. "I'll lock the door so you can dress in privacy," she said. "Call me when you're done."

Once she was clothed, and no longer in the hospital shift, Ruth felt better – less a patient and more a doctor. And she had a number of visitors in quick succession. First John Sutton, who called in case David Peters was not able to make it. He looked at the chart that held her details, temperature, blood pressure and pulse over the time she had been there. Then he checked the bumps and bruises, apologising for any pain he caused. Finally he checked her eyesight and that she was indeed feeling better. He was satisfied and said that he would tell the nurse she could be discharged the next day, unless Doctor Peters said otherwise when he called in. He also told her that the hospital was using its high-security protocol because there had been a reported intruder who had been violent, and that Sir Francis Oates had been calling David Peters about Richard. Ruth made no reaction to the news of the security measures. She was sorry that staff and patients would be inconvenienced by the locking of wards and offices, especially when the violent intruder was a fiction of her devising, but she still felt it was the right decision on her part. She hoped that David Peters would look in because she wanted to know more about what Oates had said to him.

No doubt he was trying to get Richard transferred again – but why was he so intent on achieving this?

Next to visit her was Frances, who brought some fruit and chocolates with her and made a great point of how much the invalid Ruth was in need of them. But Ruth was starting to understand her humour, and put the gifts away in her bedside cupboard for a while to deny Frances any share in the gift. She relented after a while, and they both indulged in the boxed chocolates. Frances told her that the hospital had been in some turmoil because the deputy superintendent had made the administrators type up, print and distribute to every ward and office the instructions for the security measures, and she herself had delivered a good number of the sets of rules. Then the porters and orderlies had had to carry out a check of the grounds and the wooded area at the bottom of the grounds because it was assumed that the intruder had gained entry there. Finally, the deputy superintendent had issued an instruction that the porters were to check every vehicle entering the gates and everyone's pass going in and out. She herself had persuaded him that it would be best to start this tomorrow because so many staff were accustomed to turning up without their passes and relying on the porters' knowledge of them to gain access and egress. She warned him that dozens of staff could be left stranded at the gate that evening if he enforced the rule immediately. But when she asked Ruth to explain what she had said to the deputy superintendent that had led to all this chaos, she declined, saying only that she had remembered more of what had occurred and had told him what she had remembered.

"The least said now, the better," she concluded.

"I'll accept that for the moment," Frances said, "but only if you tell me more about why I'm playing Cupid with part of my time."

"I don't know what you're talking about," Ruth protested, struggling to keep a straight face.

"Oh, don't you? Cryptic messages about where an escaped patient was found, about apologising for being upset, no, for being wrong, and that he's right, and that you're going to tell the deputy superintendent some things he won't want to hear. It all sounds like lovers' secret chat to me, not something I should be intruding on."

"Your tongue is sticking so far in your cheek it's showing," Ruth laughed. "We're not lovers, Michael and I."

"Not yet, but that's one of his helmets under your bed, and I don't think that jacket is yours. When a woman starts wearing a man's clothes, well… you know what follows."

"Stop teasing me. I'm supposed to be an invalid."

"A recovering one, I think. But I must go – no doubt there'll be some more chaos emanating from the deputy superintendent's office, thanks – I think – to this particular invalid." Ruth smiled again as she left. She had not really had a friend with whom she could share jokes in this way since her schooldays. She was again reminded of the more lonely aspects of the past ten years. Some parts of her seemed to have dried up and only now to be coming to life in the bracing waters of Black Roding. How odd that was.

Her thoughts were interrupted by a knock on the door. The nurse was in the male part of the Infirmary, so she herself called out, "Come in," and the door opened in response, but no-one entered at first. The door swung shut a little and then stopped. It was evident that someone was coming in, but awkwardly. The first thing she could actually see was a Dansette record player, and then she realised it must be Michael's, and then she saw that it was he, and that he was struggling because he was carrying the record player and balancing some records on top.

"Hi there," he greeted her. "I thought you might be here for a day or two and that you would get bored. So I brought this in, or rather, someone else brought it in, and I lugged it all the way up here. How are you?" He looked at her and winced slightly as he saw her face. "You look like you just went ten rounds with a boxer. My goodness, he caught you hard on your face, didn't he?"

"Who did?" she asked, slightly anxious to have it confirmed that he had understood the message.

"The mysterious intruder, of course. The one responsible for the whole hospital becoming a secure block. I haven't seen anything like it for years. Do you have this effect everywhere you go?"

"Don't make me laugh. It hurts when I laugh. I had to tell the deputy superintendent about the intruder, once I remembered what had happened. And I guess you told him how you found Richard?" This was the second part of her plan, and she was still nervous about how he would reply.

"Yes," he said, "I told him that I came across him trying to cross the road in the forest, and obviously in pain. That I stopped to see if I could help, and only when I got close to him did I recognise who it was – the man who wheels the newspaper trolley around every day – and that he must be trying to get back to the hospital. Jennings was so angry then. He kept asking questions, but I just stonewalled, and then I started asking him why on earth he was questioning what I'd said when it was obvious that the man must have chased after whoever attacked you, left the hospital by the same route as the intruder and then got hurt and lost in the forest and the fog. He backed down then. I'm glad… glad your memory came back, otherwise I'd have been on my own in explaining what happened."

"And I'm glad I remembered it as I did, even if everyone's paying a price for it."

"Oh, don't worry about that. It's just inconvenient for people, but it'll pass soon enough. Within a week, I'd guess, if nothing more happens. You're not planning any more events, are you?"

"No, but I think I'd better get back to work and find out the full truth about Richard. I'm very concerned about him."

"He was in a very bad state. He can't have eaten or drunk anything since he left you on the corridor. Is he on the ward now?"

"No, he's still next door. I was surprised and shocked at first, but when I thought about it, and when I remembered what had happened…." she paused, before continuing, "yes, when I remembered, it seemed okay for him to be there."

"Jennings wanted to put him in one of the old cells, when I brought him back, but I persuaded him that he was too weak. They're terrible, the cells, cold, damp and dark. He might have died there."

For a few moments there was silence between them, until she asked, "And the record player?"

"Oh, yes, I thought you'd be bored here, so I brought it in for you to listen to something. That Bob Dylan record you liked – it's on the top of the pile. One of the nurses in the block has a car, so we went to get it this afternoon. I hope that's all right with you."

"Yes, thanks, it is… It was thoughtful of you. I hope I won't be here too long though."

"Well, get the porters to carry it to your room when you leave. I can pick it up another time." Again there was a silence between them, a slightly awkward one. This time he spoke first. "I am really sorry I didn't walk with you to your room when we got back here. It didn't seem…" He seemed unable to find the right word to complete the sentence. "Well," he continued, "I'm sorry anyway."

"No, it's not your fault. It's just an accident of timing that I was there then. But I've got to work out why it happened… Thanks again."

"I must go," he said, "my shift isn't finished yet. I'll call in again, if you're still here. Otherwise, you know where to find me." He leaned forward and kissed her on the left cheek, the unhurt one, as a brother might kiss a sister. But as he left, she could not help wishing that it had been a different kind of kiss, not a brotherly one, however much it might have hurt her.

Her final visitor was David Peters, who told her that he had managed to work a full day for the first time in over a week, but that he still couldn't tell from one day to another if he would even be able to leave his wife. "Enough of my troubles, though," he said, "how are you? John said you were feeling better." She acknowledged that she was and that he had checked her over and was happy to see her discharged the next day. He told her that either he or John Sutton would come in to confirm this, but he checked the clipboard at the end of her bed and quickly checked her eyes, as well as feeling the bump on her head. "I heard it was an intruder who did this, although everyone thought it was Richard Simms," he said. She felt troubled for a moment. It was not good to deceive her own colleagues. "But I had that civil servant calling me yesterday, and he was quite rude, especially about you."

"What did he say?"

"That all this would not have happened if you had agreed to transfer Richard. He seemed particularly well-informed about what has been going on. I refused to say anything and said that he was your patient. Your decisions were my decisions, you know the rule. But today, after it became known that there was an intruder who had attacked you, he called me again. He was much more polite, apologised for being cross and said that he would invite you to visit him when you'd resumed your duties. He said he'd explain about Richard then. So, would you take up his offer?"

"Yes, I would, straight away. Maybe Thursday, if he calls tomorrow. I know there's a lot else to do, but I think I must sort out his history before I complete his review."

"Do you want someone to go with you?"

"No, no, I'll be fine by then. Intriguing, isn't it?"

"It's a strange case, Ruth. Take care, won't you? I'm not sure we shouldn't take it to the deputy superintendent now."

"No, don't do that." She did not want to have any more discussions of Richard with him! "Let's find out what he has to say first."

"I'll go along with this for the moment, but if there's any cause to take it higher once you've met this Oates fellow then I'll have to take it up."

"I agree. It's just that I don't think I'm Mr Jennings' favourite doctor at the moment, nor Richard his favourite patient." She was pleased by the way events had fallen once she had made her decision. On Michael's prompting she had done so, she remembered, and felt again the pang she had felt when he'd kissed her cheek.

"I can see that you're a bit tired," David said. "If I'm in tomorrow, I'll look in during the morning and confirm your discharge." Ruth thanked him, but her thoughts were moving beyond that discharge. She would find out what she had not been able to discover by any other means, and she only had to go into London to do that.

CHAPTER FORTY-ONE

Richard could hardly understand what the nurse had said. He had been exhausted when he returned to the hospital, and had slept most of the first day in the Infirmary hardly knowing where he was. On the second day he had eaten breakfast and the nurse had told him he could not get dressed that day. He had to rest his ankle because it was still swollen, but later in the week he would be able to return to Ward 44. "Back to the ward?" he asked back, trying not to reveal his astonishment. He had expected to be transferred to the Secure Block, perhaps even put into isolation. Attacking a doctor, knocking her down, hearing her head crack against the hard floor, running away and hiding in the forest, these were the actions of a violent lunatic who should be locked up. He should not just be transferred back to the ward.

"What… what happened?" he asked, hoping that the nurse would not notice his inquisitiveness. "To me?"

"They think you chased an intruder away, Richard, after he'd attacked one of the doctors. You must have climbed over the wall after him and then got lost and hurt your ankle."

The nurse looked at him with interest. He should be careful, he thought. Perhaps she'd been asked to take note of his reaction. So he gave no reaction at all. But he was sure that Doctor Appleton had seen him, had spoken to him, before he hit her. Surely she could not have forgotten that? But of course, he had no idea how she was. But again, how could the idea have taken root that he had chased an intruder away? There had been nobody else on the corridor to see him, but surely they would just have assumed that a missing patient was responsible for the attack. He could not think how this untruth had been constructed. And then he tried to work out how he had been found and brought back to the hospital. He'd thought that he would die in that shed. He had finally found the shed when he realised he had stumbled onto the playing field. The cut grass was so different to any other part of the woodland, and he knew where the shed was. But how did the nurse from the Secure Block know he would be there? He lay back on his bed to try to think these things through.

For the next two hours Richard worried about the matter silently. Many times he reconstructed the events of that late afternoon on Sunday, seeing Doctor Appleton in the corridor and feeling impelled to enact what Oates wanted him to do. She had not for a moment anticipated the blow, and she had allowed him to come close to her without a challenge. He had seen that his intended blow, to her stomach, would not have had the effect that Oates wanted, and at the last moment he had twisted upwards and punched her in the face. But there was no intruder. She could not have seen anybody else but him. Nobody else could have claimed to have seen an intruder. And finally he realised – the only possible explanation: she had lied about what had happened. Whereas Oates had been sure that the reaction of a doctor to being attacked would be enough to ensure that Richard was not transferred, he had been wrong. She had decided to lie, to cover up for him. And what's more, she had probably suggested to the motorcyclist that he might look in the shed in that playing field in the forest to find him. She, after all, had seen him there. And she had, apparently, been out on a motorcycle before he struck her. She was wearing a leather jacket and holding a helmet.

He felt humbled by what he now assumed she had done. She had prevented him from being punished, and she had helped – probably – to save his life. She had lied about what he had done, and if anything she had turned him into a kind of hero. And that made him feel ashamed. The very last thing he wanted was for anyone to think well of him. He could not think well of himself. How could he, how should he, now react to her? He had hit her because of Oates. A sudden despair swept over him, but after the despair there was a moment of realisation. He hated the man, Oates. He somehow represented all the duplicity of government representatives, of politicians, of others he had worked with who had lied to him. Lied and deceived, persuaded him to do their work, telling him that it was all for the good and that he was wrong to see the evil of it. All the others who had deceived him had moved beyond his realm, and he had not seen them for many years, all except Oates. At that moment he determined that he would not be afraid of him, or of what he might do to him, ever again.

CHAPTER FORTY-TWO

Ruth returned to work on the Wednesday. David Peters had come into work and discharged her from the Infirmary before he had to leave, his wife being unwell again. Although he had urged her not to go into the wards, she had said that all she would do was be available if needed. She would not do any rounds, nor meet with staff or patients, nor carry out any review work. Having made these promises to David, she felt she could hardly break them, so she stayed in the doctors' room writing up records, completing file reports and putting the files into the out tray. John Sutton looked in and was pleased to see her back, but was not very sympathetic about her bruising, claiming that the first lesson he'd been taught when he started psychiatry was how to duck.

"I must have missed that lesson," she said. He replied that David had told him to restrain Ruth physically if he saw her working on the wards or meeting with patients or nurses. "Why?" she asked. "Why would he say that? Even in jest?"

"Could it be something to do with the reputation you've earned?" John said sarcastically, even as he beat a retreat. She made a mental note to ask him later what he meant by that. What reputation could she have earned? She had only been at the hospital for a little more than three weeks.

She re-engaged with the files, and had worked her way well down the pile when she came again to that for Richard Simms. If she had been strictly adhering to David's instructions, she would have set it aside immediately. Richard was under review, and she was not to do any review work. But she had already written up some ordinary notes in the files of other patients under review – not part of their reviews, but just completing records of recent observations and noting small changes in treatment. And so she picked up the file and started to reread it, perhaps more closely than she had first done.

The writing in the file was difficult to interpret. Winstanley's handwriting was often impossibly scrawled in many of the other files she had opened since her arrival, but in Richard's case he seemed to have surpassed himself. Many words became nothing more than a flourish of the pen after the initial letter or two, so that she had to guess the possible words from their immediate context; and as she was already guessing other words, it became more like a parlour game than a medical rereading. She had passed some of this over when she had first read the file, she recalled, because it had seemed so laborious and time-consuming. Now she tried to read every line, and each word, to make sure she had not overlooked something in her haste.

It was slow-going. The first page did not add anything. It indicated that Richard had attempted suicide and that the depression that led to this act might be related to his work, but it did not specify what that work had been. Richard had been referred to the hospital by the police. Winstanley had confirmed this and had admitted him to Black Roding. But Ruth could not find out what the full process of admission had been. There should have been more doctors than one involved in the process, just as a patient referred now to the hospital would come from a practitioner outside the hospital to the doctors in the Admissions Unit, and only after that to the doctors in the ward to which the patient was finally admitted.

So at present, at least three, and arguably more, would have been evident in the process of admission. But there was no evidence of others, and Winstanley's notes appeared to be contemporaneous to the admission. She looked up one or two of the older files that were in the out tray. Sure enough, there was always evidence of two or even three doctors signing the records concerning admission to the hospital.

She returned to the slow reconstruction of the file after admission. The first entries were factual. She had read them previously. They described his physical details, his initial behaviour, and also summarised nurses' observations of Richard rather than Winstanley's, as if he were simply noting what they had reported to him. Entries such as "slept badly", "seen weeping to himself", "angry outburst" characterised the whole page. But the behaviour they described was not untypical of a patient newly entered to an asylum, and she understood that the Black Roding of thirteen years previous was a quite different institution and no doubt much more terrifying. The new drugs of the past decade had done so much to modify behaviour.

She read on. Winstanley had obviously held some one-to-one sessions with Richard. These too were summarised, with no detail. "Patient resentful", "unco-operative", "unwilling to discuss suicide attempt" were among the phrases she could decipher, and she remembered she had picked out one or two of these when she had scanned through the file earlier. And then came the first marginal entry of the meetings with Oates. Ruth studied it and could make out some words – "unstable in high-risk situations", "unwilling to accept responsibility", "security status withdrawn" – but others she simply could not read. The writing seemed hurried, as if perhaps Winstanley were recording things being said to him. At the end there were three legible words – "Not for discharge". It was a stark statement of what had, in effect, been Richard's status for the past thirteen years. She tried to read the other words, isolating them with some blotting paper so that she could just see the individual shape of each word. But even then, only one new word seemed to emerge, and she was not sure of it because it had not been mentioned to her in any discussion of Richard and his problems. It seemed to be the word "homosexual", but she could not be sure, and she could not think why it appeared among the other phrases. And the other phrases seemed incongruous as well, not really medical or concerned with a man's psychiatric state, but rather a work-related appraisal of a man in government service. They had to be Oates' words, surely, and not Winstanley's? But how would they fit with the word "homosexual"?

She was so deep in her thoughts over this that the telephone startled her when it rang. She jumped, and paused before she picked up the receiver just to make sure she didn't sound startled. "Is that Doctor Appleton?" a voice asked suavely. She recognised Oates immediately. *In his polite, calm mode*, she thought.

"Yes," she answered, "speaking."

"It's Francis Oates here," the man said, and his unctuous tone nauseated her. "I hope you're well. I understand that you had an… accident." The pause while he seemed to search for the right word was deliberate, she was sure. "An intruder, wasn't it?" He was annoyingly well-informed, and despite his sanctimony she could detect his irony. "Saved by our mutual friend, I believe you were."

She tried not to seem perturbed by his knowledge and his ironic offensiveness. "Yes, that's right. I was fortunate that Richard was close by. Were you calling me about him?"

"Yes, I am. I feel that we've not been able to tell you everything about him, but I can't say more over the phone. I wondered if you would come into town tomorrow and meet with me. Then I could, I think, help you to understand the situation a little better."

"That's a little unusual, you know," she said, wondering if she should fob him off. The image of a long-legged spider came into her mind, standing still on its web, each leg tensed to sense the vibration of the web as a victim encountered it. And she felt that she was the small fly that had just touched the outer strand but was being deflected towards the centre.

"I've cleared it with the deputy superintendent. He understands the situation. He thinks it's the right thing to do."

That did not comfort Ruth at all. She felt inclined to the view that whatever the deputy superintendent thought was best was most likely to prove disastrous for her. But her curiosity was aroused. The prospect of answering the many questions around Richard Simms, and particularly what to do about him, was alluring. And surely Oates could not do anything in his office to make things worse? And yet the image of Oates as a spider, made large and terrifying as if in one of Gulliver's adventures, still held her back.

"I don't know if it's that easy to come in. I'm covering a lot for my consultant whose wife is unwell. I couldn't really leave it to my junior to be on his own with five wards any more than I already have."

"But isn't your consultant working tomorrow? He isn't off sick himself, is he? If he does come in to work, why not just agree with him that you'll come into town, and I'm sure we can answer your questions here."

She felt she was on the spot now. Oates seemed to know even about David Peters' working arrangements. "All right," she said. "At what time, and where?"

"Twelve o'clock, at our offices. Do you have a pen and paper?" He dictated the address and gave her a cheerful farewell before cutting the line.

Ruth looked at the address with a mixture of dread and fascination. It was, evidently, at the heart of government. "Bastard," she muttered, as she put the receiver down. And then she laughed at herself. Her language, it seemed, had grown coarser from her association with Black Roding.

She resumed her close reading of Richard's file, but now she felt less anxious to interpret every word. The next day might bring better answers than studying the file. But she thought she should be as well informed as possible, so it was not wasted time. As she read, she fingered the bruising around her eye. It was very tender, and no doubt the bruising was becoming even more colourful. It would mean that people would look at her with surprise as she went in and out of London the next day, assuming that David Peters was in. But that would be a small price if she could resolve the situation around her patient.

She was close to giving up her reading of the file, which had had reached 1957 by the dates of entries, when she suddenly realised that two words which she had not previously deciphered said "Stop treatment".

She had previously thought that Richard was receiving no drug treatment throughout his time at Black Roding. That had been her view after her first reading of the file, where the only treatment listed had been the electric shock therapy that she had talked about with the other doctors. And now, again, she had not found any mention of commencing a drug treatment in the file. Perhaps it lay in some of the lines she had not been able to read at all. She looked closely at the words after the two she had decoded, saying half-aloud, "Stop treatment of patient with DES for homosexuality." Was that right? That he was homosexual and had been given drugs to subdue his sexual drives? But she was not sure and wondered how she could resolve her own uncertainty. David Peters might know; John Sutton certainly would not; she could have asked the superintendent, but he was away and not contactable; she would not ask the deputy superintendent, nor his registrar. So, who could she ask? The pharmacy! They might know; well, they might know if someone still working there had been working there in 1957.

The pharmacy was on the ground floor beneath the administrative offices. She thought it best to go there in person and to take the record card from the file, so that she could show the pharmacist what was puzzling her. It was half past four so there was still time for the principal pharmacy staff to be at work, and not just the night cover, who would more likely be a junior. So she picked up the card and hurried off, walking with her face down like one of the patients, to avoid the embarrassing looks she knew she would attract.

The pharmacy was constructed in a peculiar way. Through the doorway there was a small waiting room and a counter. Behind the counter was a single doorway into the store, where the staff made up the prescriptions that came in from every ward in the hospital. But the waiting room had no chair, no reading material and no decoration of any kind. The counter did not have a flap to allow entry, and Ruth assumed that the pharmacy staff must enter the store by another route. It was all designed to prevent patients, or others, from entering the storeroom. The drugs were too dangerous, and too precious, for anyone to be allowed access. Ruth had to ring a bell that was on the counter, to indicate that she needed someone's attention. Some moments later a white-haired and ruby-faced man, almost as round as he was tall, edged into the area behind the counter.

"I'm sorry to trouble you. I need someone to tell me what this old record from a patient's file means." Ruth showed him the record card.

"You must be the famous doctor who was attacked by an intruder," he said, scrutinising her face.

She was still recovering from the shock of being known to everyone. The "famous doctor"!

First John Sutton, and now this pharmacist. Was there anyone who did not know what had happened to her? She wished she did not have this notoriety. "Yes, my face does give me away, doesn't it?" she said. "But I was puzzled by an entry on an old record card, and I wondered if someone here, you perhaps, could help me work it out."

"Let me see it," he pointed to the card and took it from her. She pointed to the particular entry, and he immediately muttered, "Winstanley," then looked at her. "The worst writing I ever encountered in this hospital was Winstanley's. Impossible at times to make out what he wanted, and I often had to send prescriptions back because even I couldn't read them. Let me look at it more closely." He took out a pair of spectacles from his top pocket, perched the glasses on the top of his bulbous nose and placed the record card on the counter beneath the solitary light in the ceiling. He looked closely at the writing next to his finger, but then he moved his finger across to the date. "I remember that date," he said. "That tells me what the entry is. The superintendent, Verity, issued an instruction to every doctor and to the pharmacy. It was to stop a treatment that he no longer wanted in the hospital. It caused a lot of trouble among some of the doctors. They didn't like being told what they could or couldn't do. But he was adamant it had to stop, and I was not allowed to order it anymore, so the doctors couldn't prescribe it any longer. It was DES, and it was given to patients who had been involved in homosexual acts. That's what was done then, you see. It changed their… er… their feelings." He looked a little flustered to be talking of such things to her. "I think the superintendent was right, but it was very controversial then. Now, well, the drug isn't used anymore. I've read that it had some very bad effects, even if it stopped people getting into trouble with the law."

Although her own guess at the words had proved correct, Ruth was still taken aback by the confirmation. Richard's records, she now thought, had not been properly written up. Winstanley had prescribed a treatment without confirming it in the records, an act that could have led to him appearing before disciplinary boards. He had only recorded its ending, no doubt prepared, if ever confronted about it, to claim that all the time he had prescribed it he was only continuing a treatment previously arranged by some other doctor. She thanked the pharmacist, picked up the record card and left the room. Now she was determined to go and visit Oates, and to find out why her patient had been subjected to such treatment.

CHAPTER FORTY-THREE

It made it easier for Ruth that David Peters was in work and did not seem to think he would be called away. His wife was feeling well, and generally he knew when it was likely that he would be summoned home. So he agreed that she should go to see Oates, especially when she told him of her discovery the previous evening. "I should have read the file more carefully the first time," she said apologetically, but David waved away her apologies. No-one could read Winstanley's writing consistently, he asserted, and he himself had experienced no end of difficulty because of it.

She took a coat, because a cold wind was blowing, and tucked her hands in her pockets and hurried towards the porters' lodge. The gates were open, and one of the porters was standing in the doorway of the lodge. He watched her with deep interest, then disappeared into the lodge. She realised that the porters were probably one source of Oates' information. He could easily have suborned them against her. Just stopping at the lodge with his assistant and reminding them of their military service would have been enough. She could almost hear the telephone being lifted off its receiver as she walked through the gates.

She found her way to the station with a lot more ease than when she had made the opposite journey eighteen days before. And the journey into London was straightforward. But the building in which Oates worked was not the Georgian palace she had expected from the address but a dull red-brick building that looked out of place among the grander centres of government surrounding it. She had to pass three desks, and answer questions from a clerk at each, before being waved forward. Eventually, on what she thought must be the third or fourth floor of the building, she reached Oates' secretary, who was busily typing on a modern electrical machine. "Sir Francis is expecting you, but he's busy and asked you to wait," she said. Ruth looked around. It was not obvious where she was to wait. "Back there," the secretary pointed without stopping her typing, "there's a chair." Ruth retraced her steps and saw that in the open corridor there was indeed a single, hard, wooden chair. Just like school, she thought, being forced to wait outside the head's study. She was determined to resist Oates in every way possible, but all the same she felt more than a little daunted. And no doubt that was what he wanted.

Twenty minutes later, and fifteen after their midday appointment, the secretary led her into Oates' office. It was spacious and well-carpeted, with paintings on the walls which she felt vaguely she should recognise – a nineteenth-century politician, a three-masted sailing ship, and a rural, Scottish-seeming landscape. Oates was seated behind a dark, polished desk. There were two sofas set to one side, and a tray of drinks bottles, and another of glasses, on a low table between them. He was wearing a dark suit with a regimental tie, although she had no idea which regiment it might be. In front of his desk another wooden chair had been placed so that she could sit. He waved her towards it and greeted her.

"My goodness, you did take a blow, didn't you?" he said. She made no comment in response. "Before we start our discussion, Doctor, I have to ask you to read this," he held up a typed document in one hand and a single sheet in the other, "and then sign this."

"What?" she answered. "Why? What are they?"

"This is a summary of the Official Secrets Act," again he held up the first document, "and this is your acknowledgement that you are bound by the terms of the Act."

"But why do I need to sign that?" She was wrong-footed by his opening. She had heard of the Act but knew next to nothing about it. "I'm not a civil servant. I thought it was just government officers who signed that."

"No. Anyone who is about to be given classified information has to sign the agreement and be bound by the Act. Otherwise you can't be given the information. Here, read them first."

She picked up the two documents reluctantly. The first was indeed a summary of the Act and told her that revealing classified information was a criminal offence and could lead to a lengthy prison sentence. It informed her that it was her responsibility to ensure that the information was not conveyed in any form to another person or organisation.

"No doubt you've been puzzled by Richard Simms' records or, perhaps one should say, his lack of records. But that is because Winstanley signed up to the Act all those years ago and agreed that his records would therefore not reveal information about Simms that was classified. But I had not anticipated his untimely death, and I was not informed of it, or we might have avoided any difficulty."

"How, by spiriting him away from the hospital?" her tone was half-challenging, half-fearful. The image of the web had come to her mind again, and she felt the sticky lines of thread starting to pull at her, drawing her inwards fatefully.

"No, no spiriting, just ensuring that his care was planned and secure. And not unstable, as it seems to have become."

"By getting him transferred to another hospital, by another one of your toadies? Winstanley broke the rules, you know. He didn't record his treatment until it was being stopped."

"Yes, I remember his telling me that the new superintendent had issued an order banning it. He was very annoyed. Said it was a treatment that had the effects that were sought, and it had controlled Simms well. But he couldn't override the superintendent because the drug was not available at the hospital. He said he would arrange something different that would…" here the civil servant paused and sought briefly a particular word, "that would be similarly effective."

"Effective? Is that what was important? And effective in what way?"

"Well, I can't answer that question unless you sign the second document and pass it back to me." Oates sat back in his chair and stared at her. She remained silent, thinking, weighing the conflicting arguments in her head. To sign and be drawn yet further into this web, but perhaps to learn the information that would be the key to unlocking her problems with Richard Simms; or not to sign, and escape the web, but risk Oates going to the deputy superintendent, removing Richard from her care and subjecting him to some further, and no doubt inappropriate, treatment. She read the agreement quickly and, having made her decision, took the pen Oates offered her and wrote her name and profession, the date and her signature before she passed it back to him.

"Thank you, Doctor. I will be brief. The difficulty around Simms is that he had a job, both during the war and afterwards, that gave him a great deal of secret information. I cannot tell you what that job was, but the information was very highly classified. During the 1950s he appeared to have some kind of a breakdown, and he was also breaking the law by indulging in homosexual acts, in particular what was called 'cottaging' in the vernacular. It was discovered that he was about to reveal secret information to a third party. In war, as he knew, it would have been called treason, and he would have been executed. In peacetime, it is just a criminal offence, but a trial and a long sentence awaited him. He attempted to kill himself as a consequence. He had done great service to the country during the war, so it was decided that he should be offered the chance of admission to an asylum and treatment after his attempted suicide, rather than face the ordeal that was otherwise inevitable. But he understood then, and he understands now, that he cannot be released from the asylum without facing the trial that he otherwise avoided. And that's why he has been so upset by the work you are doing, making him remember his past and threatening to release him and discharge him. And that, I imagine, is why he attacked you."

Ruth started at this last remark, rocking first forwards and then back, so astonished was she. "He did not attack me!" she protested, but she herself felt that her tone was unconvincing.

"I'm sure you have good reason for saying that, but my own view is that he did it. Perhaps the blow to your face, or your concussion, has deceived you. But Richard Simms is a dangerous man, who has lived a dangerous past, and who has tried to do extreme violence to himself. It would be no surprise if he were violent towards you in the circumstances I describe."

Ruth was silent. Whatever she had expected to hear, or had guessed might be the case, had been far surpassed by what Oates had said, and yet even then she had a hundred more questions she would have liked to ask but felt too overwhelmed to do so. She shook her head, as if to clear it, but also to interrupt Oates.

"No," she blurted out, "no! I am not going to agree to him being locked up any longer if he is not ill. I will make the right recommendation for him and then see how he reacts and what he wants to do. I am not going to make decisions about him behind his back just because you ask me to."

"But I haven't asked you anything yet." Oates was almost meek in his reply, but she mistrusted that more than any other attitude. "Although it's true that I would like you to agree to his being transferred, as I suggested when I visited you before, so that a further assessment of him and his situation can be made."

There was a long silence. Ruth bowed her head even, so that she could think without looking at him. Then finally she stood up. "No. I must work through his review, in the light of what you have said, and then make my recommendation to the superintendent. Then you'll have to talk to him and not to me."

She made to go, but he stopped her before she turned away. "I hope still to find some way to persuade you. And don't forget, you've signed this agreement. You can't repeat this to anyone. If it gets to the superintendent, I may have to have Simms arrested."

"That's your decision," she muttered, as she left the room hurriedly.

She walked down the stairs and marched out of the building without stopping at any of the desks at which she had been checked in as she arrived. She was angry, confused and anxious, all in around equal measure, and at first she just walked to try to calm herself, paying no heed to where she was or the direction she was taking. At one point she walked near a park, because she could recall later the green of the lawns, but she was not sure which park she had passed. When she had regained some sense of herself, she stopped to order coffee in a café that she glimpsed down a side street. She took a pen out of her handbag and found some paper, so that she could write down some of what she had heard. War service, secret information, preparation to communicate that information, spying, the Official Secrets Act, cottaging, attempted suicide, trial, imprisonment. It made little sense to her, but she could see how the past few weeks must have strained her patient. Winstanley had been his partner in concealment, in hiding him from the world, and had been the only person he ever met who knew some of the truth, except perhaps for Oates on his periodic visits. Winstanley's death, and the uncertainty that must have followed it, and the lack of any appearance from Oates, would have created great anxiety. And then her arrival and the threat of removal, of discharge, which carried the threat of trial and imprisonment. Michael had been right. A violent assault on her had been Richard's only response, his only way to try to direct what happened to him. But the questions that remained, now she knew a little of his background, were very large, and she wrote them down. Was Richard ill, or sane? How conscious was he of his own concealment? How deliberate was his unwillingness to communicate? What should she do next? Should she report all this to someone? And if so, to whom? And what would Oates do next? All she could think of, and it did not seem attractive as a course of action, was that she should hurry back to Black Roding and report it all to the deputy superintendent. But what could she say, having signed the agreement to the Official Secrets Act?

She paid for the coffee, which she had hardly sipped and which had gone cold while she scribbled her note to herself, and asked for direction to the nearest station. She left the café and followed the directions she had been given. At the station the ticket inspector checked her ticket and said she was allowed to return from that station, so she took the escalator down to the platform. There were more people on the platform than usual – there was obviously a delay between trains – and she was anxious to get on the first train, so she moved through the throng of travellers to the edge of the platform.

She was still thinking about all that she had heard and all the questions she had written down. The platform was warm, despite it being October, and she was near the mouth of the tunnel. As she looked down, she saw that there was a mouse playing, or at least scurrying about, beneath the metal rails that carried the train and the electrical current that powered the trains. She looked more closely. There was a pit beneath the rails, around two feet deep, and it was there that the mouse, no, the two mice, she could now see, were running hither and thither. She marvelled that the creatures could live there, and be there, in full view of all the Londoners around her, in such a hostile and dangerous environment. What on earth could they live on? And it was just as she was wondering that, how could they live there, that she felt the violent shove in her back that sent her tumbling forward into the space beyond the platform's edge and down towards the deadly rails below.

CHAPTER FORTY-FOUR

As early as he dared on the Thursday morning, Richard asked the nurse in the Infirmary if he could have some paper and a pencil or a pen. He had stuttered that it was something his doctor had asked him to do, as part of his treatment, to write down all he could remember. She had shrugged but a little later had brought him some lined paper and an old pen and left him to it. He had pulled his bedside chair up to a small table in one corner of the room and had commenced writing. The first paragraphs were slow to write, and painful, since he was forced to contemplate the wrong he had done to Doctor Appleton, to try to explain why he had been led, almost forced, to strike her, breaking a lifelong taboo in the process. At school he could remember getting into one or two fights. And he had boxed a little, as a young man and student. But he had never hit a girl or woman in all his life.

He wrote a little about how he had gone to university and not been called up because his course was relevant to the government's military strategy. He wanted to write down all that had happened to him since he had left grammar school. Some of it had been written down before in the journals he kept in the water tower. Some of it he had never written before, and it would be painful to recall those events. But he thought that it was necessary, that he was nearing some unknown moment when he would be called to account for all he had done, and he needed to have recorded it because he would never be able to say it all. And he wanted Doctor Appleton to know the truth.

His thoughts were interrupted by the nurse. "Goodness me, you've been busy," she said, looking at the three sheets of paper already covered in his writing. He was going to need more paper, he thought. "I should think they'll send you back to your ward later on. You seem much better now, almost fully recovered. He ignored her. He had already started writing the rest of his life.

CHAPTER FORTY-FIVE

It was that thought of life that saved her, she realised afterwards. The thought of the mice, the small scurrying creatures, alive there beneath the rails, meant that her body somehow sought to slide between the rails to find that same space beneath, in which they lived, so that she too could live. She did not make it there unscathed. Her shoulder hit the non-live rail, and then her hip did too, and she crashed to the floor, bruising her hands and knees as they hit the concrete base first, but somehow she avoided all contact with the live rail that would almost certainly have brought her life to an end. And her head did not strike the concrete that supported the rails. She lay there, face down, and heard a woman scream, and several agitated shouts, but then, above the other noises, a man's voice was yelling at her, "Don't move, don't try to get up, keep your head down, stay there, don't move! We'll get help!"

She had felt a breath of hot air, the first warning of an oncoming train, and then the sound of the rails vibrating. There was more shouting and agitation on the platform, but she could not respond to it. The noise of the oncoming train was growing greater, its clanking wheels and undercarriage causing the rails to vibrate all the more. Then she heard the hissing of brakes somewhere behind her. The train, she thought, was coming along the platform, and perhaps the driver had seen her. It had not come at speed from the tunnel and travelled over her. Instead, she sensed, the train was coming from the far tunnel and had stopped somewhere short of where she was lying.

Again the man's voice was yelling at her. "Still don't move. You mustn't move. The train has stopped but the rail is still live. Don't try to stand up. Just stay there until the power is turned off. Don't move!" Then he dropped his voice a little. "I saw you fall. I think you're all right. Just shake an arm if you can hear me."

She tried to pull her right arm out from beneath her, but it would not budge beneath the weight of her body. And she did not dare to raise herself.

"That's enough," the man said above her. She thought he was probably kneeling on the platform's edge. "I saw your arm move. We'll get you out of there." He seemed then to be talking to people on the platform. "She's conscious," she heard him say, "and she could probably get up if you can get the power turned off." Then he appeared to turn back towards her. "They're trying to get the power off now. They'll deal with you now."

She wished she could thank the unknown man, but he was replaced by a different voice. "Don't worry, miss, we'll get you out of there in a jiffy. Just you keep still a while longer." She waited for what seemed an age, although later she reckoned it might have been no longer than five minutes. The second voice kept talking to her, but if she just shifted her body a tiny amount he shouted to her to keep still. At last she sensed that someone had come down from the platform and was standing near her head. "I'm here now," it was the second man, "and I'm going to help you to kneel, but with your head still down. I don't want your head coming up until we're ready to manoeuvre past the rails." She felt him crouch down and his arms reaching under her shoulders. "Now, as I lift, just kneel on all fours. Keep your hands on the floor." As he lifted her shoulders she was able to force her body upwards, as he had asked, and to shuffle her legs forward so that she was indeed kneeling on all fours. "And now lift your head up." She did so, and she could see him crouching in front of her. On each side she could see the two rails through which she had fallen into the gap and onto the floor where she now knelt. "Now you need to kneel up, and then, when I've stood up, I'll help you to stand." And, slowly, that was what they did, and as she stood up a few of the passengers watching the scene even applauded. The man completed the task by lifting Ruth up and passing her to two others who were on the platform. Only then did she see the train that had stopped some ten yards short of her, and she shuddered at the thought of what might have happened.

They sat her down on the platform for a few moments while they questioned her. It was evident that nobody had seen the push that had caused her near-death, so she had to explain three times that she had not jumped on the line but been pushed by someone on the platform. She had simply tried, when falling, to reach the space beneath the lines. Then they led her up the escalator and through a brown wooden door into a staff area, where they sat her down and offered her some tea. "You'll have shock," one of the staff said, "so heap some sugar into that cup." For once, she did as suggested. She felt that she was suffering from shock – the shock of a second assault on her in the course of just a few days, and the shock of what Oates had told her – and she could hardly think anymore of what she should do. She put down the cup and suddenly burst into tears, deep sobs coming from within her chest, causing tears to drip down her face. She tried to stem the flow by squeezing the corners of her eyes, but it seemed not to work. She was too upset, and the station staff allowed her to cry for a while, before one of them put a blanket around her. "We're calling an ambulance for you. Best to get you checked over, we think."

And so it was a few hours later that she found herself in an argument with a houseman at the Central Marylebone Hospital – he wanting to keep her in hospital overnight for observation, while she was demanding to be allowed to go home, not that she was letting on where home was. The merest mention of Black Roding, she thought, and she was likely to be locked up for her own safety. She had not told the hospital her real name, and she had not revealed that she herself was a doctor. It had taken until the ambulance came for her to realise that what had happened to her might not have been the accident that everyone else was assuming it had been; that Oates had said that he wanted still to persuade her to do as he asked, and perhaps this was his doing. That one of his minions, perhaps the shifty, evil-looking one who had accompanied him to the hospital, might have been instructed to follow her and put her out of action one way or another. And in the ambulance she had decided against revealing to the hospital staff what had happened, so that she could get away and find somewhere safe to work out what to do next. She did not want to complain to the police about the push. That seemed a sure way of alerting Oates to where she was. And she most definitely did not want to stay overnight, when Oates could be checking the London hospitals for her.

"Look," she exclaimed, "I know you think it's best that I stay here, but I really can't, and won't, and I need you to tell someone to bring me my coat and bag so that I can go home. I'm feeling better; I was not knocked out, and I was conscious the whole time."

"But the ambulance men reported that you'd broken down crying, and you seemed confused about what had happened." The houseman was anxious, she understood entirely why, that something might go wrong if he allowed her to walk out. He would be held responsible, even if she had simply exercised her right to leave.

"Well, that's not surprising, is it," Ruth tried not to sound petulant, "given what happened? The crush of people on the platform led to me being pushed in front of a train. I was lucky not to be killed."

"Is that what happened?" the young man asked. "Only, the ambulance crew said you claimed someone pushed you. If so, we need to get the police to take a statement before you leave."

"No, no, I only meant that someone in the crush must have pushed up against me. No, I want to leave. Please bring me my things so that I can leave."

"Very well, but I will put down that it was against my advice." He left her, and Ruth heard a conversation with a nurse a few yards away. It caused her more concern. "It may have been a suicide attempt after all. I need a senior doctor to consider whether she needs to be prevented from leaving."

That was not going to happen, she decided. She stood up. Her coat and bag must be nearby. If she could just get them, she could leave and get away, and not face the humiliation of being subjected to a restraining order denying her freedom. Imagine, a psychiatrist who fell under a train and gave a false name to the transport staff, the ambulance crew and the hospital treating her. She would never survive it professionally. She looked out of the cubicle in which the doctor had been talking to her. It was a general area, in which there were a couple of wooden desks and chairs, and a trolley and wheelchair for patients. On one of the chairs sat her bag, and her coat was slung over the back of the chair. The two nurses seemed occupied, one of them writing down records at a small counter, and the other making a telephone call at the second desk. She went slowly but as confidently as she could to the bag, picked it and the coat up and immediately turned away.

"Hey, where are you going? You've not been discharged yet. You can't go," the nurse making the telephone call shouted at her back. But Ruth had seen an Exit sign and was already hurrying away and out to the street beyond.

The evening was drawing on, and people were hurrying home, so she was able to join the throng of commuters and hope that they would lead her to a station. She only had to walk two or three streets in this crowd before she saw the external sign for the London Underground system. Now she slowed down, moved in towards the wall she was passing by and stopped. It seemed a relief to have found her way of getting home, but she was not relieved at all. For a start, she was sure she had been pushed onto the rails in the station, and she could not separate that from her meeting with Oates and what he had told her. Now she would have to face going down onto a similar platform. What if whoever had pushed her was still following her? She looked around but could not see anyone standing still as she was. And would it really be right to go back to the hospital? By now Oates might again have been talking to the deputy superintendent and placing him under an obligation to remove her from Richard's case; and perhaps telling him of her 'distressed' state as she left him, hinting at her taking some drastic action, when it was he who had arranged it. It was a shock to her to realise suddenly that the norms of her life had been transformed. Usually she would have trusted the hospital authorities at Black Roding to do the right thing; she would have believed implicitly in the integrity of a senior civil servant; she would have trusted the station staff, the ambulance crew, the doctor and nurse in the hospital, and told them who she was and what had happened truthfully. But now she trusted none of them. And her life was at risk, it seemed. But why this was the case, she still could not understand, and she felt that the only way to solve the problem of Richard finally was to confront him with all that she knew about him, and perhaps with some of what had happened to her, and hope that she would penetrate the silence with which he had surrounded himself. But she knew she could not do that until the next morning, and meanwhile the problem remained to find a safe haven for the night.

Ruth first thought of the one or two people she knew in London, former fellow students and medical colleagues. But she did not have their addresses on her. She would have gone to Frances's home, but she did not know where that was. She could go back to Princes Risborough, but they would be astonished to find her back, and then she would have to try to get to Black Roding at an impossible time in the morning. The trains would not even be running. There was no other recourse, then, but Michael's. And what might he think of her turning up and asking to stay the night? Well, she would have to find out.

CHAPTER FORTY-SIX

It was not easy to find Michael's flat. She had only visited it once, on the back of his motorbike, and she had taken no notice of the address. She tried, in looking at the Underground map on the platform, to work out what was likely to be the nearest station. Then, she hoped, she might be able to reconstruct the motorbike journey by picking out landmarks. She picked the right station but took the wrong direction on exiting the station, not realising that there were two exits. When after twenty minutes she had seen nothing that she could recall, she retraced her steps and discovered her error. By taking the dank passage through a pedestrian tunnel under the railway, she almost immediately saw a public house that she thought she could recall. She walked on and passed a Conservative Club which she also recognised, or at least the small driveway and lawn that led to it. Somewhere, she thought, she needed to take a left turn into more residential streets, and she was pleased to see a large private house that she had noticed on her previous visit. Bushes and small trees masked it a little, but she realised from the plaque on the outer wall that it was a doctor's house and surgery combined. She was nearly there, she thought, and pulled her coat more tightly around herself. Yes, she better had be nearly there, or she would have no alternative but Black Roding.

She walked down the road, trying to recall which direction Michael had then taken the bike in. The houses were a long terrace of two-down, three-up properties, their bricks grey and their windows curtained against the darkness and the cold. Full of families, she thought, all completely unaware of her and of what had happened to her. She tried to think how she had got herself into this extraordinary situation which had transformed her life into such a tangled mess. It was not like her at all. Her life had always been ordered, regular, controlled. Now it had drifted into turbulence so violent that she was nearly broken.

She had reached the end of the road, and her thoughts had distracted her. She looked around. The roads crossed here, so she had a choice of three directions – forwards, left or right – and nothing to guide her decision. She tried to think again. She was sure Michael had reached this point, and it seemed to her that they had then turned right. But in the dark, and now with just the meagre light spilled out by the streetlamps, it was harder to recognise the buildings or the streets. She tried to re-imagine the final part of the journey. Yes, she could remember it up to this point, but she really wasn't sure. And she felt exhausted and wanted to sit down and weep again. But just as despair seemed about to overwhelm her, a young man approached from the opposite road. He was whistling and smoking alternately and did not immediately notice her, but suddenly as he crossed the road and approached her, he spoke.

"Well, well, if it isn't Michael's mad woman!" He looked closely at her. "It is, isn't it? You were the woman walking in the forest?"

"Tich?" she asked. She could not see him clearly.

"Yup, that's me," he said cheerily, but then he seemed to recognise that she was in some difficulty. "What's up? And what are you doing here?"

"I had an accident," she almost cried as she said it, "and I was looking for Michael's flat."

Another time he would have made a joke of this. But he understood the urgency behind her gasped words. "I just came from there," he said.

"He needed my advice on that scrambling bike he's doing up. He's taken on more than he can chew there, you know."

She could not reply, and she felt as if she might faint. But she felt him take hold of her arm, quite tightly, and hold her up. "Come on. I'll take you there. It's only a short walk." He put his other arm around her, again tightly, and tucked it under her armpit, and she was grateful that he did so and let him support her.

She had been wrong. The correct route was straight on, and the road curved to the right. And then she recognised the block of flats and saw Michael's bike. "I can make it from here," she said, not wanting Michael to see her in Tich's arms. Why did she not want that, she had time to ask herself, before he laughed.

"No, no, I'll not leave you until he opens the door. If he's fallen asleep already, you might never waken him."

Despite her weariness, she had time to feel slightly ashamed. This was the young man whom she had taken instantly against because of his constant jesting, his lack of seriousness. But now his jokes were light and well-intentioned, and his concern for her obvious. He had not made the kind of rude, or even crude, jokes that she might have expected when she was lost, looking for Michael's flat.

He helped her through the main door of the block and up the stairs, leaning his hand against her back as he followed her up the narrow staircase. She knew the door of Michael's flat, and lifted the door knocker and let it drop against the brass frame. Tich no longer held her, but said quietly, "You all right?"

She nodded and waited. Then Michael answered the door. He was in an oil-stained shirt and was wiping his hands with an oily rag. "Ruth?" he said, astonished. "Tich? What happened?"

She said nothing, but Tich had time to say, "She said she's been in an accident. Was looking for you," before she stumbled forward. Michael was quick enough to catch her and to pull her into the flat. He led her to a chair in the living room, and she sat down. Tich waved a hand to indicate that he was leaving, and Michael acknowledged it. But his attention was focussed on her.

"I'll make you a drink, and you can get warm. And then you'd better tell me what happened."

She remained hunched in the chair while he went into the kitchen. She heard the tap running to fill the kettle, and the match that he struck to light the gas ring. But they seemed to be sounds coming from another world. Her world still seemed to be one of bruising hurt, of unexpected assaults, of mysteries she could not fathom. And she felt crushed. Soon he was back with a drink for her, and he passed it to her, making sure that her fingers were tightly encircling the mug he gave. She sipped it; and then, for the first time since coming into the flat, she looked at him. "I'm sorry, it was all I could think of, to come here. I couldn't go back to Black Roding."

But he stopped her going further and asked if she had eaten. When she shook her head, he went to start some food preparation in the kitchen. "Give it a while, eat some food, then tell me about it," he said from the doorway into the kitchen.

So, half an hour later she tried to make some sense of all that had happened to her. She reminded him of Richard, and told him why she had been summoned to visit Oates in London. But when she mentioned that she had signed a statement about the Official Secrets Act, he stopped her and made her re-tell it.

"I don't know enough about such things," he said, "but I think you now need to be careful. If you tell me something that they think is secret, it could get you into trouble. Though how on earth you've got into this, I don't know. Do you?"

She shook her head. Then she told him in the most general terms what Oates had told her about Richard. She also told him that she had refused to do what Oates had asked of her.

"You're an obstinate so-and-so, aren't you?" he asked, but there was no criticism in his voice. "I know a lot of doctors who would just have caved in at that point. But go on, why come here?"

She told him then what had happened to her on the Underground platform and how she had survived the fall. He listened to her, touched her shoulder when she indicated that she was hurt there too, then simply held her.

"Have I got this right?" he asked. "You think this was not an accident?"

She pulled back a little to look at him. He had moved towards the same conclusion as her. "It was a push," she said; "whoever did it, I can't say, but it wasn't just a crush on the platform. It was a definite push. And I was distracted just looking at the mice on the floor. So either it was someone doing what Oates asked, or it was a random attack by a lunatic. What should I believe?"

"And that's why you didn't want to go back to the hospital, to Black Roding, that is?"

"Yes, I went to a hospital to get checked, but once that was done I didn't want to stay there. They might have forced me to stay there."

Despite the shocking nature of what she had told him, he snorted a laugh that he could not stop. "I don't suppose you'd have made that very easy for them."

She looked to see if he was mocking her at all. He was not. "What are you going to do, then?" he asked. He had let go of her, and now pulled a chair up near her and sat on it. He took one of her hands and squeezed it. "I'll help you, but I don't know what's best to do."

"Can I stay here? That's the most important thing. I need to talk to Richard as soon as possible in the morning, but not now. And I don't trust Oates. He might be at Black Roding even now, causing trouble for me, but I think it's likelier that he'll leave it until the morning as well. But someone at the hospital has been telling him what's going on, so it's best if I don't go back there tonight."

"Hang on, hang on, you lost me there," he protested. "Someone's telling him about the hospital?"

"Yes, he knew all about what had happened to me. And he insinuated that he knew it was Richard who attacked me."

"So the minute you turn up in the morning, he'll know?"

"I think so. But perhaps you could help me disguise myself, at least until I get to the ward. I'll have to go in early, be there by six thirty, so that I can change my clothes."

"The gate is opened at six, by the porters, because lots of the nurses who live outside the hospital arrive between then and seven, to start their early shifts. If we waited for a car that was going in, I could probably drive down the side of the car where the porters couldn't see us clearly from their lodge. They don't like standing outside when the mornings are chilly. And what will you do then?"

"I'm going to have to confront Richard with some of what I know. See if I can break down the communication block, or the memory block, whichever it is. If it works, I'll have to decide what to do on the basis of his reaction. If it doesn't, well, I suppose I'll have to report all this to the deputy superintendent, but I don't suppose he'll believe me. He'll send me back to Buckinghamshire, but I can't see what else I can do. I did try to think all this through on the train back – once I was safely inside the carriage."

She had made the first, just slightly, humorous comment on all that had happened. She took it as a good sign, as did he.

"OK," he said, "you had better stay here, and I'll drive you in in the morning. Do you want the bed or the settee?"

This was the one thing she hadn't decided upon as she sat on the train struggling to come to terms with all that had happened. Michael was a friend, undoubtedly a friend, but did he mean something more than that to her? She was not resolved on that; so, while the thought of a bed rather than an uncomfortable sofa was attractive, it seemed a step too far.

"I'll sleep there," she said, pointing to the settee. "If you've got something to wrap me up for the night."

"I've got a sleeping bag here somewhere. I'll find it now." He went away, and was gone for a few minutes, before returning with a quilted sleeping bag and a pillow. "It's all I've got, but I'll find you an extra blanket. And I'll set the alarm for earlier than usual." He stretched out the sleeping bag on the settee and tucked the pillow next to its arm. Then he wandered off again, coming back with a blanket which Ruth guessed he had pulled off his own bed.

"No, look, the sleeping bag's enough for me. Take the blanket back, I'll be fine with just this." She tried in vain to persuade him, and eventually shrugged when he still refused.

"I think you'd better get some sleep. And I had too. I'll wake you early. I found a spare toothbrush in the bathroom, and I've left it out for you."

She was tired and grateful. She quickly availed herself of the bathroom and saw that he had already withdrawn to his bedroom. His door was shut, but in the other room she could see the engine parts that he and Tich must have been working on before she interrupted his evening. And not just his evening. She had effectively asked him to risk his job by helping her, because she could see that her own job was probably lost. She took off her shoes, climbed into the sleeping bag, which she zipped up, pulled the blanket over herself and fell into a deep sleep.

Some hours later she was awake again. It must have been the middle of the night. She had been hot and sweating under the blanket. First she had thrown it off, and then she had wriggled out of the sleeping bag and taken her clothes off down to her underwear. But now, back in the sleeping bag, she was no longer hot but she could not sleep. The difficulties and incidents of the previous day still troubled her, but they were not the immediate cause of her wakefulness. She was thinking of taking a big step, one she would not have considered possible just three weeks previously. But the more she thought about it, the more it seemed the right thing to do. She was shocked at herself, because it was not at all her way. But then her way had not been very successful, had it? So, even if things went wrong, what harm, or what more harm, could it do?

She unzipped the sleeping bag and climbed out. It felt colder now than when she had fallen into that first sleep. She crossed the room slowly, trying to remember where the furniture was, and found the door handle. The door creaked a little, but she did not mind that. In the passage outside Michael's room she found the handle to his door and turned it. The room beyond was almost completely dark, but she could make out his bed. He was asleep but disturbed by the sounds she had made. She lifted the blanket and sheet and sat on the edge of the bed. It still felt right, however surprised she was. He woke as she twisted herself into the space next to him, and mumbled his surprise.

"It's OK," she said. "I need to sleep here." She sensed that he was becoming aroused, and was turning more towards her. "No, not now, another time will be right. Just let me sleep here," she said, pushing him to turn away so that she could hold him from behind, just as if on the back of his motorbike. And as he fell back asleep, so did she.

CHAPTER FORTY-SEVEN

THE MORNING MIGHT HAVE PROVED EMBARRASSING IF THEY had been doing nothing, but when the alarm clock sounded Ruth awoke and left the bedroom to find her clothes. Michael was left to get up a little more slowly, while she, once she had pulled her rumpled dress back on, put a kettle on to heat. When she sensed that he was in the hallway outside the bedroom, she called out to him that she would get the breakfast ready if he wanted to use the bathroom. She found cups, and some sliced bread which she placed on the grill pan to toast. She was keen to get going but anxious that her arrival should be well timed, when Richard would be waking and preparing to go to breakfast, and the nurses would be waking other patients and chivvying them to get dressed. She would ask Richard to talk to her in the doctors' room, for privacy, and tell him that Oates had told her that he had worked for the government. She would not immediately tell Richard what had happened to her, but if it was necessary she would bring in the potential threat that Oates represented. If he still could not communicate anything about himself, she would have to go to the deputy superintendent and tell him what had happened.

She was so absorbed in thought that she almost burned the toast, and only Michael's shout from the bathroom brought her back to her task. "I'm almost done here," he had obviously put his head round the door of the bathroom to shout this at her, "so if you want to freshen up…"

"No, I'll wait until I get to the hospital," she shouted back. "I'll change before I go to the ward, if I've got time."

They ate the toast and drank the tea quickly, both preparing themselves for the journey. He looked her up and down once she had put her coat on.

"It's going to be cold for you," he said. "I'll drive slowly, but you are still going to get cold. And I haven't got a spare helmet, so hold on tight."

He was true to his word, driving much more slowly than he had done before. There was very little traffic, and before they set off the vapour from her breath was already forewarning her of the cold air that would rush past her. It seemed to penetrate her clothes, particularly where she had hitched her skirt up in order to sit on the bike at all. But at least she was on the way towards a final confrontation with her patient and she had avoided any contact with Oates overnight. If she could get to speak to Richard before any intervention – that was the main hope she had. She hardly had time to think about the night that had just passed, until they stopped at a traffic light and Michael put his feet to the ground to hold the bike upright. Then she found herself thinking of how she had held him in the night, and how it had seemed so right to her that she had been able to sleep immediately. Despite the cold, and her anxiety to complete the journey, she smiled to herself as the traffic light changed from red to amber and then to green.

Near the hospital Michael slowed the bike down. He looked behind and said that there was a car coming up behind them. The bike was going so slowly that she feared it might topple over, but she kept her confidence in him. As the car overtook them and entered the hospital grounds, he picked up speed and moved across to the left of its rear, so that as it went in and the driver slowed to wave at the porters' lodge he was able to swerve around it and accelerate up the drive. They passed nurses on pedal bikes along the drive, but Ruth was not concerned about them. If anyone was collaborating with Oates, it was surely the porters.

In the car park they had the chance to talk. He asked her if she really wanted to go so directly at the problem, but he had to admit that in her place he would probably do the same. She asked if she could come over to the Secure Block if she needed to check anything with him, and he said that he'd ask the doorkeeper to look out for her. She thanked him and then, again surprising herself by taking the initiative, kissed him full on the lips. He laughed at her action and held her tightly to him.

"Take care," he said softly as he let her go.

She walked quickly to her room to change and make herself more presentable. She knew that if Oates had not yet called the deputy superintendent, her colleagues and the nurses on the ward would not know that anything was amiss. They would have assumed that talking to the civil servant yesterday had taken longer than expected. She was cold, and put some warmer clothes on than those she was discarding. She pulled a brush through her hair, frowning as the tangles caught in the bristles, and patted some powder on her face, thinking that otherwise she looked distinctly pale, perhaps after the ordeal she had faced. But there was no hiding the blue-black bruising that still surrounded one eye, and the bump on her head was still tender, though not visible, and her shoulder also hurt. But she put aside any thoughts of pain in order to focus on what she now had to do.

As she walked towards the wards she resolved to take this slowly and not reveal too much too soon. She would prefer him to tell her what had happened to him, if he could, because that was the more therapeutic way. And revealing what had happened to her, if she had to do that, was somewhere near – and perhaps beyond – the boundary edge of professional conduct, since it could traumatise him.

As she had hoped, the nurses were busy with the patients when she entered the ward, and she was able to enter the men's dormitory area without being noticed. She approached Richard's bed and saw that he was already up, dressed and seated in his chair, reading. He looked up as she approached, and she saw the pained look on his face. But she tried to keep things as close to normal as she could.

"Good morning, Richard," she beamed a welcome. "I wondered if I could just check something with you before you go to breakfast?"

He nodded his assent and stood up slowly. He could not disguise his anxiety, and he seemed to her to be trembling. She guided his arm towards the communal area, and as he shook less she let him go so that he could half walk with her, half follow one step behind. They walked through the doors of the ward and she led him to the doctors' room.

"Sit down," she said, pointing to the chair and patting its seat. He did so and looked at her as she sat down as well. He was trembling again. She felt sorry for him and was herself anxious about what she was going to do. "Richard, I was asked to go and see Sir Francis Oates yesterday."

If it were possible to look more anxious, he immediately did so. But he looked down and would not meet her gaze. "He told me something about your past, about your job. Things you couldn't remember. Would you like to remember them?"

He neither nodded nor shook his head. He seemed to have breathed in but not exhaled, holding his breath as if waiting for her to proceed. "He said that you'd had an important job working for the government. Do you remember that?" She stopped there. It was up to him how he responded, but she had to play the silence, let him feel the vacuum that she wanted *him* to fill rather than her.

He looked up at her, and she saw that he was crying. He seemed about to speak, but then stopped and looked down at the floor again. But she too stopped and let the silence between them linger. Then, just as she thought she would have to say something more, he spoke.

"I'll tell you," he said. "I'll tell you but not here. You must come with me, to where I can tell you."

She had to make a great effort not to show the astonishment she felt. "I don't understand, Richard. Where else would we go?"

"I'll show you," he said. Although his words were clipped, he seemed to have more control over himself than previously and to be speaking with an authority she had never seen in him before. "You follow me, and I'll show you." She raised her hands in acquiescence and followed him out of the doctors' room. He was not walking slowly, she noted, although he was still limping, and he was looking around the corridors in an alert way quite different to his usual manner. She had to walk more quickly just to keep up with him.

He led her back towards the reception area and then down the main corridor. But as he did so, he slowed down and looked around even more, checking to see who was on the corridor. But they were past the canteens, and there were no patients this far down, and it was still too early for the administrative staff to be arriving for work. Past all the shops and services, he stopped. The corridor was empty. He went towards a doorway that appeared to lead into a cupboard. He unlocked it with a key that he had in his pocket, pulled the door open and beckoned to her to follow him. She was reluctant, wondering what on earth he was doing, and she paused in the doorway to try to see what was there. He had a torch, and he reached past her to shut the door. Then he pointed to the corner, where she saw that there was a half-door. Within seconds he had entered it and started to descend a set of steps that were obviously there. He turned back towards her. "This way," he said, and continued his descent. Ruth shivered. It was she who seemed afraid now.

It was hard for her to follow because he held the torch. She had to feel for each step before committing her weight to the descent. But once they had reached the last step, he set off along what seemed to be a passageway. She tried to orientate herself, thinking over the initial direction of the staircase and then the passageway. *It must lead away from the hospital*, she thought. A spider's web caught in her hair and she almost shouted, but stopped herself.

"Slow down, Richard, please," she said, "you're getting too far ahead of me."

He did so, but a little further on the light from his torch suddenly disappeared. She had to feel her way forward until she realised that the passage had turned, and she could see the torchlight again. And then he stopped. She caught him up, and he used the torch to show her that there was a flight of steps upwards. She followed him still, and he opened a door that was obviously at the top. On the other side there was some light coming in through cracks in a wooden door, and there were more steps upwards. But Ruth had lost her sense of direction, and she asked him where they were.

"In the water tower," he answered, "and we'll go up there."

She followed him up the stairs, but she was very worried now. She had not anticipated being so withdrawn from the rest of the hospital, even when he had suggested talking elsewhere than in the doctors' room. She had thought that he might want to talk in the chapel, or on one of the seats in the reception area, or even on a bench in the hospital's gardens. But she certainly had not thought of the water tower, fenced off at the bottom, potentially unsafe, and in the sole company of a man who less than a week ago had attacked her. She felt foolish to have left herself so exposed, but she was intrigued. How had he gained access to the tower, and how often did he come here? He had a torch in that cupboard, a sure sign that he used the passage regularly. Her instinct remained to go on, to find out what lay behind the mystery, but she was still afraid.

Above her she could see that there was some natural light, and then she heard Richard pushing open another door, and more light burst through at the top of the stairway. *There must be a window at least*, she thought, and she too ascended the final stairs. She tried to calculate the height. She seemed to have gone up six or more flights of stairs, enough to make her slightly breathless. She could be ninety or a hundred feet in the air. She saw that there was a room there, but it was very bare. Richard seemed to be standing face to the wall, his back towards her. He did not seem intent on assaulting her again, so she took a couple of steps into the room. And then she saw the open space that served as a window, and the remains of the winching mechanism through which things had been hauled up to the room. And beyond that she saw the view, the sensational view, beyond the trees and the red-roofed houses, past the fields and marshes that ran either side of the river, and the electric pylons that carried power to this part of the London suburbs, and beyond to the City of London itself, and no doubt the Thames nestling in the hidden distance, beyond which there was a horizon of hills. It caught her attention immediately, and she was entranced. If this was Richard's refuge, the view alone might make it worthwhile spending time here. A movement of his startled her out of her momentary rapture, not least because she was still fearful of him and aware now of the open space beyond which was a very long drop.

He was holding towards her a sheath of paper. She saw that he had a makeshift desk of planks and crates, and a set of writing booklets sitting on the desk. There was also a pile of newspapers, weighted down with an old brick. And near the open winching space was an old wooden chair. The place was clearly a refuge, but what did the man write here?

"I wrote it in the Infirmary," he said, still thrusting the papers in her direction. "Please read it." She took the sheets, and he gesticulated towards the chair. He looked distressed, and for a few moments she wondered if she really should proceed. But he sat down on the floor with his back against the wall, and she took the chair and started to read.

> Doctor Appleton, I assume it will be you who reads this. No other doctor in the past thirteen years has been as determined as you in trying to reveal the secrets that for many years Doctor Winstanley helped me to conceal. I am deeply sorry that I struck you the other day, and I am writing this in part to explain why I did so. I don't suppose that my explanation will in any way take away the pain and hurt that it must have caused you.
>
> I have been a voluntary patient at Black Roding for thirteen years. I certainly needed treatment of some kind when I was admitted, because I had tried to kill myself. Whether or not I had the right treatment, I don't know. But Winstanley agreed to allow me to stay at Black Roding when I needed some such place, and he arranged for my treatment.
>
> I came to Black Roding because of things which started when I was a university student and the war had started. I was allowed an exemption from joining the armed services because of the university course I was doing. It combined physics and engineering at Birmingham University. I was a good student, and I had been particularly interested in the work of two migrant scientists at the university, Rudolf Peierls and Otto Frisch. Because they were not native British, indeed Frisch was still technically a German citizen I believe, they were

not allowed to work on the projects that many British scientists had left the universities to work on radar and coastal defences. So they were working together on some ideas that had been developing among a small group of scientists before the war, and they thought enough of me as one of their students to talk with me about their ideas. They wrote a document together which convinced Churchill and others in government that a major new source of energy, explosive energy, could theoretically be developed, and they produced the first blueprint for such a weapon. But they also talked of the dangers of such a weapon, and of the effects on civilian populations of such a weapon. They were moral men, exiled from their own country and concerned that the right country should win that war, but in the right way. They believed it possible that the Germans were already developing a fission bomb. But things only developed slowly, because the British government and the American government were too slow, even after the Americans were dragged into the war by the Japanese. I completed my degree and had started a postgraduate project on designing bombs, conventional ones, to maximise the destructive waves of the explosion. My work was funded by the government, and I was still at Birmingham when Churchill and the Americans agreed in the summer of 1943 to collaborate in the building of the first atomic bomb. They called it the Manhattan Project, and the Americans had already started the work, but the Birmingham scientists brought a lot of the expertise that was essential to the project. To my amazement, I was given three months to complete my project and was told to join them in America. Rudolf Peierls had asked that I be included in the Manhattan Project, and I was proud to go.

After crossing the Atlantic I had to make the long journey to Los Alamos in New Mexico. I felt excited, no, exhilarated to be there, to be part of a project that might save the world.

I can't write those last words without a sense of irony. But we did think that. There was a belief that we and the Germans were in a race with them to complete our work. And my two mentors both believed that nuclear energy was the real goal and that the necessary development of the bomb would bring an answer to the world's need for new energy sources. Control fission, we thought, and we solve the future shortage of electricity perhaps forever. But there was also anxiety, even then, about the secretive nature of the development. Some of the scientists, the European ones mostly, wanted the Russians to be involved or, failing that, at least to be informed about the project. There were arguments about that even after we reached Los Alamos.

It was my job, along with many other engineers, most of them American, to try to make what these theoreticians were dreaming about. Multiple simultaneous explosive devices, engineered to a thousandth of an inch, for example. The work I had been doing in Birmingham was in somewhat similar fields, I guess, so I was useful. And when the whole project meetings were held, I was allowed to attend, to be a kind of go-between for them. Imagine, me, a young scientist, listening in to the cream of the world's physicists and mathematicians. Afterwards, I thought it was the best education I could get, from the best people in my field of work. And men even younger than I was, coming later in 1944 from Cambridge and Birmingham and Liverpool, said how different it was to work there. In England it was all theoretical; in Los Alamos Oppenheimer and others simply made us feel that it was going to happen, we were going to create a bomb and change the world forever.

That's all a bit of a digression, isn't it? The point I really want to make is that I became a nuclear scientist in Los Alamos, something I wasn't before I went there. I was given experience and knowledge that only a few people in the world had.

Ruth paused in her reading. She had hardly moved from the moment she read of his transfer from Birmingham near the start of his account, except when she finished one sheet and moved to the next one. He was watching her intently. She looked at him, as if to ask if it was true. He nodded, understanding her surprise and possible disbelief.

The people in Santa Fe, the nearest city, would wonder about Los Alamos. I went down there regularly just to feel what an American town was like, to buy things I couldn't get in Los Alamos and to drink a few beers. In the bars they'd sound you out a little, because they were aware of the vast project going on nearby, but when I clammed up, which I always did out of fear, let alone anything else, they stopped asking questions. And yes, I was afraid of American security, even though everything else made me happy. They questioned everyone, or almost everyone, regularly, asking me questions about my background, my education, what I'd learned from others and then about those others, especially the émigrés. They were the special focus of the FBI and of the military intelligence officers. And I guess they were proved right in the end.

    I've hesitated to write this next part, but you need to know it to understand what happened later. While I was in Los Alamos, I discovered that I was homosexual. Well, I didn't so much discover it as have it revealed to me. All the time I'd been a student I'd not had time to meet any women, as I thought I was supposed to do. And I wasn't really interested in any women. And only when I got to Los Alamos did I start to feel, well, what did I feel? Something, anyway, for or about one of the men I was in the dormitory block with, Tom Grainger. The thing is, he was experienced, and I most definitely wasn't. So he talked to me, not mentioning anything about his feelings for me, just I guess testing me out. Then one Sunday, when everything was shut down, as happened on Sundays, he suggested we go hiking in the hills. Lots of people at Los Alamos did that. It was different walking to any place I'd walked in England. It was rough scrambling, hot, dusty work, and you could climb some high peaks with spectacular views over the surrounding country. He knew a small stream and pool around six miles from the base, and when we got there he suggested we swim. I didn't hesitate, and after a long soak he introduced me to an encounter I'd never previously understood. He started by drying my back and front with my own shirt and then laying it on a bush to dry. And then he asked me to do the same for him. Which I did, and

I found myself getting aroused by it. And when he saw that happening to me, he showed me what else to do. I think that I would have felt ashamed if he'd done this in some London toilet – I found out what they are like later – but there, just as with everything else I was doing, it just seemed right.

Of course, with this discovery came the need for more secrecy. He told me that if security got even a whisper of something queer about us we'd be thrown straight out of Los Alamos. They were scared of blackmail and thought that any queer would be open to blackmail, and even then they were trying to stop the Russians finding out about Los Alamos and the project. So, for a year, I guess it was, I had a completely secret relationship with him. We weren't reckless at all at first and only got together when we went hiking. But then he started to want more, and he'd arrange for us to meet in the showers, during the night, and he even made me use a toilet cubicle with him. I didn't like this, and I tried to stop it. And then he got to know another man, a newcomer to the base, and the two of them were discovered by security. And sure enough they were thrown out very quickly, and security remembered that I'd gone hiking with him. I had the hardest and longest interrogation I'd ever had. And I had to deny it all. No, I didn't know he was homosexual. No, we never did anything homosexual. No, he never tried to seduce me. No, I didn't know he was meeting another man in the showers. No, I hadn't married or got engaged, but that was because I was too busy working. Yes, I expected to meet someone back in England after the war and to have children and live happily ever after. I think it was touch-and-go whether they believed me or not, but in the end Peierls or one of the others must have intervened because they suddenly said I was lucky, that I was so important to the project that they wouldn't be sending me back home, but they'd be watching me, and they'd put my interrogation on my record. That's how Oates knew about me years later – what those security guys put on my record.

I have to tell you about how much work went on at Los Alamos. They – the top scientists – didn't know how to start the reactions that would become fission, and we had to conduct a lot of experiments to model the ways in which they thought a reaction might commence. That meant engineering parts with precision such as I had never seen in practice before, and I learned so much from the American engineers when this work was done. And a lot of the time, even though we were working on the practical part of the project, there was no actual explosive material, and so it was still a kind of informed guesswork. But I liked that, thinking of ideas and then preparing to implement them. Some of the scientists were particularly good at working from theory to practice, and I tried whenever possible to work for them. And Otto Frisch got me to work in a special assembly group in the canyon next to the base for several weeks in late 1944 and early 1945. We had some uranium for this, and we were probably lucky not to kill ourselves. I know that after the war some scientists were killed repeating his tests. Someone called the test 'the dragon experiment', because it felt like tickling the tail of a sleeping dragon. They had a special name for everything, or if they didn't someone made it up.

Alamogordo, that was one place they re-named, calling it Trinity site because it unleashed the power of the Trinity, as in the poem by John Donne — "Batter my heart, three-person'd God". I was one of those sent to prepare the site of the first ever nuclear explosion, and then to help in reassembling the bomb itself — they called it the 'gadget' because of security concerns — before ignition. That was the moment that was the summation of all the work that had gone on, testing the implosion. The whole desert lit up for a few seconds, brighter than any daylight, with a whole spectrum of colours, and then we felt the heatwave from the explosion, like opening a giant oven, and the sound of the bomb, as if some sleeping monster had raised itself from the desert floor and roared. One of the scientists next to me said, "What have we done, what have we done?" I had perhaps the first of many feelings of guilt over what I had participated in. What have I done? I thought. What monster have I helped to unleash?

 You know what followed. The first real explosion was over the city of Hiroshima, destroying it. I'd assumed, like some others, that the President would select somewhere less populated, but they had been dropping fire bombs on Tokyo and other cities for some time, so it was not that great a surprise. And then the second bomb on Nagasaki, suggesting that we had a regular supply of these bombs that would destroy Japan one city at a time. We didn't, of course, but the Japanese didn't know that. I and some others thought that the second bomb could certainly have been dropped somewhere much less populated, and there was a lot of discussion at Los Alamos about the implications. Many of the scientists, and I was one, hoped that seeing these effects would bring all countries in the world to end future wars, and that the benefits of these nuclear experiments would follow in terms of energy and medicine. But while there were such benefits, it did not really work out like that, did it?

 In the aftermath of the bombs I must have experienced some feelings that others did not. I read all the stories in the newspapers and tried to listen to whatever radio reports there were. I started to dream about the explosions, and in my dreams to see the victims of the bombs and the radiation that ensued. I still suffer those dreams, even though Winstanley did try to treat me to stop them. He did try, in some ways at least, to help me. But the thoughts of what I had contributed to were too strong, and they still are, I think.

 Whether it was the pressure of the work I had been doing in the almost two years at Los Alamos, and of my studies before that, or the guilt and anger about what the bombs had actually done, I don't know, but some combination of these things caused me to have a breakdown. I couldn't eat, and I found it hard to express what I thought and felt. I think I hated myself for what I had done. I took to my bed and wouldn't get up. I lost weight, and I couldn't read, the one thing that I had always done. I couldn't try to share someone else's view of the world, and I thought I'd become something less than human, I suppose.

So I did not return to Britain but was sent to a convalescence unit. The Americans I had worked with gave me a set of tools – I think you've seen that, in my tallboy – and they gave me a Los Alamos arm patch which the nurses sewed on my shirt. The American soldiers, who as GIs were due to have tried to invade Japan, or were from units where their colleagues would have been involved in such landings, treated me like some form of celebrity when they saw the patch! I'd saved them and their buddies, they said, from the most awful task. Compared to landing in France, which was a picnic, they said, invading Japan would have been a catastrophe for the GIs. They had all been dreading it, and among themselves had talked of losing one in two of their companies. They brought me gifts – cigarettes, chewing gum, illicit whisky, candy – and they shook my hand and slapped me on the back. I was introduced to every injured soldier in the unit, I think, and all of them wondered why I was there. I said I'd overdone it in my work, and they accepted it to my face. And I suppose it helped to give me some sense of balance about what I had done, and made me feel a lot better, so that gradually my appetite came back, and I was able to talk about what had happened. One doctor, who was interested in what he described as the nervous effects of war, sat with me for several sessions and got me to talk about my work and how I felt about it. He helped me to come to terms with it, I think, and to accept that I was not responsible for what had been done in Japan. That was a decision that fell to others, I came to accept. But realising that made me also realise that someone like me, working for the government, can't really trust the government and the politicians who run it. The President didn't ask us about the morality of using the bomb, and the suggestion that it would be deployed in as humane a way as possible was part of the deception that was worked on us, or that we worked on ourselves.

By the time I got back to Britain, which was not until mid-1946, I was too late to pick up a job in a British university. Those jobs had all gone to those who were demobbed from the European sphere, and no-one was interested in an academic who'd been working

> in the States. But the government was picking up some nuclear developments, and I was recruited in 1947 to the research and development that started in Kent and then moved to Aldermaston. William Penney knew of my work in Los Alamos and was instrumental in my appointment. But I had to have medical checks and psychiatric checks before I could start work.
>
> I have in the years since then wondered why I accepted working again on nuclear developments. I guess I was disappointed that my university career had simply fizzled out because of the war. I couldn't see myself being successful in a career like teaching, although they were recruiting a lot of teachers in those years. And I did not want to start all over again in some completely new field – I had no confidence that I could do that. Now they seem inadequate excuses for what I did. At the time, though, it was pressing that I should find some employment, and the offer from Penney seemed to answer my problem. Maybe I hoped that I would be able to extract myself in time. And maybe I thought that the benefits of nuclear power could be realised through the government's research. However it happened, my die was cast the day I accepted the post, and I think now that I should have refused, at whatever cost that might have been.

Ruth stopped reading again at that point. Richard was still looking at her. She felt it necessary to say something. "You've suffered a lot for what you did in good faith, I think, haven't you?" He said nothing. He could see that she had not finished all the papers. She resumed her reading.

> I found that the concerns that many of the scientists at Los Alamos had held were right. The governments all wanted to undertake their developments in secrecy, whereas many of the scientists had wanted to share the work with others so that no one country thought that it held the lead over others. That's what did for Fuchs, of course. He had believed in sharing the secrets, to the extent that he gathered information about all the work at Los Alamos and handed it on to agents who took it to the Soviet Union. And

he wasn't caught doing it. He'd come back and like me was working again for the government when the Americans tracked him down by going back through secret records they had. But he was prepared to confess everything he'd done - well, perhaps not everything - in fact he confessed to breaking the Official Secrets Act and handing on information, but the Americans had to track down the rest of his network. And I'd spoken to Fuchs several times at Los Alamos. He was not the most vocal on the matter of sharing information. In fact he must have been among the most quiet on the topic, perhaps because he'd decided actually to do something about it. When he was tried it was not for treason, because we were not at war with the Soviets. And the many other secrets he had - for example, what he'd been working on for the British government until the day of his arrest - he did not reveal, and the trial did not reveal. I attended the trial for one day and thought of visiting him in jail, but I decided that I'd just be drawing unwanted attention to myself.

The difficulty I had was that the British work was all carried out secretly and not reported to parliament, and was not even in the budgets approved by parliament. The secrecy came, I think, from the culture of Los Alamos and the fear of the Americans that the Soviets would be given information. It seemed to carry over into our work, which was divided up between Aldermaston, Harwell and Windscale, and the authorities became even more anxious when the Soviets did explode a bomb in 1949. The Labour government, and then the Tories under Churchill, continued to fund things secretly. I, and one or two others, had drawn attention to this secrecy by asking if what we were doing was legal, inasmuch as we were preparing materials and weapons of a deadly nature without any democratic approval. But the authorities simply said that everyone who needed to know and to approve the work did know and had approved it. But to cover myself I kept a record of everything that I was being asked to do, and by whom, so that I could explain my actions if there were ever an inquiry. I've always kept diaries and journals - even at Black Roding - and I had done so at Los Alamos without thinking of any possible consequences, but they had been lost at the time of my breakdown. They surfaced again, as I will tell you, in the most uncomfortable of ways.

Finally, in 1952, Churchill revealed that the secret work that had been done would result in an atomic bomb test later in the year. But if anything his announcement only served to increase the anxieties of the security agents. My laboratory and office were searched as the first part of a series of random investigations, and the notebooks in which I had been keeping the instructions and orders given to me were taken away along with other papers, for analysis. Three weeks later I was asked at no notice to attend a meeting. That was when I first met Francis Oates, now Sir Francis Oates, who was working for Military Intelligence at the time. And that was the start of my downfall.

It was not a meeting, it was an interrogation. Oates and the head of security at Aldermaston conducted it. They'd brought all my security files from the States, which I guess the FBI provided — the notebook from my office, and the journals and diaries I'd kept at Los Alamos. I don't think the FBI had them, or I would have been questioned before I left the States. Probably the American army kept them in some box and was asked for anything they held on me or about me and came up with the box in which I'd stored them.

The first questioning was polite but insistent — what were all these journals, diaries and notes for? Surely they indicated that I'd meant to do the same as Fuchs and hand them over to the Soviets by some Communist Party channel? Surely my notebook revealed that I was intending to break the Official Secrets Act and inform someone about my current work? Didn't I know that it was an offence to compile information with a view to transmitting it even if I hadn't yet done so? That I'd committed the same offence in the States and in Aldermaston? And then the questioning developed into personal matters. Why was I not married? Why did no-one know of any woman with whom I had gone out? Was I homosexual? With whom had I had relationships, both in Britain and in the States? I denied everything, which of course proved part of my undoing because they were not revealing things which they did know.

I was held overnight while they analysed my answers. And then Oates interrogated me, on his own this time, with just another soldier there, someone who I think is still working for him as a driver. And the interrogation took place in a different place, to which I was driven, somewhere away from Aldermaston, an army base I think, and a desolate room with a table, three chairs and a bare electric bulb shining above us. Oates revealed that Tom Grainger had told the Americans that he had had a homosexual relationship with me, and so they now believed that everything I'd told them the previous day was a pack of lies. And then they started questioning me about my knowledge of and contact with a lot of people I had never heard of. There were some who had been Fuchs' contacts in the States – Gold, Greenglass, the Rosenbergs – they were executed in the States, you may know. But I really had no contact with any of them, and had never to the best of my knowledge even met them. And then there were British names as well, some of them in the anti-nuclear movement, and some of them left-wing people, from the Communist Party or the Labour Party, I'd guess. But I had not been political in my objections about what was happening, and I didn't know any of these people, except by name.

And then he started again with questions about my being homosexual. Lots of questions about Tom Grainger and how I had lied my way out of an interrogation in the States. With how many other men had I had a relationship? Had I been blackmailed, either when I was in the States or back at home, by any of the men? Where did I meet them? How did I engage in sexual activity? And then he introduced the name of a man whom I did not know, a man he called Jimmy. This Jimmy was prepared to swear that I had had sex with him three times in a toilet in Reading. (I knew I hadn't, but I knew that sometimes homosexuals were lied about in this way.) With my security records, and my having lied repeatedly about my homosexuality, I would not be believed by the courts. I would be sent to jail and then I would be charged under the Official Secrets Act. He kept on and on about how I would be shamed and how I would be treated, what other prisoners would do to me, assault me and rape me, force things up my anus. It was a kind of psychological battering that he gave me, and I broke down, I broke down repeatedly. My denials were no good, they were just making things worse, he said. And then I was left alone.

I still don't know if it was deliberate on his part, leaving me alone. I think it probably was. I'd been sobbing, and I didn't even notice them leaving. When I looked up, they had gone; and when I went to the door and banged on it, no-one replied. I'd been left with my tie, my belt, my shoelaces, all things with which I could do away with myself. And that is what I tried to do. I tied them all together and put the belt around my neck so that it would choke me. And I stood on a chair beneath the light bulb and tied it all to the wire holding the bulb. But when I kicked the chair away the wire gave way and ripped out of the ceiling. I collapsed on the floor, and only then did Oates reappear. He kicked me and said, "You sorry bastard, you couldn't even do that right."

I was left in a cell overnight, although they took away all the things I'd used to try to hang myself. I had eaten almost nothing, and had just drunk some water, when they spoke to me the next day. Oates did not want me to have to go through a trial, he claimed. The police would be called to charge me later in the day, but he had a proposal for me that might prevent my being charged. That he would allow me to be admitted to a mental hospital because I had tried to commit suicide, so I could avoid being charged with homosexual acts and with breaking the Official Secrets Act. But I had to agree to keeping myself anonymous and not seeking to come out from the hospital. I was broken and had no resistance, so I accepted what he proposed.

They brought me to Black Roding, and Doctor Winstanley, as he was then, arranged my admission. There was no central admission unit in those days, and each consultant could admit patients to one of his wards. It was a very frightening place at first, and Winstanley arranged for me to have first drugs and then shock therapy. I hated both, and in the end the new superintendent banned the drugs, and Winstanley stopped the shock therapy when I said I'd go to the superintendent and ask him to stop.

Over the years the hospital has become a better place, and the wards are much less terrifying places. I dare say the Secure Block is still difficult, but I found things I could do to help to make the hospital a better place for some patients. I was made a trustee, and I do jobs like delivering the newspaper trolley, or running the bar at the dances. I was in a strange way content with these roles, because I have been troubled over the years by dreams linked to those two atomic bombs; and having something to do keeps the dreams away for a while. I also know that I felt ashamed about what I had done, both as a scientist and as a man, and I did not want to appear in a trial. And over the years Oates has visited me and always threatened me with a trial if I were ever to think of being discharged.

Winstanley's death was not expected. That was obvious inside the hospital and, as you heard, Oates did not know about it. Winstanley had obviously never told anyone about why I was admitted or kept here. He told me not to allow any other doctors to try to talk to me, and they didn't. So you came into a situation where no-one, not even the superintendent, knew the truth about me. And you tried valiantly to discover the truth, but the more you tried the more anxious you made me that I would be tried for my 'offences'. In the end Oates said that I had to do something violent to ensure that I was kept in the hospital. And he strongly suggested you as the target. I put it off and tried not to think about it, but then when I saw you on the corridor I decided to do it. I meant to hit you in the stomach, to wind you but not to harm you. But you had those bags protecting you, and I changed my aim, with the consequences that you know.

I was afraid that you had been permanently injured, or were even dead, and I ran away using a route that I'd spied out in case I *needed to run away. I used a branch that had been left overhanging the wall in the woods at the bottom of the hospital grounds. But I hurt myself landing, and all I could do was find some refuge. I managed to get to the shed in the forest at the sports ground there, as you know, but I couldn't go any further, and I lay down ready to die. I'd done such a bad thing to you, and it seemed to come together in my mind with the horrors of the two bombs I'd helped to prepare.*

You, Doctor Appleton, were my saviour. You sent someone to find me, imagining that I might have gone to that shed. And you did not tell the hospital authorities what I had done. It was an act of forgiveness that humbled me, that a young doctor, a woman, should not report me to the deputy superintendent or the police. It changed my view of what I should do, and I vowed that I would not let Oates tell me what to do anymore. I'd seen you stand up to him. Now I will. If it means that I have to stand trial, well, I'll stand trial and tell the world what he has done. I cannot thank you enough for working this change in me. In a peculiar way you have healed me.

The pages and the writing ran out at this point. Ruth was so surprised by what she had read that she could not think what to say. She glanced again at some of the individual sheets, as if rereading some sections of his account. But really she was just thinking. What could be done? Now that she knew his story, she wanted to help this man even more, but how to help? Even now Oates might be on his way to the hospital, ready to persuade the deputy superintendent to hand Richard over to him, no doubt citing national security in some way or another.

"I'm thinking about all of this, Richard," she said, trying to smile at him, trying to pretend that everything was as normal. "I've never, ever come across a case like yours. You are an unusual man, and a remarkable one, to live here all these years." She thought of something her mentor had once said in a seminar – "Can you imagine anything harder to bear than to be a sane man in a lunatic asylum?" He was telling them – her and her fellow trainees – that their job was to root out any misdiagnosed patients and find better ways for them to be looked after. She had forgotten that until now, but now she knew that it was indeed her task to unravel the steely threads with which Oates had snared Richard. But, just as she had found when confronted with the Official Secrets Act and the agreement she had signed, she did not know enough about the law to work out how to help him.

"I want to help you get out of the situation he, that man Oates, has put you in," she said to him. He leaned forward as if to hear how she was going to do this. "But I don't know enough about the legal situation here, Richard. When we are trained we are taught about the laws by which hospitals such as Black Roding operate, but we are not trained in the Official Secrets Act. I think I will have to get some advice from somewhere."

"What about?" His voice had become a whisper. "Who from?"

"From someone I know." It had suddenly come to her. Her personal tutor at her Cambridge college was a lawyer, not a doctor. Margaret Lodge, now the vice-principal of New College, could answer Ruth's questions. But, she realised, she would have to go to Cambridge. She could not just call her on the telephone and explain all this. And Oates might arrive at any moment, stopping her from getting her answers. "Richard, I think Sir Francis Oates is a dangerous man. Do you agree?" He nodded his response. "And it would be dangerous for you to be left to him to decide what happens to you?" Again he nodded. "So, if I have to go somewhere to find out about the legal aspects of your situation, would you stay here, up here, where he can't find you?"

He seemed to her to think through the implications of what she was asking, because he did not reply for quite some time. "Yes," he said at last, "though it will be difficult. I don't have any food or water up here."

"I'll ask someone to bring you some food." He looked worried at this suggestion. "The same man who found you in the shed in the forest. He already knows some of this, but he does not know about this place. I'll have to tell him."

That reassured him. "I will stay here. But if Oates finds me, I will not do what he says anymore. I would rather…" He glanced towards the open space, through which cold draughts of air constantly blew into the room. Ruth shuddered.

"No, don't even think of that. He won't find you. No-one knows about this place."

"Very well, then, I will wait here. I can read some of the newspapers, some of the stories I haven't read."

She tried to estimate how long it would take her to get into London, then to Cambridge, to cross town and meet with Margaret Lodge, then to get back. Eight hours, perhaps more if the train times were inconvenient. But if Michael could take her to a station on the line to Cambridge, that would be much faster than going into London and back out.

"I don't know how long it will take. It depends on my meeting someone, and I can only hope that she is available. Can I take the torch, to help me get back? I'll bring it back, or Michael, the man who found you, will return it. And should I take the key, so we can keep the cupboard locked?"

When she left him, he had not moved from his position seated on the floor, his back to the wall. She hoped that nothing ill would happen to him in the coming hours. Her task, she worked out as she edged through the passage beneath the hospital, was threefold. Talk to someone on the ward about leaving again to find out more about Richard; tell Michael what she wanted him to do; and get to Cambridge. But first she had to emerge from the cupboard into the hospital corridor without drawing attention to herself. And even that was not going to be easy.

CHAPTER FORTY-EIGHT

Explaining events to others in a partial, limited way was not at all easy, she concluded as she waited on the platform for her train. She had found David Peters in the doctors' room and had said that she could not explain everything but that she had found out something about Richard. When she had tried, this morning, to discuss this with him, he had walked away saying that he had to do his rounds. She did not like lying to her colleague but judged that it was better to spread the lie than to reveal any of the actual situation. The difficult part to explain was that she had to go off-site in order to follow up what she had learned the previous day. But when he asked how she was going to do that, she said she was not allowed to tell him, that he would have to trust her for today. He asked if there was any likelihood of her agreeing to stay on duty, if he told her she could not leave the wards. She said no, it was too important, she was that close to solving all the uncertainties around her patient, but it could not be done if she simply stayed at Black Roding. So, clearly anxious for her

– she must be showing the signs of all that had happened to her, she thought – he allowed her to go.

Next, Michael. And he was even more anxious about her. She had quickly told him where Richard was, to his astonishment, and she gave him the cupboard key and asked him to take him some food and water. But when she said that she wanted to travel to Cambridge to pursue some legal aspects of his case, he tried to argue with her about her decision. She had only just survived what looked like an attempt on her life the day before, and now she was proposing to travel again on her own and to leave the safer environment of the asylum. Wouldn't it be better now to tell the authorities about Oates? But, she argued, the authorities would side with Oates. She was a junior doctor. Oates had all the power of a senior position in government service. And she had no evidence at all that her fall onto the Underground railway lines had been instigated by Oates. Oates had a legal case against Richard, and only if she could discover how strong that case was could she find an alternative for him to lifelong incarceration. In the end, Michael had shrugged and asked what she needed to be done. He would take the torch and get some sandwiches and water to Richard, but first he would drive her to a station from which she could get a train to Cambridge. That would save several hours and help her to get back as quickly as possible to the safety of Black Roding. She joked about the asylum being intended for the patients, not the doctors. But she did appreciate his concern and was determined to be as quick as possible in her errand.

Ruth had gone quickly to her room and put on the motorcycling gear she had never returned – the leather jacket and helmet that Michael had loaned her. Then he had met her outside the hospital. They had agreed that they could not avoid the observation of the porters this time. But if they were communicating with Oates, at least they would not know where they had gone. Michael would lie if he was asked where he had taken her, saying just that she had caught a train into London. And this time Michael had not spared her inexperience as a pillion rider. He had driven quickly through the forest, forcing her to lean into the bends as he took them without slowing and then accelerated when they reached a trunk road, overtaking lorries and vans with calculated movements that made her feel breathless. And when they came to the station, he made her look up the timetable and agree the train on which she would return, so that he could transport her back to the hospital. Before he left her he had taken off his helmet and held her and then kissed her, not violently but she had felt the strength of his desire for her in the kiss. And then he had returned to Black Roding, taking her helmet but leaving her in the leather jacket, promising to take food and drink to Richard in his lofty hideout.

In Cambridge it was term time, and the station and streets were quite busy, so she decided to take a taxi. She gave her destination and then sat back to think carefully about the questions she needed to ask, finding no pleasure in the familiar sights of the town. The taxi stopped at the front of the solid red-brick buildings of New College, the female-only institution she had attended to complete her first degree. Its small barred windows and narrow entrance reminded her how crowded it had always felt, the bedrooms tiny and without facilities, the cold queues for the bathroom in the mornings, the cramped dining hall where one felt one's elbows had to be kept in for fear of making the next diner uncomfortable. Uncomfortable it may have been, but she had a lot of affection for it. The tutors had valued learning above all else and had made it their priority to support the students in their endeavours, especially ones like her who had come from a family unaccustomed to university study. The snobbery and elitism she associated with some of the men's colleges had never prevailed at New College.

She asked the porters – they were called that even if they were female – how to find the vice-principal's office, uncertain whether Margaret Lodge would have moved from the rooms she had used as a personal tutor and director of studies in Law. She was indeed directed to a new location, near to the Principal's House, the poor equivalent of the Masters' Lodges of the male colleges. But first she had to reassure the porters that she was a former student and so formally a member of the college. Only by offering information about her student days, and naming some of the porters from those days, was she able to gain entrance. But once they had accepted her she had the freedom of the college. A quaint belief in the trustworthiness of former students, Ruth concluded, although she was grateful not to be questioned further.

The principal and vice-principal shared a secretary, who controlled access to a room to her left, which housed the principal, and to the room to her right, which was for the vice-principal. She was thin and her skin had a ghostly white character that suggested to Ruth that she never saw daylight. A cold atmosphere seemed to surround her, and she was not helpful.

"Have you an appointment?" she asked sharply, staring at Ruth hard. "If not, you'll have to make one; the vice-principal's diary is full for today."

"No, I don't have an appointment. I have a very urgent matter to consult Doctor Lodge on. So I had to come here without an appointment."

"Well, what is it about? Doctor Lodge is very busy and can't be dealing with just anybody who turns up, you know."

Ruth tried hard not to let her exasperation show. When Margaret Lodge had been her personal tutor, she could drop into her room any time of the day or night, well, the evening at least. She was sure that this obstructive attitude would not have come from her.

"No, I can't tell you that. It's confidential. She was my personal tutor and always said that I could come back if I needed help. And I do… need help, that is." She tried to smile at the secretary, though she was not sure that a smile would be recognised, let alone reciprocated.

Fortunately, at that moment Margaret Lodge herself came into the office. "Hello Ruth," she said instantly, having recognised her, "what brings you here?" Ruth turned to greet her, and she said at once, "And what have you been doing to your eye, to your face?" She started to reach towards it, so shocked was she by the bruising on Ruth's face. Ruth herself had forgotten about the injuries, and now understood perhaps why the secretary had wanted to ward her off, and why the porters had quizzed her. She must look suspicious, turning up with a blue and black eye like a prizefighter's and wearing a leather jacket. "Come in to my room. Would you like some tea?"

The secretary frowned. "You have appointments with the admissions tutor and the bursar, Doctor Lodge."

"Then cancel them. I can meet them another time. I don't suppose Miss, no, it must be Doctor Appleton has come all this way without a good reason. So, could we have some tea?"

It was clearly a hypothetical question. Ruth was glad to see her tutor so unchanged in her approach to her. "Thanks, Margaret, I'm very grateful to you," she said as she sat down. She looked around briefly as the vice-principal took off her coat and scarf, shuffled the papers on her desk and looked quickly at the letters in a tray on her desk. The room was lined with bookshelves, everywhere that could hold one was fully equipped. And it was Margaret Lodge's collection of law books, history books and English literature that covered the shelves. Some of the books were in red and blue leather, obviously series of treatises and commentaries on aspects of the British legal system. Others were individual textbooks, some of them looking well-used and others more pristine. The history books were all in chronological sequence, just as they had been in the rooms that Ruth could remember visiting as a student – the first time so daunted at the visible learning and culture of her tutor, and on other occasions so grateful for the interest of a woman who was dedicated to her students and her vocation. She thought briefly of the superintendent at Black Roding – they had things in common, her two mentors. She sighed at the thought of Black Roding.

"Something tells me you haven't come to see me with good news, Ruth. I'm not going to hear your marriage plans, or about your first baby, which is what I often hear from former students. Indeed I sometimes think I hear them too often. New College girls seem to forget all their education and training and go off and get married and have babies. And no career!"

Ruth laughed. It was an argument she had heard before. New College wanted its former students to be out in the world, working for its and their betterment. And Doctor Lodge did not think that marriage and childbearing were the best choices for the graduates of New College. Then she frowned.

"You're right, of course. It must be obvious from my appearance that I have encountered a few problems. But I don't really know how to start."

Doctor Lodge raised her eyebrows but said nothing. She waited, interestedly focussing on Ruth, who felt foolish in asking, "You'll know all about the Official Secrets Act, I should think?" Again the listener said nothing, but acknowledged that she did know about the Act with a brief nod. "Well, I signed an agreement to it the other day, in order to find out more about one of my patients who's been a mystery to me. Oh, I was transferred to a hospital called Black Roding recently, to fill a vacancy. It's a large general mental health hospital on the edge of London."

"I've heard of it," Doctor Lodge said. "I've not heard anything bad about it for some time."

"I don't really know how to talk to you about someone concerning whom I've signed this agreement." Ruth felt a little despondent. She did not wish to compromise her old tutor and wondered if she had been right to come.

"When we lawyers are a little unsure about confidentiality we often talk in general terms or hypothetical ones. Can you do that?"

Ruth thought for a few moments, then she said, "What if I had a patient who was up against the Official Secrets Act himself? If he had been working for the government and had some concerns about his work, and had taken some notes down about what he was being/ asked to do and when. Would that on its own be a crime, an offence, something for which he could be tried?"

Doctor Lodge smiled, more to herself than to Ruth. "I'm going to say what we lawyers often have to say, and that is that it depends… it depends on the circumstances, the nature of the work and the content of the notes. I'll check in a minute or two. Can you tell me anything more, again in a general way?"

"Well. My hypothetical patient had been involved in top secret work during the war, work that caused him some mental and emotional trauma. He couldn't find any other form of work after the war, and carried on. But everything was cloaked in secrecy. My hypothetical patient says that he was concerned that his work had not been properly authorised, and he had raised concern about this but nothing had changed. So he recorded the instructions he received and the details of who gave the instructions.

He said that he wanted to be able to explain why he had done his work, if he ever had to. But the security officers, sorry, the hypothetical security officers said that he was going to reveal all the information. So they intended to charge him. And my hypothetical patient has a complication. He's a homosexual, and there is mention of this in his records, sorry, his hypothetical records. And the security officer said that he could be tried for 'cottaging', I think it's called, and that put a lot of pressure on him. My hypothetical patient tried to kill himself and chose then to be admitted to hospital rather than be tried. But I want to release him, my hypothetical patient, because I think it's wrong for him to be locked up, unable to take his place in the world. At least, that's what I understand."

Ruth was glad to have blurted it all out, even if she might have overstepped the mark and revealed something she should not have done. "Can you tell me the name of the security officer?"

"Yes, I think so. He'd revealed himself before I signed the agreement. He came to the hospital. He's called Sir Francis Oates."

Just at that moment the secretary brought in the tray of tea. Doctor Lodge took it and said, "Could you just bring in the copy of *Who's Who*, Olivia? It's one of the reference books on the shared shelves."

While the secretary fetched it, Doctor Lodge explained that the shared shelves were the ones used by both her and the principal, an economy to avoid reduplication of expenditure. Once she had the volume in her hands, she leafed through it quickly, muttering the name to herself. "This must be it," she said, finding a particular entry. She read through the lines quickly, without informing Ruth of the contents. "Oh dear, Kenya," she said, and again, "and oh dear, Malaya. He's been in Military Intelligence in both Kenya and Malaya."

"But what does that mean?" Ruth asked. "I don't understand."

"Well, it could mean nothing, he could be a perfectly upright man, full of good intentions and motives."

"But…" Ruth said, "you want to say 'but', don't you? What about Kenya and Malaya?"

"I'm sorry to say that there have been stories and rumours about what our intelligence officers did in those two countries, rumours of atrocities, of torture and cruelty, murder even. I don't myself know anything more about it than that. But what do you make of this man, Sir Francis Oates?"

Ruth thought. He had terrorised Richard and caused him to attempt to kill himself. He had arranged for a man to be wrongly incarcerated in an asylum, a terrible one at the time Richard was first admitted. He had bullied him into silence over thirteen years, and perhaps arranged for Winstanley to be honoured for services rendered. Then he had tried to bully her, and had intimidated Richard into attacking her. Not content with that, perhaps, and now she thought it much more likely, he had arranged for her to be pushed in front of a train on the Underground.

"Yes," she said, "I think he's a man capable of torture and cruelty. I've become frightened of him, and my hypothetical patient is terrified of his hypothetical security officer. Or at least he was. I think he may not be so frightened anymore."

"Let me just make sure I'm telling you these things correctly." Doctor Lodge picked two or three books off the shelves, consulted contents lists and indices, and looked up individual page references. She marked one or two with some scrap paper that lay in a tray on her desk, no doubt there for just such a purpose. She wrote her lectures in her rooms, Ruth recalled, only going to libraries to pick up additional or esoteric references. At last she looked up and, having paused as if to clear her mind and make sure her message was accurate, she said, "It is pretty much as I said. A government employee, say, may keep notes about his work within his workplace and, provided those notes do not represent any attempt to collate information for handing to a third party, the courts are unlikely – though this is not guaranteed – to consider it an offence against the Official Secrets Act. If there was clear contact with a journalist, say, that would make compiling such notes potentially much more like an offence, and if the security officers can point to any threat to publish, or to hand over the notes to a third party, that too could compromise your hypothetical patient. But I think that a concern that one may not be acting in an officially authorised way would be a good reason to compile a list of the kind that you mention. It's crucial, I think, that the information is only within the hypothetical patient's sphere of work. If the notes concerned instructions to others, that too could compromise him. But I must say that all of this is hypothetical. It is possible that some lawyers, and so some prosecuting agents, could see it as an offence, if they can argue that the context makes it so. It might then have to be tested in the courts. Sometimes, of course, the government would prefer cases not to go to the courts."

Ruth had listened carefully to the explanation. The final point, though, provoked a reaction. "You mean they might not want all the background to come out, the decisions being made secretly, not reported to parliament?"

"The hypothetical decisions, Ruth, remember, we're talking only hypothetically, just so you understand your situation. And if anyone asks, I'm your lawyer. Remember that as well. We are entitled to some confidentiality as a consequence. But yes, they might not want such decisions to be aired in public. Or someone might think that actually the case does not look strong enough to stand a trial in court. The hypothetical security officer might prefer the hypothetical patient to be secluded, isolated, removed, whatever word you want to use. I can't say so for certain though."

"Margaret, you've been very helpful. I think I understand my patient's situation, and I now need to talk to him. I hope I haven't disturbed your day too much." Ruth stood up and made to put her coat on. She was finding this difficult, and Margaret helped her to pull it on but in the process nudged the bruise on her shoulder. Ruth reacted, pulling her shoulder down and away from her friend and half-crying in pain.

"What is it? Are you hurt there as well? What have you got yourself into?" Margaret was horrified. But Ruth buttoned up her coat quickly, feeling embarrassed at having revealed further the physical damage she had suffered in the past week.

"It's nothing. I'm all right. I've just had a bad week."

"I don't believe it's just a bad week. You've been badly hurt. Is it because of this case?"

"Let's just say that I've learned for myself what kind of man Sir Francis Oates is."

"My God! Are you sure you should be doing this? You seem on your own in what's going on. Should I do something? Call the police, or the superintendent at your hospital?"

"No, no!" Ruth cried in alarm. "No, don't do that. I think it would jeopardise me, and especially my patient, if you did that." Margaret raised her eyebrows by way of questioning her further, so she went on, "My superintendent is away on a visit to America, and his deputy would just transfer me out of the hospital. Then my patient would be locked up in another hospital. And any chance of freeing him would be lost."

"And does he want that freedom?"

"If he's not threatened by a trial and the humiliation and punishment that that could bring, then yes, I think he would want that freedom. And if he is not mentally ill, he should not be in a mental hospital. He needs to talk to a lawyer, but I don't think I can arrange that until the superintendent returns."

"A solicitor could seek to negotiate with Oates, you know, or with someone else from the government, to keep him out of the courts. Let me know if you need a name. I could find you someone with some background and experience in that if I asked around. And if you find yourself in any trouble, call me. In fact, call me to let me know that you're not in trouble."

They hugged, Margaret making sure that she did not put pressure on Ruth's shoulder. Ruth walked back through the college and out into the busy Cambridge streets. Students were rushing to and from lectures, and they mingled in the busier lanes with shoppers and office workers. Ruth could not help marvelling at so many lives that intersected in the university town, but she also felt lonely that so few people knew of her situation and the difficulties she sensed she was about to face when she had completed her return journey to Black Roding.

CHAPTER FORTY-NINE

Ruth was so grateful to see Michael waiting for her at the station that she embraced and kissed him in the most uninhibited fashion, so that two women passing near them tut-tutted at their public display. But whereas the Ruth of a few weeks previous might have been made anxious by their reaction, now she was completely unconcerned. Michael was still holding her when he asked, "Did you find out what you wanted?"

"Yes, I think so. She couldn't be absolutely sure, because I couldn't tell her all the details. But I think I know what I've got to do. It means I'm not going to report what I'm doing to anybody else, though, until the superintendent is back. So I might have to get Richard to hide out where he is until then, unless I can get a lawyer in to see him. But I've got to explain it all to him, and it must be his decision that tells me what to do. If he doesn't want to be free, there's no point me forcing the issue."

They drove back to Black Roding much more slowly than they had covered the same ground earlier in the day. She confessed to feeling exhausted, and she had not eaten anything except a bar of chocolate purchased at Cambridge station. She lacked the strength to sway with him if he took a bend quickly, and so he kept the bike as upright as possible, slowing at each curve of the road and only accelerating when the route ahead was straight. Near the hospital, but not yet in sight of the porters at the gate, he stopped and suggested that they just think about what to do. It was late afternoon, and the light was just starting to drop. In the forest, the first grey wisps of mist were just visible.

"The porters will know who we are, even if I drive in without stopping," Michael said. "And if Richard has been reported missing, the gates will probably be locked and manned, so I would have to stop."

"I can't see any alternative," she answered. "I've got to get back to see him. But we have to avoid anyone seeing the entrance to the passage to the water tower. If they find that out, I've no chance of concealing him any longer. We'll just have to risk the porters."

The gates were locked, and there were two porters checking vehicles and pedestrians in and out of the hospital. Ruth saw that they were the same two with whom she had clashed on the day of her arrival. She pulled the helmet she was wearing down over her eyes, hoping she could conceal her identity and just be mistaken for a nurse. Michael, by contrast, took his helmet off to show who he was and to talk to the porters. "Everything OK?" he asked.

"There's a patient missing. Second time in a week he's gone on the run. But we don't think he's got away, so we're checking everyone using the gates."

Michael pulled away as quickly as he dared. He drove through the car park and along the road that extended towards the further parts of the East Wing. "I think you should go in by the back door of the Main Wing. You don't want to be seen in Reception, and probably not on the West Wing, before you go up to the water tower. Then I'll go in and see Frances. I'll wait for you in her office. People won't look for you there."

He drove around the Secure Block on a road Ruth had not seen or used before. It ended in a small, dingy loading area in front of the block. There was no-one there, and no windows to overlook the area.

"I leave the bike here sometimes, when it's quiet. If you just walk round the corner you'll find the perimeter path starts there and you can follow it to the Main Wing. Then you'll be right next to the cupboard and the passage entrance. Good luck."

They embraced only fleetingly. She was too anxious now, and frightened that she would be discovered. She hurried around the corner, but when she had found the perimeter path and walked around the rear of the Secure Block she hesitated and tried to look ahead to see if anyone was in the hospital grounds, or using the same path as her. It was quiet, and the mist was rising so that she could not see along the full extent of the path. But she could see that there was no-one between her and the Main Wing, and so she walked as quickly as she dared towards the back door. It was unlocked, to her great relief. When she opened it fully, she would be visible to anyone walking towards her on the corridor. She therefore opened it just a little and attempted to peer through the gap. The corridor was dingy, with only a couple of lights illuminating the long space. She could see people moving further down the corridor, but towards the end where she was it was quiet. She pulled the door more widely open and, still seeing no-one near her, entered the corridor and pulled the door closed as quietly as she could.

She edged along the corridor, almost touching the wall with her left arm, watching ahead of her the whole time. She was concerned that anyone coming towards her would notice her withdrawing towards the cupboard and might then be surprised not to see her when they came to the cupboard itself. Near the cupboard she half-knelt down, as if to tie a shoelace but really to allow herself to look ahead. Judging that she could still not see anyone coming towards her, and that those in the distance would not notice her, she stood and hurried to the cupboard door. She reached into her pocket for the key. It was not there. The key! She had forgotten the key, which she had given to Michael so that he could take some food and drink to Richard. She pulled the cupboard handle, and yes, it was locked. She would have to find Michael and get the key before she could enter the passage to the water tower. Cursing herself for her forgetfulness, she returned to the corridor and headed for the stairs so that she could get to the administrative offices.

Was it seeing Oliver Smythe walking towards her that made her feel suddenly sick, or did that feeling only arise when a slight and sinister smile appeared on his face? She was not sure, but she knew that he meant her no good when he saw her. He focussed on her as he approached, and stopped in front of her, momentarily barring her progress.

"Everything well, Doctor?" he asked. "Only, the porters came around all the wards in the last couple of hours asking if we'd seen you… oh, and a patient of yours. Very odd! In fact, I can't recall it ever happening before. Where have you been?"

She did not know how to answer him. The search for Richard must have included her, or she had been added to the search. But Michael had not mentioned that. Perhaps it had taken place after he had left to pick her up. "Just a misunderstanding," she muttered. "Don't worry about it, Doctor." She could not conceal the contempt in her voice.

"Oh, I wasn't worried, but the deputy superintendent must have been. It was he who told the porters to look for you." Smythe was enjoying his superiority over her, and she wanted to put him down with some quick wit, but she judged that it would not be helpful. She brushed past him, conscious of the grin now on his face and raging inwardly that she could not do anything about it. Discovering that the deputy superintendent knew of her absence made things even more difficult. Yet she still felt that the most important thing was to talk to Richard. So she climbed the stairs to the administrative offices and almost ran the final yards to Frances's office. She went in without knocking.

Frances and Michael were in the office, he still in his motorcycling gear but without the helmet. There was no-one else. He looked surprised to see her. Frances, it seemed, had just been talking. She jumped up from her seat and rushed to Ruth.

"My God, are you all right?" she asked, and she took hold of Ruth and held her tight. "Michael has just been telling me what happened."

"I'm fine, but I need the key." This last remark was addressed to Michael, who instantly understood their error and started to fumble in his pockets for the key. "The deputy superintendent started a search for me!"

This time she was speaking to both of them. "I'll have to do something about that in a while, but first I need the key."

"What for, Ruth?" Frances asked. "What key?"

"He hasn't told you everything then, but I think it's better if he, if we, don't. Just for a while it's best if no-one else knows. Then they can't get into the kind of trouble I think I'll be in."

"I don't understand, but I don't think that's going to change, is it?" Frances asked.

Ruth shook her head. She took the key that Michael offered her and looked in apology at her friend. "As soon as I'm able to, I'll tell you everything. I'm sorry I can't say more. Would you both stay here, though? I'll get back as quickly as I can. I may need to do something more then." She rushed off, desperate to get back to the passage beneath the hospital and not looking around to see if she was being watched at all. Back at the cupboard, she did check behind her, and when the corridor seemed clear she unlocked the door and went in. She picked up the torch and opened the further door that led into the staircase. In her hurry she almost slipped and had to check and regain her balance. "Slow up," she muttered to herself, "or you won't get there at all."

The darkness felt more sinister and threatening as she made her way along the passage. The torchlight only seemed to make her path more frightening, suggesting that there were other creatures lurking at the edge of the penumbra – rats perhaps, or some other creatures of the dark. But she was past the point where such concerns could have slowed her. Now her every intention was to get to her patient and tell him what she had learned, and then, whatever happened beyond that, she knew she would have met her obligation to him.

As she climbed the steps of the water tower she started to call to Richard, letting him know that she was approaching. But she heard no response, so that when she finally reached the level of the room where he should be she was becoming anxious. Opening the door she saw him lying on the floor, on his back. For a moment she feared the worst, but then she saw the rhythmic breathing of his sleep, and she was relieved. She stood and watched him for a few moments and then called his name gently, which drew no reaction. She had to raise her voice to make him stir, and he came to consciousness only slowly, gradually realising where he was and then that she too was there. He sat up, puckering his mouth, and reached for the tin mug in which Michael had obviously brought some water. There did not seem to be much left, for he turned the bottom of the mug up in taking a drink. Then he looked at her.

"Richard, I visited my friend. She is vice-principal of a college at Cambridge, and a well-known lawyer. I couldn't discuss your case in detail, only in general terms. But what she told me is important, and I need to explain it to you as well as I can. Are you awake enough now to take it in?"

He nodded in reply, pulling his body back so that he could rest against the wall to listen to her.

"It seems that the notes you took down could be a breach of the Official Secrets Act, but it is not certain that they are, not certain at all. If you wrote them in the course of your work, perhaps just as a confirmation of what you were being instructed to do, then they would not be a breach. They would have to prove that you were going to publish them, or hand them over to someone who was going to use them, for it to be a breach. But if the notes were about more than your work, they would be able to prove that more easily. Only you can tell me into which category the notes fall. So, a big question, can you recall the notes and what they were about? And then, can we work out if they would be, or could be, a breach of the Act?"

Richard did not need long to recall the details. "It was only concerning me. It was all the instructions given to me in the development of the weapons we were working on, and who gave me the instructions. If they came by writing, I put a copy of them with the list. If they were given orally, I wrote them down immediately. I suppose I anticipated having to defend myself if there were an investigation. Because the work had never been formally approved, never budgeted, it was completely secret from parliament. It was not like Fuchs, where he had information about what others were doing. I had probably broken orders by putting all the instructions together; but if what you say is true, Oates was lying to me all those years ago. He said that what I'd done was illegal, because I was producing a collection of information that could be used by a journalist or by another country. Well, the other country was not really true, I knew that, but I could see how the instructions could be used by a journalist. A 'secret government conspiracy' it would be called. And there would have been a lot of names involved, both in the political class and amongst the top brass. How can we confirm all this?"

"Well, I think we've got to stop Oates taking control of you, which is what he's been trying to do since he heard of Winstanley's death, and then find a lawyer for you, to check all this. And then—"

He cut her off before she could go further. "Do you still intend to discharge me from the hospital?" he asked.

She hesitated. She had assumed that once the prospect of freedom was put to him, he would show only eagerness for it. But his question suggested otherwise. She thought back over her reflections about this man, and what she had thought before she had learned so much more about him. He had found a role and purpose in the hospital as well as escaping a role that had caused him great distress. He had worked in a research laboratory, a giant organisation set in the desert for the specific purpose of channelling the most secret powers in the natural world into weapons, bombs that had killed tens of thousands of people, and injured and disabled for life thousands more, and he had clearly not been able to adjust to what he had done in the manner of many of his co-workers. He felt himself responsible – at least in part – for all the death and destruction caused by those bombs. And he had found no alternative to continuing to participate in such research. Who was she to deny him that asylum?

"It's up to you, Richard. If you don't want to leave, I'll describe you as still at risk of suicide if left isolated. That should ensure you stay here, at least for a time. But you know, you can live outside the hospital. I'm sure you are capable of that, if you want to. And there must be other work you could do, other engineering, not the military research. But you have to want to do it."

There was a silence between them. He was obviously thinking about all that she had said and what she was offering him. Freedom – he had gone to America to work on a project to try to guarantee freedom – and he had worked for his time there as he had never done otherwise, with energy, enthusiasm, learning, application and drive. He had served some men with brilliant minds but little practical ability, and had put their ideas into physical shape. That was freedom. He had found himself, and then lost himself, as a result of the work he had done. And then he had found no freedom. He could find no other work than to continue to use his knowledge to make more weapons, despite what the first two had done. Doing that work was not the freedom he had gone to America to defend – secret, unaccountable work for others who were too frightened to talk openly about what they were doing. And then, peculiarly he thought, he had found a freedom in the hospital, a freedom to serve the other patients and to live his life without the guilt that came from his work. Only his dreams, and the visions of his victims, disturbed him here. Or so it had been, until Winstanley's death. So, where was his freedom now?

"If I agree, you would find a lawyer, and we would talk about my situation? And if he could fight Oates off, and guarantee no trial, you would send me from Black Roding, is that right? But I could still be an outpatient and do some work here, if I can't find work out there?" To each of the questions she answered with a nod. And again she nodded when his last question was, "And you would have me re-admitted if I wanted?"

"Is that your decision then, Richard? That we get a lawyer to sort matters out with Oates and then discharge you as an outpatient?" She could feel relief and gratitude surging through her, but before they could go any further they were disturbed by the door being suddenly opened.

Richard immediately made to stand up. Ruth was frozen where she stood. The door crashed against the wall, and Sir Francis Oates stepped into the room, followed immediately by his driver. "Well, well," he said, "the porters were right, weren't they? There was indeed a passage through to the water tower, and that had to be where you were hiding! I am disappointed by you, Richard. You should not have drawn all this attention to yourself. And you, Doctor Appleton, you would meddle in this matter instead of doing as I asked you?"

"What are you doing here?" she said, having found her voice even though she still stood just as she had when the door opened.

"I've come to witness the tragic conclusion to the adventures we've been having because of Richard here."

"What do you mean, tragic conclusion? There's no tragedy here, except what you've done to him over the years. He's going to be free, though. We've discovered the truth behind all the lies you told him." Ruth tried to sound more assertive and more confident than she felt. Oates simply sneered at her words.

"Did what happened to you the other evening not warn you, not tell you that it's gone further than that? He's not going to be freed, to go telling everyone how he was wronged by a government intelligence officer. He's going to succeed where he failed before and end his life here, on the ground out there." Oates pointed to the open gap in the wall. It had grown dark, but the feeling of danger around it made Ruth shudder.

"Don't threaten him. He's finally free from you." Ruth stopped abruptly. "What do you mean, the other evening, warning me?" Her whole body seemed to go cold. "What warning?"

"My colleague here was a bit over-zealous. He was only supposed to scare you, not push you right down on the line."

Ruth heard Richard's gasp. She tried to speak calmly, but she could feel her heart beating, and a vein or artery at the back of her head was pulsing. "So, it was you."

"Yes, it was us. There was a time when we would not have done anything to you, but we found over the years that letting some people go free just meant there were too many loose ends. You're not going to be a loose end, I'm afraid. You're going to be his victim tonight." Oates waved his pointed finger at Richard. "Yes, the tragic case of a mad patient, and his doctor who tried so hard to help him but ended up being dragged by him to her death. Perhaps even a double suicide. I'm sure it will read well in the newspapers. How we tried to talk him out of it while he held you by the open window. How he admitted that he had already attacked you once because you had upset the tranquillity of his treatment here. How he had a self-destructive urge that had led to him being admitted here in the first place. And no doubt there will be some hints in the stories about his nature – a single man who never had a girlfriend, perhaps even going so far as to suggest that there were also allegations against him thirteen years ago, and that he might have jeopardised security when working with the United States army during the war. And I'm sure the hospital will say nice things about you, Doctor Appleton, but they will also say that you broke all the rules in your treatment of this particular patient and paid the price for your naivety. Yes, it will make a very good news story. But in a week everyone will have forgotten all about the two of you. That's what happens in those madhouses, they'll think, and then get on with their lives."

Fear had overtaken Ruth and she could not speak. All she could think was that she had indeed left herself, and Richard, open to this attack. She had not thought it would involve her death, even after she had been pushed on the lines. Somehow, she had believed she would come through this, even if the price was her job and place at the hospital. She had not anticipated Oates coming right to the place where Richard was hiding.

"The porters were very helpful, you know. Of course, they're all ex-servicemen, aren't they, predisposed to disliking a traitor, such as this man? And so ever-ready to help their country when asked to. And we were waiting in the hospital because the porters were so sure that he could not have got out this time, that he must be hiding somewhere. And then one of your colleagues, Doctor Smythe, said that he'd seen you on the corridor. That's when one of the porters remembered an old story about a passage to the water tower. And remembered that Simms here had a cupboard in that very corridor you'd been on. Well, it wasn't very hard to find you then, was it?"

"You wouldn't do this," Ruth protested weakly. "They won't believe you. My colleagues won't believe you."

"I think they will," Oates said coldly. "All the evidence will point that way. You even gave a hospital a false name when you tried to kill yourself the other evening and failed. And ran out of that hospital when they wanted to keep you there. So, your story will just seem like the lies of a mad psychiatrist, overwrought in her work." He turned to the driver behind him. Ruth could see that he was sturdily built. Against the two of them, she and Richard probably had no hope of stopping their plan, although she was more ready to put up a fight than she had been a few minutes earlier. "Come on," he said, "let's do it now and get it over with, before anyone thinks to interrupt us. You take Simms and I'll take the girl."

Then events seemed to move so quickly that Ruth could hardly understand them. Oates advanced on her, and she backed away from the window and towards the wall. She had her arms out to put up some defence. But Richard did not back away. He edged towards the window, almost drawing Oates' colleague forward towards the open air. Then he moved quickly and grabbed the chair that was standing by the window, where he was accustomed to read. And he moved quickly enough to surprise his intended assailant, because he lifted the chair and smashed it down on his head before he could move out of reach. The chair shattered, and Richard was left with one of the legs in his hand. But he did not hesitate, and using it as a cudgel he brought it down hard on the head of the driver, who moaned at the first blow but was silent after Richard hit him three or four times more.

Oates had made a lunge at her, and Ruth had tried to grapple with him. Frightened for her life she had lashed out at him with her feet, and scratched his arms and face with her nails. Oates had been distracted by Richard's sudden movement, and when he heard the blows behind him he pushed Ruth to the floor, and she struck the back of her head against the wall. The next few moments seemed to her to pass slowly in an unreal fashion. Oates was wary of Richard and circled around him. But Richard, realising it was the chair leg he was scared of, threw it out of the window. Oates moved towards Richard, making as if to strike him, but Richard again moved with a speed that surprised Oates, and grabbed hold of him. And then he started to pull Oates towards the open space. Oates realised the danger and tried to escape Richard's grasp, but the years of pushing the trolley had made his arms surprisingly strong. From where she lay Ruth could see the look of surprised horror on Oates' face as he seemed to dance with Richard. She had not been the only one who had not considered all the possible outcomes from the case. And when she realised what Richard intended to do, she managed a weak shout, "No, Richard, no!" but her cry was wasted. Richard had obviously decided his intentions while she had argued with Oates. With a shriek of triumph he turned their slow waltz into a quickstep, and ran himself and Oates across the final yards into the black night. Ruth saw the two suspended in the opening, before they disappeared downwards, and a few seconds later she heard the dull thump with which their bodies hit the ground. It was some minutes before she could stand, and as she was gathering her strength to try to go down the stairs Michael came rushing up, followed by two orderlies. He held her as she sobbed. She tried to explain, and to point to the space through which the two men had fallen, but all she could do was cry her grief.